'. . . his invented world is one of the m . . . date sh . . ng and dangerous it has been my pleasure to enco . . . . r'
The Times

'*Sea of Ghosts* is wonderful meaty stuff from Mr Campbell again – he's a true original . . . engages you from page one and never lets go'
Neal Asher

'Rich, detailed, vibrant and totally unlike anything that you've read before . . . Endlessly imaginative and impressively ambitious, but it's also a hugely fun adventure story that keeps up a relentless pace, leaving you with a cliffhanger ending that will have you gasping for the next book in double-quick time'
Sci-Fi-London.com

'Rampant imagination is allied with unusually rich writing'
Morning Star

'*Sea of Ghosts* is a highly entertaining novel highlighted by cinematic pacing, exhilarating action sequences, and unexpected moments of dark violence'
Fantasy Book Critic

'Book one of the Gravedigger Chronicles should mark a watershed moment in Alan Campbell's career. *Sea of Ghosts* is a stonking good time, rip-roaring and boundlessly ambitious'
Speculative Scotsman

THE ART OF HUNTING

Alan Campbell was born in Falkirk and went to Edinburgh University. He worked as a designer on the hugely successful Grand Theft Auto video games before deciding to pursue a career in writing and photography. He now lives in Lanarkshire. His novels include the Deepgate Codex series: *Scar Night*, *Iron Angel* and *God of Clocks* and the first novel in the Gravedigger Chronicles, *Sea of Ghosts*.

By Alan Campbell

The Deepgate Codex

SCAR NIGHT
IRON ANGEL
GOD OF CLOCKS

The Gravedigger Chronicles

SEA OF GHOSTS
THE ART OF HUNTING

ALAN CAMPBELL

THE ART OF HUNTING

BOOK TWO OF THE
GRAVEDIGGER CHRONICLES

TOR

First published 2013 by Tor

This paperback edition published 2014 by Tor
an imprint of Pan Macmillan, a division of Macmillan Publishers Limited
Pan Macmillan, 20 New Wharf Road, London N1 9RR
Basingstoke and Oxford
Associated companies throughout the world
www.panmacmillan.com

ISBN 978-0-330-50879-7

1 3 5 7 9 8 6 4 2

A CIP catalogue record for this book is available from the British Library.

Typeset by Ellipsis Digital Limited, Glasgow
Printed and bound by CPI Group (UK) Ltd, Croydon, CR0 4YY

Visit **www.panmacmillan.com** to read more about all our books
and to buy them. You will also find features, author interviews and
news of any author events, and you can sign up for e-newsletters
so that you're always first to hear about our new releases.

ACKNOWLEDGEMENTS

Thanks to Simon and to Julie, Ali and Jessica and everyone else at Pan Macmillan. And also to Maugan Rimmer, who helped me with aspects of the first book, and who I forgot to mention.

PROLOGUE

LADY OF CLAY

The soldier walked to the edge of the compound to sit in the dirt and drink the last of his rum and think about how he came to be in this dismal hole on the final morning of his life. He found a munitions crate on which to rest but he couldn't see much beyond the low mud-brick palisade wall. This sand storm had been raging since dawn and his goggles were already scoured so badly they were practically useless. He perceived his surroundings as uncertain shapes in a red haze. Only the dim circle of the sun offered him some sense of orientation. It hung there like a plague lantern. You couldn't fight in this weather because you couldn't see what was coming for you.

That was probably for the best.

In the compound behind him he could hear his commander barking orders at the other men. They were loading the gunpowder mortars with nails pulled from the wrecked farm-stead over by the southern wall, for all the good that would do. Seated on his crate, the soldier scooped up a handful of sand and let it pour out between his fingers until it was all gone. This struck him as a fitting metaphor for a morning like this. He wondered, briefly, if he ought to construct a poem along these lines. He could carve it into an earthen brick so that others would know what happened here in the Adad Godu

1

wastes. But then he dismissed the idea. It sounded too much like the sort of thing an Unmer soldier would do. Leave a poem. Leave a legacy. Instead, he took a long draught of rum and spat out sand. Sand got in everything here – your food and drink and even your leathers. You couldn't escape from it. As inevitable as time.

The soldier sighed. This is what happened when you had too much time to think about things and you hadn't yet drunk enough booze to blot it all out. He raised his canteen to his lips again, but halted.

He had spotted movement out there in the crimson murk. His muscles tautened. His hand shifted instinctively to his sword. His heart was suddenly racing. Had he . . .?

There.

He saw it again. However, this time he was able to relax somewhat. It was only a solitary figure: an archer, probably another one of Queen Aria's mercenaries lost in the storm. The stranger was tall and wore a woolspun cloak wrapped around his head and shoulders to keep the blowing sand from his eyes. He reached the compound's low earthen barrier and vaulted lightly over it. And then he came strolling up towards the place where the soldier was sitting.

The soldier offered his canteen. 'How's things in Jabanin?'

The archer looked down at the canteen, but did not reach for it. He was carrying a white bow carved from a dragon's rib and had a fine and unusual quiver – a black glass cylinder patterned with runes – lashed to his belt. 'I didn't come from Jabanin,' he said.

'I thought everyone passed through Jabanin.'

The stranger did not reply.

The soldier grunted. 'Well, it makes sense, I suppose. It explains why you're here. You won't have heard the news.'

'What news?'

'You'd better take a drink, my friend,' the soldier said, 'because I'm afraid you've just walked into the most dismal and dangerous backwater shithole in the entire world.' He thrust his canteen up towards the other man.

'Have you sighted the entity?'

The soldier blinked. Slowly he lowered the canteen. 'You know? You know about the slaughter at Arrash and Morqueth?'

'I know Jonas Marquetta's sorcerer has summoned one of the entities that you refer to as the elder gods. I know there have been two confrontations at the villages you mentioned. And I know that it's now headed this way.'

The soldier looked at him. 'You came here deliberately?'

The archer nodded.

'The last person I'll ever speak to,' the soldier said, 'and he's a lunatic.' His shoulders slumped and he took another drink. 'Until three days ago I thought we'd won this war. An end to bloody Unmer rule. An end to two decades of slavery.' He glanced at the archer, but couldn't see his face behind the wrappings of his cloak. 'I was sold twice, you know? Twice in three years, to two different Unmer masters, though one of them was a woman.' He let his mind wander back to those days. 'And when the Haurstaf fleet arrived in Losoto, I didn't believe it. I didn't believe those psychic witches could do what people said they could do. And then I saw it myself.' He smiled. 'Two women, just girls really. I saw them paralyse two whole divisions of Unmer soldiers – and their unit commanders and attendant sorcerers. All those armed men writhing in agony on the streets of the capital, unable to think, barely able to breathe under a psychic assault.' He shook his head. 'And that was just two little girls.'

The archer continued to observe him.

'When they drove the Unmer out of Losoto or rounded them all up into their ghettos, I thought that was an end to it,' the soldier went on. 'The Haurstaf's dominance over the Unmer was every bit as complete as the Unmer's dominance over us.' He took another swallow from the canteen. 'Didn't figure on this long drawn-out conflict.' He shook his head. 'But now it's obvious why the bastards have been stretching it out, running and hiding. They were buying themselves time for their bloody schemes. Enough time to summon that . . . thing.'

'The war isn't over yet.'

The soldier shot him a fierce look. 'If the stories we've heard are true, then the war is very definitely over. The Unmer have a god on their side.'

'A goddess,' the archer said. 'And gods fall as men do.'

The soldier coughed and shook his head. 'You know how many Samarol were in Morqueth? Didn't so much as slow it down. You have heard what happened there? You heard what this goddess is riding?'

'An entropic beast.'

The soldier grunted. 'A what?' He frowned. 'That's not what I'd call it.' He paused, his brow still furrowed as he studied the other man. 'You know, you never did say where you were from. I've been trying to place that accent of yours. I've heard it before, somewhere, but . . .'

But his ruminations were disturbed, for at that moment a new sound could be heard over the gusting wind and the rasp of the sand. Both men turned their heads towards the northwest. At first it was faint, like a low tone plucked by gales from a cave or a hollow in the rocks, but as the moments passed it quickly became unmistakable: a distant, steady pounding, like something huge stalking the earth. And overlaying this was another sound, of a higher pitch – as though the wind itself had grown keener.

The soldier put his canteen to his lips and upended it, finishing the last of his rum. Then he dusted sand from his hands and rose unsteadily to his feet. Back in the compound he could just perceive the dim silhouettes of his brothers in arms rushing to and fro. 'I suppose this is it,' he said.

The archer nodded. 'This entity can manipulate entropy at will,' he said. 'This storm is its voice. The men whom it killed have become its teeth. And when it bares them, it will be to strike terror into your hearts. Do not let it, or the beast upon which it rides, touch you. Doing so would condemn yourself to an eternity of unimaginable horrors.'

'I wasn't planning on going hand to hand with the thing. That's what our cannons and mortars are for.'

'Cannons and mortars can't harm it.'

'Well that's a damn shame,' the other man muttered. 'Because cannons and mortars are what we have.'

'The most sensible course of action,' the archer said, 'would be for you to flee.'

The soldier grunted again. He scooped up another handful of sand and then opened his palm, watching as the glassy powder flowed out between his fingers. 'I'm not paid to run away,' he said. 'Besides, I'm hellish tired of this desert. I could do with seeing a bit of action. What about you?'

The archer half-turned as if to reply, but his attention remained on the distant pounding. *Boom. Boom. Boom.* It seemed to have grown louder. The accompanying sound had become louder, too. Now it sounded like a cacophony of wails and screams.

'What *is* that?' the soldier said.

The archer strung his bow in one smooth movement and

5

removed the cap from the quiver at his belt. A sudden crackling sound came from that black cylinder, and air rushed inwards, drawing tails of dust and sand into the opening.

The soldier stared at the quiver for a moment, then looked up at the archer. 'So, I've finally remembered where I've heard that accent before.'

The archer selected an arrow from his quiver. It had only a threaded metal cap where the arrowhead ought to be.

'What are you?' the soldier said. 'A saboteur?'

'We need to do something about this storm,' the archer said. He reached inside his cloak and pulled out a fist-sized object. It looked like a bulb of amber glass, full of miniature machinery. Among the gears and wires could be glimpsed a phial of liquid. He sealed the quiver again and the torrents of air around him abruptly stopped.

Next, he fixed the glass bulb onto the arrow, screwing it onto the threaded cap. When it was secure, he notched the arrow and raised his bow towards the heavens. The bow string quivered as he released it and the arrow shot high into the air.

After a moment, the dust clouds above them flashed blue as the strange device detonated. A heartbeat later they heard a concussion. 'If you have any powder,' the archer said, 'best see that it's covered.'

As he said this, the first drops of rain began to fall.

The soldier understood that he was witnessing Unmer sorcery. The archer's accent was the same as the accent of the men and women who had owned him.

Lightning ripped across the darkening skies, followed by the boom and rumble of thunder. And suddenly the air filled with the growing rush of water. The rain became a torrent. It drenched the two men and turned the sand to dark mud and hammered the palisade walls.

And it cleared the air.

The soldier could see his comrades now, crouched by their cannons and mortars. They had covered the barrels and flint-locks with sack cloth or anything else to hand – helmets and shields and crate lids. Other men squatted behind the defensive wall, their rifles and bows ready, staring out across the dirt plains.

Now the soldier could actually see storm clouds overhead and with the rain they brought they pushed a chill wind down across the cracked earth plains. It howled and gusted and drove sheets of water through the uncertain light. To the south lay squat red dunes and bars of sand like the veins on the back of an old man's hand. Striding across the plains towards the soldier's compound was a creature from a nightmare.

It had roughly the shape and the muscular proportions of a pit hound or a bear – a blunt head on massive shoulders – but was far larger than any land beast of this world. It was hairless, with flesh as pale as dead skin but oddly rippled and covered in countless red bruises or contusions. It walked on four squat legs, turning its head this way and that as though sniffing out its prey. Its bristling teeth gleamed in the half-light, although it appeared to have no eyes. There came from it an odd sound, a dire chorus of shouts and wailing as of people in great pain.

Seated in a saddle on the creature's back was a pale woman with long dark hair that blew behind her like a pennant. She wore some type of faceted silver armour – so brightly polished that it flashed as she moved. In one hand she held the reins of her beast, in the other she gripped a whip that crackled and fizzed with constantly forking electrical fluids.

'The Unmer know her as Duna,' the archer said over the screams and cries that accompanied the approaching beast.

'Queen of the realm of thorns and at least three other minor dimensions. Daughter of the shape-shifter, Fiorel, whom some people call the Father of Creation and the God of Cauldron and Forge. Those who fear to utter Duna's name call her Lady of Clay, for it is said her father moulded her and cast her in the furnace that raged at the birth of time.' The archer's brows lowered. 'Make no mistake. She is neither furnace born nor a lady. She is an entropath. And the beast on which she rides is no mortal creature. It is the Agaroth, another of her father's creations. It is undeniable, unstoppable, eternal and – like its creator – it has the ability to assume any physical form.'

'Entropath?'

'The entities you call the elder gods. Fiorel and Duna are entropaths.'

The soldier turned to him. 'Why is she here?'

'She has a lust for war,' the archer said. 'Perhaps Marquetta's sorcerers have made a deal with her. I do not know. Whatever her reasons for being here, her father cannot know she is in this realm. Travelling between their cosmos and ours uses vast amounts of energy and the entropaths cannot afford to waste their dwindling reserves. Fiorel would never have allowed her to come here just to sate her battle lust.'

'How do you know all this?'

The archer unwrapped the cloak from his face and rubbed rain from his forehead. He was Unmer: cadaverous with sharp, almost severe features, a long narrow nose and a prominent bony brow. His skin and hair were as white as salt but his eyes were crimson and intelligent and seemed to burn with a fierce inner light. The soldier recognized him.

'Conquillas,' he said. 'You are Lord Argusto Conquillas.' Conquillas the betrayer. The dragon lord who had abandoned his own people for the love of Aria, the Haurstaf queen whose witches had so recently put an end to decades of Unmer rule. Aria of the Ether – the living ghost – a telepath so powerful she could bathe her mind in the thoughts and dreams of millions. She must have learned of Duna's coming through espionage.

'It has long been my ambition to hunt the Agaroth,' Conquillas admitted. He opened his quiver again. Again, the air around them twisted and became suddenly violent, rushing into the maw of that black cylinder at the archer's hip.

By now the air had cleared and the goddess, Duna, and her hellish mount had drawn near enough to the compound that the waiting soldiers could see them more clearly. And when those men perceived the Agaroth as it truly was and understood what it was composed of, many of them lowered their weapons and wailed in terror.

The great beast now lumbering towards them was composed entirely of the bodies of those it had slain. Its massive limbs were full of mouths and faces and scraps of armour, swords and shields. A great mess of flesh and metal. And yet those bodies from which it was composed were not dead. Hundreds of slaughtered soldiers gazed out from its knees and its shoulders and gnashed their teeth and screamed.

'How do you hunt *that*?' the soldier exclaimed.

'With bow and arrow,' Conquillas said. He notched an arrow and aimed it at the approaching fiend, sighting along the shaft. The tip of this missile was a crackling black dot that appeared to be sucking in the very air around it.

Void arrows?

The soldier had heard of such sorcerous creations. It was said that only one hundred and eleven had ever been made. One hundred and one of them had been lost forever, fired through the world or sent into the heavens, never to be seen again. Another was in the palace of Emperor Ji-Kai of the

Golden Domain. He had bought it from a pirate lord, giving the man one full tenth of his empire – an area of land equivalent to a small country. The remaining nine were in Conquillas's possession.

And one of those was now aiming at the beast on the plain.

Conquillas loosed his arrow and it shot away across the ground with a crackle and a shower of black and white sparks.

It struck the beast in the centre of its head and vanished. Although he couldn't chart the missile's progress after that, the soldier imagined it tearing through the creature's skull and emerging from the other side. It would keep on that same trajectory forever, plunging through the Alhama Mountains on the distant horizon and then onwards out into the endless void behind the sky, until it reached the ends of the cosmos and passed beyond.

The beast let out a baleful roar and swung its head towards them, baring its massive teeth. And that alien queen whose name was Duna, daughter of Fiorel, now turned her attention upon the soldier and his companion. She lashed her whip above her head and a sudden burst of lightning poured down from the thunderclouds and connected with that sorcerous cord.

'Would it offend you if I flee?' the soldier said.

'You are only human,' Conquillas said.

'I thought a void arrow could stop anything.'

The archer's gaze remained locked on Duna and her mount. The Agaroth was a maelstrom of living corpses and metal – a great howling juggernaut that loomed high above the flat earth and the pockets of withered scrub. Its huge hooves drove deep into the muddy earth as it came lumbering towards them at a frightening pace.

Conquillas loosed another void arrow.

The arrow shot over the palisade wall and struck the

oncoming beast again. This time it pierced its chest where, presumably, its heart would be located. But again, the sorcerous missile had no effect. The ground around them shook as the Agaroth's speed increased.

The soldier glanced at his companion's quiver. Strangely, there seemed to be more than nine arrows in there. 'How many of those do you have?' he asked.

'A score or so,' Conquillas said, pulling yet another free and notching it to his bow string.

'I didn't think there were that many left in the world.'

Conquillas sent a third arrow whizzing across the earth towards the goddess and her mount. This struck the beast in the left eye. The Agaroth screamed and huffed and batted the air with one massive hoof, but it barely slowed. A moment later it came charging at Conquillas with even greater urgency. Now that there was less than three hundred yards between them, the other soldiers started firing their mortars and cannons. Concussions sounded all around them. Smoke filled the air.

'I retrieve them,' Conquillas remarked.

'The arrows? From beyond the edge of creation?'

Conquillas raised his bow again. 'Fortunately, time does not exist outside the cosmos,' he said. 'The void arrows are always present.' He loosed the fourth arrow and then a fifth and sixth in quick succession, but each missile plunged straight through the creature without harming it. He frowned. 'Nevertheless, getting them back is not straightforward. It can sometimes take hundreds of years to find them, so I do not like to waste them.'

'How many do you have left?'

The archer lowered his bow and stared at their oncoming foe. Duna and her mount were now less than two hundred yards away. Most of the other soldiers in the compound abandoned their guns and fled, despite shouted orders from their commander to remain at their posts. Conquillas ignored the commotion. His full attention remained fixed on the enemy. 'I suspect the Agaroth lacks a brain and any critical organs,' he muttered. 'It is not living in a sense we recognize. But if it is an abstract creation, then it must be formed by the will of its rider. And there lies the problem. The only way to destroy such a fiend will engender grave repercussions, I fear. I must have more time to think of a better solution.'

He reached into a pocket in his padded tunic and took out a small silver whistle, which he proceeded to blow into. It made no sound, or at least none that the soldier could hear.

But he heard the shrieks that soon filled the skies above them.

'Dragons,' he cried.

The winged serpents must have been waiting in the thunderclouds above them. There were three of them, all monstrous, each wearing horned and spiked helmets and dark metalled armour over their scaly red hides, war dragons if ever there had been any. Now, at Conquillas's behest, they tore down through the air, diving towards the oncoming foes at reckless speeds.

'Dah'le ne kustol,' Conquillas muttered. 'Ne kustol.'

'What was that?' the soldier said.

'They must tread with care.'

One of the dragons broke to the west, its vast wings thumping, while the remaining two continued to swoop downwards. These began to loop around each other in helix formation. At the last instant one banked sharply aside, while the other rushed at the goddess, its great black claws seeking to rip her from the saddle of the monster she rode.

Duna flicked her lash skywards, and there was a flash of white light. As that cord of energy swept up to meet the attacking serpent, it grew to a hundred times its length.

Crackle.

The whip passed straight through the onrushing dragon, slicing it in half from neck to rump. The pieces fell amidst a cloud of blood and smacked into the ground behind the goddess, where they lay with the great wings still twitching.

The remaining two dragons shrieked as they wheeled around their fallen comrade.

The goddess lashed her whip above her head in triumph. It ripped through the air like lightning. And then she reined her beast around and brought it over to the fallen serpent, whereupon the Agaroth lowered its head and began to devour the remains.

A chorus of shrieks filled the heavens and both surviving dragons now turned and swept in from the north, flying so low their claws raked the ground.

And the Agaroth began to change.

'Mercy,' the soldier said. 'What's happening?'

As the entropic beast gorged itself on dragon flesh, it was growing larger with every passing moment. And as it grew it altered its shape. Its head became elongated, developing into a snout full of black teeth. Ears sprouted from its skull. Hooves became claws. Its rump stretched out, writhing snake-like across the earth, until it took the form of a tail. From its back there unfolded enormous fans of bone that shuddered and grew sheets of translucent skin.

'It looks like a dragon,' the soldier said.

In half a hundred heartbeats the Agaroth had transformed itself into the likeness of a great winged serpent. Now it thrashed its newly formed wings and lifted itself airborne. Gales blew around it, raising clouds of grit and tearing leafless shrubs from the earth.

Conquillas's war dragons did not falter, but came straight at the monster, raking its neck savagely with their claws and teeth.

'Ne kustol!' Conquillas cried.

But it was already too late. As the war dragons engaged Duna's mount, a strange and terrible fate befell them. The entropic beast *absorbed* them. One instant the dragons were involved in savage combat, the next they all but vanished inside the monster. The soldier saw red wings flapping uselessly, a tail thrashed, and then nothing remained in the air but the goddess and her hellish mount.

The Agaroth grew larger still. And from its shoulders it sprouted two new necks and two new heads and two new maws crammed with glassy black teeth. It turned its baleful eyes back towards the men in the compound.

'Shit shit shit,' the soldier said.

'Run,' Conquillas cried.

'What about you?'

Duna and her mount came surging through the air towards them, and the soldier could see that its forelimbs comprised great swellings of corpse muscle and human bones and blood-black organs still dripping. Scores of the living dead gaped out at the world from the beast's chest and shoulders or shuddered and howled and chattered in madness. It came at them, furious, dragging behind it a storm of dust.

All of the other soldiers were now fleeing, the commander included, but Duna did not even seem to notice them. Her dark and savage eyes were fixed on Conquillas.

Who raised his bow.

'Daughter of Fiorel!' he cried. 'Halt there or die!'

The beast's wings thundered, and it slowed, halting its dive. Its three necks writhed like snakes, its mouths hissing and snapping at the air. And upon its back Duna looked down and laughed.

She was pale and achingly beautiful with a soft, tapering face and elegantly arched brows, and yet to look upon her was to feel horror. There was no glimmer of humanity in her eyes: merely raw and inhuman power. She wore armour fashioned from mirrored silver and sculpted around her small breasts. Her lash crackled constantly and scorched the air around it. Her hair blew out behind her head like silk funeral pennants, lifted by winds that seemed not to exist in this world. The hand that clutched the Agaroth's saddle horn was covered in tiny runes that looked red and painful. The soldier could see scratch marks and old scabs there, as if those imprinted designs caused her endless irritation. On her left hand Duna wore a ring that seemed composed of nothing but white light.

The shape-shifting beast lowered one of its heads towards Conquillas.

'I warn you, Duna,' the Unmer lord said.

'You may yet appeal to my mercy,' she said. 'Kneel now and beg that I might end your life rather than prolong it.' Her tongue tasted the air. 'The worth of such an appeal shall be determined by how entertaining you can make it, Lord Conquillas.'

'I have no quarrel with you, Duna. But you have no right to be in this realm. Return to your garden or I will have no choice but to stop you.'

The Agaroth's wings pounded.

'My very existence grants me that right,' Duna said. 'Power grants me that right. Why do you think you can stop me, Conquillas?'

'I will shoot you dead.'

She smiled. 'And my father will remake me and scorch this world for your insolence. I'm growing bored with this conversation, archer.'

'Fiorel would not destroy this world,' Conquillas said. 'I believe he has plans for it.'

She raised her eyebrows. 'You *believe*?'

The Agaroth was edging closer to them. They would soon be within range of the goddess's lash.

'I also believe that, were you to die, he would not remake you,' Conquillas added. 'He does not love you, Duna. Your lusts embarrass him. You have risked the lives of your kin by coming here.'

Suddenly her face twisted into a snarl. 'How dare you!' she cried. 'You mortal! You . . .' Her voice choked off and she let out a growl. 'You dare lecture me? I am a god!'

And then she swept back her lash, as if to strike the archer.

Conquillas shot his arrow.

It scorched through the air and struck Duna between the eyes and passed through her head without pause. The soldier could hear it fizzing away into the sky even as he saw the goddess topple forwards and lie slumped across her saddle horn.

Without her will to sustain its form, the Agaroth abruptly collapsed into its component parts. A great deluge of bones and corpses and dragon flesh fell from the air and struck the ground before them.

The soldier gaped. 'You killed her,' he said.

'She was arrogant to assume I wouldn't.'

'You killed a god.'

'An entropath,' Conquillas said. 'But a young one, and not particularly powerful. I myself am considerably older than Duna was.'

'But she was the daughter of the creator!'

Conquillas nodded. 'That was unfortunate,' he admitted.

The soldier couldn't tear his eyes from the goddess's dead body, which now lay in a pool of gore and dragon guts and among the corpses of soldiers who had been killed at Arrash and Morqueth – men who had at last found peace in death. 'What do you think Fiorel will do?' he said.

'I do not know what he will do.' Conquillas regarded his bow for a moment. 'Fiorel is a terrible meddler. He certainly has plans for this world, and possibly plans for me. He might attempt to strike me down tomorrow, or three hundred years from now. Or he might simply ignore the matter. Duna was always causing him trouble.'

'You think he might just ignore what you've done?'

Conquillas shrugged. 'I will retrieve my arrows, just in case.'

272 YEARS LATER

CHAPTER 1

THE GIRL BENEATH
THE WATER

She found herself in a high corrie where the granite mountains reared over her like dark and monstrous waves. Their snow-topped crests blazed with the light of a billion stars, of constellations scattered across the vacuum like pulverized glass. The air here was razor-thin and elemental, so cold it hurt her lungs. She could hear freshets crackling through broken stone – and the wind, keening as it ripped plumes of ice from unassailable heights. The crystals fell as curtains of scintillations, shimmering against the dark and the stars. She breathed in and nearly sobbed.

Down here the base of the corrie had been artificially levelled and excavated everywhere to form scores of deep depressions in the rocky ground. Each had been filled with a poison from a different sea and then illuminated from below. They glowed like the stokeholes to chemical furnaces. She recognized cherry-red Mare Regis brine and the bottle-green brine of the Mare Verdant and there the vinegar gloom from the Sea of Lights. And yet more held poisons unknown to her, the pits shining in the dark with chromic and gunmetal hues or throbbing pinks and lilacs.

In the centre of these excavations there lay like some storm-flipped skiff a shack constructed from dragon bones. A fierce and bloody light burned within its walls and cast across the earth great clenching seams of flame and shadow. She glimpsed someone or something moving about inside and she thought she heard a noise like a whetstone drawn across steel. But then the wind cried out again and drowned all other sounds.

Ianthe began to make her way towards the shack, but then she halted.

Amber seawater filled the pit to her right. A fathom down there toiled a stooped and scrawny figure more corpse than man. He was naked above the waist and bent over, his fists and muscles agleam like nodes of bone as he dragged an iron plough through the sediment under his feet. His skin was milk white, his hair a diaphanous foam. Whenever he reached the limit of his prison he turned his plough and worked in the opposite direction. Gem lanterns set in each corner threw spider-like shadows across mortared walls, and as Ianthe peered closer she felt that she recognized this figure from somewhere. *Something in his gait.*

He must have sensed her presence, for he halted and lifted his head.

Ianthe shuddered. The man had no eyes.

The pit opposite held brine as pink as starfish meat. A table had been placed in the middle of this pool and dressed with plain farmhouse plates and cups. A woman and a young girl stared down at their crockery, but there was no food set out before them. The waters gave their flesh a febrile aura. Watching the scene tickled a memory of Ianthe's childhood. This pair, like the Drowned farmer, were familiar.

Don't look up, please, don't look up.

Both woman and child looked up at her.

Ianthe cried out.

She hugged her stomach and ran towards the shack, shaking

her head as if she might dislodge those crow-picked visages from her mind. She hurried onwards, the lights from the open pits glazing her skin. And as she ran she saw men, women and children below the waters, some unmoving and some engaged in simple tasks: a blind greybeard shaping a table leg; a blind schoolteacher turning blank pages; two blind men wrestling upon a coppery mulch of keys. She recognized them all, for they were her own memories corrupted in some dreamlike fashion.

At last she reached the shack. Here she stopped and tried to steady her shuddering heart. Red furnace light bled through the latticework of bones. She glimpsed flames crackling within, part of a rusted metal desk, hooks and loops of chain depending from the ceiling. She laid her hands upon the smooth black joists and peered between them. Hundreds of small glass phials – ichusae? – stood glittering in wire racks upon the desk. And there she spied the whetstone she had heard. But no sword. No owner.

'So it's you.'

Ianthe spun to face the voice.

The Unmer prince stood outside the shack door. He was every bit as handsome as she remembered: young and pale and slender, strong of jaw and with a rickle of hair as golden as summer hay. He wore a white uniform brocaded with silver cord and crusted with gemstones around the collar and lapels. His posture averred the calm confidence and arrogance of his noble heritage. His violet eyes, so clear and sharp, crackled with a hint of cruelty. They were very old eyes indeed, at odds with his youthful appearance. His hand rested on the pommel of a curved sword lashed to his waist by a red silkspun cummerbund. His gaze lingered a moment on her torn and bloody

Haurstaf robe, then snapped back up to meet her own expression of wonder.

'Do you know where you are?' he said.

'I'm dreaming?'

'*I'm dreaming*,' he said. 'My dream. You're the interloper.'

Ianthe felt herself wilt under his unflinching scrutiny. She was suddenly acutely aware of her sorry state of dress, her bruised and naked feet. She raised a hand to hide her swollen lip. 'Maybe it's *my* dream,' she said, 'and *you're* the interloper.'

'How could *I* possibly invade *your* mind?'

'How could I invade yours?'

'You're Haurstaf.'

'I'm *not* Haurstaf.'

A sudden rumble of thunder broke across the mountain tops, startling Ianthe. It seemed to her that this dream world had just voiced her anger. And now it looked to be assuming her mood. The stars above, so clear mere moments ago, were being swallowed quickly by dark reefs of cloud.

The prince glanced up and gave a mirthless smile. 'You're already changing things,' he said, 'asserting control, asserting your own dominance. It's a Haurstaf trait.'

Another crack of thunder. Lightning ripped across the north, illuminating the corrie and the mounded mountains around them. In that instant it seemed to Ianthe that they were standing in the heart of an ocean tempest, that those granite peaks would come crashing down and obliterate them both. But then cold, quiet darkness returned.

In a low, measured tone, she said, 'I told you, I'm not Haurstaf.'

He studied her for a moment longer, his brow furrowed in thought. Then he turned and swept a hand towards the luminous pools. 'These mountains are the Lakuna Aressi. The pools . . .' He gazed at them with the detachment of someone lost in their own memories. 'My father told me stories of this place when I was young, that's why I dream of it.' He hesitated again, idly rubbing a tiny white brine scar on the back of his hand. 'The real brine pools didn't contain *these* people. You brought them here with you. They're your memories.' His white teeth flashed. 'May I ask why you have imagined them all to be blind?'

Ianthe looked away, her heart quickening.

The storm in the heavens began to dissolve. The thunderclouds thinned to a haze and then to nothing and moments later the stars had been restored to their full brilliance in that cold clear sky.

'What is your name?' he said.

'Ianthe.'

'I am—'

'Paulus Marquetta,' she said.

'You know of me?'

If only he knew the truth. How many times had she gazed on him from afar? She had seen him through the eyes of his own captors, a lonely prisoner kept in a cell deep below the Haurstaf palace. She had looked upon his sleeping face, the golden tangle of his hair upon his pillow, so peaceful and beautiful, and him so utterly unaware of his power over her. And through his own eyes she'd read the letters he'd written to his dying princess; *I was with you when she died*, she wanted to say. *In your loneliest moments, I was there beside you. In my mind I held your hand and kissed your brow and loved you.* But she couldn't talk of this, not even in a dream.

'Everyone knows you,' she replied. 'Son of King Jonas the Summoner and Queen Grace.'

'Jonas the Summoner,' he said. 'That is one of the kinder

25

epitaphs you could have chosen. Those who blame him for the downfall of my race call him Jonas the Whiteheart.' His brow wrinkled and he pursed his lips. 'I've seen you before, Ianthe.'

She shook her head.

'Yes. Twice. Once with Briana Marks . . . and then again at the palace entrance, after the attack. A man carried you away.'

A man? Ianthe couldn't recall anything about that.

'You were unconscious,' the prince said. 'Your rescuer wore Unmer armour and carried Unmer weapons, but he was human. A soldier, but not Haurstaf, his flesh had been badly scarred by brine. He looked . . .' The prince snorted. 'We have a saying in Unmer . . . The closest translation is: he looked like a battle-field.'

Granger? She had peered through his eyes often enough, observed his brine-scratched hands gripping the wheel of the emperor's stolen steam yacht as he pursued the Haurstaf men-o'-war. *And destroyed them.* She recalled the battle, the cannon fire, the smoke and screams. Granger had harpooned their own vessel and dragged it behind him like a dragon carcass, until Ethan Maskelyne had severed the cable. But then they had abandoned the sinking yacht. Granger had earned his death, for all his greed and for the suffering he had caused Ianthe and her mother, and yet she had felt no desire to watch him drown.

He had returned for her?

'My family owe this man a debt of gratitude,' Marquetta said. 'We would reward him handsomely.'

'Why?'

'He freed us.'

'No.' She tried to recall what had happened, but her memories of the attack skirled like snowflakes in the wind. There had been a concrete cell. A Haurstaf soldier. A man in a white coat. She remembered the door slamming shut, the soldier perspiring heavily.

'Are you with him now?' Marquetta said. 'Does he watch over you while you dream?'

They'd hurt her and she'd cast her consciousness away from that terrible place, dislocating herself from her own suffering. She had drifted through the Sea of Ghosts, that great void of perceptions and in her anguish and fury she had . . .

Oh, god.

'Will you bring him to the palace at Awl?' Marquetta said.

What have I done?

'You have my word that neither of you will be harmed.'

A gust of wind lashed her hair. She felt hail sting her face. The returning thunder boomed like cannon fire. *A battle at sea.* And all around her the mountains appeared to swell. Why had Granger taken her away? Why couldn't he have just left her there to die?

Marquetta glanced between Ianthe and the heavens. 'I have made a mistake,' he said. 'This man . . . He didn't rescue you. He abducted you?'

Ianthe felt tears welling in her eyes. 'He's my father,' she said. 'You don't understand. *He* didn't free you. It was me. I killed them.' She began to sob. 'I didn't mean to, I . . .'

She turned and ran.

'Wait!'

He seized her wrist.

She shrieked.

But he held on. 'Ianthe, wait, please.'

And suddenly she felt pain – an acid burn, as though his touch was scalding her. She saw blood trickle between his fingers, heard a crackle as his sorcerous touch banished her skin to non-existence. He looked at her with horror, then immediately released her. 'I didn't,' he said, his violet eyes fixed on her bloody hand. 'I didn't do that. It's your dream, you've imagined this, I swear.'

Ianthe struck out – not physically, but with an instinctive mental blow intended merely to push the young man away. He flinched and then gave a sudden violent shudder. His face became slack and he dropped to his knees.

Ianthe turned and fled. The wind howled and the hail beat the frozen ground and chopped the surface of the brine pools into colourful froths. And from the depths of those pits the Drowned gaped blindly up at her, their faces distorted but full of accusation.

In her panic and terror she lost her footing and stumbled. The world rolled. She hit the ground, her face mere inches from the edge of a yellow pool. The metal stench of it filled her nostrils and throat. She found herself gazing down at her own self. Not a reflection, but a real person trapped beneath that sunflower-coloured brine. The Drowned Ianthe sat upon a chair, gazing at something cupped in her hand. It was a locket, opened to reveal a tiny portrait. A young man with golden hair? Her prince? She could not be certain. The girl beneath the water didn't look up at her air-breathing counterpart, merely stared wistfully at the image in the locket, her other hand resting on the pregnant swell of her belly.

CHAPTER 2

GRANGER

After four hours of using the replicating sword, Granger's nose began to bleed. He pressed the back of his gauntlet against his upper lip, then withdrew his hand, only to see the red stain disappear into the shallow whorls etched across the metal surface. A moment later the armoured glove began to thrum with power in response to the increased entropy. The whorls shifted, scattering rainbows. Moments later he sensed the power in the gauntlet flow into his sword, as if the Unmer blade was drinking it in. The gauntlet shivered, resisting the drain, and for several seconds he felt a tug-of-war between the two artefacts. The muscles in his hand tightened painfully, pressure built inside his head, and then abruptly it was over. The sword had won, as it always did. Granger tried to relax. He wanted to release the weapon, but he didn't dare do so until he knew they were safe. The blade was his security. The sorcerous replicates it created were too useful to dismiss.

The nearest of them was breaking wood and stacking it in a pile beside the fire, while another hunched over the flames, boiling tea in a spent shell casing. Both men were identical copies of him, summoned from *somewhere* by the hellish blade, versions of which they both gripped even as they toiled. Both of them wore Unmer power armour identical to Granger's own, giving them the same increased strength and endurance he now possessed. They looked like him in every way – the same lean frame and tough, brine-scarred skin, the same savage and haunted eyes – and yet it was hard enough to think of them as men.

He watched his duplicate boiling tea in one of the thousands of shell casings that had been scattered throughout the forest around the Haurstaf palace. Some of those shells had been fired at Granger's own chariot during his decoy assault.

The sword replicate reached into Granger's kitbag, pulled out a handful of birch grass and sprinkled it into the steaming water. The Unmer shield Granger had taken from the transmitting station rested against a fallen log twenty paces away. He'd placed it over there to avoid catching a glimpse of the hellish visions that occasionally appeared within its colour-shifting glass. The last time he'd looked into that cursed shield, it had seemed to be filled with shadowy figures gazing out.

Granger's third sword replicate leaned against a tree and watched over Ianthe, while the remaining five were out in the deep woods, checking his snares or patrolling the perimeter of his camp. In the back of his mind he could smell the earth and feel the mulch give under their boots and sense the flickers of autumn sun, dreamlike, upon their faces: sharp, painful perceptions that raked the periphery of his nerves. The Unmer sorcery was sustaining him and draining him at the same time. He felt exhausted, edgy.

Granger exchanged a glance with the third replicate, but then tore his eyes away. It wasn't the wretched, brine-scarred face that horrified him, but the other man's empty stare. It had been like looking into the abyss itself.

Birds darted through the woods, whistling and chattering. Shafts of sunlight broke through the canopy and lay in gold green pools upon grass and moss or illuminated bursts of wild flowers. Puffs of midges hovered in the dappled shade. The boles and boughs were warm and hoary to the touch. Granger could smell the wild psellia and nettles and even the shorn hay from the fields further down the valley, but these late summer scents were corrupted by the sulphurous tang of cordite and gunpowder. He hadn't heard any gunshots or cannon fire for a while now. Whatever fighting there had been between the freed Unmer and the Haurstaf battalions had now ceased.

He was just wondering whether he should wake Ianthe, when he noticed her stir. She groaned, then raised her head and groaned a second time. She sat up, slowly and with great effort, and gingerly touched the bruises on her face. Her lips parted.

'Where are my lenses?' she said in a dry, cracked voice. She shook her head and immediately began groping the grass around her. But then, abruptly, she stopped what she was doing.

'It *is* you,' she said. 'Granger.'

'Don't call me that,' Granger said.

'It's your name, isn't it?'

Granger said nothing.

'Where are my spectacles?' she repeated. 'The Unmer lenses? What did you do with them?'

He wandered over to his kitbag. After a moment of rummaging, he found the small Unmer lenses and brought them over to where she sat.

She held out her hand.

But he hesitated. 'These are Unmer.'

'Give them to me.'

Granger examined the small wheel fixed to the side of the frames. He touched it with the thumb of his gauntlet, but didn't spin the cursed thing. There was sorcerous energy here. His own armour was already reacting, powering up in order to wrestle energy from the lenses. 'They're probably dangerous,' he said.

As he spoke, a jolt of pain shot through his left arm and hand. He dropped the lenses. It had seemed as though those Unmer spectacles had tried to wrest a massive amount of power from the gauntlet.

'Give them to me!' Ianthe cried, snatching them up from the ground. She put them on at once, then turned the wheel and blinked several times.

'Be careful,' he said. 'You don't know what—'

'Oh, what do you care?' she said. She was staring at him now.

Staring *right* at him.

Granger had grown used to the blankness in her eyes, the dissociation evident whenever his blind daughter pretended to see through her own useless eyes. But there was no evidence of that now. Something had happened to her the moment she'd turned that wheel. Her eyes looked normal. They appeared to react normally to her surroundings.

'You can see me,' he said.

Ianthe made a face, somewhere between an impudent smile and a sneer. She seemed about to say something, but then her demeanour changed abruptly. She frowned. 'That's odd,' she said. 'I sense . . . There are nine people nearby, but . . .' She hesitated, her brow furrowed in confusion. 'What *is* that? It's like they're all the same person, nine perspectives, but . . .' She raised her eyes and looked at Granger. 'They're all *you*,' she said. 'How are you doing that?'

Granger felt the weight of the sword in his fist. A familiar sensation of unease crept over him, that same feeling he got whenever he realized Ianthe was looking out through his eyes, hearing the world through his ears. Part of him was repulsed – it instinctively wanted her out of his head – but his pragmatic side urged him to remain calm. 'An Unmer trick,' he said. 'I don't really know how it works. How do those lenses help you see?'

She shuddered. 'God, that's creepy. They're . . . empty.'

'What?'

She shook her head dismissively, then winced again. Gingerly, she touched the back of her neck.

'Where did you get the spectacles?' Granger said.

'I found them. What does it matter?'

'On an Unmer ship?'

Her silence confirmed his suspicions. Ianthe had been aboard the same icebreaker that had taken Granger north to the transmitting station in Pertica. The same ship that brought him to the very weapon horde that had allowed him to rescue her. *The ship with a dead captain.* Something Herian said came back to him, an offhand remark the Unmer operator had made about that long-gone mariner: *That didn't stop him from delivering his package and then bringing you here, did it?* Had the Unmer somehow *placed* those lenses in his daughter's hands? And the rest? Granger finding the transmitting station, his training with the power armour, phasing shield and replicating sword, his escape and subsequent journey to Awl – had it all been *planned*?

After all, the result of such unlikely series of events was that the Unmer were now free, their Haurstaf enslavers either dead or fleeing for their lives.

The more he thought about it, the more he felt sure they had both been manipulated, moved like pieces on a chessboard. Herian's remark made it impossible to dismiss as mere coincidence the events that had brought them to this place. And yet the logistics of engineering such an operation confounded him. How had the Unmer even known about Ianthe in the first place? Herian had described himself as an operator. Now Granger wondered exactly what kind of operator he was.

'Where are we?' Ianthe said.

'A few miles south of the palace,' Granger replied. 'A league or so. The fighting has stopped.'

'What fighting?'

'The Unmer have seized control of the palace,' he said. 'They used some weapon – something that cut through the Haurstaf psychics like a scythe. Hundreds dead, thousands. Those who survived fled to the military camps in the forest or on to Port Awl. Haurstaf military units went to the palace to investigate. There were skirmishes. I saw leucotomized Unmer gunned down in the woods, but there's been nothing for a while now.'

Her thoughts appeared to turn inward again. Or had her consciousness merely drifted off into the mind of someone else? He could never be sure whose eyes his own daughter was peering through at any given moment. But then she shuddered and Granger noticed anguish in her eyes.

She sniffed and wiped her nose on her sleeve. 'What are we doing out here?'

'We're leaving.'

'To where?'

He shrugged.

'You don't even know?'

'Port Awl,' he said. 'We'll find passage on a ship—'

'Which ship?'

'I don't know.'

'You've really thought this through, haven't you?' she said with surprising bitterness. Her red-rimmed eyes now glared fiercely up at him. 'Do you even have any money?'

He said nothing.

'I suppose you were counting on *me* for that?'

Granger had had enough. 'I got you out of that damned place,' he growled. 'Now shut up and leave the rest to me.'

'*You* got me out?' she said, with incredulity.

The truth was that he'd found the palace in chaos, with Haurstaf corpses strewn everywhere and leucotomized Unmer freed from their torture cells to wander half-mad and gibbering through corridors choked with the dead. His arrival at that time had to have been more than just fortuitous. Again, he sensed the hand of a hidden manipulator at work, and it deeply unnerved him. It was time to get as far away from here as possible.

'Can you walk?' he said.

'I'm not going anywhere with you,' she replied.

'You don't have much choice.'

'I'm going back to the palace.'

'No, you aren't.' As soon as the words had left his mouth, he saw his daughter's jaw clench and her nostrils flare and he knew what was coming. When Ianthe dug in, she really dug in.

'*You* don't have any right to stop me,' she said. She tried to rise from the ground, but then winced and let loose a pitiful wail as her beaten limbs railed against the sudden movement. At once she looked much younger than her fifteen years. Or was she sixteen now? Only a few years younger than her mother had been when Granger first met her. Yet here she was now, a wounded child, sitting on the grass, about to cry.

Granger's nearest replicate crouched down as if to comfort

the girl, although he hadn't consciously instructed it to do so. He was about to pull it back when Ianthe reacted.

She shrieked, 'Get that *thing* away from me!' And then she began to sob.

Granger willed the replicate to leave. His control of them had become intuitive by now. It was like having numerous waking dreams running simultaneously in the periphery of his mind. He could switch over to any one of them (finding himself marching through the undergrowth and breaking branches and crouched over a fire) and yet they seemed to undertake the tasks he'd set for them without much conscious direction from him. He wondered if this was close to the way Ianthe saw the world.

He stared at her dumbly for a moment, unsure of what to do, then he left her and went over to the fire, where his other replicate was straining tea into a tin mug. He couldn't bear to speak to the thing, to treat any of these sorcerous manifestations as human, so he simply lifted the steaming brew from its hands and carried it back over to Ianthe. He could feel the warmth of the drink through his alloy gauntlets as a prickling sensation in the palms of his hands.

'Drink this.'

'Go away!'

'It'll numb the pain.'

She blew her nose on her sleeve and wiped tears from her eyes. For a moment he thought she might lash out and knock the tea away. But then she seemed to calm down. She reached over and accepted the mug.

'Smells like grass.'

'Mostly it is,' he said. 'Birch grass, a couple of other things. We used to use this stuff in Aramo when . . .' His voice tailed off. She didn't want to hear about that.

He left her sipping her tea, while he assessed their situation. They were deep in the wooded foothills below the palace, but still surrounded by Haurstaf army encampments. Now that the fighting had ceased, there would have to be negotiations between the Haurstaf's military commanders and whatever Unmer force had decimated the Haurstaf. On his way out of the palace, Granger had seen one Unmer lord still in possession of his mind. That single escapee ought to be enough to give the Haurstaf soldiers pause. Conventional warfare was woefully ineffective against these eastern sorcerers. What's more, with their paymasters dead or fleeing, he doubted that the Haurstaf military would be in a mood to fight on principle alone. Some sort of parley was inevitable. It was the perfect time for Ianthe and him to escape.

He looked back at his daughter, only to see her flinch. Had she been looking through his eyes then, even with her physical sight restored?

'I won't do it,' she said.

'Do what?'

Ianthe actually growled. 'I won't find trove for you. Why does *everyone* think they know what's best for me?' She set down her tea, which toppled and spilled over the grass. And then she struggled to her feet, wincing and gasping.

'Which way?' she said.

'What?'

'Are you being stupid on purpose? *Which way back to the palace?*'

'We're not going—'

Granger stopped suddenly as an image of men on horseback flashed across his vision. *Four, five riders.* Metal tackle and buckles gleaming in broken sunlight. The huff and snort of the beasts. In a moment of confusion, he thought they were moving through the trees directly beyond his camp, but then he realized the truth. One of his sorcerous replicates was watching the riders from a distant part of the forest.

He raised a hand to Ianthe. 'Wait here a moment.'

Then he shifted his full attention into the replicate.

And suddenly he found himself crouched among ferns, thirty feet up on one side of a defile. It was cooler here than back in the camp. Below him he could see part of the trail he had walked that very morning, about half a league from where his real body now stood. Steep, heavily wooded banks rose on either side of a narrow track, the trees growing amid jumbles of great lichen-marred boulders.

The riders were a mix of Unmer and human, he could see that now – five of them, relaxed in their saddles as their mounts stepped along the track below. The two in the lead were Unmer: tall and pale and wearing silk hose and shirts of light forest greens and greys and darker quilted tunics the colour of earth and rock. As they moved towards Granger's hiding place, he spied gemstones glittering – their sword belts like seams of anthracite and emeralds, exquisite dagger hilts and jewel-encrusted quivers on their backs. The rider at the head of the party was a slender youth with golden hair. Granger recognized him as the young lord he'd encountered in the palace antechamber when he'd carried Ianthe to safety. Immediately behind him rode an older man with a noble forehead framed in white hair, a long jaw and the same dark violet eyes as the youth. Behind this pair came three human palace guards, clad in plain mail and steel epaulettes whose surfaces had been polished over many years to a dull metal grizzle.

The presence of these turncoats with the Unmer lords clearly indicated the presence of some sort of agreement or truce between them.

The boy raised a hand, halting his comrades. Then he looked directly up at Granger's hiding place and called out: 'I hope you haven't been clutching that blade *all* this time. Those swords have a nasty habit of cooking men's minds.'

Granger felt a twinge of surprise and shame that the lad had spotted him so quickly, but now that he'd been detected he saw no reason to remain crouched among the undergrowth. He stood up and called down to them: 'What do you want?'

The young lord observed him for a moment. 'I am Prince Paulus Marquetta,' he said. His violet eyes continued to survey Granger while he waited for a reply. When none was forthcoming, he smiled. 'Actually, I was looking for you, sir.'

'I don't know you,' Granger said.

'Nor I you,' Marquetta replied. 'And yet it would seem that I owe my freedom to your daughter.' Tackle clinked as he urged the horse forward. Marquetta's jewellery gleamed in the dappled shade. 'My uncle, Duke Cyr of Vale, and I are the last of the Unmer royal line on Awl,' he said. 'The Haurstaf have either murdered our kin or imprisoned them in Losotan ghettos. Or else taken their minds entirely.' As he came forward, he touched the side of his left eye, indicating the place where the Haurstaf drove in their leucotomy blades. 'Now we would not see our saviours struggle on through the woods on foot like fugitives,' he said. He stopped his horse on the path below Granger. 'Please, return to the palace with us and enjoy our hospitality. We will provide you with a carriage to Port Awl whenever you wish to leave.'

Granger showed no emotion, but inside his thoughts were racing. *Ianthe?* The prince thought her responsible for the devastation that had set him free? He felt a sudden coldness in his heart, quickly followed by an overwhelming surge of despair for the girl. Every shred of his being yearned for it not to be true, and yet he feared it was the truth. The Haurstaf had been probing deep into his daughter's mind – a mind with uncanny and possibly untapped powers. A mind they feared, that they were vulnerable to. They had been trying to discover Ianthe's limits. What had they unlocked?

The prince was frowning now, the searching look on his face turning to puzzlement.

To purchase himself some time, Granger said, 'You say the roads are open?'

'We have reached an understanding with the palace guard, and a provisional agreement with the Haurstaf commanders,' Marquetta said. He shrugged. 'Although there still remains much to discuss, hostilities have now ceased. The roads are a good deal safer than they were last night.'

'Then I don't need your help,' Granger said.

'I'm quite sure of that,' Marquetta replied. 'But what about your daughter? The poor girl needs time to recover from her ordeal. Why walk all the way to Port Awl, when you can dine with us at the palace and sleep in feather beds?'

'She's fine as she is,' Granger said. 'We're going home.'

The older Unmer lord behind Marquetta now urged his horse forward until it was abreast of the young prince. He leaned over and whispered something to him.

Marquetta nodded and turned back to Granger. 'We will escort you to Port Awl.'

'I don't need an escort,' Granger said.

'It would be our honour.'

'I said no.'

The prince regarded him for a moment longer, his gaze lingering on Granger's sorcerous sword. He possessed an arrogant twist to his lips that wasn't quite a sneer and wasn't quite a smile, and it seemed to Granger that the young man's violet eyes now held within them a spark of anger. His face was as pale as spider silk, his hair like a burst of gold wire. The older lord was similarly gaunt, but carried himself with the confidence of a veteran warrior. On the back of his right wrist Granger spied a tattoo of the geometric design favoured by Entropic sorcerers and yet this man carried none of the amplifiers or other magical devices employed by those devils. The two Unmer men exchanged a glance and there was a moment in which it seemed to Granger that some unspoken communication passed between them. Suddenly Marquetta shook his head and said, 'So be it. We will not force our hospitality upon anyone.' His glass-shard eyes held Granger's own for a moment longer, before his gaze returned to the replicating sword. 'Be wary of that blade, sir, or it *will* consume you.'

With that, he reined his horse around. The other riders parted to let him through. He set off back down the trail without as much as another glance at Granger.

Granger stood there, gripping sorcerous steel in a hand that wasn't his, and watched them depart. Once the riders had disappeared from sight, he took a deep breath and then shifted his consciousness from the sword replicate's body back to his own.

He had been inside the replicate too long. Returning his mind to his own body was like coming to after a sound beating. The environment slurred and then abruptly changed. Sunlight pierced his retinas, bringing with it a sound like clattering carriage wheels that faded quickly but then lingered at the periphery of his nerves. For a moment, nothing seemed real. His stomach bucked, and he came close to vomiting. Instead, he fell to his knees and clutched the warm grass to steady himself. He retched and spat saliva, and then his nostrils filled with the odour of warm earth and wild flowers.

'We'd better go,' he said, turning to look for Ianthe.

But she was nowhere to be seen.

CHAPTER 3

RETURN TO
THE PALACE

Granger cursed his own lack of foresight. How long had his attention been diverted? Mere minutes, it had seemed, and yet . . .

A frantic search of the woodland all around yielded no sign of his daughter, so he closed his eyes and ground his teeth and let the perceptions of all of his sword replicates come crashing into his already exhausted mind.

The green glow of ferns.

Yellow leaves among inkscrawl branches.

Insects drifting like plumes of pollen.

Grasses nodding.

Knuckles of green stone.

Earth. Lichen.

A butterfly flitting drunkenly between white flowers.

With a growl of pain and exasperation, he tore his own mind back from the onslaught. His ears rang with echoes like clashing steel, like raiders with war chariots ravaging through his thoughts. He tasted blood on his lip.

Not one of those sorcerous creations could see Ianthe.

But of course she could see through *their* eyes if she chose to do so. She'd know where every one of them was, and thus be able to avoid them easily.

43

Granger leaned against his sword and squeezed his temples as if that might alleviate his pounding headache. He gave a deep and weary sigh. How do you find someone who doesn't want to be found and always knows exactly where you are looking for them? Did he even want to try? His eyeballs felt raw, scratched, his limbs leaden. His eardrums still reverberated with the smash and rattle of imagined steel while flashes of his replicates' perceptions pulled his own thoughts away on wires of pain.

He spied his shield resting against a fallen tree, and his heart fell further. Its crystalline facets now smouldered with green and black fire. No leaf nor bough nor blade of grass found its likeness in that glass. To look within was to stare into the fuming heart of the cosmos. And there lurked insanity. Granger considered leaving the hellish thing where it was. The merest touch of it clawed at his nerves. He wasn't even sure if he currently possessed the strength to pick it up. And yet Herian had spoken of unimaginable powers spun into its prisms – far more subtle and dangerous than his stolen sword and suit. Nothing could penetrate that abyss-forged glass, not even a void arrow. Nor could it be unmade by the destructive touch of the Unmer. Such feats were possible, Herian said, because the shield existed in multiple places at once, shared by warriors across more than one cosmos. Granger could not be sure who else carried that same shield, or where in the vastness of the heavens they would presently be located, only that he would not recognize them as human. And then Herian had hinted that the shield possessed a still greater and more frightening power. He had implied that it might be possible to summon its other bearers.

How could he abandon such a treasure?

He picked up the shield and pulled the leather straps tight

around his forearm. Colours boiled over the surface of the glass and, in a moment of sickening disorientation, its myriad facets became a great burst of scintillations upon a green and black ocean. He found himself turning around, staggering and dazed, suddenly uncertain of his actual location. He was at sea? Caught in a raging storm? *But there had been a woodland.* And then the trees and the flowers returned in a swirl of hot colours. The vision faded and the shield once more became a solid mass of glass. It had almost no physical weight and yet he could barely lift it. It exerted a different sort of pressure that – like a clutch of needles – cinched around his consciousness.

He coughed and was not surprised to see blood in his spit.

Granger raised his shield nevertheless and he slung his kitbag over his shoulder and gripped the replicating sword more firmly. And thus both hideously encumbered and unnaturally empowered he set off through the forest at a hard run. His bones and skin crawled with sorcery. Sorcery scratched the back of his eyes. But he forced his mind to focus on the task at hand. He might not know where Ianthe was now, but he knew where she was going.

Despite being blind and deaf, Ianthe was rarely lost, for it was her habit never to venture too far from other people. After all, it had been their eyes and ears she'd always used psychically to perceive her own surroundings. All her life she'd struggled with the one frustratingly limited aspect of her ability: when nobody was looking at her, she couldn't see her immediate surroundings. This constant yearning to be observed had led to what her mother had called *attention-seeking behaviour*. In Ianthe's case, however, the attention seeking was a necessary survival skill.

Her Unmer lenses had changed all that. She could see as well as anybody else. She could see the sunlight piercing the forest canopy overhead, the butterflies flitting between flowers, the warm moss and lichen-scarred boulders. A fly buzzed past her head and she batted it away. It still felt strange to be directly aware of such things. However, Ianthe's unique supernormal senses continued to augment her newly won perceptions of the world, adding a comforting layer of normalcy to what still felt strange and unnerving. When she closed her eyes she could perceive the palace several miles to the north. For Ianthe, it existed as a great patchwork of light suspended in the darkness, a combination of the perceptions of everyone inhabiting the building.

Weirdness aside, her Unmer lenses had opened up a world of freedom she could never turn her back on. They were, like most such spectacles, psychically linked to a particular sorcerer who had lived in the past. By turning the tiny wheel on the edge of the frames, she was able to perceive everything the original wearer had witnessed at any given moment during his lifetime. Her mind was linked, across time, to his, and she could roll back through a lifetime of his perceptions at will. The spectacles allowed her to see through his eyes and him to see through hers. For a normal, sighted, wearer of the lenses, the ensuing paradoxes resulted in a complete breakdown of the sorcery – what Ethan Maskelyne had called *terminal feedback*. The cosmos would not permit someone to see their own future.

Ianthe was blind, however. She couldn't use her own eyes to observe the world. But she could use his. And somewhere amidst these myriad loops of time and sorcery and metaphysics, lenses that were cheap and commonly regarded as useless gave her the power to see and hear the world she inhabited.

As she marched onwards through sunlit woodland, a pang of misery clenched her heart. She recalled the moment Ethan Maskelyne's men had thrown her mother, Hana, across a brine-flooded cell in Granger's prison, leaving her badly wounded by the toxic water. Ianthe had been leagues away by then, crouched against the bilge of a boat heading for Maskelyne's fortress on Scythe Island, but she had been looking through her mother's eyes.

Ethan Maskelyne – trove expert, metaphysicist, crime lord, psychopath. He had just been another link in the chain of people who'd wished to own Ianthe or use her peculiar talent for finding treasure. Her life had been a succession of such relationships. Ianthe had earned the money by which she and her mother had survived on Evensraum after the war. They had escaped cholera by working for a trove scavenger and smuggler. But Emperor Hu's navy had put a stop to that illegal operation. She'd been passed through Interrogation and then shipped to Ethugra with thousands of other prisoners of war. God knows what would have become of them if Hana hadn't identified Granger among the jailers.

She had mixed feelings about having Granger as her father. Even though he had given them refuge, he'd still tried to sell Ianthe to the Haurstaf, which was hardly surprising. That was before he'd known exactly what she was capable of – before he understood her value to *him*. But by then it was too late. Knowledge of Ianthe's powers had reached both Ethan Maskelyne and Haurstaf leader Briana Marks.

And so the course of Ianthe's life was, as always, channelled by the needs and desires of others. The Haurstaf had taken her from Maskelyne for the same reasons that Maskelyne had stolen her away from Granger and then subsequently tried to wrench her back from the Haurstaf by bombarding their palace. Ianthe lived her life like a shuttle in a loom. And now Granger had come to take her away from Awl again. An endless cycle.

Ianthe had had enough. She was tired of doing what other people wanted. Tired of being a victim. Tired of being that shuttle in the loom. When the Haurstaf realized the scale of Ianthe's powers, they'd understood how much of a threat she could be to their whole way of life. But rather than trust her as an ally, they chose to kill her. And in their torture cell they'd dug so deep into Ianthe's mind that they'd triggered something inside her. By trying to understand her powers they had inadvertently unleashed an even greater power. Ianthe had used it to devastating effect. Her rage had decimated her captors, giving the Unmer the chance to escape their prisons.

When she thought of Paulus Marquetta, her heart took a fluttering leap. In him she recognized a kindred spirit. He, too, knew what it felt like to be enslaved. He wouldn't judge her for what she'd done, she felt sure.

He wouldn't despise her.

If Ianthe could find forgiveness anywhere, then it would be with the Unmer.

With her prince.

Ianthe halted in a forest clearing where a great profusion of tiny white flowers had sprung from the grass, carpeting the earth in swathes and hummocks so bright they might have been crystals of salt or ice. She recognized the delicate scent from the Evensraum woodlands of her childhood, but had no name for it. And she stood for a moment, filling her lungs with that natural perfume and marvelling at the freshness and intensity of the colours.

But then she sensed movement nearby. One of her father's

replicates was close. She hurled herself into its mind and glimpsed its metal-shod boots compressing the soft earth, and suddenly she was in another part of the forest. Putting her mind inside these sorcerous creations felt odd – quite unlike the sensation of occupying another person. All the senses were there, but still something was missing. Something indeterminable. Ianthe looked out through the replicate's eyes and realized that it was getting too close to her physical body for comfort. She vacated the thing at once.

And ran.

She avoided the replicates easily and soon found herself picking her way along a deep gully in a quieter part of the forest. Granger's sorcerous copies were off to the west – near one of the gun emplacements, where numerous tracks made the terrain easier to traverse. But Ianthe had come to know the forest trails well during her time as a Haurstaf student and this short cut would see her reach the palace before any of her father's copies. Occasionally she heard the snap of gunfire. Hunters, probably. She sensed deer moving a few hundred yards further up the slope to her right, and when she closed her eyes and let her mind perceive the forest through its birds and insects, the world became a soft and dreamlike labyrinth of light and sound.

For several hours Ianthe wandered onwards through the forest and finally, as the sun was heading for the mountains, she reached a rocky outcropping overlooking the former Haurstaf palace.

Smoke still rose from the shattered eastern wing of the palace, where Maskelyne's explosives had reduced the grand carved façades and tall windows to a great clutter of rubble. Dozens of palace guards and servants were working in teams, clearing away the debris as they hunted for survivors. Several lines of men and women passed stones and buckets of dust and grit down and emptied them beyond the area of destruction. Ianthe was surprised to see a few Unmer among them.

As she watched, a group of riders approached through the forest. She recognized Prince Marquetta among them. There could be no mistaking his regal bearing and sunburst yellow hair. The prince dismounted and went over to the nearest line of workers. He spoke with one of the palace guards and then turned and waved his riding companions over.

Ianthe watched with delight as the majority of the riders, along with Prince Marquetta himself, joined the guards and servants moving rubble. Any fears she might have had regarding the reception she was likely to receive from the Unmer were somewhat allayed.

They were still clearing rubble an hour later when Ianthe strode out of the woods.

The prince and two palace guards were squatting on a great mound of stone and mortar, using a beam to lever up a fallen section of wall when Ianthe approached them. He was covered in dust and sweat and so preoccupied with his exertions that he merely glanced her way at first. But then he suddenly stopped what he was doing and turned and gaped at her. The palace guards looked up, too, and reacted at once, dropping the beam in what was almost a panicked scramble to reclaim the bows they had placed nearby. Their hands went to the hilts of their swords.

Ianthe realized she was still wearing Haurstaf robes. 'Wait,' she said. 'I won't harm you.'

The guards continued to watch her cautiously. But then Prince Marquetta's eyes suddenly widened and he said, 'It *is* you. Ianthe. The girl from my dream.'

She gave a nervous nod.

'But your father . . .'

'My father and I have come to a disagreement over my future.'

The young prince climbed down from the rubble and dusted his hands. He approached her, his violet eyes burning with curiosity. 'I have the chance to thank you, at last,' he said. And then he took her hands and grinned and dropped to his knees right there. 'So thank you, my dear Ianthe. We Unmer owe you a debt of gratitude we can never repay.'

Ianthe felt her face blush. Everyone was looking at her.

'We Unmer use dreams to speak to our patrons,' Marquetta said. 'The entities your kind call *elder gods*. I was in such a dream when we met. You interrupted my conversation.'

'I'm sorry,' she said. 'I didn't—'

'Please don't be,' Marquetta said. 'Gods can be tedious. You, most certainly were not. I remember it vividly. And how delightful it is to discover that you are even more beautiful in the flesh.'

Ianthe felt her cheeks burn with even greater insistence. 'Thank you, Prince Marquetta.'

'Call me Paulus,' he said, and kissed her hand. 'Now tell me, Ianthe: where is your father? I imagine he's looking everywhere for you.'

In his present state of physical exhaustion Granger had no option but to allow his power armour to do the work for him. The suit augmented his limbs and made him inhumanly strong. The razor-thin whorls etched into the metal plates scattered light, endowing the suit with a patina of rainbows. His boots pounded the soft earth, leaving deep depressions in his wake. He weighed, he supposed, more than three men combined.

And as he ran he let a part of his overworked mind control his eight replicates.

He used them as he would have utilized a small unit of real soldiers. The five furthest away he forced to fan out ahead and to the sides, flanking his position through the forest while maintaining a defensive perimeter. The others he called closer. He wanted them near: three more blades to bear upon whatever dangers he might run into.

He looked for Ianthe but did not spot her and soon he had reached the place where he had, through one of his replicates, encountered the Unmer prince and his retinue.

Bursts of sunlight lit the forest canopy to the west, the greens and yellows now beginning to shudder at the edges of his vision. He felt that his eyesight might fail him. But down in the defile wherein the riders had passed it remained restfully gloomy. Earth-scented mulch compressed under his heels as he climbed down, his great mass sinking his boots in deep. He ordered his sorcerous companions out into the forested slopes on either side, and then proceeded along the firmer ground of the trail itself.

He had not gone far when a shot rang out.

A bullet glanced off his armour at the shoulder and pinged into the woods. *No . . . Not* his *shoulder.* It took him a moment to realize that one of the sword replicates had been hit, and in that instant of confusion came the *crack* of two more shots. He felt the bullets strike the replicate's chest plate and heard the metal emit an angry buzz and crackle that sent involuntary spasms through his own muscles. His subconscious reacted, willing the replicate to dive for cover, while he amassed and collated feedback from the others in order to locate the source of the gunfire.

There.

They were crouched behind boulders on the summit of a rise, a hundred yards or so north of his current position. Haurstaf riflemen: most likely scouts or simply soldiers on hunting detachment. Each of them possessed a light carbine rifle. Their location offered them a good view of the trail and a good place to ambush travellers, but it was on the forest east of the trail that their attention was now fixed, the very spot where one of Granger's replicates now crouched behind a smooth grey boulder. They did not appear to have spotted the others.

Granger sensed his other replicates, now moving to flank the gunmen. Had he ordered them to do so? He could not recall. His thoughts stuttered. And suddenly he found himself standing a dozen yards further along the path, with no memory of having actually moved. Instantly he felt dizzy. Another ten yards would have brought him into plain view of the ambushers on the slope ahead. In a moment of terrible confusion it had seemed to him that he was a replicate himself, a slave to one of the others.

Were they using him as a distraction? A target to draw the riflemen's fire?

He gathered his willpower.

Crack.

Something slammed into his eye and knocked him round. Green and golden sunlight whirled, fractured by branches. As he turned, he glimpsed ferns spattered with blood and brain and fragments of his own skull. He fell. His face struck warm ground, felt earth between his teeth, the smell of wood and dirt, liquid trickling down his neck. Was that his blood? His mouth was dry – a crabbing pain moving up the side of his head.

And he was standing at the bottom of the rise again with the blade clenched in his fist and the echo of the shot that had killed him rolling away through the forest. The Unmer sword shuddered faintly, expelling the fallen replicate to non-existence. And then it trembled again and, with a hideous sensation of dislocation, a fresh copy of himself appeared on the trail before him. The thing simply materialized out of thin air, its arrival announced by a faint *pop* and an inrush of wind. It looked at Granger with its corpse-flesh eyes before turning towards the riflemen and loping away up the slope in their direction.

Again, Granger could not recall having ordered it to do so.

Stop. His mind groped for the other replicates. *Stay where you are.*

Suddenly he was running again.

Why?

He stopped, unsure.

When he heard screaming, Granger finally understood that he had lost control. He sat down on the ground and began to laugh. Images flashed through his mind: of wide white eyes and teeth and flesh cleaved open. The steel barrels of carbine rifles bent double by powerful gauntlets. He was no longer in a woodland of sun and leaves but in a forest of green glass, a mass of shards that split his vision into innumerable planes. Rifts of shadow clashed with light as white as pain. And some-where in that frenzy of broken images he witnessed the brutal murder of the Haurstaf riflemen on the rise.

Drop the sword.

He wanted to drop the sword, but he could not.

Drop the sword.

Some part of him begged his hand to release his grip on the weapon. But yet another part was using the blade up there on the summit of the slope – in three hands, in four hands, in six of his hands. And that part of his mind refused. He growled with impotent rage, powerless to do anything but watch as his replicates hacked and hacked at the unfortunate men and his splintered vision turned from green to red.

They gave Ianthe a suite of chambers overlooking the meditation garden in the westernmost courtyard. This accommodation had previously belonged to a high-ranking Haurstaf official, and Ianthe wondered if the prince had chosen this suite merely because the official was as close to Ianthe's size as the servants could find. Everything in the wardrobes fitted her like a glove.

On the morning after her arrival here she paced back and forth before the mirror on the gilt and onyx wardrobe and tried on the clothes of a woman she had probably murdered. In addition to the white Haurstaf robes were scores of other garments: gowns in gold and silver and alabaster colours and spider-silk blouses and quilted hunting outfits and shoes by the dozen woven with fine precious metals. A dragon-bone chest in the corner of the room held enough jewellery to buy a house.

However, as beautiful as they were, none of clothes felt right. She would try something on, and stare at herself and then inevitably feel guilty and miserable. How could she delight in wages of her sins? She stood in the bedroom and gazed around at the myriad piles of sumptuous fabric. And then she piled it all unceremoniously back into the wardrobe and went through to the bathroom. There, she removed her own threadbare and mud-stained robe, washed it in the bath using hand soap and hung it up to dry.

The servants brought her bowls of fruit for breakfast and she dined at an elaborately sculpted glass table beside the window. The light pouring through the window made the table sparkle like a frost-crusted bush.

Ianthe was so nervous about breaking the blasted thing that she became tense and clumsy. It was probably inevitable that she should knock her mug over, spilling coffee that dripped down through the transparent intricacies. In her panic to mop it up, she knocked over a vase, which chipped the table surface and then rolled off and hit the floor and shattered.

She stopped, breathing hard, and stared at the destruction she'd caused and almost wept.

When the servant girl came to collect the breakfast plates an hour later she found Ianthe sitting on the floor in her damp and wrinkled robes, scrubbing at the glass table with a napkin.

'Please, ma'am,' the girl said. 'Let me.'

Ianthe stopped what she was doing, and said, 'I'm so sorry. I didn't mean . . . I . . .'

'The prince has asked for you,' the girl said.

Ianthe stared at her.

'He's waiting for you in the garden below the window.'

'He's there *now*?'

'Yes, ma'am.'

'Please don't call me that. My name is Ianthe.'

'Yes, Miss Ianthe.'

'You say he's waiting there now?'

'Yes, Miss Ianthe.'

'Can you take me there?'

'Yes, miss. Now?'

'Please.'

The servant studied her a moment. 'Would you like to change first, miss?'

Ianthe looked down at her miserable robes, then glanced at the wardrobe again.

She found Paulus sitting waiting for her on a bench beneath a whitewashed wall against which the Haurstaf gardeners had trained fans of pears and almonds. He was reading a small leather book in Unmer, but looked up when she approached.

'Ianthe,' he said, rising and taking her hand. 'How wonderful you look.' His gaze wandered approvingly over her pale silk skirt and a cream quilted jacket with its gold filigree. 'I see that everything was the correct size?'

'Thank you, Your—'

'Call me Paulus,' he said. 'I insist.'

He led her along the crushed-shell path and under a vine-smothered arbour dripping with plump grapes. Fruit, he explained, that was ripening earlier in the season, thanks to sorcerous heat blades driven into the soil. Yet another aspect of Unmer culture borrowed by Haurstaf.

And so they walked among the lavender and sage and inhaled the scent of wallflowers and Paulus talked eagerly of the future Ianthe had given his people. The air seemed ripe with possibilities. His uncle Cyr had, he explained, come to a provisional agreement with the Haurstaf military. Some four thousand soldiers in bases around the palace now had new paymasters – a transition that had been remarkably uneventful. There were enough riches in the palace to keep an army that size paid for decades to come, with enough left over to build a fleet of ships should the Haurstaf navy prove less cooperative.

'However,' Paulus explained. 'Our priority is our people in Losoto.'

Thousands of Unmer remained imprisoned in the ghettos there, under the guard of a unit of Haurstaf psychics – an arrangement which was paid for by Emperor Hu himself at Guild insistence. Presumably Hu had heard of the Haurstaf's demise in Awl, but as yet there had been no response from him.

There had been survivors among the Haurstaf in Awl, but almost all of them had fled to join their sisters in Port Awl and arrange passage away from the island altogether. Paulus had sent word to these estranged psychics, offering a truce. Since none of the Haurstaf knew what had really been behind the slaughter at the palace, they had naturally assumed that Maskelyne's bombardment had been a decoy to allow the Unmer to launch their own attack using some as yet unidentified sorcery. This worked to the Unmer's advantage. The Haurstaf now feared them enough that they accepted Paulus's terms and were unlikely to retaliate.

They left the garden by a small wicket gate and stepped out into the forest. Ianthe knew the woods around the palace well. On any given day you could be sure to find students wandering the worn pathways or sitting studying in quiet glades. Now it seemed woefully quiet. Ianthe let her consciousness reach out, out of habit, and search for anyone around her. In the back of her mind she sensed the birds and insects, the skittish deer. She could see and hear the work of palace guards and manservants still clearing the wrecked palace wing, and further away a unit of soldiers marching along a trail further down the hill.

But then she sensed something horribly familiar. A group of people with unnaturally sharp perceptions – and yet edgy, corrupted, tainted by sorcery. She had missed them initially because they were moving around the shattered wing where so many other people worked. She had overlooked them in a crowd of perceptions. But now those workers had stopped clearing rubble and were staring at the newcomers. Eight men. They were close enough to make her stop suddenly and clench Paulus's arm.

'What is it?' he said.

Ianthe looked along the palace façade to the corner. She knew what was coming and almost stamped her foot with frustration. It wasn't fair. Why should her perfect moment be spoiled?

'Can we go,' she said.

'Why? What is it?'

But then it was too late. Granger's replicates came into view around the corner. Their identical faces each bore scorch marks caused by immersion in brine. Their eyes were hot and red and utterly devoid of human emotion. They wore bulky power armour that whirred faintly and altered hue in the patchy forest light, as nacreous swirls danced across sorcerous alloys.

The lead replicate was holding the body of a man before him, supporting him as easily as if he weighed nothing. And suddenly Ianthe's breath caught in her throat. She'd seen the replicates from afar, but she had overlooked the figure they carried. She'd overlooked it because the man was dead. He didn't have perceptions she could hijack, nor even a consciousness she could inhabit.

But of course Ianthe recognized him at once. His face was well known to her. A face that would have been identical to the seven other replicates, were it not for the bullet hole in his eye.

Paulus beckoned the replicates inside, and they followed without a word. He got them to lay Granger's body on a large table in one of the schoolrooms and then he sent a servant to fetch his uncle.

Ianthe stood beside her father's dead body while his eight ghoulish likenesses looked on. They unnerved her. Just looking at them filled her with nausea and revulsion. She resented them being here, sharing this moment. Her hand hovered over her father's breastplate – the scorched and battle-scarred metal, with its weird rainbow patina – but she couldn't bring herself to touch it.

She felt hollow, as if some great part of her future had been wrenched out of her. And, as she looked at his shattered face, anguish came to fill the emptiness. Suddenly her tears welled and flowed freely down her cheeks. She hid her face in her hands and sobbed.

'I'm sorry for your loss,' Paulus said.

She sensed his hand on her shoulder. She turned into him and sobbed against his chest, trembling, her breaths now coming in great uncontrollable heaves.

'I hated him so much,' she managed to say.

He held her closer. 'That emotion is often a companion of love.'

She let out a soft wail. She had started to shake and so she let him hold her for a long time, feeling the warmth of his chest against her cheek.

'Your Highness.'

Ianthe recognized Duke Cyr's voice. She sniffed and looked up to see him striding over to the table, his brow creased with concern. He glanced at the sword replicates standing mutely around the table and then back at her father's body.

He stooped over Granger and examined the wound in his head. And then he reached down and pressed his hand against the side of Granger's neck. After a moment he gave a soft grunt of approval. 'Dry your eyes, my dear,' he said. 'Your father is alive.'

Ianthe gaped at him for a moment. 'But the wound . . .?'

'Is as fatal as I've seen,' Cyr replied. 'The eye and most of his brain are gone. Nevertheless, he is alive.'

*

That night Ianthe lay in bed and tried to unravel her thoughts. They had moved her father to an empty chamber and laid him upon the bed. She thought of him lying there with that gaping hole in his face, his brains exposed.

And still alive.

It was the armour, Cyr had said. The armour was keeping him alive, regenerating him, forming new tissue to replace the stuff that had been damaged. Growing him a new eye.

A new brain.

She shuddered.

Did her father dream, she wondered. Was he aware of his surroundings, his condition?

And how had he ended up here? How had the replicating sword been able to create the replicates who had brought her father here when he had been unconscious? She recalled that they were, in this instance, not exact copies of him. None of them had displayed the same mortal wound.

She didn't understand any of it.

Moonlight glimmered beyond the gauze drapes. She could smell the jasmine growing in the garden below her window. Normally she would have found it soothing, but sleep eluded her tonight. It must already be three or four bells past midnight. She found herself on edge, listening out for something.

But what?

And then she realized what it was. She was listening for the approach of her father's replicates. Sword phantoms, Paulus called them. They were empty, mere sorcerous husks, but they still terrified her. She imagined them standing out there in the dark of the garden, their ghoulish faces staring up at her window, and the thought made her shiver.

Ianthe wrapped the bedclothes more tightly around her. Of course they weren't out there. Why would they be? Her father's brain was in pieces. He could neither summon them nor control them. They were here at the will of the blade itself.

She wondered where they were right now. Had Cyr sent them away? Had they merely evaporated back to non-existence now that they had accomplished their task and brought Granger here?

Ianthe listened to the silence.

They weren't outside. It was foolish of her to think so.

Perhaps she should just check, to put her mind at rest.

Ianthe shook her head and buried herself further under the bedclothes. She was being ridiculous. There were no ghouls out there in the dark. She was alone and it was four bells after midnight and she ought to get to sleep. Paulus had promised to take her riding tomorrow, if she felt up to it.

She wasn't going to feel up to it, if she didn't get some sleep.

Ianthe growled and sat up in bed. She stared at the window. The moonlit curtains glowed faintly. Nothing moved. There were no sounds. Not so much as a breeze to disturb the utter stillness.

Ianthe got out of bed and padded over to the window. She reached for the drapes, but then hesitated. Fear prickled the back of her neck. The stone floor felt icy beneath her toes. She could feel her heart racing.

Really. She was just being ridiculous.

Ianthe pulled back the curtain.

She saw them at once, standing in the garden below her window. Eight dark figures, their brine-scarred faces upturned, their eyes mere pits of shadow. They were all looking up at her.

She screamed.

Moments of confusion followed. Ianthe did not remember

backing away from the window, nor how she came to be on the floor beside her bed, but suddenly she was kneeling on the cold stone, gripping the bed sheets and shrieking.

She heard noises in the corridor outside and then the door burst open.

'Ianthe?'

It was Paulus. He rushed over to her and she seized him and held on like a drowning woman clutches a buoy.

'What is it?' he said.

'The window,' she replied. 'The garden. They're in the garden.'

'What are?' He tried to extricate himself from her, but she held on fiercely. 'Ianthe, please, I have to see who's out there.'

She choked back a sob, but let him go.

He hurried over to the window and peered out. After a moment he said, 'I see nothing.'

'The sword phantoms,' Ianthe said. 'They were out there.'

Paulus leaned out of the window and scanned the surroundings. After a few moments he ducked back into the room. 'Well, there's nothing there now. Are you sure it wasn't a dream?'

'They were there!' she said.

He came over and took her hands in his. 'All right,' he said. 'I believe you. They must have run off when you screamed.'

'I'm sorry,' she said. 'They startled me.'

'Ghouls like that would unnerve anyone.'

'I'm so embarrassed.'

He kissed her forehead and squeezed her hands more tightly. 'Don't be.'

She raised her chin and her nose brushed his cheek. His skin was cool. He smelled clean, a hint of some fragrance. In the gloom she could just make out his sharp features. His fair hair seemed almost white in the dim glow of the moon. For a moment they were silent, listening to each other's breathing. There was something tangible in the air between them, almost electric. She knew he felt it, too.

She kissed his ear, gently, and then again on his cheek. And then she kissed his lips.

'That's it.'

A blur resolved itself into the face of a handsome young man whom Granger recognized. *Marquetta.* The prince's violet eyes glinted with dark mirth as he looked on. Beside him stood an older, grey-haired man, whom Granger recognized as the second Unmer lord in the prince's riding party. This man leaned back from the bed. He was holding a long silver pin, which he now inserted into a spherical device held in his other hand. The device appeared to be constructed of thousands of silver filaments each as fine as gossamer. As the pin slotted into place, the sphere emitted a gentle sort of clattering noise, like that of a Losotan abacus. The silver-haired lord peered at it very intensely. Then he held it aloft and released it, whereupon it remained hovering in the air a few inches from his face.

'Shoo,' he said.

The device wafted away like a silver soap bubble.

'His mind is functioning again, sire,' he said to the prince. 'Although to what degree remains uncertain. Time will undoubtedly tell.'

Granger was lying on a bed in a white marble chamber, still wearing his heavy power armour. His gaze moved from the prince to his older companion, to the tattoo etched on the back of that man's right hand. He'd seen such geometry inked on the skin of Brutalist sorcerers, and yet this frail fellow did not look much like a combat sorcerer. He possessed a tall, aquiline face and unusually small bird-bone hands. Upon his head rested a circlet of dull but faintly nacreous metal. A scholar's pronouncement, perhaps? The silver sphere drifted past his nose. He batted it away with a nervous fluttering gesture and then folded his hands precisely against his plain black tunic.

If the older man's attire suggested quiet restraint, Marquetta's gave him a somewhat dandyish appearance. He looked to Granger like a court jester in his pink and white quilted jerkin and his jewels and his countless rings of precious metals on his long white fingers.

'At least he's alive,' Marquetta said. Then something occurred to him and he turned to the older man. 'He *is* alive, isn't he?'

The other man shrugged.

Another voice came from behind Granger, and this one he recognized with great relief. 'Thank you, Duke Cyr,' Ianthe said.

Granger turned to find her standing before a wall of sunlit windows. Morning light enveloped her in a golden halo and poured through her pale gown so that it glowed like ether. Either he was still dreaming, or she had been healed in some unnatural manner, for she bore none of the bruises from her ordeal at the hands of the Haurstaf's torturer. She gazed at him a moment, her brow furrowed nervously, then looked away with embarrassment.

The grey-haired Unmer lord said, 'Do you recognize the girl?'

Granger made no reply.

'He's confused,' Ianthe said.

'I recognize all of you,' Granger said. He looked at the old man. 'You were with the prince.'

'This is my uncle,' Marquetta said. 'Duke Cyr of Vale.'

'Is this the Haurstaf palace?' Granger said.

Marquetta nodded. 'It is.'

Granger moved to sit up, but his head swam.

Duke Cyr raised his hands. 'Any unnecessary movement will merely delay your recovery,' he said. 'You must remain still, Colonel Granger.'

Granger took a deep breath and pushed himself up into a sitting position. From the temperature and the angle of the sunlight outside, he estimated it was early morning.

'Do you never follow the advice of others?' the prince remarked.

Granger grunted. He could see Ianthe more clearly now, her dark impetuous eyes and olive-coloured skin. Hair as black as fuel oil. The change in her was remarkable. No trace of her injuries remained, and yet the way she stood with her arms clasped around her waist was stiff, guarded. It seemed to Granger that she was afraid of something.

'How long have I been here?' Granger asked Marquetta.

The young prince cast a questioning glance at Duke Cyr, who spoke up. 'You were suffering from delirium, Colonel,' he said. 'And violent episodes. So much so that we were forced to sedate you while you healed. I'm afraid it was a lengthy process.'

'How long?'

'You were brought here eleven days ago.'

Eleven days? 'How? How did I get here? Who found me?'

Marquetta gave him a cold smile. 'Nobody found you, Colonel,' he said, with just a tremor of satisfaction in his voice. 'The sword replicates brought you here.'

Granger stared at him with mute incomprehension. He could still feel an ache in the back of his head, a persistent dull pounding that continued to muddy his thoughts. How could the replicates have brought him here without his knowledge? How could they even have *existed* if he'd been unconscious?

'It was indeed fortunate that you were wearing such a remarkable suit of armour,' Duke Cyr said. 'It preserved your body after you were killed, and then it repaired it.'

'*What?*'

'You died, Colonel Granger,' Cyr said. 'A bullet entered your left eye and passed out through the back of your head. Had it not been for the peculiar combination of your armour and that sword, you would not be here now.'

'I didn't die. A replicate died.'

'That was you, sir,' the duke insisted. 'No doubt you were confused. However, since you were wielding a sword that creates eight copies of its owner, and wearing armour that regenerates the body, you appear to have suffered few ill effects from the experience.'

'Provided he is the original,' Marquetta said.

'Well, quite,' the duke agreed.

Granger's gaze travelled between the two men. 'What?'

'Prolonged use of a replicating sword almost always leads to a transposition,' Cyr went on. 'The sword consumes the original wielder and then replaces that person's physical body with one of its own replicates. Because the replicate is essentially identical to the original, physically and mentally, he is usually unaware that he has been replaced. But he is in fact merely an extension of the sword and is thus compelled to obey its will for as long as he lives.'

'What will? How can a sword have a will?'

The duke grunted. 'Such swords were created by sorcerers far older and more cunning than you,' he said, 'and many yet possess the will of their original masters. If I were you, Colonel

Granger, I would be concerned by how I came to own such a weapon. Was it mere chance? Or was the blade placed into your hands?' He smiled thinly. 'Such swords are psychically chained to their owners. They cannot move on until the present owner dies. Usually that's not an issue for a replicating blade, since it gradually consumes its wielder and replaces him with a copy it can control.' His grey eyes studied Granger carefully. 'A blade that has complete control over its wielder can choose when that man dies. If it wishes to move on, it could simply compel you to remove your armour and cut your own throat. It would then be free of you. However, this particular sword seems quite attached to you, Colonel Granger. It brought you to us so that the armour could have time to restore you.'

'I don't understand. What does it want with me?'

'A sword like that is intelligent,' Cyr explained. 'It has desires, a plan. No doubt it regards you as a useful resource to achieve its goals. While you live it will continue to exert pressure on you, forcing you to bend to its will, until one day you find that you are no longer Thomas Granger. You are a sword replicate. A slave to the blade.' Cyr stroked his chin. 'Assuming that hasn't already happened.'

'Then I'll throw the blade away.'

'The chains that bind you to it are psychic, Colonel. The distance between it and you is irrelevant. When it finally enslaves you, it will merely summon you back to retrieve it.'

'Then I'll throw it into the ocean.'

The duke merely smirked. 'You can try,' he said. 'But it will certainly stop you.'

'That's assuming you're not a replicate already,' Marquetta added.

'Naturally.'

'You *don't know*?'

'If there's no severe mental or physical degeneration in the next few days,' Cyr said, 'then we'll know for sure.'

Granger shook his head in disbelief. 'There's a chance I might not be me?'

Cyr nodded again. 'It is possible,' he conceded.

'This from a sword?' Granger said.

Cyr glanced at Marquetta.

The young prince pressed his lips together and stood in thought for a long moment. He appeared to be scrutinizing Granger. Finally he said, 'How old are you, Colonel? Fifty years? Or less?'

Granger took the young man's estimate to be an insult and failed to see any point in answering him.

'The sword and the armour that restored your life,' Marquetta went on, 'are both vastly older than this world. Older even than the stars in the heavens. It is . . .' He hesitated. 'It is hard for humans to comprehend. They look at a blade or a suit and see metal, steel, plates of alloy . . . or . . .' Marquetta sighed, trying to find his way. 'Both artefacts are ideas,' he said to Granger. 'Conceived long before this particular cosmos was born. We Unmer try to realize such concepts to understand universal truths. Truths that often pre-date the universe – in the case of your armour, the concept of entropic order by design. Of course that is quite incompatible with the natural order of the universe, just as life itself is. The universe is decay. Life resists decay. However, nature is undeniable. Even something designed to empower a body or preserve it from decreation cannot help but affect that body in ways which are often not . . . entirely healthy. Wearing such armour is like drinking water tainted with a drop of brine: it will keep you alive for a long while, but it is always going to kill you in the end.'

Granger felt a pang of panic. 'And the sword? What did you hope to learn from that?'

The young prince gave him an enigmatic look. 'As I did not create it,' he said, 'I cannot say. But it would be a grave mistake, Colonel Granger, to continue to assume that *you* are the one wielding *it*.'

'Where is it now?'

'The armoury.' The prince raised his eyebrows. 'You wish it returned to you right now?'

Granger said nothing. God, how he wished they would give him the sword back. His fingers itched to feel its solid weight. He wiped a bead of sweat from his brow.

'I see it is working its will on you.'

Granger looked away, embarrassed, then turned his attention to Ianthe. In truth he was glad to see her looking so well. Beautiful, even. Her hair had been cleaned and tamed. She looked like a lady of court. It surprised him how relieved he felt to note the perpetual hint of insolence in her eyes; it seemed that every glance was a wilful challenge to his authority. She did not respect him, and she certainly didn't trust him.

So much like her old man.

But if she *was* truly responsible for the decimation of the Haurstaf, then he knew that the Unmer would try everything to prevent her from leaving them. The Unmer were vulnerable while there yet remained a single living Haurstaf psychic to threaten them.

'You must rest until your strength is fully restored,' Duke Cyr said. 'I think it is safe to remove your armour and let your body continue to heal naturally. In another two or three days we will know if you are the original Thomas Granger,' he smiled, 'or if you are merely a sorcerous copy of him and a slave to the sword's will.'

'And what if I turn out to be a copy?'

'The sword will use you for whatever purpose it desires.'

Great, Granger thought. *I might not be me.* He certainly felt like himself, albeit exhausted and somewhat foggy headed. But if he was merely a copy of his real self, then wouldn't he feel exactly that way? *If I'm not a replicate already, then it's only a matter of time.* The sorcerous blade was exerting its will on him night and day, trying to overthrow his own mind. And the Unmer had kept him asleep for eleven days already.

So he wouldn't cause trouble.

They'd made a mistake in waking him up, because he wasn't about to let his daughter be held to ransom by anybody. 'I'll heal faster standing on my own two feet,' he said, swinging his legs out of bed. His armour whirred, the metal plates refracting a kaleidoscope of light before his eyes. A moment of dizziness caught him unawares and he grasped the bedclothes to steady himself. At once the light from the windows seemed too harsh, too hot. Some of the disorientation he'd felt in the forest returned. But then it passed. He took a deep breath and said, 'Ianthe, we're leaving.'

Marquetta merely blinked.

'We're not leaving,' Ianthe said.

'We can't stay here.'

'Why not?'

He had to get out of here. He had to figure out a way to beat this sword. Maybe he could snap the bloody thing. Or melt it down. But whatever it was, he had to act quickly. And he needed Ianthe with him. He looked at her in her fancy robe and he wanted to tell her that they didn't belong here, but was embarrassed to speak such words in the present company. Where did they belong? He wasn't even sure if she belonged with him. And he couldn't tell her the truth – that he didn't want the Unmer to have her. To use her. Too many people had used her. 'I promised your mother I'd look after you,' he said. 'And that's what I'm going to do.'

'I don't want you to look after me,' she said.

He grunted.

Marquetta intervened. 'You are, of course, welcome to leave whenever you choose,' he said. 'However, given your eh . . . Given the unusual circumstances of your situation, don't you think it would be prudent to remain under observation for a few more days? Until we know for sure.'

'If I turn out to be a sword replicate,' Granger said. 'Then how does staying here help me? Can you reverse it?'

Marquetta shrugged. 'Unfortunately—'

'That's what I figured. Ianthe, get your things.'

'I'm not going anywhere with you.'

He bared his teeth. 'Yes you damn well are.'

'No, I'm not missing the ball just because you wake up and want to leave. We've been planning it for days now.'

Granger shot a quizzical look at the prince.

Marquetta explained. 'We have organized a ball tonight as a gesture of peace and friendship with our neighbours. Every nobleman, official and landowner in Awl will attend. Will you not at least stay until then?'

A ball? Mere weeks after the Haurstaf slaughter and the takeover of Awl's military, and the Unmer were having *a ball*? Granger was about to protest when he saw the look of fierce determination in Ianthe's eye. It was almost a warning. *Don't embarrass me.* But she was too young to understand the dangers of remaining here. She hadn't seen the corpse piles the Unmer had left in Dunbar and Dorell and a hundred other places before the dragon wars. She hadn't been in that transmitting station in Pertica and seen the entropic horrors Herian had summoned from god knows where. Whenever you stumbled upon one of the Unmer in some remote place, as Granger had done while following Ianthe to this palace, there was always trouble. Herian had likely been in that war-ravaged station for centuries, working away like a weaver on the looms of fate, manipulating events for his otherworldly masters – those eternal god-like creatures the Unmer called entropaths. Granger still didn't know why the Unmer operator had manipulated events to bring him there, or what the entropaths wanted of him, but he suspected it had everything to do with Ianthe. The Unmer were a dangerous, secretive race. His daughter was too trusting, too naive to deal with them. Hell, half the time Granger felt that he was too naive himself. No. Even one more night here was too long.

He was about to tell Marquetta just what he thought of his damned ball, when a second wave of dizziness overcame him. The room tilted and blurred before his eyes and he nearly toppled to the floor.

'Colonel Granger?' Marquetta said. 'Do you require assistance?'

'I'm not a colonel,' Granger said. 'Not any more.' His head was reeling so much he could barely see the others in the room now. Their three forms seemed to merge into one and then separate. And for a horrible moment he thought he saw eight more figures. His sword replicates, standing at the back of the room. But then his vision returned to normal, and the replicates – if they had ever been there – disappeared. Ianthe was looking at him anxiously. The duke had his eyebrows raised and wore a faintly questioning expression. And it seemed that Marquetta's smile evinced arrogance.

'Stay one night at least,' the young prince said. 'Until these dizzy spells stop.'

Granger could only nod.

'Excellent.' Marquetta smacked his hands together, denoting an end to the matter.

Ianthe's face was full of joy.

A flash above the young prince's shoulder caught Granger's attention. It was the tiny silver sphere. It hung there in the air, bobbing slightly and emitting a crackling hum that sounded disturbingly like a chuckle.

'He seemed overly keen to be reunited with the sword,' Paulus said, as they strolled along the corridor beyond Granger's room. 'Not a good sign, I fear.'

'You think he has succumbed to its will?' Ianthe said.

'I don't know,' the prince admitted. 'Does he seem like the man you know? Is he normally so rude, obstinate and irreverent?'

'Yes.'

'Then perhaps he still has some time,' the prince said.

'What will happen to him?'

'When weapons possess a will, they almost always seek power. Many tyrants through the ages have been steered by the ghosts of long-dead sorcerers.'

'But he can resist it?'

'Only for a limited time.'

Ianthe stopped and clutched Paulus's arms. 'Please, isn't there anything you can do to save him?'

'I am sorry.'

Her eyes welled with tears.

Paulus hugged her. He held her head against his chest and smoothed her hair. 'At least you will make him proud tonight, Ianthe. He will leave this earth knowing that his daughter is in safe hands.'

She sniffed, nodded.

They walked on and passed through a grand portal into one of the central palace thoroughfares. It had been nearly a month since the westernmost wing had been destroyed by Ethan Maskelyne's bombardment, and a great deal of the rubble had been cleared, exposing a maze of roofless chambers to the open skies. But there still remained several weeks' worth of work to do before any reconstruction could begin. The workers had erected temporary tarpaulins and tin sheets to keep any rain out, although they had been fortunate with the weather so far. Early summer was generally calm and sunny in Awl. Paulus had by now recruited the military to assist in the task and, as Ianthe walked beside the young prince and his uncle, she passed groups of former Haurstaf soldiers carrying chucks of black marble along the corridors or out through gaps in the walls to carts waiting outside. Every one of them, she noted, avoided Cyr's glare.

Those who wished to continue to earn a living had had little choice but to accept Unmer rule, but it seemed to Ianthe that these men did not yet trust their new masters.

Once they reached the grand antechamber behind the main palace doors, however, there was no trace of destruction. The floors, staircase and pillars shone like black glass, as pristine as the day Ianthe had first seen them. The corpses had been removed to one of the army bases to the south of the palace, where they had been burned. The main doors had been thrown open to admit sunlight and cool, pine-scented morning air. A palace guard wearing a grey cape over boiled leathers bowed to Paulus and then to Cyr as they approached.

'Our guests are on their way, Your Highnesses,' he said. 'A convoy of carriages approach on the Port Awl road.'

Cyr chuckled. 'We must ensure that our effusive Commander Rast does not have them shot at one of his checkpoints.'

The guard bowed. 'Your wife requests your presence in the hospital,' he said. 'She says she is at a loss as to what to do with the leucotomized and begs your assistance.'

'My ideas on the matter would only distress her,' Cyr remarked. 'Besides, we have more pressing issues. Three weeks, and the Guild commanders are still bumbling around like raw recruits. Trust must be fostered and strategies must be set on course if we are to call Awl home.'

'Losoto is my home,' Paulus said.

The old man smiled. 'And we will reclaim it in good time, Your Highness.'

But the prince's expression only darkened. 'Sooner, rather than later, I trust.'

Cyr dismissed the palace guard and waited until the man had gone before he addressed the prince. 'My dear Paulus,' he said, 'do you think I could bear to leave our people trapped in those ghettos for a moment longer than is absolutely necessary?' He steepled his fingers under his chin and regarded the young man with a look that suggested great sadness and wounded pride. 'I yearn for safe reunion just as you do,' he added, 'but we must lay the necessary foundations to ensure success. We mustn't go rushing in like impetuous young men.'

'Every moment we delay puts our kin at greater risk,' Paulus replied. 'What if Hu decides to act before we get there? He might simply panic and leucotomize all of them.'

'The emperor will not harm them,' Cyr insisted. 'Even Hu is not that foolish. He'll keep his own psychics close by. He'll wait and he'll watch. If we're lucky, he'll use our kin to make the only sensible political move he can make.'

'What move?'

'To ally himself with us,' Cyr said. 'With Ianthe on our side, the Haurstaf can no longer threaten us. The emperor can no longer use them as a shield.' He gave a sudden chuckle. 'That will save him vast amounts of money at least,' he added. 'A clever ruler would release his Unmer captives as a gesture of conciliation.'

Paulus shook his head. 'But that's my point exactly,' he said. 'Hu is not a clever ruler. You overestimate him, Uncle.'

Cyr raised his eyebrows. 'And perhaps you underestimate me, Paulus.' He gave a short bow. 'I will personally guarantee our people's safety. You can have my head if I'm wrong.'

The young prince laughed. 'You see how he manipulates me, Ianthe? My own uncle? I should hope he is wrong or else fear for my throne!'

Ianthe smiled sweetly. The duke merely nodded.

Paulus took his uncle's arm and moved to lead him away. 'About this extravaganza . . .' he said quietly.

'Diplomacy is hardly an extravaganza,' Cyr replied. 'We must cement our relationship with both the Guild soldiers and the Port Awl authorities. An empire is like a palace: it must be built upon solid ground.'

'Yes, yes. Buy them, you mean.'

'With Haurstaf money, My Lord,' Cyr said. 'Such a delightful irony, don't you think?'

The prince nodded impatiently. He glanced back at Ianthe and then whispered something in the duke's ear. Cyr smiled once more and then rested his hand on top of Paulus's own. A gesture, Ianthe guessed, designed to reassure the young prince. Then he said loudly, 'But come, if it pleases you, release me to answer my wife's summons. I feel stricken with a sudden and brief sense of mercy, and thus temporarily and inexplicably endowed to cope with her poor crippled charges.'

'You? Merciful?' Paulus said. 'This we have to see.'

They left the grand hallway and strolled along a corridor in the north-west wing of the palace, which had wholly escaped Maskelyne's bombardment. Ianthe knew these lesson rooms and libraries well from her time as a student here. They were all empty now, the desks and chairs stacked away, the chalkboards wiped clean. Paulus led her to the far end of the wing, towards the dormitories formerly occupied by year one students.

She heard the patients before she saw them. From the last few rooms there came a great maniacal howling and then a cacophony like the cries of wounded beasts. This, then, was what had become of those Unmer upon whom the Haurstaf had experimented. The leucotomy process involved severing the link between the lobes of the brain, thus stripping the recipients of their innate and peculiarly destructive powers, as well as most of their higher functions. Leucotomized Unmer were used to train Haurstaf combat psychics in safety.

They walked through the first dormitory door and there found rows of pale men, women and children strapped or chained to beds. Each bore a scar upon his or her forehead, a mark showing where the Haurstaf surgeons' knives had done their work. *Decreation*. That was what Paulus called the process by which his kind could extinguish whatever they touched. Matter was not destroyed, he said, but simply displaced through entropic manipulation. Through will. Nothing vanished from the cosmos; it was merely scattered and displaced. Sometimes he referred to it as *entropic trade*. A simple punch from an Unmer warrior could send a fist-sized lump of his opponent to the other end of reality.

Upon sensing the presence of new arrivals the patients turned their wild and haunted eyes on Paulus, Cyr and Ianthe. They gibbered. They grinned and spat and frothed at the mouth. One man screamed terribly and rattled his chains. Another started to howl like a dog. Ianthe grabbed her prince's hand.

'Don't be afraid,' Paulus said. 'I won't let them harm you.'

They were bound, impotent, and she could have destroyed every one of their minds with a single thought, but she accepted this unnecessary offer of protection without comment. If it made him feel better . . .

'Now where's Anaisy?' the prince murmured.

They found the duke's wife in the second dormitory, a room which turned out to be a good deal quieter than the last one. She was fat and grey and restless and her hands fluttered endlessly, scrunching tissues and mopping her brow and scrunching and mopping and wringing the air with despair. She sniffed and wiped her nose, which was as red as a boil. Her eyes were as dull as puddles. She sat at a table in the centre of the room, writing in a journal, while the patients around her writhed and groaned and made muted sounds. The ones in here, Ianthe noted, were all wearing gags.

'Anaisy,' Paulus said, opening his arms.

She looked up and beamed. 'Paulus? Where's Cyr?'

'You really do need glasses,' Cyr replied, coming through the door behind the young prince.

'I see perfectly,' she said. 'My mind . . .'

'Engages the voice without sharing information?' he enquired. 'Or tactics?'

'My mind,' she said, 'was engaged.'

'The new book?' Paulus enquired.

She shook a hand dismissively. 'Oh it's nothing really.'

'But I'm sure it's marvellous,' the young prince insisted.

She blushed. 'I suppose I could let you read some.'

Paulus held both of her plump little hands in his. 'You know I'd love to,' he said, grinning. 'But I'm not going to. Affairs of state and all that.' He dropped her hands.

She nodded vigorously and then in an almost conspiratorial tone said, 'I completely understand.' Her gaze then fixed on Cyr and she opened her mouth to speak.

'My dear,' he said, raising a hand to stop her. 'Don't make me choose between honesty and love.'

'But what's been going on?' Paulus said. 'I'm told you require assistance.'

'Well, yes. No,' she said. 'Yes and no.' She clenched her fists in frustration and sucked in a deep breath. 'The noises they've been making . . . And the smell, oh my dear.'

'But then you must leave,' Paulus said. 'The palace staff can see to their needs.'

'Oh, I don't trust the staff,' she said, leaning closer. 'Some of these patients were my friends.'

'I see you've gagged them,' Ianthe said.

Anaisy turned her wet eyes on Ianthe and gave her a blade-like smile. Then she turned back to the prince. 'How am I to cope? The gags aren't particularly effective. I've asked for drugs, but there isn't anything suitable.' She lowered her voice. 'I've been thinking about this a lot, and it seems to me that the best thing would be to put them on a boat and send them somewhere.'

'A boat?' Paulus said. 'Where would you send it?'

'Oh, I don't know,' Anaisy said. 'It hardly matters, I suppose. Somewhere nice, where they can . . . you know.'

'Frolic and drool,' Paulus said.

'Precisely. The important thing is that they don't return. Better that than have them killed, don't you think?'

Cyr guffawed. 'You want to exile our kin?'

She shot him a murderous look. 'Absolutely not. How dare you even suggest that?'

'My apologies,' he said. 'You don't want to exile them. You merely wish to send them away, never to return.'

'Well, yes,' she said. 'What choice do we have? Killing them wouldn't be acceptable at all.'

'We're in agreement there,' Cyr said.

'After all,' she added, 'what would people say if they knew what we'd done?'

'I'll wager the words would not be kind.'

Anaisy nodded. 'So, do you think you could arrange it?'

'Consider it done,' Paulus said.

She beamed at him again. 'Oh, Paulus, you'll make such a fine king.' And then she turned to Ianthe. 'And you . . . my dear . . .' She grabbed Ianthe's hands and smiled. 'You must not fret. We can always do something about your presentation.'

Ianthe frowned. 'What do you mean?'

Cyr intervened, steering Ianthe away from the woman. 'The dear girl must prepare for the ball,' he said. 'As young and beautiful as she is, we must have her looking less seductive and more regal. This is, after all, a formal affair.'

'Of course.' The duchess spoke through a smile that seemed cemented into her jaw, but then the smile faded and she was abruptly thoughtful again. 'What if it was an old ship?' she said.

Paulus raised his eyebrows.

'Well then we couldn't be blamed if it sank,' she said. 'Could we?'

'Ethan?'

When Lucille shook his shoulder, Maskelyne realized that

the light in his laboratory had changed to a deep umber. He looked up from his desk to find her eyes pinched with worry.

'You've been staring into that thing for hours,' she said.

Hours? He glanced at the large crystal sphere in his hands as if seeing it for the first time. Had he been daydreaming? The crystal shone weirdly, reflecting light that didn't appear to emanate from his environment. Through its facets he sometimes glimpsed dark waves and sometimes a tower standing on an outcrop of rock in an endless sea. 'This thing,' he said, 'is quite possibly the most important object that has ever existed.'

He had found it in the chariot that one of Granger's replicates had crashed into the mountainside at Awl – a crash that had destroyed the gun Maskelyne was using to turn great chunks of Haurstaf palace into great mounds of powdered Haurstaf palace. A crash that had nearly killed Ethan Maskelyne himself.

But his wife only raised her eyebrows in a manner that bordered on pity.

'I mean it, Lucille,' he insisted. 'This artefact is no mere ichusae or chariot. It is, as far as I can tell, a lens – refracting light, but not from this world.' He held up the magnificent object so that it gleamed wickedly in the evening sun, cycling through a kaleidoscope of otherworldly hues. 'Look at it. See these waves, the colours. The view . . . it's from several hundred yards above the surface . . . an island, perhaps. The ocean you perceive through these facets is not on this planet.'

'How can you be so sure?' she said. 'One ocean looks much like another.'

'And one sky does *not* look much like another,' he retorted. 'I have watched the night stars, Lucille, such as they are. This world – if indeed it still exists – belongs to a far less crowded part of the cosmos than our own, or even another cosmos altogether.'

She looked at the crystal anew. 'Another cosmos?'

'Many scholars believe that the Unmer are in contact with intelligences beyond our world, perhaps even beyond our own universe,' he said. 'There are too many tales of godlike beings to dismiss readily. Argusto Conquillas is said to have murdered a goddess during the dragon wars. You know the story?'

'The shape-shifter's daughter,' Lucille replied. 'Oh Ethan, you don't believe that, do you?'

'Why not?' He held up the crystal. 'Is this not evidence enough of otherworldly life?' He spoke with passion, but not complete conviction. Admittedly, there was no real proof of this. Conquillas collected legends like the Baruch tribesmen collected their enemies' daughters. However, the artefact here in his hand *was* something tangible. 'This lens might well be a method of communication,' he ventured. 'If it is, then it represents nothing less than the key to the survival of our own race.'

A trace of fear came into Lucille's eyes.

Maskelyne grumbled and shook his head. 'Look . . . come.' He leaped from his desk and bounded to the window, which had been thrown wide to admit the breeze. His light summer jacket and cotton trousers flapped in the metal-scented wind from the sea. The gauze curtains wafted like smoke around him. Between the horns of Scythe Island the evening sun scattered its rays across the dark brooding waters of the Mare Lux, forming countless gold and honey sparkles. Under his fortress and directly beneath this very window there lay a silver crescent of beach bisected by a long stone quay. 'You see the high-tide mark?' he asked her. 'Where it runs along the quay?'

She joined him. 'I see where the stone is stained.'

'It's up to fourteen yards,' Maskelyne said. On either side of the quay, gentle bronze-coloured waves broke across the metalled shore, leaving tails of yellow froth. 'A yard in the last eight years alone. Regardless of how many ichusae I pull from the depths, the seas continue to rise faster than ever. The rate is accelerating.' Something among the breaking surf caught his eye. 'Look at that!' he cried with evident delight. 'There's a twitch of fate for you. The Drowned conspire to strengthen my point.' He pointed furiously, jabbing his hand at the beach below. 'Their mad compulsions have been increasingly fervent of late.'

From out of the waves there crawled a figure – a scrawny woman with rough grey skin and hair like spilled green paint. She was naked above the waist, but wore a wrap of some tattered red material about her hips. She clawed her way up onto the beach, moving slowly and painfully. Three yards above the shoreline, she reached out her hand and deposited something on the metal shingle. And then she turned slowly and began to make her way back to the poisoned water.

'In broad daylight,' Maskelyne said. 'In broad daylight!'

Lucille had covered her mouth with her hand. 'The poor thing. Why do they do it? Why endure such agony to leave all those keys?'

Ethan Maskelyne watched the woman drag herself back into the sea. 'I suspect the answer to that has become more important than ever,' he said quietly. 'The Drowned sense that something is coming. They sense it instinctively, even if they don't know what it is. I would—'

He stopped talking as something out in the great shimmering sea caught his attention. Out to the north-west he spied a flash of white canvas: a square mainsail and then a spinnaker.

'We have company,' he said.

'Emperor Hu?'

'I think not,' Maskelyne replied. 'I must assume that this is Briana Marks come to beg my assistance.'

'Assistance with what?'

Ethan Maskelyne smiled. 'A small matter of genocide.'

Granger must have slept for hours because the lozenges of light that had been on the wall had now slid far across the marble floor.

In another two or three days we will know if you are the original Thomas Granger.

And what if I turn out to be a copy?

The sword will use you for whatever purpose it desires.

Sudden panic overcame him. He wrestled the bedclothes away and then lay there panting, his brow clammy with an unexpected and surprising fear. What was he afraid of? He knew who he was. Thomas Granger of Anea. Son of Helen and John Granger. Brother of John junior. The man who had led Imperial Infiltration Unit Seven, the Gravediggers, for all those years. He remembered Evensraum, the farm in Weaverbrook where he'd met Ianthe's mother, Hana. The same place where he buried John and three thousand others. He thought about the men in his unit who'd survived the bombing: Creedy, Banks and the Tummel brothers. He recalled his own trial in Ethugra. How could he be a sorcerous copy of another man and yet remember all of these things? He had lived through those events. His limbs were tired beyond belief and it was all he could do to support himself on one elbow. But he was alive. Real.

A rich and cloying floral scent assaulted his nostrils. He grabbed a fistful of his shirt and sniffed. Then he smelled his arm. Evidently someone had bathed him while he'd been asleep, and then slathered his skin with perfume.

They had removed his armour.

Was that why he felt so exhausted?

His thoughts groped through a fug that felt like a whisky hangover. Who the hell had been in here? And how had they managed to do this without waking him?

Nothing at all came back to him. His mind remained blank.

A series of clicking noises grabbed his attention, and he looked over to see the silver sphere Duke Cyr had released floating near the windows, some eight feet from the floor. It gave out a few more clicks – the sounds eerily reminiscent of language – then bobbed up and down in the air. Had it stirred because Granger had woken up? It occurred to him that the device might allow the Unmer to observe him remotely.

Before he could contemplate this any further, the door opened and a young servant girl came in. From the look of her, he took her to be one of the Port Awl locals who had previously been under Haurstaf employ. She was carrying a pile of neatly folded – and rather extravagant – clothes. She blinked with surprise at seeing him awake, then quickly lowered her head and scurried across the room, depositing the clothes on a chair beside the dresser.

Granger frowned at her. 'Did you . . .?' he began.

'Sir?'

'Who bathed me?'

'Your servants, sir.'

'What servants?'

She looked at him blankly for a moment. 'Four of us, sir.

Are you ready to be dressed? Shall I activate the somnambulum again?'

'The what?'

She turned to the floating silver sphere and beckoned to it. The little device moved immediately, whistling through the air, and stopped a few inches away from her face. She opened her mouth as if to speak to it . . .

Granger awoke – again, with no memory of having fallen asleep. Changes in the angle of sunlight suggested that an hour or so had passed. The servant girl was no longer in the room, but now he found himself lying flat on the bed, fully dressed. He was wearing a padded plum-coloured tunic over a pink silk blouse and pantaloons patterned with green and yellow diamonds. He raised his head and gazed down at this riot of coloured cloth – every bit as fetid and febrile as the perfume they'd forced upon him. The material shimmered with arabesques of silver and gold thread. And upon the finger of his left hand there now rested a silver-mounted ruby the size of a bullfrog's liver.

A chattering sound came from the corner of the room. There. Granger spotted the little silver sphere – the *somnambulum*, she'd called it – hovering a foot below the ceiling. It sounded like it was mocking him.

Or was it summoning someone? This premise seemed suddenly more likely, for no sooner had the device stopped, than the door opened again and the servant girl reappeared. She cowed her eyes from Granger and then hurried over to the sphere.

'Wait,' he said.

'I beg your pardon, sir,' she replied. 'It isn't supposed to wake you. I don't know what's got into it.'

'What? Wait! Stop, get away from that.'

She halted. 'Sir?'

'What is that thing? Why do I keep falling asleep?'

She looked at him dumbly.

'The somnambulum,' Granger said. 'What does it do?'

'It removes the necessity to suffer the touch of one's servants' hands upon one's person.' When it became clear to her that she'd baffled him, she added, 'Allowing the lady or gentleman to complete their toilet without being forced to endure the discomfort of physical contact.'

'I want it out of here.'

'Sir?'

'Get rid of it.'

Her brow crinkled with confusion. 'You wish to be *conscious* when you are bathed and dressed?'

Granger growled. 'I don't *wish* to be bathed and dressed at all. I can manage on my own.'

She frowned again.

'Where is my daughter?' he demanded.

'The Lady Cooper?'

'Ianthe!'

Granger's anger quickly turned to chagrin. *Cooper* was a name he knew. It had been Hana's surname, and so of course it now belonged to Ianthe. And he hated it because it exposed his own inadequacies. It marked her as part of a family he didn't know and hadn't cared to find out about – family he had no real connections to. Who were Ianthe's Evensraum grandparents? Her uncles, aunts and cousins? Were they still alive? Ianthe's given surname represented a heritage about which he knew nothing. The name Cooper implied her family had been barrel-makers in the past. As decent and as skilled a profession as any. And yet how ridiculous the name sounded here among all these gilded halls and servants. Lady Barrel-Maker.

Granger had gone to Ianthe's homeland on behalf of a conqueror, to take everything from the Coopers and the Smiths and the Dukas and all the other families his daughter had been raised among. His daughter had been a child of war – a combination of what had defined Evensraum and what had destroyed it.

'She's in her quarters, sir, preparing for Prince Marquetta's ball.'

'What ball?'

The servant girl hesitated. 'The ball tonight,' she said. 'Don't you remember? You announced your intention to attend, sir.'

That ball. Granger now recalled his earlier conversation with the young prince. Why hadn't he been able to recall it a moment ago? Had they drugged him? Or was this merely the aftermath of severe exhaustion? Now that he thought about it, he remembered some talk of diplomacy. It seemed to him that the fog engulfing his mind was clearing, but not particularly quickly.

Or was the sword taking control of him? He imagined it lying there in the palace armoury, reaching out psychic tendrils that wrapped around his mind, pushing, pushing.

'I want to see her,' he said.

'She's with the prince and Duke Cyr.'

Granger swung his legs out of bed. A moment of giddiness sent his senses reeling, but it passed quickly. He took a deep breath and then settled his bare feet on the cold stone floor. The pain in his joints took him by surprise, forcing a gasp from his throat. 'Where are they?'

'I don't know if I should . . .'

'*Where are they?*'

She flinched. 'Their Highnesses are taking the Lady Cooper on a tour of the palace dungeons.'

'The dungeons?' Granger frowned. 'Whatever for?'

'He's showing her his former quarters.'

'Where are we going?' Ianthe said.

The prince continued to follow his uncle Cyr down the stairwell. 'It is important that *you* understand the scope of my desire to rebuild our empire,' he said to her.

'But I do.'

They reached the bottom of the steps, where they came upon a metal door. 'Nevertheless, I wish to demonstrate my intentions.' He nodded to Duke Cyr, who drew the door bolt back. *Clang.* The sound resounded around the gloomy subterranean chamber and made Ianthe shiver. She had heard too many of such noises during her time in Awl.

'Highness?' the duke said.

Ianthe realized that her prince had halted before the open doorway. Paulus's face seemed paler than usual, his lips narrow and dry. *He's more afraid than I am.* She reached over to take his hand, but then stopped herself. Such a gesture would not be appropriate, she felt, in the presence of his uncle. It might hurt his pride.

Not yet.

The duke coughed. 'Have we . . . forgotten something?'

'Forgive me,' the prince said, turning to Ianthe. 'This place stirs terrible memories. The Unmer . . .' He sighed and shook his head. 'I will not speak of such things in your presence, Ianthe.'

She gave him a supportive smile. *You have nothing to fear while I am here.*

He nodded. 'If we are to set sail on a new course, we cannot be anchored by past fears. Let us continue.'

They stepped through the doorway and into a low tunnel

hewn from the naked rock. They were now deep in the mountain below the palace. It was warm here and the air held a faintly sulphurous odour that made Ianthe think of dragons. Gem lanterns suspended at ten-pace intervals cast pools of alternating green and yellow light on the levelled stone floor. Black scuffs on the rock underfoot suggested the passage of many rubber wheels.

Paulus explained. 'This is one of many service corridors the Haurstaf used to move prisoners around out of sight.' In this light his eyes were very dark indeed. Despite his fierce determination, it was clear to Ianthe that he remained haunted by this place. 'I find it shameful that we know them as intimately as our former captors.'

'Why should you feel ashamed?' she asked.

'We were slaves,' he said. 'And yet . . .' His voice tailed away.

'We were unharmed,' Cyr said.

The prince was suddenly angry. 'Do not . . .' he said. 'Do not presume to answer for me.'

If the duke was surprised by this unexpected outburst he didn't show it. He merely bowed with grave humility. 'Forgive me, Highness,' he said. 'It was not my intention to offend you.'

The prince regarded him for a moment longer, then turned away.

At the end of the tunnel they reached another metal door, this one inlaid with bone geometries and facets of red glass. It opened into an enormous chamber which Ianthe recognized at once. Near the centre there stood a wooden chair set atop a scaffold – like a miniature watchtower – from which someone could survey the surrounding floor. This floor alternated between expanses of marble and great rectangles of clear glass, through which could be seen a series of rooms and corridors constructed below: the very same quarters in which Ianthe had first seen her prince. These transparent ceilings had allowed a Haurstaf observer to watch him at all times.

Briana Marks had once brought Ianthe here. She had explained that the prince's quarters were suspended above a deep pit, lest he decide to use his odd talent for matter destruction simply to obliterate a section of the floor and thus escape. In the end such precautions had been deemed insufficient. The Haurstaf decided it was necessary to observe their captives, either physically or psychically, at all times. Standing here now, Ianthe felt suddenly afraid.

'Why are we here?' she said.

'To meet a prisoner,' he said.

Ianthe stopped. 'Who is it?'

'Nobody. A girl, a Haurstaf survivor.'

'Who?'

'She claims to have had no prior friendship with you.'

'Then why do I have to meet her?'

The prince's expression remained grimly serious. 'If we are to begin to forge new relationships with our former enemies, we must first confront them.'

'You want to make peace with the Haurstaf?'

He turned to her. 'The idea offends you?'

'No,' she said instinctively. 'I just . . .' The truth was she didn't want to meet any of the survivors, because of the shame she felt for what she had done to them. She looked between Paulus's questioning expression and the duke's earnest face, and it occurred to her that they had both, by coming here, exposed themselves to danger. Walls would not stop a Haurstaf combat psychic from destroying any Unmer minds in her proximity. They had also, she realized, placed their lives in her hands, for she was the only defence they possessed against such an attack.

It was an overt display of trust.

Trust in her.

'Our new allies found her wandering in the woods,' Paulus said. 'Quite distressed.'

'But why bring her here?'

'It is the most comfortable cell in the palace, bar one other, and I could not bring myself to keep her in *there*.' A pained look flitted across his face, but then his expression hardened, as of one determined not to show weakness or grief, and Ianthe could see thoughts racing behind his eyes. After a moment he shook his head dismissively. 'But then you never knew Carella.'

Ianthe could not tell him that she'd watched the Unmer princess die in confined quarters much like these. Nor could she tell him that she'd peered out through his eyes and read the letters he'd written to her. He'd been forced to write in Anean, so that his Haurstaf captors could vet his words before passing them on to the princess. The thought of it now merely compounded her guilt.

'There was no reason to keep us apart,' Paulus said, 'none but that we should suffer all the more.' For a moment he seemed sad and distant again, but then his resolve returned. He straightened and looked squarely at Ianthe. 'We Unmer believe that compassion is the primary measure of worth,' he said. 'Mercy is the second. Please.' He beckoned her to follow him.

They walked over to the glass slabs. Duke Cyr, however, chose to linger by the door.

The room beneath the window had not changed since Paulus had been imprisoned here. But now in his place there was a Haurstaf girl. Ianthe's breath caught in her throat. The girl was a few years older than her and seemed all elbows and knees and great dark hollows for eyes – a sapling of a girl with skin as white as a winter birch, but mottled by bruises. Even her hair was thin and pallid, almost translucent. She looked familiar. Ianthe was sure she'd seen her around, but they had never spoken. She had been sitting on the edge of a red plush settee, fidgeting with her hands, but stood up when Ianthe and Paulus came to stand at the edge of the glass ceiling. She regarded Ianthe with absolute fear.

Paulus looked down at her. 'I'm told you are a combat psychic.'

Her gaze moved between him and Ianthe. She moistened her lips.

'Your name?'

'I don't want to harm anyone,' she said.

'Please,' the prince said. 'We merely require your name.'

'Genevieve Greene.'

He regarded her calmly. 'You were lucky to survive the uprising, Genevieve.'

Uprising. That struck Ianthe as an odd choice of words. There had been no uprising as such, merely liberation as an unintended result of her psychic attack. They'd hurt her and she'd hurt them back a hundredfold. And now the Unmer were free as a result. She could, however, see why Paulus might utilize that particular term for political gain.

Genevieve's gaze was fixed on Ianthe. 'Please don't hurt me,' she said.

Ianthe felt her face redden with shame.

'We're not here to hurt you,' Paulus said. 'We're here to offer you a job.'

Genevieve's eyes snapped to him, now smouldering with distrust.

'You are wondering why you should trust me,' he said. 'Why, after all your kind has done to mine, should I grant you

94

your freedom? Why would any Unmer risk having an enemy psychic around? It is, after all, within your power to cripple me here and now. You might, with one thought, inflict unbearable pain on me or reduce me to a . . . gibbering wreck. The fact that you refrain suggests that you are smart enough to know that such actions would not be in your best interests.' He glanced at Ianthe, a half-smile on his lips. 'However, this impasse – albeit tenuous – nevertheless provides me with an invaluable opportunity.' Now he paused, perhaps to give weight to the words that followed. 'The simple truth is,' he said, 'I need the Haurstaf.'

She frowned.

'Our last conflict cost my people dearly,' Paulus said. 'We had no defence against your mental weaponry, and no appeal. My father Jonas begged the goddess Duna, daughter of Fiorel, for assistance, but Argusto Conquillas put an end to that desperate ploy. And all was lost. We could not engineer a way to shield ourselves. Conquillas raised his dragons against us. His lover, Aria, raised her Haurstaf to war against us. Faced with genocide, my father turned to Fiorel for help. They conceived of one last way to save us.

'If we couldn't protect ourselves from you, we would make ourselves invaluable to you.' Paulus looked again at Ianthe. 'Fiorel taught my father's best sorcerers how to create ichusae. He sent them as far from Haurstaf interference as possible. They worked in secret, in remote camps in the mountains, producing them.'

'The grave pits,' Ianthe said. 'My dream.'

He smiled suddenly. 'Dear Ianthe, it was not your dream.' He turned back to Genevieve. 'Your kind always liked to promote the idea that we poisoned the oceans out of spite. But the truth is that we did it to ensure our own survival. We really had no other option. We seeded the oceans with ichusae to give you a reason to keep us around.'

'To counter the magic you unleashed?' Ianthe said.

'Only we knew the location of every last ichusae,' Paulus said. 'The Haurstaf would need us to delay the end of the world. They could not destroy us without dooming themselves.' He shrugged. 'The problem was: as the seas rose, less land became available. Which meant more conflict. And the more conflict there was, the more money and power came to the Haurstaf. We made them rich beyond imagining. It turned out that ever-rising seas suited the Haurstaf just fine.'

'But now you're free . . .' Ianthe began.

'Now it's too late,' Paulus replied. 'There are not enough of my people left to accomplish the task ahead. We have no empire, no ships, no resources of any kind, and no time left to establish them. The Haurstaf have allowed the world to reach the brink of death. And if we're going to pull it back, we need friends, Ianthe. Even among those who have tortured and enslaved us.'

Ianthe's heart filled with love for him. And such admiration. And hope. If Paulus could show such forgiveness and compassion to those who had tortured and murdered his own family, then was it inconceivable that the Haurstaf might one day forgive her for what she'd done to them? She would have thrown her arms around him had it not been so inappropriate.

'Will you help me, Genevieve?' he said.

'Yes,' she said without hesitation. 'Thank you.'

Paulus smiled.

Just then a door at the far end of the chamber opened, and a party entered. Three former palace guards, now in Unmer employ, escorted two more Haurstaf prisoners across the chamber. The telepaths were both young, of an age with Ianthe. Both wore the white cowled robes of recruits. One was snow-blonde and slender, the other dusky and rotund. Ianthe vaguely recognized them, but – again – had no knowledge of their names. The palace guard commander halted a few steps in front of Paulus and clasped his own shoulder in salute. 'There are four more in the north hall,' he said. 'Commander Artenso is due to . . .'

'Tell Artenso to hold off until I've had a chance to speak with him,' Paulus said. 'In the meantime I'd like to meet the girls myself.' He turned to indicate the sunken quarters beneath the glass floor slabs. 'You may rescue this young lady from the clutches of extreme luxury and add her to your party. See that they are settled quickly.' He turned to the two recruits and gave them an amiable smile. 'You are both invited to tonight's ball.'

The dumpy girl curtseyed, 'Thank you, Your Highness.'

Her slender blonde companion glowered at this for a moment, before she turned to Paulus and addressed him in a voice twisted to sarcasm, 'Thank you, Your Highness.'

Paulus observed her a moment. 'Have I offended you?'

She snorted and raised her chin. 'Of course not, Your Highness.'

Paulus's gaze lingered on her a moment longer, before turning away. He had, it seemed, no desire to provoke a confrontation. But then he stopped suddenly and winced. He shook his head again, this time in apparent response to some minor pain. And suddenly he reached up and clamped his hands against his temples. His eyes snapped shut and he staggered forward.

Ianthe caught him. 'Paulus?'

The young prince gasped and collapsed to his knees, pulling Ianthe down with him.

From the other side of the room came a sudden cry. Duke Cyr pointed wildly at the Haurstaf girls. 'The blonde girl,' he yelled. 'She's doing this. She's attacking.'

The dumpy girl who had curtseyed mere moments ago now backed away, her hands raised defensively, her horror-struck eyes fixed on the prince's agonized writhing. Her fair companion remained rooted to the spot. The malice had disappeared from her expression, replaced by what appeared to be genuine shock.

'An assassin,' the duke cried. 'An assassin.'

The palace guard wheeled and struck the slender girl across the face with the back of his gauntlet. She crumpled like a pile of sticks, her body splayed across the floor, her hair a lick of yellow flame. She moaned and raised her head and gaped back in terror at her assailant.

Paulus cried out in agony.

'Stop her,' Cyr cried. 'She's killing the prince.'

Even as the palace guard raised his boot to strike the girl, Ianthe reacted instinctively.

She closed her eyes and let her consciousness slip from her own body until she was floating in that dark and endless reservoir of perceptions she had begun to think of as the Sea of Ghosts. She could still perceive the chamber she physically occupied, but now through the eyes and ears of everyone present. It was like being in the room, but removed from it at the same time.

At the focus of each person's vision, the young blonde Haurstaf assassin lay upon the stone between the feet of the palace guards, her perceived surroundings shining like a beacon before Ianthe's own discorporate soul. The chamber seemed to flicker and swell around Ianthe as the Haurstaf girl cast her gaze around. Was she even now looking for escape?

There would be no escape.

Ianthe's own consciousness flitted through the dark like a phantom. She fell upon that young Haurstaf mind and curled her anger and desperation around it. Through the ears of those others around her she heard screaming, but she could not tell from whose throat it came. She heard a sudden sharp intake of breath. *Paulus?* And then she felt a stab of agony at the base of her spine. Her spine? She wanted to cry out, but she had no lungs, no body. No spine. She was nothing but a ghost. A male voice roared, 'Kill her!'

Ianthe snuffed out the Haurstaf mind like a candle.

She opened her eyes again to find Paulus staring at her intently, but her thoughts scrambled through dizziness and nausea. Someone had tried to attack her. The prince was holding her shoulders, keeping her drunken limbs upright. 'Ianthe?'

'My love.'

'Hush, you're confused.'

Her sense coalesced. And suddenly she heard sobbing. She glanced at the floor. The Haurstaf girl lay there, unmoving, one hand pressed against a wound at the base of her spine from which blood was pouring. One of the palace guards crouched over her, a bloody knife in his hand. The girl lay in an awkward attitude, her torso twisted strangely, her robes scattered about her naked legs. Her mouth was open but still. Her dead eyes stared at nothing.

The other girl sat on the floor nearby, weeping uncontrollably into her sleeve.

Ianthe failed to stifle a wail.

'You saved me,' Paulus said, holding her more tightly. 'Do you hear me? You saved my life.'

'I killed her,' Ianthe said. 'Before the knife. She was dead before her blood even started to flow.'

'She was trying to kill me. Another heartbeat and it would have been too late.'

Ianthe rested her head against his chest and began to sob.

Maskelyne's smile stuttered momentarily when the door opened and his servant Garstone admitted the Haurstaf witch out onto the terrace. The face beneath that white Haurstaf cowl was not that of Briana Marks at all, but rather the face of a beautiful young woman he had never seen before. It took the metaphysicist a moment before he realized what was going on.

'My dear Briana,' he said to the stranger. 'You're here by proxy.'

The young woman extended her hand. 'Thena Althorpe,' she said. 'I will telepathically relay the conversation between Sister Marks and yourself.'

'I'm envious of your talent, Miss Althorpe,' Maskelyne said with a smile. 'But not the task before you.' He offered her a seat at a table by the edge of the sea cliffs. They were on a little-used terrace on the eastern side of his fortress, high above the darkly plunging waters of the Sea of Lights. Waves boomed and fizzed against the rocks far below, sharpening the air with vapours that had long ago corrupted the ironwork of the patio furniture and the railings, giving them a furred bromide texture. In the waning light the Mare Lux glowered heavily.

Over their heads Maskelyne's fortress of pink and purple quartz stood atop the island's spine like a monstrous lantern or even a great crystal skull. Its translucent façades and buttresses and inner spaces hoarded and amplified the last rays of sunlight so that the whole building glowed fiercely against the darkening skies.

'May I say,' Maskelyne said, 'what a pleasure it is to see you again, Briana. You're looking especially radiant.'

Thena blushed. 'Sister Marks asks that you . . . uh . . . refrain from patronizing her, sir. And she requests that you address her as Miss Marks.'

'She asks and requests?' Maskelyne grinned. 'That hardly sounds like her at all.'

The telepath opened her mouth to speak, but stopped.

'Yes?' Maskelyne said.

'I will relay her words exactly.'

'Harder than it sounds, I imagine.'

'Sir, I am a trained . . .' She fell silent again, then recomposed herself. 'Stop baiting the girl,' she said in a voice clearly intended to mimic Briana's own. There was even a harshness to the tone. 'I need to speak with you urgently, Ethan.'

'My dear Briana,' Maskelyne said. 'This pretty voice can't mask your anguish.' He took the young telepath's hand in his own, resting his finger on her pulse. 'Tell me where you are and how I may be of assistance.'

The telepath barely flinched at Maskelyne's touch. Her eyes remained focused inwards. 'I'm at sea,' she said. 'My exact location is irrelevant and secret. You need only know that I'm far from Awl and far from you.'

Maskelyne released the telepath's hand. 'Some wine? Is this woman able to convey the taste and smell of a rare Losotan vintage across the leagues to you?'

'Of course not,' the young woman said. 'Don't waste wine on her.'

'Of course,' Maskelyne said. 'We wouldn't want her slurring your words. Still, I hope you don't mind if I have some.' He signalled to Garstone, who was waiting beside the door. Garstone disappeared inside.

Maskelyne leaned back in his chair. A cool breeze blew off the sea and ruffled his hair. He could see that the telepath seated opposite him was trying to distance herself from the conversation, removing her own will in order to act as a conduit between himself and Briana Marks. Of course she could not accomplish that completely. The blankness she'd adopted in her expression was merely an affectation. This girl might be trained, but was certainly not in the same league as Ianthe. 'Why send such a pretty one?' he said.

'She happened to be available,' the young woman said.

'The only one available?'

The telepath hesitated. 'If she pleases you, you may . . .' She paused again, swallowed, then resumed her conversation in a rather bitter tone. 'You may have her after our business is concluded.'

'Have her?' Maskelyne said. 'You mean fuck her?'

'That's exactly what I mean,' the telepath said in a voice now edged with anger.

Maskelyne couldn't help but smile. 'Thank you, Briana,' he said. 'That's most kind.'

'Think nothing of it.'

At that moment Garstone arrived with a tray bearing a decanter of red wine and two goblets cut from the same quartz as Maskelyne's fortress. The glassware burned with a pinkish light. He set them down on the rusty table and was about to pour the wine, when Maskelyne dismissed him.

'What do you want from me, Briana?' he said to the telepath.

The telepath waited until the servant had gone. 'Simply what's in our mutual best interest, Ethan,' she said. 'Neither of us can risk letting the Unmer regain their power.'

Maskelyne watched her over the lip of his glass.

'An alliance makes sense,' she went on. 'As soon as the Unmer have gained a foothold in Awl, they'll look towards the empire. Hu has no way to stand against them, but he'll rally the warlords anyway. He'll summon you, Ethan. With your knowledge of Unmer artefacts and an army of prisoners at your disposal. You won't be able to refuse him without Haurstaf help.'

'How many of you *actually* survived?' Maskelyne said.

The telepath took a deep breath. 'Enough of us to make a difference. Enough of us to be useful in a war against the Unmer.'

'Assuming Granger's little girl allows it,' Maskelyne said. 'Ianthe destroyed your Guild without raising a finger. And from what I understand about her abilities, she could very well be listening to this conversation right now.'

'No,' the woman replied. 'Ianthe's abilities don't stretch to telepathy. If she's watching me now, then she's watching a woman gazing out at the sea. She can't hear my thoughts. And she doesn't know about this proxy. I've never met the woman you're speaking to. Why should Ianthe choose to spy on her?'

It was a reasonable safeguard, Maskelyne conceded. If Ianthe was spying on Briana Marks, as seemed probable, then the use of a proxy meant that the girl wouldn't necessarily be aware of this conversation. 'You can be quite cunning when you want to be,' he said. 'But you forget that Ianthe could be spying on *me*.'

'Your ego truly is remarkable, Ethan,' the telepath said. 'It's possible, but highly unlikely. She can't eavesdrop on the whole world at once.'

Maskelyne took a sip of wine. 'Presumably, you want her killed?'

The telepath was silent for a moment. 'She can't be allowed to stand between us and the Unmer,' she said at last. 'They've already tried to enslave mankind once.'

Maskelyne sighed. 'Spare me the melodrama, Briana,' he

said. 'Why should you care what happens to mankind? The Guild's top priority has always been its own survival. Ianthe's power over you is the only thing preventing you from dominating the Unmer. So while she's allied with them, this is their one and only chance to get rid of you.' He snorted. 'The Unmer are doomed if Ianthe dies. The Haurstaf are doomed if she doesn't.'

'How did you know she was with the Unmer?'

Maskelyne smiled. 'You just told me.'

'So you'll help us?'

Maskelyne swigged more wine. 'No.'

'What?'

'Why should I care if the Haurstaf disappear?'

'Uh . . . Didn't you hear the part about the enslavement of mankind? I said it just a minute ago.'

'Really, my heart bleeds.' The metaphysicist set his glass down and leaned forward. 'The greatest threat to our species is not the Unmer, but the consequences of the sorcery they unleashed in their final, desperate hours.' He saw that she was about to object, so raised his hand. 'The seas are rising, Briana, and neither you nor I know how to halt them. Has it occurred to you that the Unmer's liberation might actually be a timely blessing?'

'Don't make an enemy of us, Ethan.'

Maskelyne waved a hand. 'Spare me the threats, please. I have work to finish here. When that is done, I intend to go and see the Unmer myself.' He looked deep into the telepath's eyes. 'If they do possess a way to reverse the rising seas, then I will offer them my assistance.'

'You think they care about this world? After everything they've done.'

The metaphysicist smiled. He thought about his crystal and

the lands he'd seen through its facets. It was entirely possible that the Unmer had no intention of saving this world – that they would ultimately abandon it for another. Either way, Maskelyne intended to be on their side. 'I think they care about themselves,' he said. 'Now, I'm sorry I couldn't be more helpful, Briana.' He rose to his feet. 'If you'll excuse me, I have work to do . . .'

The telepath stood up, her face red with embarrassment. 'You're making a foolish mistake, Ethan.'

Maskelyne smiled again. 'Garstone will see you out.' He gave the young woman a curt bow, then strode off towards the terrace doors. After a few paces he turned back and said, 'The problem with you, Briana, is that you've got into the habit of using people indiscriminately to get what you want. I won't submit to it.'

'It's always served me well, Ethan.'

'That's exactly why I won't submit,' he replied. 'I intend to follow your example.'

The servant girl brought Granger to a banqueting hall in the west wing of the palace, where hundreds of guests sat at long tables below a raised stage. Servants moved like bobbins through a tapestry of commotion, of clashing sounds and smells. Glasses clinked and sparkled by the light of a thousand candles. Men and women murmured, gossiped, roared out laughter. A fire crackled in the hearth, snapped, settled. By the fine cut of their clothing, Granger took the guests to be wealthy landowners, farmers, shipowners, bankers and other business people from Port Awl or the river valley.

They were, he supposed, used to such excess.

And yet, their noisy chatter diminished as the girl led Granger down an aisle towards an empty table upon the stage.

It occurred to him how strange he must look to them. All the finery the Unmer had thrust on him could not disguise his blood-red eyes or brine-scarred face nor his invalidity. Without his power armour to help him he moved like a cripple, leaning on the servant girl as he would have leaned on a crutch. His legs trembled and twice he was forced to clutch her shoulder to keep himself from falling. The first time this happened she started with fear, but then she saw his shame and weakness and permitted him this indiscretion.

They climbed three steps to the stage, every one of which threatened to unbalance him and bring him toppling to his knees before the assembled nobility. In his panic he put too much of his weight on her tiny bones and he heard her give a soft gasp. And yet she seemed aware of his embarrassment and made an effort to hide her own exertions as she struggled to support him. When they reached the table, Granger stopped and leaned against it with the pretence of reading the name cards set upon the linen tablecloth. The girl waited without complaint and when he was ready she helped him to a seat at the far end and then departed, leaving him alone to suffer the stares of the curious and indignant diners below.

He waited for what seemed like an age. He kept his head down and tried to ignore the other guests. Bowls of bread, olives and dried fruits had been set upon his table but they were undoubtedly for his Unmer hosts and, anyway, he had no appetite. A male servant brought wine, and he sat there rolling the goblet between the scarred grey hide of his palms, grateful for even this small distraction. Occasionally he would glance up and catch the eye of some Port Awl socialite who happened to be looking his way. There seemed to be a lot of them looking his way. The dark part of his imagination supplied words to their conversations.

And suddenly his glass was empty of wine.

The servant refilled it. And then a second time.

Finally, the grand doors at the top of the hall opened and a long-nosed man in a silver-trimmed frock coat appeared. He clapped his hands together three times. 'Ladies and gentlemen,' he announced in a loud and confident voice. 'Valued guests. Please rise and welcome their Royal Highnesses Prince Paulus Marquetta, Duke Cyr of Vale and his wife, the Duchess Anaisy.'

Chairs scraped the floor. Hundreds of guests stood in unison. The announcer stepped aside and bowed deeply as golden trumpets blew a fanfare. The royal entourage swept into the hall in a procession of glitz and bombast. First came the young prince, with chin raised and violet eyes sparkling, his slender torso resplendent in a tunic of crystals and platinum thread, his long sleeves glimmering. He walked arm in arm with Ianthe.

Granger's breath caught in his throat.

His daughter was a vision of beauty. She wore a gown of emerald and blue and a diamond tiara set upon hair that gleamed as black as anthracite. At her neck she wore a single ruby as large as a child's heart. Her brass-framed Unmer lenses flashed in the candlelight as she cast a nervous glance about her. And then she blushed and lowered her eyes and clung to Marquetta all the more fiercely. Marquetta noticed this and patted her hand and smiled. He whispered something in her ear.

Behind them came the prince's uncle, Duke Cyr of Vale and his wife. The Duchess of Vale was a enormous woman with stone-grey hair pulled back so severely behind her head that the skin on her face seemed in danger of rupturing. For a nose she appeared to rely upon a red boil-like hemisphere set above a wide soft mouth. Rouge coloured her ample cheeks, and she walked with a pronounced waddle. She wore a frock dyed or painted to resemble lizard skin and black shoes that clacked like little claws against the floor. A great confusion of pearls hung about her neck – enough, perhaps, to throttle a fair-sized horse.

Her husband, by contrast, had dressed himself in plain black and grey attire – the garb of a man who wished to fade into the background.

Nobody spoke as the party made its way across the hall.

Granger stood as the duchess alighted the stage and sidled along the table to the chair next to him. He heard the floorboards creak with the strain. Next came Marquetta, followed by Ianthe and finally the duke. Duchess Anaisy eyed the bowls of food, moistened her lips, then glanced at Granger with a dark flash of suspicion that seemed almost to cry: Who is this grotesque interloper to sit at my table? There was something defensive and vaguely hostile about her attitude, as though she feared Granger might help himself to titbits she had already earmarked for herself. Once the prince and Ianthe had seated themselves, she eased herself down into her own chair. The wood under her rear groaned, then settled.

Granger sat.

'You're her father,' she said.

He nodded.

'Whatever happened to your face?'

'I went swimming,' he said. 'Turns out someone filled the oceans with poison.'

She snorted with laughter. 'Unlike my husband,' she said, grinning, 'I have never been one to stand on ceremony.' She grabbed one of the bowls and started tearing into the bread and olives as a servant attempted to evade her elbows in order to fill her wine glass. Oil dribbled down her chin. She muttered something indecipherable, waving a hunk of bread, before taking a drink and swallowing. 'Of course, I haven't been to one of these for years. None of us has. It's been terrible, simply terrible.'

Granger nodded. He glanced over at Ianthe, who was in conversation with Marquetta. He couldn't hear what they were saying.

The duchess continued to fill her face. 'The last time we were out in public must have been, gosh, it must have been nearly three hundred years ago now.'

Granger looked at her. Sometimes it was easy to forget how long lived the Unmer were. They had some natural longevity, but that would only see them to an age of two hundred or thereabouts. So they sustained themselves with sorcerous arte-facts, either worn on their person or else implanted inside their bodies. Since the duchess had survived nearly three hundred years of Haurstaf confinement, she most likely belonged to the latter group – although Haurstaf surgeons had been known to cut them out. Granger wondered briefly where the artefact that prevented her from ageing was located in her body. There was no shortage of places it might be.

He glanced over at Ianthe, but still couldn't catch her eye. She seemed to be deliberately avoiding him.

'I'm writing a book,' the duchess said.

'Really?'

'Would you like to know what it's about?'

'No.'

She stopped suddenly and stared at him. Her mouth opened and closed again. 'You are a very rude man,' she said. 'I should warn you, Colonel, that my husband the duke has a very powerful patron.'

'I'm not a colonel.'

The duchess harrumphed. 'Don't mock me, Colonel. I'm so pleased your daughter doesn't take after you.'

Granger shrugged. He was pleased she did.

Just then an army of servants arrived, laden with trays of food. The duchess's eyes lit up and the hostility evaporated from her. She clapped her hands. She accepted everything that was offered and then set to work demolishing it. Trails of juice and wine now covered the front of her lizard-skin dress. Granger allowed a servant girl to ladle some meat and fowl and apple preserves onto his plate. He stirred it around with his fork. Prince Marquetta, he could see, was choosing dishes for Ianthe, who smiled and nodded each time, but even he could see how nervous she was. She merely picked at the corners of her plate.

The duchess belched. She was already drunk. 'More wine,' she shrilled, waving to the servants. 'And bring another plate of those chicken liver things.' By now the guests had started to notice her behaviour. Granger noted more than a few glances in her direction, followed by chuckles and whispered exchanges. The duchess, however, seemed blissfully unaware of the attention.

'Is everything to your satisfaction, Duchess?' Marquetta said.

'Very good, Highness,' she replied. 'Very good indeed.'

'I've never seen our colonel so rapt,' he said.

She assumed an expression of utter disdain. 'Oh, he's not a colonel,' she said, then turned to Granger. 'Are you dear? Just a simple little man who finds himself swimming out of his depth.'

Granger made no reply.

'I was just telling him about Cyr's patron, Fiorel.'

Marquetta's face fell. 'I'm sure Mr Granger has no interest in that,' he said, in a low, warning tone.

Granger's ears perked up.

The duchess, however, did not seem to notice the prince's

warning. She crammed another handful of honeyed meat into her mouth and turned back to Granger. 'You've heard of Fiorel, I take it? The shape-shifter? The God of Cauldron and Forge? What do your people call him? Father of Creation, isn't it? It's nice when a figure of absolute power chooses to offer you patronage.'

Granger grunted. 'You mean Fiorel the meddler.'

She shook her head in disbelief. 'How dare you . . . disrespect! How dare you even utter his name? You will come to regret those words, Colonel, I can assure you. When Fiorel hears of this, and he will, you are going—'

'I told you, woman, I'm not a colonel.'

'Woman?' She stopped suddenly, open-mouthed, and then stood up and swung round to face the prince and the duke. 'Move him, or move me,' she said loudly, jabbing a finger at Granger. 'I won't be seated next to this awful man a moment longer.'

Now Cyr got to his feet. 'Anaisy, please.'

'Put him down there with the commoners, where he belongs.' The banquet hall had fallen silent by now, and the duchess's words were loud enough for everyone present to hear.

'Anaisy!' Cyr cried. 'These people are our guests.'

The duchess glared at him. Then she raised her chin, gathered up the hem of her skirt, and strode away from the table without uttering another word. She hurried down the steps from the platform and then breezed across the room with every eye following her.

A servant opened the door for her and she was gone.

Granger turned to find Ianthe staring at him with her dark eyes narrowed and brimming with murder. He sighed and rubbed his weary eyes.

The banquet continued for hours. Servants skirled around

the tables with platters of cured ham and lampreys with raspberry preserve and pheasant roasted in wild mountain herbs and served with rings of fruited bread and a dozen dark rich sauces. The excess and wastefulness of it all grated on his nerves, but he sat there and listened to the laughter and the chatter, while trying to hide his boredom and discomfort. Tomorrow they would leave for Port Awl. He'd heard enough of Marquetta's conversation with the duke to know that he planned to use Haurstaf recruits to carry messages across the empire. If that was true, Ianthe might persuade the prince to give them passage on a ship to Evensraum. Finally they'd be away from this infernal place.

Someone rang a bell, and the chatter of conversation died to silence. The servant in the silver-trimmed frock coat appeared again. 'His Highness, Duke Cyr of Vale,' he called out.

Cyr stood. He unfurled a small scroll, peered at it, and cleared his throat. Then, with his eyes on the scroll, he addressed the room. 'Esteemed guests,' he said. 'As much as we are here to celebrate our liberty and union, we are also here to mark the forthcoming coronation of His Highness Prince Paulus Marquetta, son of King Jonas the Third of Galea, known as Jonas the Summoner, Jonas the Brave and Merciful, Walker of the Infinite Paths, and Queen Grace Constance Lavern of Aldegarde, may they rest in eternal peace.' He paused and looked up.

The servant in the frock coat called out, 'May they rest in eternal peace.'

Silence filled the hall. Someone coughed. Among the diners there were a few embarrassed mutters and mumbles.

The duke returned his attention to his scroll. 'The coronation will be held on the last day of autumn, the month of Reth or Hu-Suarin in the Anean calendar, in this year of 1441.'

Granger thought it was odd to see an Unmer noble – an Unmer royal, no less – using the emperor's own calendar. But then, he supposed, nobody here would know an Unmer date from a rotten fig. Those calendars hadn't been used in centuries.

The duke rolled up his scroll, then extended a hand towards the prince and said, 'Prince Paulus Marquetta.'

The young man stood. For a long moment he regarded his guests with sparkling eyes and a half-smile upon his lips. 'Dear guests,' he said at last. 'Let me set the matter of the coronation aside for one moment, and say that today marks a turning point in history. We are not here merely to celebrate my reign, but rather the beginning of two very special relationships.' He paused, allowing those words to settle into silence. 'The first is the relationship between our two peoples,' he went on. 'For many years we have both lived under the rule of a Guild that has become rich and powerful through scaremongering, blackmail, and through the propagation of *lies*.' He stressed this last word. 'We have all, in some way, suffered under the Haurstaf. Whether directly through torture, imprisonment, or as a result of their political manipulation.' His gaze roamed from table to table. 'But mostly because of their greed. Greed that has seen the Haurstaf *allow* sea levels to reach critical levels.' He spread his hands, as if in appeal. 'Now that their regime has fallen, and the Haurstaf no longer pose a threat to my people and yours, we find ourselves with work to do. We must halt the rising tides before it is too late.

'Each of us here, in this room, possesses the vision to foresee a future of peace and mutual respect between our two peoples. Together we will prosper . . . here in Awl, and in all the lands beyond.'

Granger was dismayed to hear a chorus of muttered approval sweep through the hall, accompanied by scattered applause.

Peace and mutual respect? Couldn't they see that everything Marquetta had just said was a lie? Had they forgotten their history so soon? The Unmer poisoned the seas, not the Haurstaf. Or were they just making the noises required by their own cowardice? He recalled what Herian had told him in the Pertican transmitting station:

Brine never *stops flowing. Not in a hundred years, nor in a million; not when our air thins and boils away and this bloated planet pulls the moon and the sun down from the sky. It will fill the vacuum between the stars long after my race has departed this world and yours has perished. It isn't a weapon; it's a catalyst – the broth from which a new cosmos will be manufactured.*

The Unmer had made a deal with the elder gods, creatures they called entropaths who lived in the dying embers of another cosmos. In their desperation they had helped those gods open a door between their world and ours. The brine flowing through was somehow important to those gods. Perhaps it was the source of their power, or was used to prepare the way for their coming. Granger didn't know. They didn't need it to breathe. The entropath he had seen at the transmitting station in Pertica had breathed air. Nevertheless, these entities valued it above all else. And when they had brought enough of it through, they would follow, abandoning their own dying universe for ours.

To save themselves from genocide, the Unmer had sacrificed everything – our own world, our own universe.

The applause had died down and now the young prince addressed the crowd again. 'But we are also here to celebrate a second relationship,' he said. He turned and reached over and took Ianthe's hand, gently ushering her to her feet. She stood beside him, blushing fiercely.

Something in her eyes, her stance, warned Granger. He

found himself watching events unfold through a giddy cloud of apprehension. Standing on the brink of an abyss with a gale rising at his back, and he didn't know if he could keep his balance.

The prince smiled. 'May I present Ianthe Cooper of Evensraum, my fiancée, and the future queen of the Unmer.'

Furious applause shook the banquet hall. Granger felt the blood drain from his face. He glared at Ianthe. He wanted to stand up and shake her and say, *Are you insane?* And he wanted her to look at him so she would see that question burning there in his eyes but she avoided his eye, just as she avoided the looks of astonishment from everyone in that room. She merely stared at her plate, blushing like a foolish child.

Granger felt sick. He made to rise.

Perhaps it was a mixture of the wine and the heat and his already weakened state, but his legs gave out before he had taken two steps. He stumbled drunkenly towards Ianthe, who recoiled instinctively.

But then strong arms caught him. He found himself looking directly into the young prince's eyes.

'Steady on, sir,' Marquetta said. 'You're less than a day out of that suit.'

'I'm fine,' Granger said, trying to push away.

But Marquetta held on. 'I fear we have pushed you too, far too quickly,' he said. 'You need to lie down, rest some more, accept your present state.' He took Granger's elbow and led him along the back of the stage, waving away the servants who came rushing to assist them. Amidst the fug of his weakness and indignity, Granger spied Duke Cyr. The old man was watching him carefully, perhaps studying Granger's reaction.

Granger's head swam. He said, 'What do you want with her?'

'I want an heir, Mr Granger. Can you imagine an Unmer child with her powers?'

'You're using her.'

'She's happy, Mr Granger. Why can't you be happy for her?'

'Because I know how deceitful you people can be. You don't care about her. You're liars, all of you.'

Marquetta's face twisted into an angry scowl. He clenched Granger's elbow more tightly, and Granger felt a sudden piercing pain, as though he had been stung there. When Marquetta removed his hand, Granger spied blood on his elbow.

'Forgive me,' Marquetta said, looking at the wound he had just given Granger. 'I've displaced some of your skin. A lapse of concentration, I fear. Sometimes I forget how vulnerable your kind are to decreation.'

Granger leaned close to the young man and growled into his ear. 'Harm my daughter, and I'll kill you.'

Marquetta laughed. 'You think?' he said. 'Mr Granger, you are being consumed by a parasitic sword. With each hour that passes, it gains more control of you. Don't you feel a yearning to go and collect it? To feel its weight in your hand? Do you think that is *your* will? A week or a month from now you will be nothing but a phantom, compelled to obey the sword's every desire. And there is nothing you can do about it.'

'I'll destroy it.'

'The sword will not let you.'

'I'll cripple myself.'

'You do not yet understand.' The young prince studied Granger for a moment. 'Look at yourself. It already has too much of a grip on you. You cannot escape the inevitable. You are no longer the wielder with the sword as your weapon. Now the sword is the wielder and you are its weapon.'

Granger said nothing. He knew the prince had spoken the truth. He didn't want to destroy the power armour, nor even the hellish blade that was destined to devour him. Even now, he yearned to reclaim the weapon with every pore and shredded nerve in his body. He wanted to succumb to it.

'You might have stood a chance against it,' Marquetta said, 'if you hadn't slept so long.'

Granger growled. 'You kept me asleep deliberately?'

'But I woke you as a gift to Ianthe,' Marquetta said. 'She has been hovering around your bedside for days. She wanted you to know about her marriage. She desperately wanted you to be . . .' He smiled. 'Proud of her.' He fixed Granger with a penetrating stare. 'Can you do that one thing for her, before you die?'

CHAPTER 4

THE DRAGON ISLE

Briana Marks watched a flight of four dragons skim the seas to port, each clad in massive banded leather armour, their great aquamarine wings agleam in the sunlight. *Curse Maskelyne for his selfishness*, she thought. *The man cares more for his own neck than he does for his species.* Her last hope now lay here in this strange and treacherous place.

Her hired captain – a thin and bearded Valcinder named Acanto – wrung his hands and clicked his tongue against the top of his mouth for the umpteenth time. He'd been making these sounds ever since they'd caught sight of the Dragon Isle.

'The flag is clearly visible, Captain,' she said.

'And yet they flew so close that time,' Acanto said.

'They're simply testing your mettle,' she replied. 'They won't attack a Haurstaf vessel.'

He nodded meekly and wrung his hands again. 'As you say.' But he didn't look convinced.

Oars dipped and rose on either side of the hull as Acanto's ship, the *Silver Flame*, rounded a fang of dark rock protruding from the red Mare Regis waters and made for a shingle beach backed by monstrous black cliffs. Briana's Haurstaf Guild flag hung limply from the bowsprit. She could see nest sites on ledges high above and great jagged cracks in the rock that led into the serpents' network of caves and the rude stone homes they'd built there. Waves crashed and fumed against massive tumbles of bone and cartilage lying under the cliffs – the remains of whales and sharks and a hundred other forms of marine life.

Acanto was peering at the beach. 'If Conquillas is here,' he said, 'then where is his ship?'

She snorted. 'Really?'

He looked at her blankly.

'You think Argusto Conquillas needs a ship?'

Acanto seemed uncomfortable. 'I always assumed the tales were exaggerated.'

'This is one Unmer lord whose exploits require no exaggeration. This is the slayer of Duna, daughter of Fiorel, the lord who rallied the dragons against his own kind.'

'You say he is a friend to the Haurstaf?'

Briana nodded. But, truthfully, she wasn't certain. Conquillas had fought for the Haurstaf leader, Aria, nearly three hundred years ago. He had betrayed his own kind because of the love he had for her, not for the Guild she presided over. And yet he would not wish to see Marquetta's heir reclaim his throne in Losoto. An Unmer king would seek to punish Conquillas for crimes against his race.

She had encountered the dragon lord three times before: twice when she'd been a young woman, the last only three years ago. He'd been in Awl to demand from her the release of a particular serpent who'd been caught in a hunter's net. Demand, not negotiate. Some pet of his, she'd presumed. She'd simply bought the dragon from the hunter and then released it to him to avoid any unpleasantness from either party. She recalled how cold he'd been.

The *Silver Flame* drew nearer to the beach, where the waters of the Sea of Kings had left a line of flesh-coloured scum running along the shingle. More remains lay scattered everywhere: the huge skeletons of whales and sharks and clusters of smaller animals. Some of the larger specimens were over sixty paces from jaw to tail, the lines of their ribs running like bleached driftwood fences. And strewn everywhere were human limbs and pelvises, the hands and feet and grinning skulls of the Drowned – the dragon's favoured prey. Briana sensed eyes upon her and looked up into the caves overhead, but she saw no sign of life in those dark rents.

When the leadman called two fathoms under the hull, Acanto's coxswain ordered the oars banked and the anchor dropped. The crew cranked winches, lowering the *Flame*'s tender into the blood-red waters. The breeze had stiffened and so Briana and Acanto donned their cloaks and goggles before descending by rope ladder.

The tender's small engine coughed into life with a puff of acrid fumes, and the small vessel bore them across seawater that glittered like rubies. The wind blew puffs of pink foam from their wake.

Briana wrinkled her nose. 'This engine,' she said, 'is it fuelled by whale oil or dragon venom?'

Acanto shot her a fearful gaze. 'Oh my . . .'

She grinned. 'Relax. I'm kidding. I doubt they can smell the difference.'

'You're certain?'

'Not certain, no.'

'May the gods save us.'

The sunlight had a peculiarly clear quality that seemed to sharpen everything around Briana, yet it was becoming bitterly cold. Again came the feeling of being watched. Acanto cut the engine a yard from land and the keel scraped tiny metalled stones. They stepped ashore with the bones of giants looming over them like sculpted ice.

'That's odd,' Acanto said. 'Weird. Do you feel it?'

'What?'

'An edge to the air, to the sunlight maybe.'

'There is a foul odour, now that you mention it,' she admitted. 'But I think it's the same one I've been smelling since I stepped aboard your ship.'

But there was *something* in the air, and perhaps even in the rock and the bones: an invisible force that enveloped the island itself. It felt as though everything here was under constant stress by some unseen power. And it struck Briana that here among the dragons of the Mare Regis she might be sensing the residue of powerful Entropic sorcery. To forge these beasts the Unmer had ripped apart and reconstructed nature, dragging the minds of their victims through oblivion, only to reassemble them in new and ghastly forms. Was she now sensing that lingering damage? That distant echo of their once-human screams? For all a dragon's terrible beauty, one could always sense in them a fatal flaw – a deep fracture or sickness lurking behind their eyes. Rarely did one encounter a dragon that was not, to some degree, insane. Like all Unmer creations, they were the product of imperfect minds striving for perfection.

She wondered why Conquillas loved them so.

Steps cut into the rock led them up towards the black throats of the caverns overhead. Briana could hear the wind keening up there and it seemed to her a chilling, forlorn sound.

After a few hundred paces they stopped to rest on a small terrace.

Briana raised her goggles and stood looking out to sea, her cloak snapping in the cold wind. Some distance to the south she could see a long dark shape skimming the crests of the waves – a serpent of considerable size. Its head turned and it wheeled inwards towards the island, wings thumping languidly.

Acanto clicked his tongue against the roof of his mouth. 'That beast is large enough to be Gruinlahg herself,' he said.

'Or one of her daughters, perhaps,' Briana remarked. 'It's said they live here.' Gruinlahg had been one of the largest and most ferocious dragons ever to hunt the Mare Regis. Unmer sorcerers had fashioned her, it was said, from the mind and spirit of a simple nursemaid. With such a humble heritage, no one could explain how she came to be such a terror. But her rage had been legendary. She sank one-tenth of the Imperial Navy and then at least twenty privateers Emperor Lem subsequently sent to kill her, before finally meeting her end in a sea battle near Praxis over a hundred years ago.

'A woman scorned,' Briana said.

'What?'

'Gruinlahg. Never underestimate a woman scorned.'

'Do you think her daughters could still be alive? After all this time?'

'Why not?' she said. 'Everything tainted by sorcery seems to resist nature's attempts to unravel it. Conquillas himself must be nine hundred years old by now.'

Acanto whistled. 'Nine hundred years.'

And as bitter as the sea, Briana thought.

They resumed their ascent and soon reached the mouth of a vast cavern, into which the path now meandered, snaking onwards through taluses of shattered black rock and mounds of white bones into the subterranean heart of the island. Now their footfalls echoed under a canopy of stone and, looking up, they could see where, on the walls of the cave, the dragons had built their nests.

'They look like limpets,' Acanto observed.

It was, Briana thought, an accurate metaphor. The dragon's nests clung to the naked rock in the manner of limpets. They were constructed of mortared stone and roughly hemispherical, and each possessed a single opening through which the serpents came and went.

'They buy the cement from Valcinder traders,' Briana remarked.

'*Buy* it?'

She grunted. 'At exorbitant prices.'

They passed through the ribcage of a whale and moved on into an area littered with post-human remains licked clean and gnawed. Skulls etched with tooth marks. Tibiae and fibulae cracked open for the marrow inside. Here and there the cavern floor bore the scrapes of claws. And soon Briana could smell the dense musk of the beasts themselves – an odour so powerful she could actually taste blood and sweat and sulphur on her lips.

Acanto pointed. 'Look there.'

Ahead of them the path meandered onwards through slopes of rock and bone, following the downward incline of the cavern floor, until it reached a relatively flat and open area. There, cradled between two specially constructed piles of mortared stone, rested a ship.

She was an antique, an Unmer yacht the likes of which had not been built nor sailed for over a thousand years. Eighty feet from bow to stern, straight and slender, her heartwood hull had faded to a bone grey and was still clad in its original metal scrollwork – filigree so exquisitely wrought it reminded Briana of the finest Valcinder concertinas. Her windows were intact, the rounded lozenges of thick yellow duskglass set in patterned alloy frames. Her single funnel, also forged from a forgotten alloy, rose behind a wheelhouse inlaid with hardwoods and precious metals and a mast with a single yard and wire-wound shrouds. On her prow there stood a harpoon gun and cable spindle, while various hunting spears and nets had been lashed both to her bulwarks and to a sturdy fore-deck rack. Her gangway had been lowered from the side of the yacht and rested on a series of stone slabs forming a rude stairwell down to the cavern floor.

Acanto blew through his teeth. 'That's a dragon hunter,' he said. 'I've never seen one so old. I'll bet that girl sailed before the seas were poisoned.' He examined the ship for a moment longer, then frowned. 'But why would a dragon lord choose to live in a dragon-hunting ship?'

'You're missing the point,' Briana said. 'It's not a dragon-hunting ship. It's a *captured* dragon-hunting ship.'

How like Conquillas to live in a trophy, Briana thought.

'How on earth did he get it up here?'

'Strange, isn't it?' Briana remarked. 'Presumably, it would have to have been carried here by something large that could fly. I can't imagine what sort of beast that would be.'

Acanto gave her a thin smile.

She smiled back. 'Let's hope he's in.'

'What? All this way and you don't even know if he's home?'

'I'm prepared to wait.'

'The place is *crawling* with dragons.'

'You should have expected that,' she replied. 'The clue is in the name.'

The yacht lay just inside the arc of sunlight defined by the cavern roof and had, Briana suspected, been placed just so to take advantage of both the low slanted winter light and the available shade in summer. As they drew near, she was relieved to hear the bright tones of a lute or similar instrument coming from within. She and Acanto climbed the rocky stairwell and strolled across the gangway.

'That's far enough,' said a voice from above.

Briana halted and looked up.

Argusto Conquillas was slouching in the shrouds, staring down at them with cold violet eyes. In his pale hands he held a bow, the arrow aimed at Briana's head. How could she possibly have missed him before?

'You won't shoot,' she said.

'I hadn't planned to,' he admitted. 'But now I'm tempted, just to prove you wrong.'

'That shot's too easy for you.'

He grunted, but he lowered his bow. In one smooth motion he slid down the shrouds and landed lightly on the deck.

Conquillas's eyes were the same peculiar hue as those of his relative, Prince Marquetta, but he was much older, with a long, almost skeletal, face and grey hair woven into a dusty plait that hung between his shoulders. Physically, he appeared to be in his late forties, although Briana knew this to be misleading – Conquillas was probably older than the ship upon which he now stood. He was tall and possessed an angular body softened somewhat by the puffs and frills of his woollen jacket and trousers. His calfskin boots made no sound as he approached.

He regarded Briana with cold intensity.

His eyes betrayed his great age; there was something both intense and deeply savage about them – a brutal intelligence coupled with a cold detachment that seemed to Briana to border on inhuman. Conquillas didn't perceive people as friends or allies, lovers or threats. When he looked at you, it was with eyes that merely determined what could be gained from your death. Briana looked away, unable to meet his gaze for more than those few moments.

Conquillas evidently had company, for she could still hear the sound of the lute playing below decks. She could not imagine who his guest might be, although a gentle mental probing determined that the presence there was certainly not Haurstaf. The playing, however, was exquisite, indicating a master musician. And now, as Conquillas approached, she heard a second sound . . . the faint crackling of void arrows in the black glass quiver looped around his shoulder. Those sorcerous missiles were, alarmingly, extinguishing the air around them. She felt her hair stir in a sudden breeze, drawn towards those ghastly arrow tips by the vacuum they were creating.

Conquillas screwed a bulb of glass across the top of the quiver, sealing it. Light shuddered within; there was a *whoomph*, and the breeze stopped, leaving Briana with a painful thrum in her teeth and a ringing in her ears. She heard Acanto gasp. There was something about that glass tube, or the arrows it contained, something that made them difficult to be near. Like the atmosphere pervading the island, but far more powerful. As with so many Unmer artefacts, it would be exerting an unnatural pressure on everyone around it.

Only Conquillas seemed unaffected. 'Why have you disturbed me?' he said.

'Forgive me,' she replied. 'I wasn't aware you had company.'

The Unmer lord regarded her for a moment. 'News of the massacre in Awl will have reached Losoto by now,' he said. 'Have you knowledge of the emperor's response?'

She raised her eyebrows in surprise. 'You've heard?'

'Dragons carry news more swiftly than ships.'

'I was unaware we had any dragons in Awl.'

Conquillas's lips narrowed. '*You* didn't.'

There was an uncomfortable silence.

'Emperor Hu hasn't made a statement yet,' Briana said. 'At least not publicly.'

'And what is the latest from Awl?'

She hesitated, glancing at Acanto, then said, 'May we speak in private?' That was, after all, the main reason she'd brought the captain along – to use him as an excuse to get Conquillas alone. She didn't want her words overheard by half a hundred serpents.

Conquillas indicated a hatch leading underneath the wheelhouse. She followed him towards it.

Acanto looked around at the shadows. 'I'll wait here, shall I?'

'If you like,' she replied.

'And . . . I'll be safe here?'

Briana turned to Conquillas. 'I need him to pilot the ship.'

The Unmer lord nodded. 'Then he will not be harmed.'

'Then?' Acanto said. 'I note your use of that qualifier.'

Conquillas ignored him. He threw open the hatch and led Briana down several steps and along a short passageway. At the end of this he opened another door and admitted her into a comfortable wood-panelled chamber.

It was a parlour, occupying the full beam of the yacht. Like the wheelhouse exterior, its walls had been inlaid with tropical woods and curls of precious metal and bone. Light poured through the duskglass portals and stretched across the floorboards in honey-coloured ellipses or else gleamed here and there on some fitment of brass – a scalloped table leg or lampshade base. The ceiling was low and the joists had been shaped to resemble whalebones and hung with many tiny gem lanterns of an eastern style Briana had never seen before. Delicate furniture occupied strategic positions around the room, overstuffed chairs and fine tables strewn with scores of books and scrolls. In one corner of the room there stood a harpsichord of pale lacquered wood. Resting upon a nearby stool was the lute Briana had heard earlier, but the player was nowhere to be seen. She realized the playing must have ceased mere moments ago.

'I'm not intruding, am I?' she said.

Conquillas gave a dismissive wave. He filled two goblets from a decanter of pale green liqueur. Briana accepted the drink graciously, but did not raise the cup to her lips. Unmer spirits were usually laced with drugs. They could affect human minds in strange and unpredictable ways. Conquillas settled into a curled gold couch. He sipped his drink and his violet eyes studied her over the rim of his glass.

'How long has it been, Argusto? Three years?'

He rolled the liqueur in its goblet and inhaled the fumes. Then he took another sip. 'How could you have allowed this to happen, Briana?'

She felt her face flush. 'No one could have foreseen it.'

'She was in your care. You were studying her.'

His knowledge surprised her. *How much did he know?*

'We thought—' she began.

Conquillas growled, 'No, you didn't think. You were negligent, arrogant, vain. That is why you underestimated her.' He observed her for a moment longer with his piercing gaze. 'Is she within you now? Can you feel her presence?'

'She might be,' Briana replied. 'I can't tell.'

'Then we must assume she is listening to this conversation.'

Briana nodded.

'As was your intent.'

'Argusto . . .'

'Say what you came here to say.'

Briana hesitated. She was walking a dangerous path here. The possibility of Ianthe spying had already forced her to lie once to Conquillas. Now she was forcing the Unmer lord to choose sides, and possibly to name his enemies publicly. 'Forgive me if it seems reckless,' she said at last. 'But even if Ianthe is not present at this moment, she would have learned of our meeting eventually. I came here, Argusto, because I know you to be a man of principle, and not one to flinch or cower from your enemies.' She watched the Unmer lord take another sip. 'Since you know about what has happened in Awl, you know what this girl is capable of. Which is why I believe you will recognize the threat now posed by her engagement to Marquetta.'

She saw from his surprised reaction that he had not been aware of this latest development. Dragons might carry news as fast as the wind, but thought carried it faster still, and a few telepaths yet remained in her former stronghold. 'The prince announced their engagement publicly last night. They are to be married after his coronation, three weeks from now.'

Conquillas gave her a mirthless smile. 'He hasn't wasted time.'

'The girl has been smitten with him since she first laid eyes upon him,' Briana said. 'Which only goes to show how well Duke Cyr has taught the little bastard to keep his true nature hidden.' She paused and rolled the liquor round in her cup. 'Or else he simply mesmerized the prince. Either way, they mean to keep the girl close and use her to shield them from Haurstaf influence. With such an ally on his side, the brat can only become . . . What would you say? Even more insufferable?'

Conquillas rose and walked across the parlour, deep in thought. He topped up his drink without offering Briana any more and stood there, staring into the corner of the room for a long time. Finally, he said, 'Have your soldiers sworn loyalty to their new paymasters yet?'

'They have.'

'And they are gathering support from Port Awl?'

She snorted. 'Cyr is up to his usual tricks.' She brought the goblet to her lips, and almost took a sip, before she remembered what type of liquor it contained. 'He's using the pretence of saving the world to recruit allies.'

'Evensraum?'

'Not yet, but it's only a matter of time.'

'He's well placed for that,' Conquillas said. 'Awl's wealth should allow him to stir up a revolt among the population, hire privateers to halt naval traffic and starve the empire.' He paused, thinking. 'Or else smash Losoto and remove Hu in a show of brute force. That's what I would do. Hit the capital hard to make a statement. The emperor is universally despised. His death will only strengthen Marquetta's cause. What Unmer weapons does Cyr now have access to? What were you hoarding at the palace?'

'Nothing . . . Minor things.'

Conquillas nodded. 'Then he can't attack without help.' He paced the floor, thinking. 'He must find an ally. Evensraum would be the most obvious choice.'

Briana gave a cynical smile. 'Did you know that Ianthe is from Evensraum?'

The Unmer Lord fixed his eyes upon her. 'Fate has indeed been kind to Cyr,' he said. 'So Hu perceives the Unmer as a threat. He must raise an army quickly and that means buying the warlords with promises and favours. He'll baulk at that and fuss and hesitate like he's always done, which will ultimately lead to his downfall.' He gazed out of the window for a long time, then turned. 'And there's no way to armour yourself from the girl's psychic attacks?'

'Not that we know of.'

He pondered this. 'We must assume that her destructive powers are not limitless. After all, she slew only those Guild sisters in her immediate vicinity. Her reach did not extend to those Haurstaf in Port Awl?'

Briana shook her head. 'Those sisters in the highest palace towers and lowest dungeons survived.'

Conquillas nodded to himself. 'An ugly war is coming,' he said. 'With Ianthe's protection, Cyr will build his empire. And then he will seek revenge for a century of enslavement and humiliation.' He gave her a grim smile. 'I dare say he won't have forgotten your own personal involvement in it all.'

'Nor yours.'

'So you wish me to assassinate the girl?'

The abruptness of his statement startled her momentarily, but she soon found her voice. 'I thought such a challenge might appeal to you, Argusto. The opportunity to test your wits against someone who can see your every move, someone who could, at a distance, murder you with a single thought.'

'And yet she is a child.'

'A child poised to become an Unmer queen.' Briana sighed. 'You once slew a goddess and brought an army of dragons against Prince Marquetta's father for the love of Aria. I beg you, please, consider her daughters now.'

'I fought Jonas Whiteheart to protect Aria, not the Guild.'

'The Guild is her legacy, Argusto. Aria built it. She strove to protect it. And you are tempted. I know you are. I can see it in your eyes. Cyr will come after you as soon as he regains enough power. Help me put an end to it now. Finish what you started. Now, while there's time to act.'

The dragon lord cradled his long chin in his fingers. 'I will kill Duke Cyr,' he said, 'and the Whiteheart's son, Paulus, and anyone who tries to prevent me from doing so.' He turned and looked deeply into Briana's eyes. 'But I will not harm the girl unless she chooses to involve herself in my affairs. Now, I must send a message to the prince and his uncle announcing my intentions.'

'*What?*'

'You said yourself – Ianthe might be spying on this conversation, but we do not know for sure.'

'She—'

'Therefore I cannot be certain Cyr and Marquetta are aware that I have marked them for assassination.'

'But that's . . .' She managed to stop herself from finishing her sentence in time. Accusing Conquillas of lunacy would not be prudent. Instead, she added, 'Why would you *give* them warning?'

He shrugged. 'I gain no pleasure from bloodshed or murder. It is the challenge that drives me,' he said. 'The sport. The greater the challenge, the greater the glory to be gained in the attempt.'

'Argusto . . .'

His eyes remained cold and distant. He was deep in thought.

'You don't like to make things easy for yourself,' she said.

'I have no interest in living a dull life.'

Briana smiled. 'Sometimes I'm glad we're friends,' she said.

Conquillas pursed his lips. 'We are not friends, Miss Marks.'

Maskelyne remained in his laboratory, working late into the night. Gem lanterns shone in their wall sconces, casting great claws and lattices of shadow between the tables of Unmer trove scattered about the place. He filled notebooks with his musings while his latest specimens gazed out from their brine tanks. Sailors had pulled two fresh women from Ethugran canals and a sharkskin child from the Sea of Kings. Both women had drowned recently, and still possessed mental acuity akin to that of the living. They hunched in that bromine gloom and watched him silently from yellowed eye sockets. The child's brain had rotted months ago and it merely walked forwards repeatedly, knocking against the glass each time. Maskelyne would normally have removed such a worthless specimen by now, but he'd kept this one because little Jontney found it so funny.

He turned the salvaged crystal over in his hands and watched the dark and alien ocean churning within its facets. There was a storm raging in there, the gales raising vast waves and smashing them against the windowless tower on its solitary rock island. What purpose did that tower serve? Was it a fortress? Or even a machine? Who dwelt within? And where exactly was *there*? Brine came from ichusae, those devious little Unmer phials more commonly known as sea-bottles. Because intact ichusae spewed forth endless torrents of the stuff, it had always seemed reasonable for Maskelyne to assume that each of these little bottles contained some sort of conduit to another part of the cosmos – or, indeed, to another cosmos entirely.

And now he held in his hands a lens that appeared to offer him a view into that very place. Were the seas there, he wondered, littered with some cousin of the ichusae – artefacts that sucked in brine rather than expelled the stuff? Or could these sorcerous bottles exist in both places at once? He set the crystal down in a wooden bowl on his desk. It lay there in the semi-dark, illuminating its immediate surroundings with a dim green glow.

A nearby sound startled him, a sharp metallic *trill*. Maskelyne glanced round and saw that an Unmer device on one of his tables had activated. Now it continued to hum and chatter as small lights played within its barnacle-crusted box. He had seen similar machines before, and knew it to be a form of pain mutator – related to the nerve manglers used by his jailers in Ethugra. This one would be able to change pain into other sensations: hunger, or – more dangerously – sexual ecstasy. He returned his attention to the crystal again. Many of his trove items had been springing to life since he'd brought it into his laboratory.

Clearly, it focused light. Did it, he wondered, focus other energies? He glanced back at the pain mutator, wondering if it had simply come into contact with some sort of energy leakage. A field? That made immediate sense. His heartbeat quickened. What if the lens didn't just focus energy, but *sorcery*? Could this simple sphere act as a conduit between the two realms? Was this the conduit through which all Unmer sorcery flowed?

What was sorcery but the wilful transfiguration of matter and energy? And yet it was clear that some sort of external energy was necessary to effect such alterations. Could the lens provide a bridge for that imported energy?

What about brine?

Could he, by destroying the crystal, arrest the flow of energy to ichusae?

And thus stop the influx of brine?

He picked it up again and stared into its facets, marvelling at the alien structure within, at the seething waters and starless cloud-torn sky. The glass felt strangely warm. Was it too much to hope that he was holding the answer to his dilemma here in his hand? Could he bring himself to test his theory by destroying such a treasure?

No.

At least . . . not until he had no alternative.

Maskelyne placed the crystal back in its bowl. He could not take such a risk. He had to know exactly what he was dealing with. He picked up a pen and wrote:

If all energies utilized by Unmer artefacts are cosmically imported and funnelled through a single point, then they must – in this world – radiate out from that point as light radiates from a lantern. And if those rays generate a field which affects change and can therefore be detected, then it ought to be possible to follow said rays to individual Unmer devices.

The flow of electrical fluids could be detected by various devices sensitive to their proximity. Copper coils and toruses could transmit electrical fluids through the air, but could also be used to sense the invisible fields created – even at great distances. And it seemed to him that Unmer sorcery must work in a similar fashion. If this crystal transmitted sorcerous energy, then it must be possible to *detect* the lines of energy surrounding it. And if he could detect these lines, then he could follow them in order to locate Unmer artefacts. He might yet engineer a way to discover every last ichusae in the oceans.

He set about testing his theory.

If sorcerous energy produced a field, then artefacts brought together might disturb each other's fields. Maskelyne slid a gem lantern across his desk and positioned it next to the crystal. *The faintest flickering, perhaps?* He couldn't be certain. There was little – if any – perceptible disruption to the light produced. He dug out some screwdrivers from his desk drawer and opened the lantern casing. He knew from experience how to adjust the mechanism to alter the flow of energy into the bulb – energy, he now hoped, passed through the crystal. Indeed, he had used this knowledge to devastating effect against the Haurstaf palace in Awl.

This time, however, he planned to reduce the flow. He removed four exterior screws and swung back a hinged door in the brass casing, revealing the workings underneath the lantern bulb. Deep in among the wires, needles and bones he moved aside a flap of human leather and located a series of miniature glass spheres on tiny, movable rods. Each of these contained a drop of amber fluid. Some of the drops rested in the base of their particular sphere, while others appeared to defy gravity by clinging to the uppermost surfaces. Long ago, he had found that he could adjust the brightness of the lantern by realigning these spheres.

He did this now, dimming the lantern until it was barely visible. By quenching the lantern's source of power he hoped it might become more sensitive to the other sources of power radiating from the crystal.

To his great delight he discovered that moving the lantern around the crystal now caused the light to fluctuate notice-ably. It did indeed appear to be reacting to the energies being funnelled through that sorcerous lens. He imagined those ener-gies to be like invisible rays of sunlight. The stronger the partic-ular ray, the more it affected the lantern's own field.

At one point in particular, the gem lantern's brightness leaped considerably.

Whatever could that *be?*

He grabbed his pen and made a note of the position. Two seventy-one degrees. Whatever it was, it must surely be an arte-fact of extraordinary power to cause such a large disruption in the lantern's field. A course of two seventy-one degrees would take him south-west, out past the prison city of Ethugra, and ultimately into the strange green waters of the Mare Verdant.

Maskelyne pulled the bell cord to summon Garstone. Then he rifled through the desk in search of quality drafting paper, rulers, compasses and set squares. By the time his servant had appeared, Maskelyne had already sketched a rough outline of the housing system he required.

'Give this to Halfway,' he said. 'Tell him to drop everything else, I want all his machinists working on this right now.'

Garstone glanced at the sketch. 'To this scale?'

'As it's drawn. And ready the *Lamp*. We sail as soon as the device is built.'

'Very good, sir.'

Garstone retreated.

Maskelyne dimmed the laboratory lights and went over to the window.

In the dark the Mare Lux shone like engine oil. To the north and south the island's headlands stood in ragged silhouette against heavens dusted with stars. Between them he could just perceive the silvery arc of the Beach of Keys. He could not spot any of the Drowned upon that metal shore, but he knew they would be there. They came in droves at night.

He turned his back on the night and approached the first of his brine tanks. The woman floating within watched him warily. She was in her early thirties, shapely enough, and dressed in a plain knotted weed robe of Ethugran design – some unfortunate jailer's wife or daughter. Maskelyne suspected she had been drowned, as many of them undoubtedly were, merely to supply him with a fresh specimen. But then, people had to make a living somehow.

He pointed to the south-south-west, to the source of the power his makeshift device had detected. 'What lies there?' he said. 'Do you know?'

She stared at him mutely.

'Is this what your kind want me to find?'

She did not answer.

He had not expected her to. She was merely a vessel into which he might tip his thoughts and thus peer at them. The Drowned who brought the keys to his doorstep were invariably those from whom the last drop of humanity had long since evaporated: the old Drowned, those from whom the sea had taken everything. They came not as ambassadors of mankind or even of the human dead but as mindless emissaries of the brine itself.

'What is it?' Maskelyne asked again. 'What lies there? Punishment? Liberation?'

But the Drowned woman did not reply.

Even something designed to empower a body or preserve it from decreation cannot help but alter that body in ways which are often not . . . entirely healthy. Wearing such armour is like drinking water tainted with a drop of brine, it will keep you alive for a while, but it is always going to kill you in the end.

Granger woke suddenly with a feeling that something was wrong. He had been dreaming about the Unmer, and Marquetta's words still reverberated through his thoughts. But there was something else. He lay there for a moment, listening to the darkness, then opened his eyes. A breeze stirred the gauze curtains covering the windows. The walls were faintly grey from the starlight reflected off high mountain snow and he could smell the bitter-fresh tang of pine from the surrounding forests. The bed sheets lay crumpled around his legs.

He was struck with an overwhelming sensation that there was someone in the room with him.

He lifted his head and looked around.

Nothing but the curtains blowing in the breeze. No sounds but the distant chuckle of water from a mountain stream.

Granger knew better than to dismiss his instincts. They had saved his life on numerous prior occasions. Quietly, he pulled himself to the edge of the bed and looked underneath it.

Nothing.

He slipped out of bed, feeling the cold stone under his bare feet, and stood there, naked. Pain wrung his joints but he ignored it. The hairs on his arms and the back of his neck were standing on end. His nerves screamed: *There is an intruder in the room.* Only there wasn't. The room was empty.

The terrace?

From where Granger stood he could see most of the terrace through the translucent curtains. He padded silently across the bedchamber and brushed aside the billowing gauze. The terrace outside was deserted. A few old pots lay under the balustrade. He could see out across the treetops, the whole valley glimmering faintly silver under a star-dusted sky.

Granger sensed something move behind him. He wheeled round.

Nothing.

But as he stepped back into the room, a wave of dizziness swept over him. He staggered, but managed to stop himself from falling. A sudden sharp pain jabbed his neck, as though something had bitten him. Granger went to move his arm to slap the offending insect away.

Only he found that he couldn't. His arm was entirely paralysed.

And then he tried to move his feet.

But they, too, would not budge. Indeed, he found that none

of his muscles responded to his will. All of a sudden he was completely unable to move.

Sorcery?

He thought of the nerve shredders Ethugran jailers used. Was he now in the clutches of some similar device? It explained the bite he'd felt, the pressure he continued to feel at the back of his neck. That bastard sphere? He hadn't seen it in here, but the cursed thing was small enough to have hidden itself somewhere.

And then Granger spied something very odd indeed.

Something thin and dark crept into the edge of his vision; it looked – for all the world – like a line drawn by an artist. But this line was being drawn through the very air itself. A very fine wire, perhaps? Or a tendril? A samal? His heart clenched at the thought, but then he dismissed the idea. He was too far from the ocean. Not even the largest samal could reach so many leagues inland.

The line grew longer, proceeding slowly through the air before him in a gentle curve. He tried to turn his head to locate its origin, but found that he could not move his neck. Whatever this was, it seemed to have originated from somewhere close behind him. In this gloom he could not determine its colour – other than that it was darker than the surrounding marble – and yet it seemed to him to have a liquid glimmer.

As he watched, the line abruptly split into multiple branches, each of which continued to lengthen. Many of these branches began to divide still further, until the whole thing resembled a large plant, or some sort of root system. It continued to grow, filling the air before him, growing until it towered over him. And then the dark lines began to coalesce in places and flow together into larger channels and shapes. And as some of those shapes became more defined, Granger realized what he was seeing. Not a root system, but the *circulatory* system, complete with blood vessels and a heart, of a large and powerful animal.

A sriakal?

Despair gripped him. Sriakals were said to have prowled the battlefields in Onlo and in Galea even before the dragon wars. They were, some veterans said, an unforeseen side effect of Unmer Entropic sorcery – creatures born from the blood-pits of failed Unmer experiments. Galea had endured a plague of them until the Unmer torched their own cities. They were invisible and yet corporeal, able to paralyse their prey temporarily with a neurotoxin sting. With horror, Granger realized that the substance flowing before his eyes was his own blood. The sriakal was feeding on him, drawing his own blood into its invisible veins.

How did it come to be *here*? He thought of the tattoo imprinted on the back of Duke Cyr's right hand. The mark of a Brutalist sorcerer.

Had Cyr *summoned* it here?

Was that even *possible*?

He desperately tried to move. He threw everything into the effort, but his muscles simply would not bend to his will. He could not escape, nor would he be able to before the creature drained the last drop of blood from his veins.

If he could but simply move a finger . . .

Such a simple movement might lead to a greater one. A finger to a hand . . . A hand to an arm . . . And with an arm freed he could throttle the damned thing.

He focused on his own hand, willing his finger to move with every shred of effort he could muster. His muscles were tight, locked. His own blood laced the air before his eyes. A gasp escaped his throat – almost a scream of frustration and regret. *He could not do this.*

Before him, the sriakal continued to take shape, its great bulk drawn by the lines of Granger's blood. Now its muscles were beginning to appear, bunched massively in its arms and shoulders. It had no neck as such, merely a thick, mouthless bullish head. Nor did it possess fingers or claws. Rather, its powerful arms terminated in a network of writhing whip-like tendrils.

Granger had the horrible impression that it was watching him. He sensed something radiating from it. An emotion.

Pleasure?

And then the door to his bedchamber burst inwards to a savage kick. And a lean figure stood there, sword in hand, the face thrown in silhouette by the corridor lanterns outside.

The figure strode forward, and suddenly Granger recognized him.

But on the heels of this recognition came confusion and horror. It could not be. That man could not exist, could not be standing there with his brine-burned skin and demonic red eyes.

Granger found himself looking into the soulless gaze of one of his own sword replicates.

His mind reeled. He stared at the figure and saw nothing in its eyes that he recognized. Nothing of Thomas Granger. There was only chaos and death. No emotion, no empathy, merely a fathomless abyss. This creature was not a part of him. It was part of the sword. It was a monster.

The replicate strode forward with devilish purpose and fury. It raised the sword high – Granger's stolen Unmer blade – and plunged it down into the invisible creature and deep amidst that mass of veins through which Granger's own blood flowed.

The sriakal shrieked and the air in front of Granger's eyes

boiled with sudden movement. At once the pressure on his neck disappeared and he fell to his knees like a man in penance.

Now, with a fever-glazed stare and white teeth bared, the replicate tore the Unmer blade clean through the pulsing tangle of fluids. The sriakal gibbered and collapsed and, with a final pitiful wail, disgorged its stolen blood across the pale stone floor.

Granger swayed on his knees. He lacked the strength to rise and merely gazed up at his hellish rescuer with mute incomprehension. Had the sword spawned this warrior of its own accord? If so, then why did it need him?

And suddenly he understood.

The sword was still feeding from him, sucking out his will and replacing it with its own. It needed to keep Granger alive until the process was complete. The sword was slowly forging him into a weapon it could use. Of course it would protect its property.

He felt a sudden and overwhelming loss, as though something far more precious than his lifeblood had been taken. He opened his mouth to speak, or beg answers from this demon, but could not force a sound past his cracked lips.

The replicate stood there, drenched in Granger's own blood, and for a moment Granger thought that it was mocking him. But then he realized that he was mistaken. Its eyes were inhuman, cold and dead – mere openings into the infinite void. It evinced no desires or motives, but existed merely as an extension of the blade itself. That was the truth.

Soon Granger would be the same.

'Didn't your father arrange to meet you this morning?' Paulus said.

Ianthe blushed. 'Last night he thought he could persuade

me to go with him,' she said. 'He's probably come to his senses. Or maybe he's still sleeping off the wine. He didn't look very well.'

'Perhaps he decided to leave.'

'Without saying goodbye?' Ianthe said. 'He wouldn't do that.'

They were breakfasting on one of the easternmost terraces. Pots of bright flowers crowded the wide space and overflowed through the black marble balustrade. The sun was shining, but the air was still cool enough to make Ianthe glad she'd worn her woollen shawl. Two servant girls hovered nearby, waiting to rush forward and refill a glass or ladle fruit into empty bowls or butter toast or perform any number of other menial tasks that Ianthe would much rather do for herself. Their presence here merely irritated her.

Paulus sipped his tea, then held out his cup to be refilled. 'He didn't seem particularly pleased by our news,' he said, as one of the servants poured more tea. 'I hope he doesn't plan to steal you away against your will.'

Ianthe looked down at her bowl of fruit. 'He wouldn't do that.'

'Well, of course not,' the prince said. 'I was joking.'

'He's not . . .' She struggled to find the right words, but failed. She began again. 'It's not easy for him. I suppose he had everything planned out for us and now that's all changed.'

'He should be happy for you.'

'He will be,' she said. 'I know he will. He's just . . .' She shook her head. 'He's stubborn.'

'Do you know how he came to be here? Equipped as he was?'

'He told me he'd found a hoard in Pertica.'

'That's quite a journey. What was he doing so far north?'

'A deadship brought him there.'

Paulus frowned. 'A *deadship*?' He thought for a moment. 'Did he meet someone in Pertica?'

'I think so. He didn't say who.'

Her father had been convinced that someone had been manipulating the pair of them from afar, moving them like pieces on a chessboard. The deadship, he said, had sought him out and taken him north to that icy wilderness where he'd found the Unmer weapon stash. Ianthe wasn't convinced. After all, who but a god could engineer such a complicated thing? And why would a god be interested in them? Her father was just being paranoid.

Paulus stood up and strode over to the balustrade. From here one could see across the forests and the Awl valley to where the snow-capped Irillian mountains rose like a mirage above the morning mists. He said, 'I sense the hand of a hidden manipulator in this.'

'Who?'

He didn't turn around. 'I don't know,' he said. 'But it's clear that deadship was steered. Someone gave your father the tools to rescue you from the Haurstaf.'

'I didn't need him.'

'Yes, but whoever gave your father those artefacts didn't know that.'

'I don't understand.'

He sighed and turned to face her. 'Nor do I, Ianthe. All I know is that there is a will at work here. Some unseen power has marked you both in some way.'

Ianthe shivered. 'But who? Why?'

He shrugged. 'Who can know the schemes of the immortals?'

★

145

When he woke he was lying in bed again and there was no obvious sign that the sriakal had ever visited him. The marble floor was clean, polished to a mirror-like sheen. There was no corpse, no tangle of invisible veins filled with his own blood. No smell. Indeed, had it not been for his profound weariness and the sickly pallor of his skin, he might have dismissed the incident as a dream.

He reached around and touched the back of his neck where the creature had bitten him. There he noted two small bumps. He removed his hand to find a spot of blood on his fingertips.

No dream.

The door opened, and the serving girl came in carrying a tray of food. The angle of the light on the terrace outside told Granger he had slept until midday. She placed the tray on the table beside his bed, then smiled, and turned to leave again.

'Wait,' he said.

'Sir?'

'Who cleaned this place up?'

'Excuse me?'

'The room,' he said. 'Who's been in here?'

She appeared to be genuinely confused by his question. 'I'm not due to clean it again until this afternoon,' she said. 'Would you like me to do it now?'

'No.' He looked again at the spot on the floor where the sriakal had fallen. 'I just wondered if someone had been here this morning.'

'Not that I know of.' She frowned. 'Is something missing?'

'No.' Granger shook his head. 'It's . . .'

Had he dreamed the encounter after all? Or worse? The bumps on his neck might indicate needle marks. Had he been drugged? Could he have experienced a hallucination? His gut instincts rejected the idea, but his mind found it hard to explain what had happened otherwise. A sriakal? In Awl? Autonomous sword replicates? Why, if he had merely imagined the attack, did he feel so much weaker than before?

'Never mind,' he said. 'Where's Marquetta? I want to speak with him.'

'I expect he is on his way to the palace courtyard right now.'

'Why the courtyard?'

She smiled. 'You obviously haven't looked outside yet.'

Paulus had been staring at the view for some time, when suddenly he smiled and looked at Ianthe. 'Is this not more appealing than anywhere in Evensraum or the Anean peninsula?'

'It is beautiful,' she conceded.

They had moved from the breakfast table to let the servants clear up, relocating to a bench further round the terrace, where a gap in the forest offered striking views south across the valley to Port Awl. Gun batteries and military compounds pocked the forest stretching out before them. And in the hazy distance between the Irillian mountains there lay a patchwork of green, gold and yellow fields and woodland copses, divided by a looping blue ribbon of river.

Paulus nodded. 'Sometimes I wish we could make our home here.'

Ianthe said nothing. The palace held unwelcome memories for her. To settle here would be to remind herself daily of the horrors she had caused. 'What about your homeland?' she asked.

'Hu's navy looted Galea,' Paulus said, 'and left the land to those warlords and pirates of the Nadima Chi – the archipelago you call the Gunpowder Islands.'

'He must regret that now.'

Paulus shrugged. 'Not nearly as much as the warlords who tried to settle there. Galea was suffering long before my people left. Our sorcerers' reach had exceeded their skills at that time. They made mistakes and the land never recovered.'

'What sort of mistakes?'

The prince shook his head. 'It is unlucky to speak of it.'

'Did your parents come from there?'

'My father, yes,' Paulus said. 'My mother was from Aldegarde in the north. She died giving birth to me five years before we left Galea.' He shrugged. 'Our race's innate abilities are a curse when it comes to bearing children. The power can too often appear during childbirth, with terrible results for the mother.'

'I'm sorry,' Ianthe said.

'My father vanished during the sea voyage from Losoto to Awl,' Paulus added. 'He must have leaped overboard. He was devastated that he would never return to Galea.'

'I've heard of Galea. Wasn't that where the first dragons were made?'

'They used to be the lifeblood of our empire,' Paulus said. 'Our dragon lords controlled two thousand leagues of ocean.' He gazed out at the distant mountains, but she could see that his vision was directed inwards. 'You should have seen the aral-coas-dimora . . . the fuming towers of the Brutalist and Entropic sorcerers. There are no words in Anean to convey the sense of grandeur and . . . sheer power. They were ripping nature open and reaching into her beating heart.'

It struck her that he was talking about places that had existed nearly three centuries ago – places he had seen with his own eyes – and she was reminded again of how much his youthful appearance belied his great age.

'We used to see dragons hunt near Fersen.'

Paulus raised his eyebrows. 'You are remarkably well travelled for a farm girl.'

Ianthe felt her face redden. 'I spent some time at sea.'

'Clearly,' he said. 'But it is good that you have seen something of the world. Once we are married your place will be in Losoto.'

'Losoto?'

'Losoto was traditionally the Unmer seat of power. A thousand years before we settled in Galea. My people sought to reclaim it from Emperor Ji-Kai of the Golden Domain three hundred years ago, and so provoked the dragon wars and the Haurstaf's involvement. Now the Guild of psychics are scattered we will reclaim it from Kai's descendant, Emperor Hu. After Hu is removed, you will remain there and hold court in my absence.'

'Your absence? But where are you going?'

He made a dismissive gesture. 'I have a kingdom to build. A king must be seen by his people. I can't stay in Losoto.'

'But why can't I come with you?' She heard the desperation in her own voice and her blush deepened. This wasn't how a future queen ought to behave.

His smile entirely failed to hide his disappointment. He rested his hand on hers and for a long time they looked out across the valley of Awl, across the lands she had already won for him. He was deep in thought, but then finally he brightened and turned to her. 'But you will see the world!' he exclaimed. 'It will come to us.'

'What do you mean?'

'Unmer tradition demands we host a spectacle of games to celebrate the coronation of a new king,' he said. 'The games offer all participants the chance to come and pledge allegiance to their rightful ruler. Do you see how we anticipate each other, Ianthe? You express a desire to see the world, only to discover that I have already planned to bring it to you.'

Ianthe frowned. Poor Paulus had misread her wishes, and yet his eagerness and passion were endearing. She asked him, 'What sort of games?'

'A competition of swordplay and sorcery,' he explained. 'We will invite every warlord in the Golden Domain. The finest combatants from across the world.' He chuckled. 'And I'll show them how to fight.'

'*You* will?'

She had not intended to insult him, but his expression abruptly darkened.

'I didn't mean to—' she began.

But he cut her off. 'Human combatants are hardly a threat.'

'I'm sorry.'

He muttered something in Unmer, then shook his head. 'We must, after all, withhold our bloodline skills. It's to be a competition, not a slaughter.'

He was referring to the particular talent that allowed his race to extinguish physical matter at will. His mention of it now made Ianthe uncomfortable. She looked out across the valley and noticed a fleck turning in the sky: an eagle, she supposed.

'People forget,' Paulus said.

'What?'

'My race has been enslaved for so long,' he said. 'The world has forgotten that we once ruled, and how we came to rule.' He stared off into the distance. 'There are still rumoured to be sorcerers in the far east, pure Unmer as well as lesser entropists of the bastard races. It is important to call them forth now and remind the world of their powers.' His gaze now settled on the farmland around the river, and yet he seemed to see something else. 'Did you know that the word "Anea" is Unmer? We named the land that Emperor Hu now calls home. The remains of the original Unmer city can still be found under the mountains a few miles north of Losoto. It was once the seat of our power, the site of many great games.'

'The Halls of Anea,' she said.

He nodded. 'We called the city Segard,' he said. 'But the arena district became known as the Halls of Anea. It was once as famous as the Shogruma in Oduma-Galea, or the Knife Galleries that once spread under the streets of Valcinder. Legendary tournaments were held there.'

'But I thought Hu had them flooded?'

'Hu is an imbecile,' Paulus said. 'After the Haurstaf drove us out, he tried to flood Segard because he feared the sorcerous creations still loose in there. The pit beasts we used in tournaments, against slaves and gladiators, dragons . . . But the fool had no idea of the true scale of the city. It is far larger and more complex than he could ever have imagined. One might walk for a month without recrossing one's own path.' A curious smile came to his lips, as though his words touched on some secret that only he knew. 'When he found he couldn't drown the halls, he merely sealed the door.'

'You mean there could be things still living in there?'

Paulus grunted. 'Undoubtedly there are,' he said. 'The halls were once a proving ground where scryers and bowmen could pit their wits against unimaginable monsters and machines, against sorcerous traps or in rooms with boundless artefacts. Some of those creatures are very long lived indeed.' He smiled again. 'All that trove, and Hu left it alone. That's how afraid he was.' He was becoming more excited. 'But can you imagine the battles my people once had in there, Ianthe? Gladiators and

Do'eskan cannibals wreathed in flame, blind Samarol and jackal women and berserker dragons . . .' His eyes lit up and he laughed out loud. 'Cutting boxes! Have you ever seen a dragon fight a cutting box? Such sport is not easily forgotten.' He nodded to himself. 'We will open the Halls of Anea once more.'

Ianthe feigned a smile. She had no desire to watch men and beasts murdering each other for entertainment, not least in celebration of her marriage. And yet her beloved prince seemed so animated. Sometimes for love to flourish it was necessary to relax one's prejudices.

But then he turned back to the view, and suddenly frowned. 'That's a dragon,' he said.

Ianthe looked to the south-east.

The dark speck in the sky had grown much larger. Now she could see that it was far too large to be a bird. And then it banked in the air and she spied its long neck and serpentine tail. As it moved, it sometimes appeared dark and sometimes the colour of the sky, yet iridescent. It was coming closer with every thump of its vast wings. 'What's a dragon doing *here*?' she asked.

Paulus stood up. 'It's heading for the palace.'

She clutched his hand. 'To attack?'

'Don't be foolish,' he scoffed. He dropped her hand and set off down the trail. 'Come on.'

The dragon had landed in the main courtyard, and by the time Ianthe and the prince had arrived, a ring of palace guards surrounded it. The men were mostly Unmer, pale-skinned, swift and lean, along with a few former Haurstaf sharpshooters who carried heavy Valcinder crossbows in their stout arms and an additional twenty-two riflemen aiming their eight foot copper-banded barrels at the beast.

THE ART OF HUNTING

It was a medium-sized creature: perhaps six yards up to the shoulders and some thirty yards long. Iridescent aquamarine scales covered its lithe muscular body, but it wore as a second defence a few scraps of rusted armour across its belly and hind thighs and also a scabrous and ill-fitting mail-curtained helmet that lent it an unfortunately comical look. As Ianthe and Paulus approached, they were joined by Duke Cyr, who came hurrying out of the palace in the company of four of his personal bodyguards. Upon seeing the duke, the dragon reared and huffed and spread its vast gas-green wings across the heavens. Ianthe smelled sulphur and the hot metal vapours of distant seas. The serpent then turned to Paulus and lowered its head again in some semblance of a bow.

The prince exchanged a grim glance with the duke. Then he looked up at the dragon and spoke a sentence in Unmer. Ianthe could not understand his words, but it sounded harsh and accusatory.

The dragon did not respond immediately. It folded its wings again and its head swept forwards suddenly on that thick, sinuous neck, and for a moment it studied Ianthe with eyes like black glass. She flinched. Its teeth were each as long as her arm, the white enamel streaked with yellow, the red gums spotted with black and glistening. Each of its exhalations pushed fetid air around her. She fancied she could hear its great lungs working and the thump of its poisoned blood. Under its nostrils she could see the calcified glands it used to spray poison or flame, but she didn't know which of those two defences this particular animal possessed. It reeked so strongly of brine that the air soon became difficult to breathe, so much so that its very presence had already started to give her a headache. She imagined invisible vapours streaming from its maw.

'You speak Anean?' it asked her, its voice huge and bestial and yet surprisingly cultured.

Her shock stifled any reply.

Paulus stepped forward and addressed it in Unmer a second time.

But the dragon kept its eyes fixed on Ianthe. 'You understand this language?'

'I do,' she replied.

The beast's eyes narrowed. 'Good,' it said. 'Because I have forgotten how to speak Vensrau.'

Duke Cyr said, 'What do you want, serpent?'

The dragon turned to him. 'You are Duke Cyr of Vale?'

'I am.'

'I bring a message from Lord Conquillas,' the dragon said. 'Word of your liberation has reached him, Cyr, and he is now reminded of the promise he once made to you and your nephew.'

The duke smiled. 'I see Conquillas was too much of a coward to come himself.'

The dragon laughed. 'You will not provoke him with words,' it said. 'But know that he *is* coming. This is the message I bring. Conquillas seeks retribution for your many crimes and thus decrees vendetta. He is coming for you, scryer, and for the false prince. He will slay both of you and any one who tries to stop him.' The great serpent turned its gaze upon Ianthe. 'Conquillas wishes it to be known that he bears you no grudge, child. No harm will come to you unless you choose to involve yourself in this quarrel. You must hereby agree not to use your gifts to shield Marquetta, Cyr or their allies. Nor must you focus your supernatural vision upon Conquillas at any time.'

'Arrogance!' Paulus cried. 'He *dares* order us?'

'These are Lord Conquillas's terms,' the dragon said.

'Now hear mine,' Paulus said.

But Cyr interrupted him. 'A word in private, Highness.'

Paulus glared.

'Please,' Cyr insisted, ushering the young prince towards the palace doors. He raised his hand towards Ianthe, bidding her to remain where she was. Paulus glanced back at the beast and then followed his uncle, scowling.

Ianthe watched them leave. She could have followed him mentally. It would have been so simple for her to slip inside the mind of either man and thus eavesdrop on their conversation. But her prince had asked her to remain here. If her beloved wanted to speak to his uncle in private, then she wasn't about to betray his trust in her. As the two men closed the palace door behind them, she turned back to the dragon.

She was going to be a queen.

An ambassador for all the Unmer.

And yet the great serpent terrified her.

It was observing her very carefully, as though trying to scry her innermost thoughts or intentions. Its blue-green scales shimmered in the sunlight with an oily, rainbow sheen; its wings lay folded against its back, the skin as thin as sailcloth. Its claws had sunk deep into the courtyard gravel – claws to rip flesh and bone or crush steel hulls and bear screaming mariners to feeding grounds far across the sea. It stank of the oceans like a drunkard stinks of alcohol, an odour so powerful and sharp that it aggravated Ianthe's nose and mouth. Each exhalation filled the courtyard with acrid fumes.

One spark, she thought. *A careless rifleman or smoker's match . . .*

'Were you made?' it said.

'I beg your pardon.'

'Did the Unmer create you? Were you cauldron born?'

'Of course not.'

It bared its teeth. 'It wouldn't be the first time they have unwittingly engineered trouble for themselves. As a culture, they are prone to leaping before looking. It is their way of exploring the unknown. It is also how they destroy worlds.'

'They have been very kind to me.'

The great serpent huffed poisonous fumes from its nostrils with what seemed like amusement. Its great chest rose and fell like an ocean swell. 'You are very young,' it said. 'I beg you not to protect Prince Marquetta. It would be unwise to make an enemy of Argusto Conquillas.'

She raised her chin. 'He doesn't frighten me.'

'That is unfortunate. It is yet another one of the countless advantages he has over you.' The dragon moved suddenly and unexpectedly, sweeping its equine head about the courtyard and past the barrels of so many weapons. A few of the younger soldiers stepped back instinctively, but the veterans moved not a muscle. The dragon seemed to grin, as though it had been testing the men and was pleased with what it had found. Had it tried deliberately to *provoke* an attack?

'Conquillas is aware of your peculiar skills,' the dragon said. 'And I know the man well enough to know that he would love to test his own prowess against such a mighty force as you. Do not gamble on his honour, for he has grown restless and the challenge now is everything to him. I beg you, child, not to intervene. For he will slay you.'

'You're asking me to stand aside while he tries to kill everyone I love?'

The dragon's eyes narrowed. 'Not everyone, surely?'

At that moment the door to the palace opened again, and Paulus and his uncle returned.

Duke Cyr approached the dragon, regarding it with some

amusement. 'I would slay you now merely to provide the servants with supper,' he said. 'However I require you to deliver our reply. Tell the traitor Conquillas that he is too keen to hide in the shadows. We seek honourable contest. It is our intention to hold games to celebrate the coronation of Prince Marquetta and his marriage to the Lady Cooper of Evensraum. Both the prince and myself will be among the combatants. If Conquillas makes the lists, he may face us in the arena. As a guest of the future king, we will guarantee his safety outside the contest.'

The dragon's dark eyes glittered. 'You would fight him openly?'

'Naturally,' Paulus replied.

'When?' the dragon said. 'And where? I see no arena here.'

'The games will be held in the Halls of Anea, two months from now,' Paulus said.

The dragon chuckled. 'Emperor Hu might object to that. I seem to recall that he sealed the halls.'

'The only power Hu has left is the power to keep my throne warm.' The young prince raised his voice to address everyone present. 'Any man who wants to swear allegiance to me will be given the opportunity to do so at the forthcoming tournament. And any man who doesn't will be given the opportunity to face me in the arena or thereafter be known as a coward.'

The dragon made a deep sound somewhere between a purr and a growl. Invisible fumes poured from its nostrils, warping the air around it. It raised its head again. 'I will spread the word for you. And I believe Lord Conquillas will agree to this. He will . . .' It paused, as though considering its next words, but then it glanced at the ring of soldiers and appeared to have decided not to voice its opinions aloud. Instead, it lowered its head again and its eyes thinned. 'It will please him. But does your fiancée agree to withhold her talents?'

'We do not hide behind women,' the prince replied.

The great beast turned its gaze upon Ianthe. 'You agree to this? To avert your gaze always from Lord Conquillas?'

Its teeth were mere inches from her face and the stink of rotting oceans nearly overwhelmed her. Her heart rushed with fear. But she was going to be queen and so she stood in the face of the monster and said, 'The prince does not need my protection. However, I will not stand idly by while a traitor threatens the life of those closest to me. His enemies are my enemies. Tell Conquillas that I will *not* avert my gaze from him.'

A profound sadness came into the dragon's eyes. It observed her for a moment longer, before it lifted its long neck and inclined its head. Sunlight flashed rainbow patinas over the scales on its neck. 'Very well,' it said. 'I will inform Lord Conquillas of your decision.'

It rose on its hind legs and unfolded vast wings across the heavens. The quality of light in the courtyard changed. 'I imagine he will agree to your terms,' he said to Paulus and Cyr. 'The idea of slaying both of you before witnesses will undoubtedly appeal to his sense of theatre.' It thumped its wings – once, twice and thrice, and then rose in a glimmering blue-green gale. Wind rushed across the onlookers and snapped the flags on the palace spires.

Ianthe watched it soar skywards, diminishing as it headed south across the valley. And then she turned to Paulus. The prince smiled and took her hand. Was that pride she saw in his eyes?

He led her back inside the palace, accompanied by his uncle. When the three of them were alone, the young prince closed the door behind them and came over. For a moment he just stared into her eyes, a half-smile on his lips.

Then he slapped her.

Ianthe gasped.

The prince clenched his fists and half-turned, fuming. 'Foolish girl,' he said.

'*What?*'

'Do you want the world to think I hide behind women?'

She stared at him in silence, her face flushing as the sting spread across her cheek. And then she said, 'I did it to help you. To show my loyalty . . . my love.'

'You helped *him* by embarrassing me!'

'I'm sorry.'

Cyr laid a hand on Paulus's shoulder, but he spoke to Ianthe. 'His Highness knows that you acted out of love,' he said. 'That you had his best interests at heart. His anger is not directed at you, Ianthe, but at himself for permitting you to be put in danger.'

Paulus closed his eyes and took several deep breaths. When he opened his eyes again, his temper had cooled. He moved to take her hand, but she flinched away from him. Suddenly his eyes flashed regret. 'I'm sorry,' he said. 'I acted . . . Please forgive me.' He reached for her hand again.

Ianthe pulled her hand away.

'Cyr is right,' Paulus said. 'I shouldn't have lashed out at you. I blame myself.'

She turned to go.

He seized her. 'Wait,' he said. 'Ianthe, please, hear me.'

She could have driven him to his knees with a single thought, or ripped his mind apart like so much scrap paper. But instead she looked down at his pale hand, his skin so smooth and cool against her own, and she forced herself to relax.

'Forgive me, please. I promise never to strike you again.'

'I'm sorry, too,' she said, blinking back tears. 'But I can't just stand back and watch you die in a tournament when I could stop it with a thought. You can't ask me to do that.'

'He won't kill me,' he said.

'You don't know that!'

Paulus smiled. 'But I do. I will come to no harm, Ianthe.'

She hesitated. 'How can you be sure?'

'You'll just have to trust me.'

She took his hand and clutched it desperately. 'But what about Emperor Hu? You've just declared war on Anea.'

The prince smiled. Even Cyr chuckled.

'Hu is the least of our worries,' Cyr said. 'Thanks to you the Haurstaf are leashed. Our only foes are human, and we do not intend to mount a *campaign* against them.'

'Cyr's patron will deliver Losoto into our hands,' Paulus said.

'Your patron?'

The two men exchanged a glance. Paulus said, 'Do you remember when we first met, Ianthe? I told you that the Unmer speak to our gods in dreams.'

She nodded.

'Cyr's patron is named Fiorel.'

Her eyes widened. 'The Father of Creation!'

'Fiorel appeared to Cyr in a dream,' Paulus said. 'He has promised to give us the means to take the city. Losoto will fall.'

'But why is he helping you?'

'All I can tell you is that it is to our mutual benefit.'

Paulus lifted her hand and kissed her fingers.

Ianthe felt a tingle as his lips brushed her skin. The sensation was so electric she half-expected to see a drop of blood fall from her palm.

'I love you,' he said. 'And I've been such a fool.' He held her shoulders and gazed deeply into her eyes. 'Do you forgive me?'

Her whole body trembled. She smiled up at him. 'Of course I do,' she said. 'And I do trust you. I'll never spy on you, Paulus. You know that, don't you?'

He leaned forward and kissed her. 'I know,' he said.

Crouched in a shadowy alcove behind a nearby pillar, Granger watched Ianthe depart. Marquetta and Duke Cyr remained in the entrance hall for a minute longer. They waited until Ianthe had gone.

'She was naive and foolish,' Cyr said, 'but you can't deny her bravery.'

The young prince shook his head irritably. 'I don't need a brave wife,' he said. 'I need a loyal one. The words she spoke out there might well come back to haunt her in the form of a void arrow.' He raised his hands before him and stared at them as though he might throttle someone by will alone. 'I cannot revoke my future queen's words. We must keep her safe and hope Conquillas intends to spare her until after the tournament.'

'We could ask him to,' Cyr said. 'Ianthe isn't his primary target. His vendetta is against you and I. If you sent him a message, I believe he would honour a request to leave Ianthe alone. He is still an Unmer lord.'

Marquetta gaped at him in disbelief. 'You want me to *beg* Conquillas?'

'Well, then we must keep our faith in the current plan and hope the archer enlists.'

'He will enlist. Conquillas will not be able to resist the opportunity to fight either of us in open combat.'

'But he's cunning,' Cyr said. 'He's known for his ability to smell a trap.'

'Even so,' Paulus said. 'Conquillas will come to Losoto anyway. He's that arrogant. Tell me, Uncle, in what form did Fiorel appear to you?'

'As a yellow butterfly.'

'Then he was in good humour. And what form will he assume at the tournament? One of our own sorcerers, perhaps? Or a humble sellsword?' The prince grinned. 'That might dampen the dragon lord's legend.'

'He would not say.'

'We will know him when he stands over the archer's corpse.'

Cyr nodded.

'Something is bothering you, Uncle?'

'I was just thinking. What if Conquillas kills him?'

The prince frowned. 'What do you mean?'

'If Conquillas kills Fiorel at the tournament, what's to prevent him from going on to kill us? We could not withdraw without losing all honour.'

'Conquillas won't kill Fiorel.'

'He killed Duna.'

'Duna was a reckless child,' Marquetta said. 'Fiorel is one of the oldest and most powerful entropaths in the cosmos, the architect of four great rifts – a being who can assume any form he chooses. There will be no contest.'

'Perhaps we should have a reserve plan,' Cyr said. 'Just in case.'

'You doubt your own patron?'

'No, I . . .' Cyr was silent for a moment. Then he said, 'But I feel the hand of more than one player in this. I think Thomas Granger has a patron too, although he doesn't know it. His acquisition of that sword and armour was not part of the plan. Someone is helping him.'

'An entropath?'

'I do not have an answer to that, Your Highness.'

'Why would Fiorel's kin contrive against him? They need this world as much as he does.'

'It might not be an entropath at all. A traitor among the Unmer? Or else the sword itself has some great designs of its own. These old blades are cunning and treacherous.'

'And how does Granger fare today?'

Duke Cyr shrugged. 'No word from his chambers.'

The pair began to walk away. They continued to converse but Granger could no longer discern the words. He had been unable to hear the dragon's conversation from his bedroom window, and so had come to the palace entrance to eavesdrop. Now he stood there for a long moment, mulling over what he had heard. *A patron?* That merely confirmed his own feelings.

As he stepped out from behind the pillar and headed off into the west wing of the palace, he was deep in thought. That the prince and his uncle were plotting to murder Conquillas came as no surprise. He could have guessed *that* without hearing it from the conspirators' own lips. Even Conquillas himself would guess as much. The dragon lord had a reputation as a formidable warrior. Marquetta and Duke Cyr knew it would be suicide to meet him in the arena.

So the duke's patron, the shape-shifter Fiorel, would be at the tournament. One of the most powerful gods in the cosmos was going to disguise himself as a mortal man and slay Conquillas in a public arena. Such a plan benefited both sides. Fiorel would rid the Unmer of their most formidable foe, while exacting revenge for his daughter's death.

Fiorel would not even have to reveal his true identity. He

might assume the form of a simple sellsword or footsoldier. For an Unmer lord like Conquillas to die at the hands of an ordinary man would be a terrible humiliation: the legendary warrior cut down in the opening rounds of a public brawl.

As Granger hurried along a corridor, he was all too aware of the weakness in his limbs and pain in his chest. It felt as if his heart was overworked. The tournament was of little concern to him; he had more pressing matters to consider. Ianthe was safe here for the moment at least. Prince Marquetta clearly despised Granger's daughter, and yet he needed her: enough to lie to her, enough to marry her, enough to *apologize* to her – which was unheard of. The poor girl was too lovestruck to see through his deceit. Granger's own safety, however, was far less assured. His Unmer hosts had already tried to kill him once. Since the sriakal had failed to do its job, they would undoubtedly find some other way to murder him if he remained here. Simple poison would suffice, or even a blade in his guts while he slept. Evidently they were not prepared to wait until the sword enslaved him. Even in his weakened and addled state, even so close to death – and for Granger enslavement would surely mean death, for there would be nothing left of his mind – these Unmer lords had chosen not to dismiss him.

That simple fact continued to give Granger hope that there might still be a way to rescue the situation. The sword hadn't taken him over completely yet. He could still resist its desires. But for how much longer? There had to be a way to halt the process. He needed an expert on Unmer artefacts. He needed to find Ethan Maskelyne.

And find him fast.

Granger arrived at the armoury and opened the door.

A stone partition wall topped by a wire grille divided the chamber in two, with a door providing access between the two sections. This would be locked, leaving a well in the stonework as the only way items could be passed back and forth between the two sections. Behind this barrier were kept the racks of Unmer and Haurstaf weaponry – including, Granger hoped, his sword, his shield and his armour. The guard behind the grille glanced up from a book he was reading, then closed it quickly and sat up. He was one of the former Haurstaf guardsmen – a native Awler by the look of him – and had probably held this position before the Unmer ever escaped their cells. His gaze wandered over Granger's brine-scarred face.

'Colonel Granger,' he said. Then he frowned. 'Are you all right?'

'Just here to collect my things.'

The guard looked uncomfortable. 'I'm not allowed to release them.'

'It's my property.'

'I appreciate that, sir,' he said. He seemed genuinely torn. 'But I can't let them go without word from the prince or his uncle.' He gave Granger a regretful shrug. 'Orders.'

Granger grunted. 'What if I paid you an obscene amount of money?'

'Look,' the guard said. 'I'm going to do you a favour and pretend I didn't hear that.'

Granger nodded. He wasn't going to get his stuff back without force, and that would cause as many problems as it solved. He'd just have to beg, borrow or steal something in Port Awl. He glanced back at the guard. 'Sorry to have bothered—'

But then his breath caught in his throat.

Ten feet behind the guard, on the other side of the grille, stood a dark and wild-eyed figure. He recognized it as one of

165

the sword replicates. It wore his power armour and carried his phasing shield and in its fist it clenched the Unmer blade.

A blade it now raised, as it rushed towards the guard.

'Wait,' Granger cried. 'No!'

The guard looked up at Granger with surprise.

But the replicate coming up behind him ignored Granger's pleas. The seated guard half-turned, in time to see the hellish eyes and brine-scarred face and teeth. The upraised blade. The replicate thrust the sword downwards savagely, puncturing through the skin under the guard's clavicle and burying the steel tip deep into his heart. He twisted it once.

A short gasp escaped from the guard's throat.

And then he collapsed to the floor, dead.

Granger stood there, his heart thumping, his breaths coming hard and fast as he watched the guard's blood spill out across the floor. He looked at the replicate and the replicate returned his gaze. There was nothing in those eyes but a savage emptiness.

And then the replicate stooped and ran its fingers through the dead man's blood and brought it to its lips and supped. It rose again and stepped forward and placed the sword into the well below the grille. He released the handle.

And vanished.

Granger felt a sudden sensation of dizziness and nausea. The light itself seemed to shift, fracturing subtly, as though the air immediately around him had momentarily possessed a different quality.

He looked at the sword with dread. It had wanted Granger to free it. It had been waiting for him to come. But had it summoned him here? Would it still serve his will? Would the replicates obey him? Or would they obey the sword? Was he, Thomas Granger, to blame for this innocent man's death?

Granger reached for the sword, but then stopped himself. The weapon wanted him to pick it up, he could feel it in his heart, but Granger resisted. His hand trembled, inches from the blade.

'On my terms,' he said. 'You hear me.'

He wanted to pick it up. Every part of him yearned to reclaim the blade. Granger hissed through his teeth.

'On my terms!' he cried.

He snatched up the sword and then used it to break the armoury lock. He stepped over the spreading pool of blood and went to look for his armour and his shield, dimly aware of the eight ghoulish figures who had appeared in the shadows around him.

Maskelyne's chief engineer and metallurgist, Milford 'Halfway' Jones, had a gift for fixing broken Unmer artefacts and adapting others to create new devices: most notably the miniature trumpet horn strapped to the left side of his own head that allowed him, after a certain amount of tweaking, to hear – or so he claimed – conversations in an as yet unidentified Losotan-speaking household somewhere in the world, and the monocle he wore perpetually over his left eye that enabled him (again, if his claims were to be believed) to determine at all times the location of his wife. Maskelyne had no doubt that these were merely fables intended to boost his reputation across the Sea of Lights, and yet he could not help but admire the man's ability as an engineer. By dawn the new device was ready and fitted into the wheelhouse of Maskelyne's deep-water dredger, the *Lamp*. He kept the ship in a constant state of readiness, but he'd had her crew working overnight on the numerous last-minute details required for any lengthy voyage. Now he stood in the wheelhouse and examined Jones's handiwork.

The crystal had been mounted in a spherical wire cage set atop a gyroscope. Around the cage, the adapted gem lantern could swing on a pivoting arm, which could be tightened or locked into place during high seas. By revolving the lantern around the crystal to the spot where it was brightest, Maskelyne's navigator would be able to follow the line of greatest energetic radiance and thus discover whatever artefact was presently drawing on that energy.

Whatever it was, Maskelyne suspected it would be in a locked case or cabinet.

It could only be the object for which the Drowned continued to bring him keys. They had, in their mindless way, sensed something extremely powerful lying on the seabed. And they knew Maskelyne to be a man who dredged up such objects by their thousands. He wondered if they even knew what the object was. Did they intend Maskelyne to have it for some unknown, and possibly unknowable, purpose? Or did they simply want it removed from their domain?

That last thought gave him pause.

So it was with a chill in his heart that he waved goodbye to Jontney and Lucille and boarded the *Lamp*. The crew were busy loading the last fresh fruit and animals, and he found himself skipping sideways to avoid a largess of maniacally bleating goats.

They steamed out from Scythe Island on a calm morning with the sea like a polished bronze plate reflecting a red sun and the scent of northern snows still sharp in the air. A sunny day still trying to shrug off its winter coat. Even the heavens seemed to shine like lacquered metal, purple ranging to gradients of orange in the east. The gentle booming of the ship's engines failed to lift his spirits as it usually did. And his mood was pervasive, for he noticed several of his crew standing quietly to aft, where they could watch that lonely rock diminish.

His first officer, Mellor, came down from the bridge. 'One sixty-eight steady, Captain.'

Maskelyne nodded.

'Are we to expect a traverse?'

'I don't know, Mr Mellor. The artefact might lie ten leagues from here, or a thousand.'

Mellor gazed out to sea. 'The weather can be unpredictable around the southern fluxes, particularly at this time of year. You know Tom Gascale?'

'Lost his eye during a storm down there.' Maskelyne grinned. 'You see? I do sometimes listen to their tales. The knowledge that my men have experience of the area gives me great confidence.' He studied the small, thin-faced officer. 'Your father drowned in the confluxes, did he not?'

'He went there looking for grandfather's ship. Never found a trace of it.'

'And your grandfather?' Maskelyne enquired. 'He didn't, by any chance, go looking for a long-lost great-grandfather?'

Mellor's lips twitched in what was not quite a smile. 'No, sir.'

'Then there's no curse to speak of.'

'I believe it takes three deaths, father to son, before a sequence of misfortunes is considered to be a curse.'

'Thank the heavens for that.'

'You ever wonder why so many ships sink there?'

Maskelyne had given it some thought before. The conjunction of two seas led to a mixing of brines, which was essentially just a mixing of different poisons. And when the sun warmed these night-cooled confluence waters, the mists could be strange indeed. He suspected there could be a psychoactive element to the resultant chemical fumes. It was either that, or one was forced to believe the fantastical sailors' tales: of sea monsters and blood-mottled sharks and jellyfish with gas bladders as large as city blocks, acting as host to all manner of other creatures; of Drowned mariners sailing undersea ships; of musical growths of crystal and dark tentacled things that supped on the brains of sleeping crewmen and replaced them with a sentient broth intent on breeding mischief. 'If fate brings us to the southern arm of the Mare Regis, then so be it,' he said. 'We will brave the confluxes and hope to pass without incident. We've been in worse places, Mr Mellor.'

'I suppose we have, sir.'

The crystal led them almost due south for three days and three nights. By all accounts it should have been getting warmer as they covered those leagues, but the sea continued to shudder under a slab of cold air from the north. On the second day a wind from the north-west picked up and blew against the *Lamp*'s hull, aiding her engines in the push south. And so they made good progress. The waters of the Mare Lux flashed and foamed, and copper-coloured spume blew against the wheelhouse windows behind which Maskelyne stood and watched his crew at work in their whaleskins and goggles.

On the fourth day they passed the Clutching Rocks, a cluster of wind-blown pillars against which the waves exploded into droplets like a million shards of amber glass. Here the boom and fizzle of the brine reminded him of cannon fire. Two generations ago this had been a temple atop a hill upon an island on which Verluya vines had grown. Now it was all drowned. There were sailors who swore the priests still prayed within those watery halls and still plucked rank malodorous weeds from the silt, with which they made a potion that was no longer wine but an elixir to turn a living, breathing, man each night into a phantasm. Other buildings yet lay beneath the surface here, village houses and cottages and hovels where a community of the Drowned existed to this day.

They left the flooded island behind and an hour later in their wake they spotted a dragon hunting the sea around the rocks. It must have been there all along, Maskelyne supposed, watching from the deep as the dark mass of their hull passed overhead. Dragons could stay submerged for hours, but lacked speed and mobility in water, preferring to swoop down on prey from the sky above, as many sea birds had once done.

The men watched in silence.

That night the stars closest to the southern horizon glimmered with unusual colours: very frail pinks and topaz and ultramarine. An illusion caused by vapours, Mellor said, yet not vapours born of brine. They were watching, he said, the deaths of a hundred million jellyfish. Where the seas met and mixed, countless numbers of these simple creatures found themselves trapped in a poisonous mixture of different brines. And so they died, and the gases released by their decomposition coloured the stars.

Mellor watched with a grim expression. 'We must be careful not to stray into such fields,' he said. 'Issue the men with gas filters for their masks.'

Maskelyne knew the dangers well. 'Men have fished such corrupted waters before,' he remarked. 'The slicks attract rare predators. I remember a ship in Raine . . . another in Losoto.'

'Carnival ships,' Mellor said.

'That's right.' Maskelyne recalled the bright designs, the scorched and painted hulls, and the wild-eyed and savage men who sailed them. 'Have we any men who crewed such ships?'

'I wouldn't hire 'em.'

Maskelyne raised his eyebrows.

Mellor simply smiled and tapped a finger against his forehead.

After consulting with Hayn the navigator about alterations to their course, Maskelyne retired to his cabin, poured himself a whisky and tried to relax. The crystal continued to lead them unerringly south. He had hoped to see a change in the brightness of the mounted gem lantern, perhaps indicating that they were nearing their target, but he could not determine any noticeable increase in its illumination. Either the ray of energy they followed was not prone to variance or the artefact was very distant.

He had been in his cabin for less than fifteen minutes when he heard a bellowing sound from outside so loud and deep that the spirit in his glass shuddered. It had to be a whale. The *Lamp*'s engines slowed at once. Maskelyne took his drink to the wheelhouse. It was a calm night and everyone but the helmsman had gathered on the deck outside. They were clustered around the starboard rail, lanterns raised, as the dredger edged forward at less than quarter speed. Maskelyne grabbed a whaleskin cloak, opened the wheelhouse door and climbed down to join his men.

The whale must have surfaced close to starboard as Maskelyne reached the edge of the ship for he heard it blow. It was near enough that he could hear the spray spattering against the surface of the ocean, but he couldn't yet see it out in that glimmering darkness. It bellowed again, a sound so vast it might have been the cry of a god, and now Maskelyne recognized it as a cry of fear and pain. The whale was in some sort of trouble.

'There!'

One of the men was pointing out at the dark ocean.

At first Maskelyne could see nothing. But then he spotted

a great long shadow drifting some two hundred yards distant, like the hull of a capsized ship. There appeared to be something snarled around it, a mass of pale rope or weed.

Maskelyne suddenly understood what he was seeing. He located Mellor in the throng and seized his shoulder. 'Have the helmsman steer us away,' he said. 'Engines full ahead.'

Mellor gave him a brief quizzical look, before comprehension lit his face. He muttered a curse under his breath. 'Full speed?'

'The time for stealth has passed. It must have heard us by now.'

'Aye, Captain.' He turned and ran back towards the wheelhouse.

Just as Maskelyne was about to address his crew, one of them spoke urgently. 'Samal.'

A few of the crewmen scrambled to get a better look. Silence fell.

Finally, one of his men said, 'That's not a whale.'

He was right, of course. The large shape drifting past their starboard side had the wrong outline to be a whale. It was too bulbous and uneven. Among the mass of flesh Maskelyne thought he spotted a limb, huge and distended, ending in a lump that might once have been a hand. Huge gas-filled sacs swelled from the skin. The sound he had assumed to be the bellow of a whale had come from vocal cords that had once been human. He said, 'We're moving away quickly. Mellor will distribute firearms. I want all watch stations manned immediately. Remain in pairs and watch your colleagues closely.'

Once Mellor had handed out the rifles, the men dispersed quickly, without a word, moving in pairs to each watch station. Each of them wore a grim expression. Sailors had been encountering erokin samal in the seas since the Unmer unleashed their poisonous brine on the world. Many thought they had once been a benign species, a form of deepwater worm or polyp mutated by the toxins. They were notoriously sensitive. It was unlikely that they had escaped the creature's attention.

Maskelyne returned to the wheelhouse. At length he found himself pacing behind the helmsman, repeatedly checking their speed and their engine oil pressure. Every few seconds his gaze returned to the window. Samal were parasitic. This one had most likely trapped one of the Drowned, and then slowly altered its host's pathology to suit its own needs. The inflated body was used as a flotation aid and a crude sail, allowing the parasite to drift with the wind. The organs within the host would have been adapted to process brine and toxic marine invertebrates into food. Large samal would often ensnare several hosts, forming whole islands of biological matter. By altering blood-flow, the creature would then create pockets of decay among the living tissue, thus allowing wind-blown seeds to take root. Vegetation grew vigorously in such a rich medium. Such islands often resembled natural landmasses, but with the parasite's slender tentacles waiting amidst the greenery to snatch unwary birds, or men. Samal could keep their hosts alive for many hundreds of years.

He heard a gunshot.

There was a commotion at the bow of the ship. One of his crewmen had just shot his comrade and was now backing away, his rifle still trained on the body. Maskelyne could see blood pooling around the fallen man.

'Was he got?' the helmsman said.

Mellor came up beside them. 'Men lose their nerve when there's a samal around. There's no—'

Another shot rang out.

'Mellor, with me!' Maskelyne ran to the wheelhouse door.

He slid down the ladder to the midships deck with Mellor following close behind, just as four more of his men arrived from aft. The sailor who had fired the shots was reloading his rifle. His target was lying on his back ten paces further along the deck, his whaleskins soaked in blood. He had two puncture wounds in him, one through the chest and one above his left eye. That eye had filled with blood. The skull behind had burst outwards, leaving a gap into which a man could shove a fist. And yet he was still moving. As Maskelyne watched, the fallen sailor lifted his head and tried to rise from the bloody pool in which he lay. The flesh around his ribs and at his thighs had already begun to swell. From his lips there came a low, mournful wail.

Maskelyne's gaze searched the gore-drenched deck behind the unfortunate man. After a moment he spotted a mass of slender white tendrils writhing within the spilled blood. They resembled fungal mycelium, it seemed to him. He watched them slide over each other with morbid fascination. They had connected with the back of the wounded man's knees and again at his lower spine. Maskelyne's gaze traced them out through the wash-gaps in the bulwarks to where they disappeared into the darkly rushing sea. Perhaps it would have been more appropriate to compare these filaments to fishing lines? They had, after all, just snagged the creature's prey.

He raised his own rifle. 'Aim for the head,' he said. 'Try to remove as much brain matter as possible.' Then he turned to those standing closest to the deck rail. 'And keep an eye out for more, will you?'

They fired upon the crewman until they had reduced his head to a rag-like clod. And yet after each volley the stricken man rose again and came lumbering towards them with his arms outstretched. His wailing was unbearable to hear until one of the sailors shot out his larynx and most of his throat. The distension in his belly and thighs continued and then moved to his shoulders so that in the space of several minutes he looked like some gruesome hunchback. His clothes ripped, revealing skin inflated and stretched to translucency. Bubbles of blood formed amid the mulch of flesh at his neck and now they could hear the whine of gases escaping from this area. Finally Maskelyne raised his hand to stop his men from firing any further rounds.

'Over the side with him,' he said.

The men drove boat hooks into their transforming comrade and, with a chorus of yells and one almighty heave, pitched him over the side.

Maskelyne watched the sea in silence for a long moment. 'Now return to your watches,' he said at last. 'And remain vigilant. Samal are notoriously persistent.'

He returned to his cabin and lay on his bunk, listening to the ever-present creaking of wood and the steady thrum and thump of the *Lamp*'s engines. He could not sleep. Something was troubling him, but he could not say what it was. Something all around him, an ambience of unease. He closed his eyes and let his mind go blank, filling it instead with the sound of the ship's engines.

His eyes snapped open, and he grabbed the com funnel. 'Mellor.'

The first officer's reply came at once. 'Captain?'

'The engines are labouring.'

'Sir?'

'I've spent long enough aboard this tub to know how she sounds. And we're not carrying enough cargo to account for the noise she's making.'

'The samal?'

'It's attached itself to us somehow, Mellor. I want our sides examined for tendrils – and a full head count. Now.'

'Right away, sir.'

Mellor came back on the com several minutes later. The head count was underway, but they had spotted samal tendrils low on the port side, amidships.

'The animal pens,' Maskelyne said. 'I'll meet you there.'

'Aye, sir.'

He caught up with Mellor and four other crewmen in the bathysphere hold and together they hurried towards the midships deck well. Every man carried a rifle. The great metal bell of the submersible loomed over them, and in the gloom all around stood shelves of machine parts and dredging hooks and nets, spades, harpoons and chains – all coated with whale oil lubricant and glistening black. To Maskelyne this chamber smelled like a cavern at the heart of the earth and the oceans – awash with that fragrance of brine and rock oil and treasure. Their boots clanged on welded iron deck plates and their gem lanterns threw grotesque shadows across the bulkheads.

The cabins and living areas occupied the stern section of the *Lamp* underneath the wheelhouse, while the salvage hold took up most of the bow space before the dredger's crane. The food stores and livestock cages were located amidships, in those low cramped decks immediately below the equipment level. All the portholes and storm shutters should have been sealed, as they were every night, although the men sometimes left volver vents open to allow the livestock some fresh air. Such an opening seemed the most likely point of ingress.

His unease deepened as the party advanced along the companionway towards the first of the animal holds, for they could hear a frightful commotion coming from ahead. The goats and pigs were greatly distressed.

Mellor cast a grim look in his direction. Maskelyne checked his rifle, upheld his lantern and then nodded to the men at the front. They took a breath and then opened the door of the hold.

A terrible shrieking noise assailed them. Something huge and fleshy bulled through the group, scattering men to either side. Maskelyne raised his rifle and almost fired, before he recognized the corpulent shape. A pig. The frantic animal scrambled up the companionway away from them, screaming hellishly, its hooves clattering across the iron.

'Hell o'brine.'

The curse had come from one of the two men in the lead. He was standing by the open hatchway, gazing into the hold. He made no effort to raise his gun, but wore on his face an expression of horror.

Maskelyne and the others joined them.

As he raised his lantern through the hatchway, his immediate reaction was one of confusion. The walls and ceiling appeared to be lined with some organic substance – a dense mat of fungus or the root system of an enormous plant. He glimpsed walls of dark fleshy swellings, all folded and creased and interspersed with white nodules and tendrils and tufts of brown scrub. *An excavation* – it reminded him of an archaeological dig he had attended on a rain-drenched hillside near Losoto: sodden clay, bones protruding from the root ball of a tree. Moments later he realized just how much of the available space this substance occupied. Except for a scant few yards in front of the party, the entire hold was full of it. It must have been sixty paces deep, by forty wide. And the smell . . .

One of the men retched. Others covered their noses. The stench was of putrescent brine or rotten shellfish mixed with something earthier, like animal blood or flesh – the musk of a menagerie.

Mellor coughed. 'What was it?'

'Goat or pig,' another man replied. 'No way to tell.'

'There may be more than one animal in there,' Maskelyne said. 'Our guns are useless here. It's grown too large already.'

The wall of tissue continued to unfurl and distend before them. In that mass of meat and gas-filled blisters Maskelyne could see veins and hair and even something that might have been a curl of horn. He guessed the thing was mostly goat. A yard below the ceiling he could perceive an eye – vastly bloated, perhaps eighteen inches across, but undeniably caprine. He shuddered and took a step back, clenching his nose. 'Seal it off,' he said.

They closed the hatch and Maskelyne posted two guards.

He met with Mellor and the other officers in the officers' mess. 'Well,' he said. 'Our stowaway appears to be quite firmly entrenched. Do we have any ideas on how we shift it?'

Jones's oil-stained fingers drummed the table. 'Looks like it got in through a volver vent,' he said. 'We might want to think about keeping those closed in future.'

'We'll see,' Maskelyne said. 'Our first task must be to sever the connection between the unfortunate animal below decks and the parasite we are now dragging through the sea. But that still leaves us with the problem of how to dispose of the . . . eh . . . matter in the hold.'

A murmur swept through the assembled men.

'Maybe it's edible,' Jones said.

Maskelyne gave him a thin smile.

They all fell to silence.

'We could burn it out,' Mellor suggested.

Maskelyne shook his head. 'I'm concerned by the quantity

of gases trapped within the host animal's flesh. There's a risk of explosion. Even if we could contain it . . .' He shrugged. 'Such a fire might taint the air in unforeseeable ways.'

'Then it's down to hatchet work,' Mellor said. 'We go in, in teams, and cut it out.'

Most of the men nodded.

'I feared it would come to this,' Maskelyne said. 'Triple rum rations for any man who volunteers for the job.'

The men used a whaler's headspade to cut the samal tendrils from the side of the ship. They were almost translucent and as fine as gossamer. They checked the other volver vents but found nothing. As soon as the *Lamp* was freed, Maskelyne noted a distinct change in the tone of her engines – testament to the prodigious weight of the parasite they had been pulling behind them. Now with the creature gone, they could begin the process of removing its host from the livestock hold. Maskelyne met briefly with the first of the cutting teams, offering instruction and advice, and then retired to his cabin. It was almost dawn and he had been awake for too many hours.

But when he slept he dreamed of monsters. He woke several hours later, clutching his chest in desperate panic. He was drenched in sweat, breathing erratically. His heartbeat felt irregular and laboured.

He took a long draught of water and lay back in his bunk, panting, willing his heart to slow. The men could not see him like this. After all, the seas were no place for cowards.

CHAPTER 5

JOURNEYS

Conquillas's dragon flew over a great blood-glass ocean and Ianthe – hiding in its mind – flew with it. The wind tore at its eyes and muzzle and filled its vast wings. And the merest tease of its shoulder muscles brought it swooping down at reckless speeds to smash froth from the tips of the poisoned waves or snatch at the brine with powerful claws. Water flashed in the sunlight. Sea spray chilled its armoured face, its nostrils. And then it would rise again, the cold metal-scented air buffeting its neck and keening in its ears.

The beast's vision was keener than that of human or Unmerkind and it allowed Ianthe a view far across the Sea of Kings to the dark and fiercely ragged island rising above the horizon like a claw reaching from a pool of blood. Other serpents were hunting there, their lithe cross-shaped bodies soaring or else folding closed and plunging dagger-like into the waters.

'Peregrello Sentevadro was once a mountain,' the dragon said. 'Now the less poetic of your kind call it the Dragon Isle.' The beast made a growling laugh in its throat. 'Are you in there, little girl? There are occasions when it seems to me that I can feel you hiding behind my eyes.'

Ianthe knew the dragon could not detect her presence. It merely assumed – correctly as it happened – that she was currently a stowaway, lurking in the periphery of its mind as it neared its homeland.

'Of course, all of this was once the Sentevadro Lowlands,' the dragon went on. 'Part of old Anea. There are many valleys below the waves here, many cities and manmade caves. The ruins of the old Marolian capital cut into a cliff, and more wonders besides. The wreckage of old bone ships and tea merchants' ships and a fort carved out of a single blue crystal. But no Drowned.' It looked down at the ocean rushing past beneath its claws – wave crests flashing like rubies. 'Not for many years now.'

The dragon flew with the wind for a moment longer, and then it said, 'If you can truly see through my eyes, then watch now.' With that it flexed its shoulders and drew back its wings and dived.

The sea rushed upwards.

And the dragon smashed through the glinting waves and down into freezing depths. Bubbles of air boiled around its snout and claws. Ianthe heard the thump and clang of the pressure difference in the beast's ears. The brine around them was pink, pierced by rippling shafts of light that played across the seabed like floral auroras. Less than ten fathoms separated the silt-smothered ground from the air above. She could see scalloped outcrops of rock and boulders furred by sediment. And here and there stood the skeletons of long-dead trees. It had been pastoral land once, for the outlines of fields could still be determined by dry stone walls now bulked and mortared by crimson mud.

The dragon swam on, past a low building from which the roof had been torn.

And then suddenly from the gloom emerged the masts and yards and shrouds of ships – a great many of them. These were mainly Unmer vessels, with a few Evensraum trawlers and dredgers and even a couple of smaller Losotan yachts. Ianthe looked on in awe. The larger ships were old, so terribly old, and clad with the bones and scales of creatures she did not recognize. Not dragon – too large to belong to dragons. Cannons still rested upon the silt-soft decks, and schools of silver fish darted between woollen rigging, scattering when Ianthe's dragon drew near. The serpent swam low over the remains of two warships whose masts had fallen into each other's and around whose open hulls there lay a scattering of crates and cables and rusted cannons. And she saw that some of the crates had been smashed open and disgorged scores of tiny human skulls upon the seabed.

The dragon raised its neck and thrashed its tail and broke through the surface of the waters in a glittering eruption of seawater. Water sparkled like a cascade of gemstones. Ahead of them loomed the cliffs and pillars of the Dragon Isle. The serpent slapped its wings against the waves, twice and thrice, and the cold wind blew it higher into the air once more.

'The Unmer modelled us dragons on the great sea snakes of old,' it said. 'Dead and forgotten seven thousand years now. But you saw the ships below? Armoured with the petrified bone and scales of those old monsters. We faced such vessels in the war.' The serpent chuckled. 'They hunted them, you know? The old sorcerers. Sea snake bones and blood were used in entropic rituals. The corpse of a worm, a young specimen, is said to reside in the gardens of Hu's palace, although I have never seen it myself. Here, my girl, we have arrived.'

Towards them rushed black cliffs pocked with the openings to many caverns and passages, the great mass of rock towering over a small bone-littered curve of beach. The dragon threw out its wings and lashed at the air, landing amidst an expanse of shattered black rock and scree. Deeper in the cave Ianthe could see an old yacht with a scrollwork-patterned hull. But here on a bluff before them there stood a tall and very pale man with striking violet eyes and a bow slung over his shoulder. He regarded them coolly.

'Does the girl ride with you?' he said in Losotan.

The dragon laughed. 'Either she does, or I've been conversing with myself over all these leagues. The truth is, Argusto, I cannot sense her presence any more than I can sense my liver. However, given the nature of my conversation with her fiancé, I'll wager she's there.'

Conquillas? He was frailer than Ianthe had imagined. His face evinced weariness, but there was something else in those eyes – cynicism mixed with an icy detachment, as if his instinct at each encounter was first to analyse a person to determine their risk to him. Strangely, this reminded her of Granger. One got the impression with the dragon lord that he was prepared, at any moment and at any provocation, to draw his bow and fire.

The beast gave a great exhalation. 'The boy prince intends to invade Losoto and force Hu from the throne. And then, as tradition demands, he will reopen the Halls of Anea and hold a contest there to celebrate his coronation. The first in over three hundred years. He invites you to face Cyr and himself openly in the arena.'

Conquillas regarded the dragon without emotion.

'You have to admire his bravado,' the dragon went on. 'Of course, he'll try to assassinate you during the competition, or else prior to it.'

'I am no stranger to assassins,' Conquillas said. 'But he's courting danger by reopening the halls. Sealing that hell was the only sensible decision the emperor ever made.'

'Well . . .'

'Where does the girl stand?' Conquillas asked. 'His betrothed, Ianthe.'

The dragon sighed. 'Firmly beside her future husband,' it said. 'She refuses to avert her gaze.'

It seemed to Ianthe that Conquillas looked sad for an instant. Then he nodded and stared straight into the dragon's eyes. 'I must assume you are there, Ianthe. I had no quarrel with you. Indeed, I had hoped to meet you under different circumstances. You will see me again one more time, and that will be during the last moments of your life.'

The Unmer lord reached behind him and pulled out a strip of cloth. Then he tied it around his head as a blindfold, obscuring his vision. 'Now look away,' he said.

And the dragon complied.

'Well?'

Ianthe hesitated. Finally, she said, 'I can't follow him.'

'What do you mean you *can't*?'

'He blindfolded himself.'

Paulus snorted. 'But how does he expect to shoot a bow? How does he expect to *travel* to Losoto?'

He stood up and strode over to the window and stared out as though he might be able to see Conquillas from here. His quarters in the Haurstaf palace were a network of bright marble cubes hung with silver cloth and silver chandeliers. They occupied most of one floor of one entire wing. The view from this particular parlour looked south across the Awl valley. The servants had opened all the windows to admit glorious golden sunlight and a breeze that lifted and puffed out the gauzy curtains. Paulus's hair shone like spun gold, his fine white hand rested upon the jewelled pommel of his rapier. His mouth was open slightly, his lips as red as cherries.

'Occupy another one of his dragons. Track him that way.'

'None of them is looking at him.'

'But how will we know what he's up to?'

She shrugged. 'I suppose that's the point of the blindfold.'

He glared at her, and she regretted her words at once. 'I'll find him in Losoto,' she added hastily. 'He can't force everyone to ignore him there. He'll attract attention. People will notice a dragon lord.'

'Not if he's in disguise,' Paulus said. He turned away from the window and paced the white stone floor. 'I had hoped to follow his movements leading up to the contest. He could be plotting to undermine us.'

'Is that likely?' she said. 'You said yourself how eager he was to meet you in the arena.'

He gave her a strange look. 'Eager to meet me on an even footing. But if he thinks you're going to protect me . . .' He hesitated. 'He might just put an arrow through the back of your head.'

'Not with a blindfold on,' she said. 'As soon as he takes it off to shoot at me, I'll see him.'

Paulus didn't look convinced. 'What if he shoots you without taking the blindfold off?'

'That's impossible.'

'Conquillas does not know the meaning of that word.'

Ianthe thought for a moment. 'How long will the tournament last?'

'Ten days or more.'

'And are all the fights to the death?'

'Only vendetta matches,' he replied. 'In competition games, a combatant may yield to his opponent.' He shrugged. 'Most fights end that way. It is considered poor etiquette to kill a man who yields. That's not to say it doesn't happen occasionally.'

'Then there's no chance he might be killed before he even has to face you?'

Paulus seemed detached. 'There is always a chance.'

She huffed. 'Isn't there anyone else with a vendetta against Conquillas?'

'I expect some will declare it,' he said, 'in the hope that sacrificing themselves will win favour for their families.'

'But that's terrible.'

He grinned. 'Actually it can be quite amusing.'

Ianthe couldn't see what was funny about that. 'But how can you be sure you'll defeat him?'

'You have to trust me.'

'If you told me . . .'

He shook his head. 'I cannot. The less you know, the safer you'll be.'

Her heart clenched. She admired his courage, and yet his determination to keep his plan secret aggravated her. The more she knew, the easier it would be to protect him if the plan failed. She would be there at the tournament, watching, ready to destroy Conquillas if it looked like her beloved Paulus was in danger. But of course she could never tell him that. He would have to believe that he had killed the dragon lord without her help. She hadn't yet figured out a way to hide her involvement, but she would. She loved him too much not to.

She smiled and reached out and hugged him.

He stiffened – for just a moment, but Ianthe felt it nevertheless. Then he relaxed and returned her embrace. His nose nuzzled her ear. 'There is something else, Ianthe,' he said. 'I must ask you another favour.'

'Anything.'

'I need you to direct your vision upon another traitor. A murderer. I need you to find him for us.'

'You need only name him.'

The prince's lips thinned. 'It is your father, Ianthe. He killed a guard and fled the palace this morning.'

Granger arrived on the outskirts of Port Awl at dawn the next day. He was weary eyed and itching from his long trek from the palace. To avoid detection he had shunned the foot-worn trails that followed the river in favour of a circuitous route through the forest, picking his way due south along the bluffs and the steep wooded slopes. His power armour alleviated physical fatigue, allowing him to move more quickly across difficult terrain, but it had nevertheless demanded concentration. Consequently he felt exhausted mentally.

Rather than head to the harbour, where the Unmer would have undoubtedly posted men to watch for him, he set off on an eastern coastal trail, where he hoped to find one of Awl's smaller fishing settlements, and a captain in need of some money.

He had to hope Ianthe wasn't watching him.

Soon the sun had climbed above the green hills and fields and beat down on him. He wore a grey Haurstaf militia cloak over the buzzing alloyed plates of his armour. The sword and shield he carried in a loose canvas kitbag over his shoulder, along with numerous smaller items he'd taken from the armoury. Among the objects he'd stolen were a pouch of dull coins from the guard he'd killed and three Unmer daggers of exceptional quality. The coins each bore an imprint of the Haurstaf seal on one side and the head of Briana Marks on the other and it was now likely they'd be worth little more than their weight in metal. But the knives were the real find: a quicksilver knife, a tempest knife and a prison skull blade, any one of which should have been more than sufficient to pay for transport from one side of the empire to the other.

He could feel the sorcery within them murmuring against his shoulder, and realized with dismay that something else – either his armour, shield or sword – was feeding on them, draining their power.

He cursed and took them out of his kitbag, but it made no difference, so he packed them away again. With luck, they'd still have some sorcerous properties remaining by the time he came to sell them.

His destination was the city of Ethugra, where Maskelyne owned and ran a number of jails. If the metaphysicist wasn't in the city itself, then he would most likely be at his fortress on nearby Scythe Island. Granger's main concern was that Maskelyne was off on one of his trove-hunting expeditions. He might be out on the open ocean for months, and almost impossible to find.

But there was no point dwelling on that possibility. Granger had no choice but to hope that the man was home. He also had to believe that Maskelyne – a man who had kidnapped Ianthe and murdered her mother – would help him, but in that respect Granger felt most confident. The metaphysicist would have sold his own son for the artefacts Granger now carried. Or even to learn the location of the Unmer transmitting station whence they'd come. If Maskelyne could free him from the sword's psychic grip, then Granger would be glad to hand the thing over to him.

The problem was reaching Ethugra in time.

He had no idea how many more days of freedom he had left. A week? A month? He could feel the weapon's presence, gradually insinuating itself into his mind. Everything he wanted to do required a stronger force of will than normal. Making decisions was like moving through quicksand. And when he slept he had started to dream of a strange faceless figure. Granger worried that a ship wasn't going to get him to Maskelyne in time. Lacking a functioning Unmer chariot, he had to find the next best thing.

A dragon.

The great serpents hunted far and wide across the Mare Verdant, but generally kept away from people. He might stumble across one out on the open water, but that was by no means certain. Trade in their meat was still commonplace, and he would certainly find a living serpent at the market of any large port or city. Ironically, dragon hunters commonly refuelled at Port Awl, and the odds were reasonable that he'd find one there. Unfortunately, he couldn't risk such an excursion. The other ports were all weeks away by ship. That left their regular haunts. And the nearest of those was Carhen Doma. This island group lay three days south-east from Awl. Sometimes called the Halls of Songs, Doma was a cluster of rocky mounds and partially submerged temples built by a Losotan cult who had tried to halt the rising seas by prayer. Now the priests were gone, dragons used the vast stone halls to nest.

Intruding on a nesting site was not ideal, and yet Doma was the nearest place en route to Losoto where Granger was certain to find one of the winged serpents. All he had to do now was persuade a local captain to take him there, and then convince a dragon to carry him the rest of the way to Ethugra. It wasn't going to be easy, but then what the hell was? He began to wonder if his stolen – and constantly weakening – knives were enough.

The trail headed east, following the base of the ridge over

which the town of Port Awl had spread like peculiarly angular coral. Buildings clustered around steep zigzag roads shrouded in the dust from horse and cattle carts. Columns of smoke rose from scores of chimneys amidst jumbled slopes of umber terracotta and white-walled hovels and faded into the blue sky. A few buildings extended from the base of the ridge, crammed around the main road into the town, but apart from this one incursion every inch of the land on the plains beneath the town had been turned over to agriculture. Sheep, horses and cattle grazed on green grass. Fields of rape and barley shone yellow and bronze in the sun.

Granger left the port town behind and continued east, walking the dusty trail with the sun climbing over the coastal hills ahead of him. To his left the immense Awl valley rose in a grand and gentle sweep into summer pollen haze penned by gaseous mountains. For the first time since he had murdered the weapon-room guard, he felt good. He removed a gauntlet and ran his hand across the dry stone walls, savouring the touch of warm stone grizzled with lichen. Insects buzzed. A smell of woodsmoke and cut hay hung in the air.

After he had walked for an hour, the land buckled and rose to join the eastern edge of the township ridge. Here the trail plunged into forest and meandered onwards and upwards through the southern foothills of the Irillian mountains. Above the trees loomed blinding swathes of broken rock and tails of scree driven into meltwater runnels.

The shade of the forest gave Granger some relief from the blazing sun, but his arms and legs were already slick with sweat and his eyes began to smart and twitch from exhaustion. He passed a peasant couple, rugged and ancient, each of them pulling the arms of a cart laden with gathered wood. They stopped and stared after him. Granger strode on without a word, his armour humming faintly, his boots leaving deep impressions in the earth, and when he reached the bend in the path he was aggrieved to find the couple had not moved from that same spot but rather continued to stand silently and watch him.

He encountered nobody else on that path, however. By late afternoon he had moved into the lee of the Irillian mountains, where the air was noticeably cooler. The land began to drop again and soon the smell of the sea permeated the forest. At dusk he reached the first of the settlements he'd been making for. It was a simple scrubbed-dirt and woodsmoke place, an uninspiring hamlet of rude wooden shacks and chicken wire dumped in an uneven clearing on the forested slope. Perhaps it had once been a river valley. Now it was a narrow coastal inlet. The Mare Verdant lapped the hillside a few yards below the houses, leaving an arc of viridian scum on the wet earth. White mist hung over green water, damp and silent. All along the shore dead trees stood like bones set in bottle glass; their white branches chalkscrawled through the haze. The villagers had cleared a patch of forest immediately before their settlement and were using this area to moor their boats against a white-wood pontoon.

Granger breathed in the stinking metalled air and studied the boats. They were all shallow water fishing skiffs and outrigger canoes, none of them large enough to attempt a journey across open waters.

'You're not the first.'

Granger turned to see an old man standing outside a woodshed next to one of the shacks. He had a splash of brine damage across his forehead and chin and long grey hair matted with filth. His jacket and breeches were threadbare and dirty. He regarded Granger with pale grey eyes and added,

'The first deserter, I mean. Four of you already come through this way.'

'Where'd they go?'

The old man shrugged. He continued to study Granger for a long moment. 'Hell, son, you look like one of the Drowned. What'd you do? Go swimming?'

Granger said nothing.

'It's none of my business where the others went,' the man said. He took out a pipe and began loading it with tobacco from his front shirt pocket. 'Evensraum would be my guess. Sure I just dropped them off in Addle.'

'Addle?'

The man jabbed the stem of his pipe east. 'Two leagues that way.'

'Why didn't they take the trail?'

The old man grinned, revealing a mouth empty of all but two teeth. 'You ain't been on Awl long, then?'

Granger made no reply.

'Addle's a sea gypsy village,' the old man said.

Granger understood. To deal with the ever-rising seas, sea gypsies lived in floating villages. There would be no trail there. He said, 'How much did you charge the others?'

The old man shrugged. 'Call it twenty sisters.'

'I'll give you two.'

The man's twin teeth appeared again. 'Fair enough. Wait here, will ye?'

He disappeared inside one of the shacks. Granger heard him argue with a woman, but the dialect was so strong he couldn't make out much of their conversation. When the old man came out again he was carrying a gaff and a basket of mushrooms. He extended a gnarled hand, his palm marred by a small tattoo of some word that had long since blurred.

'Two, you said.'

Granger dug out two coins from his pouch and handed them over.

The old man grinned. 'I'm Fuller.'

Granger nodded.

Fuller waited a moment, presumably for Granger to reply, then he shook his head and sighed. 'Aye, the other four wouldn't give *their* names neither.'

They walked down to the pontoon. Fuller clambered aboard one of the larger skiffs, set down his basket and gaff, and then cleared a pile of fishing nets to give Granger a seat in the stern. The boat rocked heavily as Granger got in, and sank down a clear three inches into the water, but she was dry in the bilge and seemed hale enough. He gripped the kitbag between his knees.

'Hell's that armour made of?' Fuller asked. 'Stone?'

'Steel.'

Fuller grunted. 'Well, then it's a bastard of a lump of steel.' He untied and used the gaff to push off.

They slipped out into the mist and the skeletal trees. It was as quiet as thought. Fuller slid his oars into the rowlocks and bent his back to pulling the small vessel gently across the mirror-glass waters. Even in the centre of the inlet the brine was less than a fathom deep and Granger could peer down into it and see moss-covered boulders strewn across the forest floor. It was like looking through a green lens. A school of long pale fish drifted away from the hull and he saw an eel wriggle and settle on the seabed. The other side of the inlet rose up out of the mist but Fuller turned the boat south and rowed them out into deeper water. Soon the trees thinned and the submerged land under their hull sank away. Even in the gloom the brine remained remarkably clear. Granger could see far into its depths. As they approached the headland at the south-eastern end of the inlet, he spied three of the Drowned seated on the wooded hillside four fathoms down: a couple and a small child – and still fresh by the look of them. But for their grey skin and the oddness of their present location they might have been a normal family having a picnic.

The Drowned man looked up and saw the boat pass over his head. He grabbed the child and carried it down the slope into deeper water, with his woman following behind.

Granger glanced up at Fuller. It disturbed him that these three looked so recently drowned. But Fuller was bent over the oars, his eyes glazed with his own thoughts, and gave no indication that he'd seen anything under the brine.

'How many of you in the settlement?' he said.

Fuller blinked, shaken out of his reverie. 'What?'

'How many families live back there?'

'Just the one,' he said. 'Big family.'

'You fish?'

Fuller nodded. 'And a bit of trade with the gypsies.'

They were turning around the headland now, which opened into a much wider bay dotted with dozens of small islands. Beyond lay the open sea: a great shimmering slab of green. Most of the islands here were tiny, mere rocks overhung with vegetation, stunted trees and bushes – but one or two looked large enough to be inhabited.

'You get many visitors?' Granger asked.

'A few deserters, as I said.'

'They bring their families with them?'

The old man shrugged. He looked uncomfortable.

'Most of the men here have wives, children, I'd imagine. Here in Awl.'

'Can't say I recall.'

'You don't remember if you carried the men alone, or whether they had their families with them?'

'Some had families,' Fuller admitted. 'Never charged 'em any more.'

He continued to pull the oars through the emerald brine. The sun was setting behind the headland they'd rounded, turning the sky to dragonfire. Angry reflections coiled in the wake of the old man's oars. The air remained still, breathless, and hung with curtains of pale green mist where the trees met the seawater. Granger noticed that they were making for one of the larger islands in the bay: a long, low, tree-covered mound, about three hundred yards from end to end.

'I was surprised you didn't haggle with me,' Granger said.

Fuller said nothing. Granger noted he had picked up the pace of his rowing.

'So what's on the island?' Granger said.

Fuller looked back sharply. 'What's this? What're you accusing me of?'

Granger shrugged.

'I got a boat stashed there,' Fuller said. 'An old naval lander with a sweet little Losotan engine.' He spat into the water. 'An' fifty quarts of whale oil. You expect me to row you all the way out to Addle?'

'Why not keep the boat back there?'

Fuller grunted. 'Thieves is why,' he said. 'The whole damn island's full of deserters looking for a way off. How long d'you think it would last back on the shore? Eh? Others have lost their boats.' He glared at Granger in an accusatory manner. 'You wake up one morning and your livelihood is just plain gone 'cos some goddamned freeloader stole it out from you in the night. It's me who should be watching you.'

They began to make their way around the island. Snarls

of vegetation crowded the waterline, their submerged leaves and branches like specimens trapped behind green glass. Wild pines shaded the interior, and now Granger could see the outline of a simple shack or fisherman's hut in there. He sniffed the air but couldn't detect an aroma of smoke. His ambushers were not complete fools, then. He supposed they would be waiting for him in the hut or in the woods nearby.

But he changed that assumption when they rounded the horn of the island and he saw Fuller's boat. He whistled through his teeth. She was stolen, had to be. Or else the old man had been robbing and drowning travellers for many years to afford such a vessel. The southern aspect of the island curved inwards, the horns forming a natural harbour in which Fuller's boat lay moored, ten yards out from the shore. She was an old naval assault craft, the type used by the empire to land horses and men on hostile beaches. Many decommissioned vessels had been converted into ferries over the years. Warlords sometimes used them to raid coastal settlements. She was forty feet long and fifteen wide, with an open deck and her wheelhouse and pilot's cabin up front at the bow. Her brine-stained and storm-battered steel hull wasn't much to look at nor particularly ideal for the open ocean, but she was a damn sight better than the skiff. These boats were as tough as they looked.

It was also, Granger observed, large enough to hide several ambushers aboard.

Granger assumed his new theory to be correct when Fuller steered his rowing boat directly towards the assault craft. They weren't going to make landfall, after all. He loosened the cord at the top of his kitbag to make it easier to reach in and grab his sword in a hurry. The old man's eyes darted to him suspiciously, but he said nothing.

Finally, Fuller's skiff clanked against the assault craft's port side. He dropped anchor and told Granger to climb aboard, using the handholds running up the side of the hull. A moment later Granger found himself standing on the vessel's open deck. Through the grimy wheelhouse windows he could see the ship's rudder and engine controls – basic and well worn – and another hatch leading down to what would certainly be the pilot's cabin in the bow.

Fuller pushed the anchored rowing boat away from their propellers and then joined him. He frowned. 'What's the matter with you?'

Granger simply looked at him.

'You're clutching that kitbag like I'm going to steal it.' Fuller eyed him suspiciously. 'What've you got in there? A sword?'

Granger reached into the kitbag and pulled out the sword. He felt a shudder in his mind as the replicates' consciences crowded in on his own: one, two, three . . . Finally he sensed all eight of them nearby, standing in the brine below the boat. 'That's right,' he said. 'You ever see one like this?'

The old man moistened his lips. 'Looks Unmer.'

'It's very rare.'

Fuller held up his hands. 'Well, fine as it is, I told you I ain't going to steal your sword.' But then he gave Granger a sudden wicked grin. 'I can't speak for them fellows behind you, though.'

Granger heard the wheelhouse door open. He turned to face his ambushers.

There were two of them: big, mean-looking types. They wore custom-made Losotan armour, scraped and bashed from countless skirmishes, but well maintained, with the plate and leather oiled against the sea air. And they carried short swords in whaleskin scabbards at their sides. Neither of them had drawn these blades, however. Instead they both clutched weighty steel hand-cannons. The weapons looked like home-made one-shots, pipes or mortar barrels adapted to fire naval large-calibre rounds. The Imperial Army called them fist mashers, on account of their nasty habit of blowing up when fired.

Granger had encountered men like this a hundred times before: mercenaries who sold their services to one warlord or another. The first of them ducked through the wheelhouse door – he had a heavy brow like a shelf of bone and fierce, deep-set eyes. His face and hands had been badly scarred by brine, although not nearly as thoroughly as Granger's own decimated flesh. The man who followed him was seven feet tall, but rangier, with a nervous gait and red spots spattered across his face – an unusual birthmark, perhaps, or even acid damage.

The pair of them cleared the wheelhouse door, and then both raised their cannons to point at Granger's face.

'Drop the sword,' said the rangier one.

'Drop the cannons,' Granger said.

'You ain't that quick, pal,' the rangier one replied.

'No, I'm not,' Granger said, 'but I outnumber you.'

The mercenaries grinned. But then their expressions turned to alarm as the boat gave a sudden lurch, and then rocked, as all around, Granger's replicates climbed out of the brine. In moments eight of them stood on the deck and the wheelhouse roof and in the stern, all clad in the same weird Unmer amour Granger wore under his cloak, all dripping poisonous water from crackling metal plates and boots and gauntlets and from their hideous brine-scorched flesh. And all of them clutched a version of that same hellish blade Granger now pointed at the mercenaries.

The two mercenaries swung their cannons around in horror

and confusion. And then suddenly the stouter man wheeled his firearm round to face Granger. 'What's this?' he cried. 'Sorcery?'

'Lower that firearm,' Granger demanded.

But the other man was frantic. And when one of Granger's replicates moved suddenly behind him, he heard the sound and swung his cannon round and fired. The weapon discharged with a flash of light and a colossal *bang*. The shell struck the replicate's armoured breastplate and burst into a cloud of spectral scintillations and fumes. The sword replicate staggered backwards against the port bulwark. But then it merely shook its head and regained its feet.

The other mercenary threw his cannon down. 'I want no part of this,' he said. 'Let me leave.'

Granger was about to order his sorcerous unit to stand down when the one who'd taken the shell in the breastplate leaped forward and drove his sword deep into the neck of the man who'd fired at it. The mercenary let out a terrible scream and collapsed in a pool of his own blood, while his attacker jerked its sword free and turned to the other mercenary.

'Enough!' Granger roared.

The replicate ignored him. It swung its copy of Granger's blade in a vicious sideways arc, opening the throat of the remaining mercenary. That man seized his neck, but could not stem the jetting blood. He dropped to his knees, gurgling and hissing, then toppled forward.

'Stop!' Granger cried. He tried to drop the blade, but his hand would not release its grip of the cursed thing. Instead, he felt his arm stir, as – against his will – he found himself raising the weapon. He stared in horror at the replicate. *It* was making these motions. *It* was controlling the sword. And Granger was now compelled to copy it. He found himself turning to face Fuller, who stood there white-faced and wide-eyed with terror.

'Run,' Granger managed to say. 'Go now.'

He gasped, staggered forward, sword out-thrust, towards the old man. He could not stop himself. Again he tried to cast the weapon down. His hand remained clenched. He heard Fuller scream. And suddenly Granger realized that he had plunged the steel deep into the other man's guts. Blood was already pulsing out of the wound. Fuller grabbed uselessly at Granger's blade with his scrawny hands, slicing the skin of his fingers. Some compulsion forced Granger forwards, driving the sword in up to the hilt. He roared, and with his power armour now crackling savagely, he lifted Fuller clear off the deck. The man had no weight at all, or else Granger now possessed inhuman strength. He merely swung the sword and cast the old man out over the side of the boat.

Fuller splashed into the water ten yards beyond the bulwark.

Granger found himself turning around again, only to discover that he was now face to face with his replicates. All eight of them stood around him and their dead eyes gazed into his own for a long time. And it seemed to Granger that he saw in those eyes a hint of savage satisfaction.

One of them strode forward suddenly and stopped, its ghoulish face mere inches from Granger's own. It reached over and clamped its free hand over Granger's sword hand, squeezing his fingers tighter around the weapon's grip.

The world gave a sudden *shudder*.

A great clattering noise rose in Granger's ears, and he became aware of replicates all around him. Not eight, but many, many more. His addled mind sensed them standing on the seabed around the assault craft, hundreds of them down there under the brine, thousands perhaps. And more were appearing with every heartbeat. Granger felt his mind being pulled in all directions. Their perceptions, the perceptions of an army, crowded into him until it was too much to bear.

He cried out in pain and terror. He was losing control.

Control.

He had to gain control over this sorcery.

His eyes snapped open. The replicate was an inch from his face, its teeth bared in a hideous leer, as it squeezed Granger's hand with brutal force. It opened its mouth and whispered, 'The sword is limitless. You can be limitless. Do not fight us.'

Granger butted it in the face, smashing its nose.

The blow broke whatever thrall the replicate had over him, for it released his hand and staggered backwards. Granger felt a sudden pressure lift from his mind. He raised the sword as if to bring it swooping down across the neck of the replicate, and the hellish thing moved to parry with its own sword. He couldn't stop it from acting independently, but now at least it couldn't control him.

The two swords met with a noise like a boom of thunder.

'*My* mind,' he hissed through his teeth. 'Mine!'

He released the sword.

As it fell from his hand and clattered to the deck at his feet, all eight of his copies vanished. The boat swayed suddenly and then settled, moved by the abrupt difference in weight.

Granger's sword arm felt as if it was on fire. Intense pain crept into his skull from the top of his spine. His chest was tight, suddenly constricted, and his thoughts reeled in a fog of pain and confusion. He could no longer count on being able to control his replicates. They were starting to exert control over him.

He stared at the sword lying in a pool of blood between

the two mercenaries' corpses. 'Why me?' he yelled at it. 'Why don't you choose someone else?'

The blade lay there, as innocent-looking as any ordinary weapon.

But Granger could never use the damned thing again. It was too dangerous, already too entrenched in his mind. He could no longer trust his replicates. He let out a deep and ragged breath and wiped sweat-lank hair from his brow. Without his armour to support him, he might have collapsed.

He found a torn oilcloth tarpaulin in a bilge compartment and used it to pick up the sword by the back of its blade, being careful not to touch the hilt. He carried it to the side of the boat and held it over the brine.

All he had to do was open his fingers and let it go.

His hands trembled, but he could not release his grip.

He focused, fighting the sword with every last scrap of his will. *Just open my fingers. Open, damn it, open!*

Finally he gasped and staggered back. As soon as he was clear of the side, the sword slipped from his grip and clattered to the floor of the boat. It lay there, covered in blood, mute, mocking him.

'You won't win,' he said. 'You hear?'

Even to his own ears his words lacked conviction.

But he gathered what was left of his resolve and, driven by a kind of numb desperation, set about preparing to leave. After he had heaved the mercenaries' bodies over the side, he drew up buckets of brine and spent the next ten minutes washing the deck down. Then he wrapped the sword in a scrap of cloth and stowed it in his kitbag. When he had removed all trace of violence, he ducked into the wheelhouse to inspect the controls.

At first glance the boat seemed old and poorly maintained. Panels had been removed from underneath the wheel console, exposing a tangle of badly worn hydraulic tubes wrapped in tape. The engine crank handle felt loose and gritty when he turned it, but the engine itself kicked into life on the second attempt and sounded surprisingly smooth. The smoke streaming from the pipes behind the wheelhouse ran grey for a few moments, then turned colourless. There was very little vibration from the props, suggesting good alignment, and perhaps even new bearings. He turned the vessel slowly, listening for any potential problems, but she thrummed as if she was eager to be pushed hard. She would do fine, he decided, provided he could purchase enough fuel for the three-day trip to Doma. The gauge indicated an eighth of a tank, which would only see him fifty leagues or so. And that wasn't enough. He set out to find the sea gypsy village Fuller had talked about.

As the light faded, he pointed the boat's bow at the centre of the bay and pushed the throttle lever forwards. She leaped away eagerly in response, churning the brine to green froth in her wake.

Maskelyne woke with a start. He was in his cabin and it was late morning. His pillow and sheets were drenched in sweat.

He sat up and clamped a hand against his wet brow and shuddered. His fingers trembled as he poured himself a drink of water from the decanter on the bunkside table. His body felt weak, as if his dreams had taken a very real and physical toll on him.

What had he been dreaming of?

A man without a face.

He could not now recall. And yet some trace of his nightmare still remained. An unshakeable feeling that something bad was going to happen.

To whom? To me?

He got out of bed and used the head and then washed quickly before going above deck.

The sun shone down from a cloudless blue sky and the sea lay flat around them. The *Lamp*'s engines sounded healthy again and twin tails of black smoke from her funnels left a gauzy stain far across the north. It looked as if they had made good progress overnight. Maskelyne found Mellor in the bow with Hayn the navigator. The pair were bent over charts spread across a hatch housing. They appeared to be in disagreement, for Hayn was shaking his head and indicating insistently towards the south-west.

'Problems?' Maskelyne asked.

Mellor looked up. 'The crystal is leading us towards the Gehnal conflux. Hayn wants to go around it.'

'But you disagree?'

'What if Gehnal itself is our destination?'

Maskelyne thought about this. 'Do you have any reason to believe that to be the case?'

The first officer shrugged. 'If I were going to hide something where nobody would find it . . .'

Maskelyne nodded. 'You'd put it where nobody dared to go.'

'It's just a hunch, but . . .'

'I'm inclined to agree with you, Mr Mellor.'

'Captain,' Hayn said. 'I propose we head a point west or south-west to confirm the destination. If the device still points to Gehnal, then we'll know for sure. Otherwise, it gives us the opportunity to skirt that conflux.'

Maskelyne shook his head. 'That would cost us a day or more,' he said. 'I'm with Mellor on this. Have the helmsman keep us on our current course.'

The young man gave a quick salute. 'Very good, sir.'

They steamed due south for the rest of the day in glorious sunshine. The dark brown Mare Lux brine surged past the hull. Every so often Maskelyne spotted jellyfish pulsing near its surface and once a shoal of bright flying fish shattered free of the waves to skim away from some unseen foe. He knew there were giants in the deep out here, whales and sharks and the great squid, but he glimpsed no such monsters today. Maskelyne remained above deck until the heat in his forehead and the backs of his hands told him he'd suffered too much sun, whereupon he retired to his cabin to write his journal.

A knocking on the door roused him shortly before dusk. He had fallen asleep with his head resting on the pages of his journal. If any dreams had haunted his sleep, he had no recollection of them. He opened the cabin door to find one of the deckhands with his fist raised to knock again. The young man looked agitated.

'First Officer Mellor is asking for you, Captain,' he said. 'There's something unusual on the horizon.'

'Unusual in what way?'

The deckhand fidgeted. 'You'd best see for yourself, sir. Half the men think it's a mirage.'

Maskelyne followed him above decks. The sun was slinking towards the horizon and illuminated high clouds in nacreous and quicksilver hues so that the whole sky seemed ablaze with strange cosmic gases. He found most of the crew gathered at the *Lamp*'s bow, staring south. He pushed through to see what had so thoroughly ensnared their attention.

It appeared to be a floating city: a great profusion of crystal palaces and temples resting on the southern horizon. The long evening light shone through these structures and caused them to shine like vast, glorious lanterns. To Maskelyne the effect did indeed seem mirage-like, febrile. But also unsettling.

Something about this struck a chord. Had he dreamed of this place?

He could not remember.

With great shame Maskelyne realized that a part of him wanted to turn the *Lamp* away right now, and flee whatever horrors awaited him in those bright palaces. But his rational mind interceded. He refused to fear the unknown. Indeed, as a scientist, his job was to seek it out, explore it, shine his light into its darkest corners. For it was the need to understand what lurked in those dark corners that drove him. And it drove him now.

As the *Lamp* drew nearer to this floating conflagration, he realized that he wasn't looking at a city at all. Those bright translucent domes were not made of glass. They were organic, gas-filled membranes.

'Mr Mellor,' he said. 'How long would you say it takes a samal to grow its victim into an island that large?'

Mellor frowned at him for a moment before realization struck. He turned quickly back to the island, his eyes widening with horror. The rest of the assembled men cursed, gasped or groaned. Finally Mellor shook his head. 'That's the largest I've ever seen,' he said. 'It must be hundreds of years old, thousands even.'

'And the crystal points directly at it?'

'Yes, sir.'

Maskelyne couldn't take his eyes off it. 'An island that large, here in the Gehnal conflux, would have been noticed by shipping long before now.'

Mellor nodded.

'But then samal do drift, I suppose,' he added. He left the rest of his thoughts unspoken to avoid unsettling the men. Nothing of that size had ever been recorded in the Sea of

Lights or its confluxes, and it concerned him that this one should appear now, barely ten days' sail from Scythe Island. He feared that if they charted its progress they would discover that it had been moving towards his home. 'Stop the engines,' he said. 'I want my ship to maintain this distance, as minimum, at all times.'

'You mean to observe it?'

'I mean to land on it,' Maskelyne said. 'I'll take one of the tenders in tomorrow morning, but we'll keep the *Lamp* well clear. How many diving suits do we have?'

'Three, sir,' Mellor replied.

'Then I require two volunteers to accompany me onto the island at first light tomorrow.'

A few of the crew exchanged fearful glances among themselves, but not a man of them protested or complained. Indeed several approached Mellor to volunteer their services then and there.

Maskelyne ordered his men to keep constant watch throughout the night and to maintain a distance of one league. At all costs. The samal in the water below would be vast, and there was no telling how far its tentacles could reach or in which direction the ocean currents might carry it. They made preparations for the expedition tomorrow, checking the seals on all three diving suits. When that was done, the metaphysicist sat on a deckchair upon the wheelhouse roof and in the last of the fading light gazed across at that vast and gaseous mass. It covered three or four acres and supported mature trees among the swathes of distended flesh and mutated veins. The great inflated membranes he had first assumed to be temples had once been skin or other organic surfaces, now regrown to suit the needs of the parasite in the depths below. He fancied he saw movement in the undergrowth, but that could only have been his imagination, for the samal would consume any unprotected traveller that set foot upon its domain.

He had to hope the suits would be enough.

'What do you think it was?'

Maskelyne looked over to see Mellor clinging to the wheel-house ladder.

'The host?' Maskelyne replied. 'I think it was human. Or possibly Unmer.'

The other man nodded. 'The men share your belief. Some of them claim they've seen a face there.'

They watched the island in silence for a while.

'If it's any consolation,' Maskelyne said, 'I doubt the brain still functions as it once did. Who can say if such a mutation has the capacity to know pain or despair? Perhaps the parasite offers satisfaction in exchange for aid. Pleasure, even. We might also posit that the human mind can come to accept even the most grievous change. Dragons thrive in their own addictions and madness. Are we not all creatures of the same cosmos? Is it not arrogant to perceive degeneration as a cruelty?'

'Not when it's imposed.'

Maskelyne shook his head. 'It's always imposed. Why is it that life is so abhorred by the universe? Why must our existence be an endless battle against entropy? There's nature, clawing at our heels, undoing life's tapestries as fast as we can weave them.' He stood up and threw his arms wide and cried out. 'The will of the universe is the will of the void and the void has but *one single intention*. To reach equilibrium like any other wave.' Slowly he sat back down again. 'Time continues to slow and space continues to stretch and thin and homogenize. And we cannot appeal to vacuum. That would be too . . .' He caught himself, smiled. 'Too unfair. The truth is that life itself is unnatural.' He raised his chin, indicating the island.

'There is a creature debased in your eyes. But would it not be true to say that the parasite has brought it closer to the natural state?'

Mellor shrugged. 'Your perception of nature is different to mine,' he said. 'Still, I hope that come tomorrow you'll tread just as carefully as the less . . . uh . . . philosophical volunteers.'

Maskelyne grinned. 'Oh, it's all just semantics, anyway. What we refer to as nature is at odds with the fundamental nature of the universe. Now tell me, Mellor, which of the men volunteered to accompany their captain into the monster's maw.'

'All but one.'

Maskelyne raised his eyebrows. 'Who was the one?'

'New lad.' Mellor grinned. 'Should I do the usual?'

'Well, of course,' Maskelyne said. 'One must learn to conquer one's fears, after all.'

'Very good, Captain.'

No dreams came that night to disturb Maskelyne's sleep. He woke before dawn and joined several of his crew on the bathysphere deck. With Mellor was Spenratter the dive engineer and the coward who had failed to volunteer – a twenty-year-old Evensraumer named Charles Pendragon. Now that this young man understood the outcome of his decision, he would undoubtedly be more inclined to put his name forward for future expeditions. It was through small steps like these that Maskelyne had long forged and tempered collections of men into crews.

A fragile pink light glimmered in the east and a profusion of stars yet dusted the sky above the ship's twin iron funnels. It seemed to Maskelyne that the ocean around them simmered with the same dark energy of the cosmos – tremulous and pregnant with elemental wrath. It was a medium of both degeneration and creation, of cold indifference to those it altered.

Maskelyne had chosen Spenratter to accompany him lest they had any issues with the suits while away from the *Lamp*. He saw no danger on the island other than the danger posed by crawling samal filaments. A well-maintained dive suit ought to keep those out. Pendragon said nothing as Mellor and the others helped him into his suit, but the terror in his eyes was clear for all to see. His hands trembled when they handed him a dragon lance. He almost dropped the weapon. His finger would be jumpy on its trigger, liable to spray flame wildly at the first hint of trouble. Maskelyne's diving suit was brine-proof, but it wasn't particularly fireproof. He thought for a moment, then said, 'That suit's a poor fit. Don't you think, Mr Mellor?'

Mellor frowned, but clearly knew better than to question his captain's comment. 'It is, sir.'

'Slack around the knees, there,' Maskelyne added, pointing.

The first officer nodded. 'Droops like my old nan's tit, sir.'

'Get him out of it,' Maskelyne said. 'Find me someone more suitable.'

Pendragon's eyes snapped to Maskelyne. And suddenly all trace of fear had vanished from him, to be replaced by sudden and righteous defiance. 'Please, sir,' he said. 'The suit fits just fine.'

'The gloves are too large for your hands,' Maskelyne replied. 'You'll struggle to pull that weapon's trigger.'

'It's not a problem, sir.'

'No?'

'No.'

Maskelyne studied the young man for a long moment. 'You know what we face over there?'

Pendragon nodded. There was, Maskelyne noted, no longer even a hint of nervousness about the boy. He held his dragon lance with the relaxed grip of a veteran.

'Why the change of heart, son?'

'No change of heart, sir. I wanted to go, and it's well known you choose new sailors who refuse to volunteer.'

'You're not scared?'

'I've faced worse.'

Maskelyne laughed. 'Worse than the mother of all samal?'

'My old man, sir, was a hell of a brute.'

Maskelyne's smile faded. He gripped the young man's shoulder. 'Mark my words, son. You have a long and prosperous future in my employ.'

'Provided I survive today.'

'You'll survive today.'

When all three men were suited up, they clambered down into the *Lamp*'s steel-hulled dory. He used this thirty-foot flat-hulled vessel primarily as a tender, but also in those rare occasions when the shallows gave up trove. She still bore the Valcinder shipyard's mark on her side, *VM22*, although the crew called her *Tutu*. Mellor passed him down the crystal locator device, which he set on his lap. A cursory glance confirmed that their destination was indeed the heart of the parasite's island.

Spenratter started the engines and soon the small boat was skimming across the tea-dark water towards the floating island. As they drew nearer, they began to smell the rich musky odour of the thing. The suits were merely for protection from the samal's gossamer tentacles; they lacked the means to pump air into them so far from the *Lamp*, and so simply breathed through the disconnected hose valves at the top of each helmet – an opening through which they were most vulnerable to ingress.

212

Nevertheless, the stench was so foul Maskelyne wished he'd possessed the foresight to have filters fitted. Young Pendragon sat in the stern, pale faced and gripping the gunwale with both hands, while Spenratter's stocky figure stood over him at the wheel.

'You'll get used to the feel of it soon enough,' Maskelyne said, his voice muffled by the heavy glass-and-brass sphere around his head. 'But if you want to vomit, do it now. There won't be an opportunity to open your helmet after we land.'

'I'm fine, sir.'

'Spenratter?'

'Actually quite enjoying the smell,' he said. 'Reminds me of the wife's cooking.'

'I've tasted your wife's cooking, Spenratter,' Maskelyne said. 'And I find that remark grossly unfair to the samal.'

The three of them laughed.

The lamp mechanism around the crystal continued to point unerringly towards the island. And soon the veined and gas-filled bladders were looming over their hull. The host flesh had been stretched and distorted over the centuries into new and grotesque forms, hillocks of bone enmeshed with red muscle and rumples of skin in which gleamed teeth. Mounds of diaphanous bubbles trembled in the breeze and gave off such hellish aromas as to make one cry out in anguish. The land throbbed and glistened and seeped and shivered. Rivulets of pink fluid trickled between pale mounds beset by black rot. And among this post-human morass there grew clutches of botanic life. The roots of grasses and other small plants found purchase in all manner of moist and yielding surfaces and so clung there and thrived. Tangles of undergrowth drank the sweat of unusual soils. And, further into the heart of the island, Maskelyne could see trees.

Trees.

Through what hives of nerves and memories did their deep roots plunge?

Spenratter eased back the throttle and the boat's engines dropped to a murmur. For several dozen yards they coasted along muscular banks packed with knuckle-like protrusions, until Spenratter spotted a suitable place to land. Here the shore was scalloped and shallower and the *Tutu*'s bow slid up onto the sticky fabric of the island. It may have been Maskelyne's imagination, but he thought he saw the entire bank give a shudder.

He stepped out onto the island.

The ground was surprisingly firm underfoot, and yet quite as glutinous as its appearance suggested. The earth clung to his soles like moist lips and educed from each step a faint supping sound, his boots parting from the soil as a bandage parts from a wound. At the top of the bank lay an expanse of red and black mounds rising three to six yards high with channels of greenery crammed between them. The substance of these mounds was not immediately identifiable, although to Maskelyne they looked like tumours. He perceived black veins under the skin of the land. Beyond these mounds there loomed an enormous grey and yellow sac, or lung, that rocked slightly in the breeze.

They dropped the boat's anchor cautiously and tied her bowline to a stout branch, before setting forth to explore this strange place.

Maskelyne climbed the bank with Spenratter and Pendragon close behind him. The defiles running between these earthen tumours were too congested with branches and vines to permit easy passage and so he clambered up on the first of the mounds themselves. The living ground under his boots felt as hard as packed earth. He stopped at the summit and shielded his eyes from the sun. His breaths echoed in his helmet and already he was blinking back the sweat. He consulted the locator. The source of sorcery lay to the north.

'Look, there,' Pendragon said, pointing down into the green channel below them.

Maskelyne spotted a white tendril moving out of the undergrowth. It was snaking towards them across the darkly mottled surface of the mound. A further two, then four tendrils appeared out of the vegetation. Each one was barely thicker than cotton string and yet they crept unerringly towards the three interlopers, guided by unseen intelligence.

Spenratter cried out suddenly and raised his foot. Another filament had crept up on him unnoticed and wrapped itself around his shin. He wrenched his foot away, but it would not release him.

Maskelyne took out his knife and cut his companion free. He did not want to use his lance until they had no other choice. 'Let's not linger here,' he said, urging his comrades onwards. 'Keep moving. And keep to the high ground.'

The three explorers proceeded by short scrambles and leaps from mound to mound, careful to keep ahead of the searching filaments that reached out from the green gullies. The geology of the landscape continued in this fashion around one side of the bruised yellow gas sac and then sloped downwards and levelled as the mounds became smaller. Behind the sac they discovered a great pink crater wherein there lay entrenched a sodden cluster of bones. It appeared that the bones had been partially unearthed from this wound in the earth, or else partially absorbed. From the enormous size of them Maskelyne supposed they could be the remains of a whale. But then they might well be part of the same unfortunate creature upon whose back they now walked. He could not know for sure.

The land behind the crater remained mostly level but was pocked by larger solitary mounds that seemed to be formed of a more elastic, greyish material. These expanded and contracted gently. The host's lungs, perhaps. Clumps of vegetation clung to the scabrous ground in places but the men kept to the open areas between them. They crossed some kind of cracked grey scurf that resembled dragon hide, and it occurred to Maskelyne, now that he thought about it, that there was something else about this particular part of the island that reminded him of those great Unmer serpents. An unwholesome beauty? An aura? The air here smelled like the breath from a serpent's lungs. He paused to get his bearings. To the north-east he could see three more gas bladders, these as red as gums, rising from low scrub. Closer, and to the east stood the trees he had spotted from afar. He was marvelling at the age of these specimens when Pendragon suddenly cried out.

He turned to find the young man on his knees, frantically hacking away with his knife at something near his shins. Maskelyne hurried over at once and immediately established that Pendragon's predicament was exactly as he had feared: the sailor had become ensnared by yet more of the parasite's tentacles. These ones had – Maskelyne now saw – emerged from between the scales of the ground. Those gossamer threads had already reached around Pendragon's thighs and pulled him to the ground.

Maskelyne looked down at his own legs.

And there saw white tendrils curling around his shins.

'Blasted things are everywhere,' he said. He dropped to a crouch and drew his knife across the tendrils, severing handfuls of them. But for every dozen he cut, twice as many snaked out of the ground and curled around his boots. They moved with terrifying speed.

'Stand.'

Maskelyne glanced over to see Spenratter with his dragon lance levelled and pointed at Maskelyne's feet. He stood up quickly.

Spenratter squeezed the trigger and a gout of flame burst from the nozzle at the end of the weapon. Fire engulfed Maskelyne's boots and lower legs for a moment, before Spenratter quenched the spray. The tentacles had all burned away, leaving the dive suit partially soot-blackened but otherwise undamaged. The dive master then turned his lance on Pendragon and burned those tendrils too. Maskelyne sensed a faint shudder under his feet. Had the island just *reacted*? If so, he wondered if that had been a shudder of pain, or fury?

'We need to move more quickly,' he said. 'Use the lances whenever you need to.'

Now ejecting licks of flame whenever the parasite's searching tendrils drew too near, the three men skirted the grove of trees and soon reached a raised hillock which offered a view of the entire island. Maskelyne checked his locator again only to discover that the source of sorcery was now somewhere behind them. They had walked past it.

Carefully, the men retraced their steps. Maskelyne now kept one eye on the locator, adjusting the lamp arm to keep the filament at its brightest. It was directing him towards the grove of trees.

'How much fire do you have left?' he asked Spenratter.

'Not much,' the dive master replied. 'But I imagine there's enough left between us. Unless you're planning on spending the night here.'

Maskelyne indicated the tangle of trees and bushes ahead

of them. 'See if you can clear that scrub,' he said. 'Our target, it seems, lies in there.'

Spenratter nodded. He made an adjustment to his lance and then stepped forward of the other two. Then he squeezed the trigger.

A huge gout of fire burst forth from the weapon, engulfing the vegetation before him. Bushes crisped and went up in balls of flame. Spenratter kept up the onslaught until the fire had taken firm hold. The lower branches of the trees now crisped and blackened as flames grew.

A violent shudder ran through the ground. Maskelyne staggered, but managed to keep himself from falling. Spenratter, however, was unbalanced by his lance and lost his footing. The stout man rolled and then scrambled upright again, helped to his feet by a hand from Pendragon just as a fresh network of tendrils snaked across the ground towards him.

Maskelyne aimed his own lance at these and burned them away.

The island moved a second time. Suddenly and with great fury, the land *bucked*, throwing all three men from their feet. As Maskelyne hit the scaly ground, he spied Spenratter roll a second time and leap upright. The dive master came quickly to the aid of Pendragon, who had fallen into a mass of tendrils and was now struggling against them. Every time it seemed he might pull away, a dozen more filaments reached over him, winding themselves around his legs and neck. The dive master drenched the young sailor in fire and then dragged him to his feet.

Then, suddenly, from the thicket came a vast and terrible moan.

Spenratter grabbed his arm, pulled him round. 'Look there!' he cried, jabbing his finger at the burning undergrowth. 'Hell have mercy, look at that thing!'

Much of the smaller scrub had burned away, allowing Maskelyne a view into the heart of the thicket. And what he saw there momentarily stopped the breath in his throat. From the ground there rose a great mass of bloated skin, in which could clearly be seen two enormous weeping eyes, a pair of fist-sized nostrils and a black gulf of a mouth as wide as a man. He realized he was looking at the face of the parasite's host.

As the vegetation around it burned away, that gross visage coughed and sputtered and fixed its terrified eyes upon the three interlopers. It opened its prodigious maw and let out a baleful howl. And then it cried out in Losotan, 'Stop it, stop it, stop it.'

Spenratter swung his lance around to torch the thing, but Maskelyne stopped him. A hundred more tendrils were snaking across the ground towards them, and he feared they lacked enough liquid fuel to see them safely back to the tender. He had a theory he wanted to test. He turned to the face and yelled, 'Recall the tendrils.'

'Please, I beg you,' it replied. 'I can't breathe.'

'Recall them, or we'll scorch your skin.'

The great wet maw shuddered and cried, 'No! Please . . .'

Maskelyne nodded to Spenratter, who stepped forward and raised his dragon lance a second time. Now it was pointed directly at the grotesque visage.

'Last chance,' Maskelyne said.

'I'll try!' the face replied. 'Please, don't . . .'

It closed one enormous eye and its other eye fluttered and its monstrous brow furrowed, as though it was struggling to untangle some mental knot or puzzle. Was it, as Maskelyne suspected, in communication with the samal? Were the two minds connected? He got his answer a moment later, when the slender tentacles halted, and then drew back into the scaly ground.

Pendragon scanned the ground around them, and then seemed to relax. The face amidst the smouldering vegetation was now wheezing and weeping and spitting ash from its lips. Tears coursed over its great soot-smeared jowls. Its bloodshot eyes rolled and flinched.

'You will note,' Maskelyne said, 'that our actions have been in self-defence. We have no reason to harm you unless you give us one.'

'Father attacked you,' the face said. 'Not me.'

'Father?'

'What did you expect?' it raged, suddenly furious. 'It's hungry!'

Maskelyne frowned. 'Are you referring to the parasite? The samal?'

Rage faded from the face as rapidly as it had appeared. It looked momentarily confused, and then appeared to latch onto some sort of understanding. 'Samal,' it said. 'That was his name once. We sailed from Losoto to fight at Galai. On the second day out it rained frogs.'

Spenratter gave Maskelyne a worried look, then circled a finger to one side of his brow.

Madness? Yes. Of course, the host was mad. Could anyone endure such profound and inhuman changes to their nature and remain sane? That this creature could still communicate with them at all was a far greater boon than Maskelyne could ever have hoped for.

'Do you have a name?' he asked the thing.

'Tom.'

Maskelyne found himself smiling at the incongruity of it all; such a simple and common name seemed an unlikely match for a dribbling monster such as this. He said, 'You fought in Galai, Tom?'

Again, the look of uncertainty crossed those gross and flaccid features. 'And who claims that I didn't?' Tom replied. 'That man is a liar. I fought, yes, and there were men who saw me fight. Is it my fault all those witnesses are dead?'

'No one is claiming you didn't,' Maskelyne said. Then something occurred to him. This creature, hideous as it was, had retained enough humanity for Maskelyne to recognize its paranoia. It had been, he felt, rather too defensive. He added, 'No one is calling you a deserter, Tom.'

The face reddened. 'I was rowing towards the enemy!' it roared. 'The wind turned me about. The currents took me. I could have ended the war that night. An assassin's blade in the dark of Rogetter's cabin. That's all it would have taken, but for the wind and the currents. And now you all accuse me of immoral conduct? Of siding with the enemy? I've done nothing wrong!'

Spenratter came alongside Maskelyne. 'If he fought at Galai . . .' he said.

'Then he's over six hundred years old,' Maskelyne said quietly.

'That's a harsh sentence, even for a deserter.'

Maskelyne turned to look at him. 'I disagree.' He turned back to study that huge distorted face; it was agitated, breathing quickly and sweating profusely. And then he examined the crystal locator. Could this hideous creature be the source of such powerful sorcery? Why, then, had the Drowned brought him so many keys? Maskelyne felt sure he was looking for a container of some sort. He thought for a moment, then said, 'We've come for the box.'

Eyes like ship-floats glared back at him.

'Let's do it the easy way,' Maskelyne said. 'There's no need for you to endure any more suffering, Tom.'

'Father won't let you have it,' the face replied.

'Then he'll have to watch you burn.'

The face squirmed with despair. 'Please,' it said. 'The box keeps us warm.'

'If it's heat you want . . .' Maskelyne nodded to Spenratter, who raised his dragon lance.

'No!' the face cried. 'You can have it. Take it and leave us be.'

Spenratter lowered the lance.

The ground shuddered again, and the face became a scrunched mass of flesh, as if it were enduring some new, internal agony. A moment later, the lamp filament on Maskelyne's locator began to flicker. The source of the sorcery was moving. The land around them bucked, not as fiercely as before, but enough to rattle the scorched trees and bushes.

With another ominous quake, the ground before the three sailors suddenly opened. The skin of the land split and drew back, revealing a deep mass of glistening red muscle-like material. Brine sprayed up through this newly formed crevasse, like a whale's exhalation, and spattered the surrounding land. Maskelyne edged towards the opening and peered down.

Through the gloomy waters he perceived a squirming mass of pale tentacles. Most were as slender as the roots of young trees, but a few were as thick as a man's waist. These could only be the veins and gullets that connected the host to the parasite in the sea below. They writhed in that poison like an endless nest of snakes. In the depths far below, Maskelyne thought he glimpsed the great dark shadow of the samal itself.

The tentacles convulsed and shifted suddenly. Something appeared below the hole. Maskelyne stepped back as the parasite thrust the object up through the gap and held it there, ten feet above their heads, in a hundred writhing tentacles.

It appeared to be a coffin, fashioned from dull grey metal. And it was hot. Even from where he stood in his suit, Maskelyne could feel the immense heat radiating from that box.

The samal set the box down on the ground to one side of the hole, and then its tentacles unravelled themselves from the object, and withdrew, flailing wildly as they disappeared back into the hole. With a final shudder and exhalation, the hole in the ground slammed shut like the mouth of a predator.

Maskelyne approached the container. 'And where, may I ask, did you find this?'

The face appeared to recover from its ordeal. It rolled its tremendous eyes upon the three men. 'Father picked it up,' it said. 'Long ago. From a place with buildings.'

'What sort of buildings?'

'The sort with food in them,' the face growled. 'Take it and leave like you promised.'

Maskelyne held his hand over the container for a moment, then pressed his gloved hand against its metal lid. It was too hot to touch for more than a few moments. He wandered around it. It clearly resembled a coffin. It was made of metal, with a handle at each end, and utterly unadorned as far as he could tell – which was itself unusual for an Unmer creation. He tried to lift the lid, but it would not shift. Then he located a keyhole in the middle of one side.

'Oh my,' he said.

'What?' Pendragon said.

'Why would anyone build a coffin with a lock in it?'

'Bone thieves,' Pendragon said.

Maskelyne looked at him. 'Are there such things?'

'You can get thirty gilders for a sorcerer's skeleton.'

'Really? Why?'

'Elixirs.'

Maskelyne grunted. He wondering which – if any – of the millions of keys the Drowned had brought him might fit that lock. For this had to be the source of their queer behaviour. *A sorcerer's coffin submerged in the ocean.* By leaving their keys on his shore, the Drowned had been sending him messages about it for years.

But whatever was compelling them to do so?

He had no intention of trying to find the correct key, if it even existed. He had gas cutting-torches aboard the *Lamp*. 'If we slide the lances through these handles,' he said, 'we should be able to carry it between us.'

They slipped the narrow ends of each of their lances through the opposite handles, and so were able to hoist the coffin between them. It was almost unbearably heavy, and yet Maskelyne found the strength from somewhere. By short stints with much grunting and cursing, they manhandled the thing back to the tender.

Only after they were half a mile distant from the parasite, did Maskelyne feel that it was safe to remove his helmet. He wiped the sweat from his brow and took a long draught of water from the tender's supply. He handed the cup to Pendragon and gave him a wry grin. 'You survived, then.'

'Seems I did, sir,' the young man replied. He kept his eyes fixed on their mysterious new acquisition. 'What do you think it is?'

Even from where he sat, Maskelyne could feel the heat radiating from the box. He shrugged. 'It's an enigma to be solved,' he said. 'We'll open it once we get aboard.'

'What if it's . . .?' The young sailor's voice tapered off. 'What if it's dangerous?'

'Everything the Unmer make is dangerous,' Maskelyne replied. 'I'm sure this will be no exception.'

When the reached the *Lamp*, Maskelyne climbed aboard and relinquished the tender over to Mellor and his team of men. They used the dredging crane to hoist up the container and set it on the bathysphere deck, whereupon Mellor examined the artefact and turned to Maskelyne. 'Do you think this is the lock for which the Drowned bring you keys?' he said.

'It's certainly possible,' Maskelyne replied. 'Perhaps even likely.'

'But which key fits?'

'Who cares?' Maskelyne said. 'We'll cut it open.'

Mellor summoned the best of their welders – a tough, grizzled little man named Teucher, who lowered his mask and sparked his gas flame to life and bent over the Unmer coffin. The crew gathered round to watch as Teucher's flame slowly ate into the metal around the lock. It was a long process, constantly interrupted by Teucher's need to back off to recover from the heat, but finally the gas torch cut away the last of the steel around the lock. A circle of red-hot metal hit the ship's deck with a clang, and Teucher stood up.

Using rags to protect their hands, two crewmen seized the front of the lid and heaved it open. Maskelyne stepped forward and gazed down at the coffin's contents.

It was full of molten silvery grey metal. *Lead?* Maskelyne squatted down and peered at the substance more closely. Hot fumes assaulted his nostrils. The heat from it was atrocious. There had to be some energy source inside that liquid, something keeping it molten.

'What is that?' Mellor said.

'Molten lead.' Maskelyne extended a hand. 'Give me something, a pole.'

One of the crewmen passed him a nearby broom.

Maskelyne dipped the end of the broom handle into the coffin. It disappeared a few inches into the hot liquid, before he felt resistance.

And then suddenly a hand burst from that molten metal and seized the broom handle. Several crewmen cried out in alarm. Maskelyne leaped back.

A second hand appeared out of the molten metal and gripped the side of the coffin. And then a figure surged upwards out of the coffin, splashing lead across the deck as it sat up. It was completely grey, covered in the hot liquid, and yet it appeared to be human. It opened its mouth, took a single hissing breath, and then it rolled out of its prison and collapsed on the deck.

'Fetch a hose,' Maskelyne said.

CHAPTER 6

ASSISTANCE

His attempts to resist the sword replicates had given him a headache. As he steered the assault craft out of the bay and turned east around the main headland, Granger could barely look at the green glare of the open ocean to his right. Even in the dusk it was a slab of tortuous scintillations – countless millions of them fizzing behind his retina like shards of mirror-glass, forcing his jaw to tighten. The boat's engines sounded distant, dreamlike; the scent of the brine in his nostrils didn't seem real, more like a memory.

He looked down at his hand clutching the wheel, still clad in the metal gauntlet. He lifted his hand and flexed his fingers, watching as a hundred tiny alloy plates slipped over each other. How long would it be before he lacked the freedom even to make a small movement such as this? Even this pathetic effort seemed to require too much of his waning energy. His fingers felt stiff, unwilling to bend.

He pulled the gauntlet off.

The skin underneath was grey and dead-looking. Now when he tried to move his fingers he found that he could not. He sensed the sword resisting him, testing its hold on Granger's mind. For a few moments the tips of Granger's fingers did not even twitch. Only when he funnelled all of his remaining strength and will into the effort could he close his hand into a fist.

The effort left him gasping.

He realized that his power armour was helping him to resist the sword. Without it, he would be helpless.

He wondered what would happen when the sword assumed total control over his body. Would he be aware? A prisoner inside his own body? Or would he simply become a mindless ghoul like the other replicates – an extension of someone else's mind?

Granger slid his gauntlet back on and found that he could move his hand again with ease. He tried to banish all troublesome thoughts from his head. He had to concentrate on the task at hand. He needed fuel to reach the dragon nests at Doma. Fuel he hoped to buy in the gypsy village Fuller had said lay two leagues to the east. What had they called it? Addle? Granger could barely drag the details from his muddled mind. *Three sorcerous daggers. One to buy the fuel he needed to reach Doma, the other two to pay a dragon to carry him to Ethugra.* Where he hoped Ethan Maskelyne could release him from the sword's grip. The pain behind his temples continued to pulse. His eyes twitched repeatedly, uncontrollably. He realized he had been staring past the bow of the vessel and seeing nothing but the points of white light flashing on the sea.

Now he made an effort to look along the coast. To port lay the forested shore of Awl, a maze of small islands and inlets disappearing between half-drowned granite ridges. Wild pines clung to the thin earth between cliffs and boulders. He perceived a pall of smoke hanging over a long peninsula to the east. The distance seemed about right. The village he sought had to be behind that spur of land.

Granger aimed the craft a few degrees out from shore,

lashed down the wheel, and ducked through the hatch down into the captain's cabin in the bow.

There was nothing of any value: old fishing nets, some tin pails, a pile of soiled blankets on a wooden sleeping shelf. He kicked empty tins around with his foot. In one corner he found a barrel of unscented dark brown liquid, but it could have been anything. Countless layers of white paint rimpled the hull interior and now bore streaks the colour of old tobacco or blood. An odour of sweat and old food made the air feel overused. Granger tried to open one of the two portholes, but the steel had corroded around the rims and fused them shut. He went back up to the wheelhouse.

The light was fading quickly now, which came as something of a relief to his tired and tender retinas. He cruised along the coast for about an hour before he drew near enough to the peninsula to perceive the cliffs and wooded slopes in any detail. No sign of habitation. He turned the boat to the south-east and powered around the southern end of this landmass, where the winds picked up and pushed green waves against rocks and half-drowned trees.

The sight that met Granger as he rounded the headland was not what he had expected. Sea gypsy villages were typically small, usually little more than a collection of wooden huts built onto rafts, tended by a flotilla of small boats. The settlement before him now was far larger than that. Indeed, it would be incorrect to call Addle a village at all. This was a bustling town.

Tin-roofed shacks and crude floating platforms clustered around the town's perimeter, where scores of pontoons radiated out like the rays of sunlight in primitive cave paintings. At least a hundred boats were moored there, from outrigger canoes to steel-hulled trawlers, dredgers and boilers and even, to his great surprise, exquisite glass barques and gold-spun pleasure yachts. The settlement swelled upwards at its centre, where clustered numerous taller timber buildings with pinched crimson and gold-leaved eaves and tiers of verandas boasting carved arabesques as intricate as lace.

Trade, Granger noted, was not restricted to the local area, for there were seven deep-water vessels at anchor nearby. And as he studied these vessels his heart began to race. Two of them were dragon hunters. He recognized the heavy steel steamships as private Anean craft, both registered in Losoto. He'd probably encountered these very ships many times during his time in the capital. They were both equipped with pressure harpoons and cranes for offloading meat from the holds.

Granger's gaze lingered on the dragon hunters. He could hardly believe his luck. Why were they here and not in Awl? But, more importantly . . . did they have any live cargo aboard?

There was a chance he might not need to visit Doma at all.

He gunned the assault craft's engine and her flat hull skipped across the glooming brine, pounding through the gentle waves and leaving behind a broad wake of inky-green foam. When he drew near, he slowed the boat again and coasted past scores of pontoons, looking for a suitable berth. Dozens of men, women and children worked, rested or played around the moorings and shacks. Sea gypsies were a handsome, wiry race of people, dark haired and sallow skinned and quick to smile. The women had tied bright printed scarves around their heads and carried loops of glass beads around their necks. Many of the men wore wide leather gun belts and patterned leather waistcoats over their naked torsos.

Granger drove past a boathouse where a man sat outside, surrounded by pieces of an engine – presumably that of the old Valcinder cruiser he spied in the shadows. He passed an open-air restaurant in which crowds of traders had gathered to eat and chat and deal and where gypsy women fried seafood in huge iron skillets. Clouds of steam carried a dozen conversations mingled with the scent of cooked fish. Granger found himself salivating. It had been more than a day since he'd last eaten.

It occurred to him that such a meeting place might be a good start and so he located a berth for his stolen vessel nearby. As soon as her hull bumped against dry wood, a young man came bounding down the pontoon.

'Normally it's three sisters for a stolen boat,' he said. 'I'll charge you two since it's Fuller's.'

Granger slung his kitbag over his shoulder and alighted from the boat. 'Maybe Fuller sold it,' he said, tying up the stern line.

The young man laughed. 'Right.'

Granger tied the bowline then dug in his pocket. 'I'll give you five if you tell me where I can find the captains of those hunters.' He gestured out towards the bay with a nod of his head.

'Can't say for sure,' the young man said. 'But they'll probably be at the Saint Jerome. All the deepwater captains drink there. Best ask their men. You'll find them hawking dragon meat at the market.'

'They have any live stock?' Granger asked.

'Usually, but they keep that for Losoto.'

Granger gave him five coins and then set off in the direction the lad indicated.

The planks and walkways of Addle creaked and bowed under his boots. Most of the town appeared to be built on oil-drum rafts and old rusted barges and even tangled mats of reclaimed wood. Rubbish and green-brown scum clogged the oily gloom between such foundations. Granger made his way past scores of tin-roofed dwellings, past groups of women weaving by oil light and men working metal over braziers or sitting smoking, their dark eyes gleaming in the light of their pipe-bowls. He edged by people wheeling goods back and forth on sack trolleys. Chained goats bleated and dogs barked and children ran shrieking over the roofs, their little feet pattering the tin like rain.

Soon the buildings became larger and his boots more often rang on metal. And all of a sudden he turned a corner and came upon the market.

It was an open area in front of the Saint Jerome – a three-storey tea house with sweeping gold eaves and intricate trelliswork. Four lines of covered stalls and canvas tents faced each other across a square in which stood a roped-off area, presumably used for livestock auctions and prize fights. Candles and oil lamps burned everywhere, filling the shops with warm yellow light that seemed at once to add wealth and mystery to the treasures for sale within. The atmosphere reminded Granger of a carnival. Most of the traders sold thrice-boiled fish or woven clothes and scarves and leatherwork, but a few had glittering shelves of trove. Granger idled past, ignoring the odd glances cast his way, one hand clenching the pouch of coins and daggers he'd stolen from the Haurstaf palace. What few artefacts he spied among the tat fetched reassuringly high prices. Provided his own stolen artefacts retained some of their power, he felt it might be possible to negotiate a good deal.

He found the dragon tent midway along the row of stalls. It was four times larger than any of the others.

The interior was hot and crawling with flies and full of the rich dense aroma of dragon meat. Granger found himself salivating unwittingly. The particular game on display here held none of the poisons that suffused other marine life. It could be cooked or even eaten raw, without the need to treat it first. And it was delicious. Slabs of meat and strips of scale-covered hide hung on steel racks all around the chopping table where the butcher worked, hacking away at a great shank of red flesh and bone as large as a goat. He was a heavy, muscular man with a face as red as the meat he chopped. If his bloody overalls had ever been white, that time was long past. He wore a tightly fitting cap, spattered with dried gore, to keep the sweat from his eyes. He turned the shank on the table and drove his cleaver into the sinew at one end and then skimmed it down between the bone and the flesh. Then he glanced up at Granger and stopped.

'Help you?'

'This is an odd port for you, isn't it?'

The butcher snorted. 'Fuel's cheaper here. Everything's cheaper here.'

Granger suddenly understood. With the Haurstaf gone and an Unmer regime yet to be fully established, there was nobody around to regulate – and tax – trade. It made sense that the captains would favour this place over Port Awl to resupply their ships. He indicated the dragon meat. 'This is a blue?'

'Caught three days ago near Doma,' the butcher said. 'Slaughtered her yesterday. The meat's still fresh.'

'You cure it normally?'

The butcher nodded. 'We cure what we don't sell.'

Granger's gaze wandered over the cutting table. The wooden surface had been heavily gouged and stained near black with blood. Flies crawled over mounds of red meat and gleaming white sinew. The butcher turned the hank again and cut from it another strip of muscle and fat, leaving the bone bare. He lifted the bone in both hands and threw it into the corner of the tent. A cloud of flies erupted, buzzing angrily, and then settled again.

'You have any live dragons?' Granger said.

'I told you, this meat was slaughtered yesterday. As fresh as you'll find anywhere.'

Granger nodded. 'My boss needs a living one.' It had occurred to him that he would seem more credible if he were acting on behalf of someone else. He didn't look like a rich man, but he looked like someone who might be hired by a rich man. His brine-scarred face gave him a fierce, dangerous look that could be useful in certain lines of underground work. He had also taken care to use the word *need* rather than *want*. The likeliest reason for someone to need a living dragon was to fight them in an arena – an illegal practice in Hu's empire. However, such an implication would answer all the butcher's questions.

'You'd have to speak to the captain about that,' the butcher said.

'You have a live beast, then?'

The butcher lifted another slab of dragon beef from the rack and set it down on the chopping table. 'We always do, this close to Doma,' he said. 'We got this one's mother in the hold. She's old, but she's a hell of a fighter. You know how they get when their calves are taken?'

'I can imagine,' Granger said. 'What state is she in?'

The butcher shrugged. 'She's alive.'

'Healthy?'

'Healthy enough for what you need.'

'Fine,' Granger said. 'Where can I find your captain?'

'Saint Jerome, third floor, look for white hair and a black jacket with blue lapels.'

234

'His name?'

'Captain Scalton.'

'Thanks.'

The butcher nodded. As Granger turned to leave, he called after him: 'I hope your boss has a lot of money.'

'Something better than that,' Granger replied.

On the third-floor veranda of the tea house, he spotted Scalton and four of his officers crowded around a table overlooking the market square. They were drinking steaming black tea and smoking fruit tobaccos from floor-standing hookahs and chewing strips of what was probably dragon meat laced with opium. Granger walked right up to them and placed a cloth package on the table. In it were his three Unmer knives: the tempest blade, the quicksilver knife and the prison skull blade.

'Captain Scalton?' he said.

Scalton was a slight man with white hair and a long and narrow hook-shaped nose that overhung a neat white beard. His face and hands were spotted with brine marks and his eyes were quick and crowded with humour lines. 'What's this?' he said.

'Part payment,' Granger said. 'If you agree to sell my boss that old blue you've got in your hold.'

Scalton exchanged a glance with one of his younger officers. This man leaned forward and untied Granger's package, revealing the three Unmer daggers. He held one up – the prison skull blade – and then passed it to the captain, who examined it carefully. 'I've seen finer examples,' he said. 'But who told your boss I was a collector?'

Granger smiled inwardly at his good luck. He shrugged. 'It's common knowledge, Captain.'

'And who, might I enquire, is your boss?'

235

'A man of means,' Granger said, 'with guests to entertain. That's all I can tell you.'

The young officer's hand hovered over the dagger, as if afraid to touch it. 'Is it Unmer?' he asked.

'A skull blade,' his captain replied. 'Sometimes called a prison skull. Nasty little thing. It cuts most things just as a normal knife would. But once it gets lodged in bone, it never comes out, never ever releases its grip. And it never stops hurting. I've heard of men hacking their own arms off to get rid of these things.' He turned it over in his fingers, then glanced at the other two blades. 'I suppose they're interesting enough to make a deal,' he said. 'A hundred for the prison skull, and forty for these other two – against four thousand for the dragon.'

Granger let out a long breath. Scalton could sell the blades for four times that in the Losoto trove market. 'That's an expensive dragon,' he said. 'You'd be lucky to get half that for her meat.'

'This one's a fighter,' Scalton said. 'So she's worth more to you than carcass value.' He leaned forward. 'I presume your boss is looking for a spectacle for his guests, rather than simply a main course?'

Granger nodded. 'I'll want to see her first.'

The captain gave a thin smile. 'As soon as you show me those gilders.'

'I won't be trading coin.'

Scalton leaned back in his chair and gave a snort of annoyance. 'Then there's no deal.'

Granger slid his kitbag down from his shoulder and loosened the drawstring. He reached inside and his fingers brushed the cool glass of the shield. He drew it out and placed it on the table before Scalton and his officers. He was pleased to hear from the men a number of involuntary intakes of breath. Every one of their gazes was pinned to the table.

'What does the sword do?' Scalton asked.

Sword?

Granger looked down. Beside the shield lay the replicating sword, cloth still wrapped around it. He had no memory of taking it out or placing it there.

Had the sword *wanted* him to take it out?

'Forgive me,' he said. 'Old habits. The sword is not for trade.' He reached over to take it back.

'One moment, please,' Scalton said. He leaned forward and unwrapped the cloth from the blade. By the light of the tea house's many candles and gem lanterns, the Unmer steel shone with liquid fire. It was obvious, even to a layman, that this was something rare and exquisite. The captain's eyes seemed to drink it in. He reached for the hilt.

'Wait!' Granger said. 'Don't touch it.' He moved forward, with the intention of snatching the blade away before the other man could reach it . . .

. . . but he found that he couldn't. His muscles froze. His hand stayed by his side, and he found himself simply standing there, watching as the captain's hand closed around the sword's hilt and he lifted it from the table.

The replicates appeared at once. However, these were not the mad-eyed and brine-scorched ghouls that Granger summoned whenever he gripped the blade. They were copies of Scalton, appearing in his image. Three of them stood in a half-circle around the table, each holding their own version of the sword in the captain's hand.

The officers all started, shoving their chairs back, scrambling for the daggers, swords or pistols they kept in their belt. Even Scalton gasped and flinched away, as even he reacted to what he must have perceived as an ambush. But then, abruptly, he understood what he was looking at. His eyes went wide with shock and disbelief. 'Good god,' he said, his gaze shifting from one sword replicate to another. 'Lords in heaven and the depths below.'

Granger was equally shocked. The sword had prevented him from simply snatching the blade away from the other man. But *why*? Was it evaluating Scalton's merits as a potential new owner? Granger felt his heart quicken. Would the sword allow itself to be passed on? Would it *release* Granger?

'Move the sword,' he said. 'Carefully.'

Scalton swept the sword in a slow arc before him, and the three replicates mimicked him in perfect formation. By now several of the other tea house patrons had noticed this spectacle, and conversations died on the terrace all around them, replaced by exclamations of surprise or fear or astonishment.

'Now think of three separate moves,' Granger said. 'A thrust, sweep and parry. When you've pictured them in your head, assign each to one of the phantoms. But keep your own sword still.'

'The phantoms?'

'The replicates,' Granger said. 'Sometimes it helps to think of them as ghosts.'

Scalton concentrated. After a moment, each of the replicates moved – this time independently. One swung its blade in a horizontal arc. Another thrust the sword tip forwards. The third, however, remained motionless, still mimicking the sea captain. Every patron on the terrace had noticed the replicates by now, and stopped what they were doing to stare.

'That's good,' Granger said. 'But true mastery of a replicating sword takes time. As your skills improve, you'll find yourself in control of more than three replicates.'

238

'More?' Scalton said. 'How many more?'

Granger recalled the moment one of his replicates had seized his own hand, how hundreds, perhaps thousands, of these sword ghouls appeared – their perceptions crowding his mind, bringing his consciousness to the edge of complete collapse.

'Depends on the wielder,' he said.

'I can command them to do anything?' Scalton asked.

'You can command them to die for you. When that happens, a new replicate appears.'

'Good god.' The captain looked at the blade in awe, completely transfixed by the shimmering steel and its three copies moving in unison. 'I can see why you don't want to part with it,' he said. Then he smiled. 'But if you're after a dragon, I'm afraid you're going to have to.'

Granger's nerves were still on edge, but he experienced a flicker of hope. He would have let Scalton have the replicating sword for free, if it would only release the psychic chains that bound Granger to it.

He was about to say he had no objection when, from the corner of his eye, he saw one of Scalton's replicates move unexpectedly. It bulled forward suddenly, and raised its blade as if to strike the captain.

Scalton flinched.

Granger reacted at once. He snatched up his shield and raised it in front of Scalton, intercepting the blow. The replicate's blade clashed against sorcerous Unmer glass with a spray of green sparks. The shield hummed and then glowed fiercely, throwing a queer emerald illumination around them. Within its facets Granger caught a glimpse of fires raging.

Scalton cried out. Those officers who had been seated now scrambled away in panic.

'Drop the sword,' Granger yelled. 'Now!'

But Scalton wasn't listening. He was gaping at the sorcerous version of himself with a look of terror on his face. Granger barrelled forward between the pair of them, shoving the sword replicate hard with the heel of his hand. Unbalanced, the replicate went over and crashed into a group of nearby naval officers. Granger spied movement to his left. A second replicate was pushing through the group of men to attack.

Granger cursed. He slammed the lower end of the shield sharply down against Scalton's wrist, knocking the sword from his grip. It clattered to the ground.

All three replicates vanished.

There was a moment of silence, while the shock of what had happened percolated through the crowd. Scalton stood there, white faced and wincing, rubbing his wrist. The younger officers seemed just as stunned.

'Like I said,' Granger said. 'Controlling them takes a bit of practice.'

Scalton fixed his wide eyes on Granger. 'They almost killed me!'

Granger shrugged. He cursed his own stupidity. Of course the sword had had no intention of letting him sell it. The truth was that it didn't want him to go to Ethugra and find Ethan Maskelyne. It didn't want Granger to be free. And so it had used whatever hold it had over him to try to sabotage his plans.

And it had almost succeeded.

This thing was more cunning than he gave it credit for. And it was growing stronger with every passing day.

Scalton rubbed his face and looked back at the table. 'What does the shield do?' he said.

*

Granger stood on the steamship deck with the captain and his men, gazing down at the dragon in the hold. She was far older and larger than Granger had expected. Indeed, it was unusual for a serpent of this age to have borne a calf so recently, which made Granger wonder if she had merely adopted the slaughtered youngster. Nor was she a pure blue, not that that made a difference. Her blue-green colouring indicated she was a mongrel, but then those were usually tougher than pure breeds. She was also in much worse condition than the butcher had implied. The harpoon that had brought her down was still lodged in her hind leg amidst a mess of blood. Her snout was bloody, too, the skin pulled back by the steel net in which she had been wrapped, revealing monstrous yellow teeth. Lacerations covered her torso, the bulk of which slowly rose and fell as Granger watched. That movement was the only sign the creature was alive. She wasn't worth one twentieth of the value of the shield he'd given up for her.

'She's half dead,' Granger said.

'Half dead is still alive,' Scalton replied, 'and these animals are tough as hell. Give it a couple of weeks and it'll be ripping men to shreds in the arena.'

'Can she still fly?'

'What d'you want it to fly for?'

Granger didn't answer. By now he had it on good authority that this was the only living dragon in Addle. The other ship had stopped here on its way *to* the hunting grounds. He might, of course, still charter a vessel and head for Doma himself, but that would cost him time – not to mention putting him in considerable danger. He turned to the captain. 'I want to speak to her.'

'You want to what?'

'I'm going down.'

Scalton looked incredulous. He shook his head. 'You know what that thing is, don't you? I mean, you're not labouring under the misapprehension that it's a puppy?'

Granger set down his kitbag.

'Saints below,' Scalton said. 'Well, don't blame me if it roasts you alive.'

Granger climbed down a series of metal rungs in the side of the hold. The hold reeked so strongly of brine that it was hard to breathe. He saw the black gleam of the beast's eye through the metal net and felt the heat emanating from her great body. As he drew near, he became aware of the heavy, ripe odour of blood, the huff and rasp of her breaths, and the stink of sulphur from her nostrils. She did not move, but she was watching him warily.

He crouched down beside her head and spoke in Unmer. 'Can you still fly?'

The dragon made no reply.

'I can offer you a deal,' Granger said.

For a long moment there was no sound from the great serpent but her laboured breathing. And then she spoke in a low, bestial hiss. 'I'd rather die here than suffer the indignity . . . of a life in the arena.'

'That's not what I'm offering.'

The dragon was silent.

'I need you to carry me to Ethugra,' Granger said.

'You would buy my freedom for that?'

'Aye.'

'Why?'

'Because I really need to get to Ethugra,' Granger said.

'So take a ship.'

'I need to get there fast.'

The dragon did not speak again for a long moment. Granger

could feel her hot breaths searing his face. The stink of her flaming venom filled his nostrils. Her black eyes were fathomless and yet it seemed to Granger that they evinced unbearable pain. Finally she said, 'If this net is removed, I will slay this crew.'

'No,' Granger said. 'I can't allow that.'

'These men killed my daughter and sold her body for food.'

'You must swear to leave this crew unharmed.'

'I cannot.'

Granger hissed. 'Then you'll die in a Losotan slaughterhouse.'

'Death would be welcome.'

Granger leaned closer and growled, 'I had no idea your species were so weak.'

The great serpent gave a snort, which might have been of resignation or perhaps even humour. 'You cannot appeal to my pride,' she said. 'I have none left.'

'I'm appealing to your reason,' Granger said. 'Make the deal and live. Hold your revenge for tomorrow.'

Her vast chest rose and fell beneath the net. 'I fail to see the appeal of logic,' it said. 'Tell me, why do you need to get to the prison city so quickly?'

'I am a victim of Unmer sorcery,' Granger said. 'There is a man in Ethugra who might just be able to save my life.'

The dragon was silent for another moment. 'You do look unwell.'

'You don't know the half of it,' Granger said.

The dragon grunted. 'My answer is no.'

'What?'

'I do not care if you die,' the beast replied. 'And I have suffered enough of this life myself. If you release me, I will slay this crew or die in the attempt.'

Granger cursed under his breath. What would it take to convince this cretinous beast to live? He'd already given away a priceless Unmer shield to buy its freedom. And the damn thing actually wanted to die. His thoughts reeled. How to appeal to her?

'You are a mother . . .' he began.

'I *was* a mother.'

'You lost a daughter,' he said. 'And I'm sorry. But if you don't help me, then I could lose a daughter too. I can't protect her if I'm dead, and right now she needs all the protection I can offer.' The sulphurous fumes down here were beginning to make him feel nauseous, but he could see that the dragon was watching him intently. 'My daughter Ianthe is betrothed to Paulus Marquetta. No doubt you've heard of him?'

The serpent huffed.

Granger went on, 'Argusto Conquillas has pledged to kill Marquetta and his uncle Cyr, and anyone else who gets in his way.' He hesitated. 'My daughter has refused to stand aside. She'll try to save her fiancé.'

The dragon's voice was a low growl. 'If Argusto Conquillas decides to kill your daughter, then she will die. There is nothing you could do to protect her.'

'You don't know my daughter,' Granger said. 'Her psychic powers are on a different level to the Haurstaf. She might actually kill Conquillas.' He sighed. 'The point is that this doesn't have to happen. I'm on the same side as Conquillas. Ianthe would be too if she wasn't blinded by Marquetta's looks. She can't see that he's using her. If I speak to Conquillas I can make him understand that my daughter isn't his enemy. And I can only do that if I survive.' He spread out his hands. 'So will you help me?'

The dragon considered his appeal for a long time. Finally it said, 'No.'

'No?'

'I have no desire to become embroiled in this mess of yours. Now leave me to die in peace.'

Granger let out a growl of frustration. He had nothing left to offer, nothing to convince the dragon to help him. He raked his memories. Perhaps there was one more thing. He leaned in closer. 'What if I told you that the prince and his uncle are planning to assassinate Conquillas?'

The serpent yawned. 'It would be more of a surprise if they weren't.'

'They have allied themselves with the shape-shifter Fiorel. He plans to fight Conquillas in an upcoming tournament, disguised as a mortal man.'

'Fiorel?' the dragon said, its voice low and suddenly tense. 'You are sure of this?'

'Yes.'

A fierce growl came from the beast's throat. 'Get me out of this net,' she said. 'I must inform Conquillas. If Fiorel is walking this earth, then the situation is far graver than anyone could have guessed.' It writhed and twisted against the steel links. 'Now release me.'

'Do we have a deal?'

'I will deliver you to Lord Conquillas. After that we part.'

'Conquillas?' Granger said. 'I need to reach Ethugra.'

'We must warn my master first,' the dragon said. 'Besides, if you are truly a victim of Unmer sorcery, then he is the man to help you. There is very little on the subject he does not know.'

Granger stood up. 'Very well,' he said. 'Take me to Conquillas.'

'Let us hope,' the dragon murmured, 'that I can still fly.'

Captain Scalton offered to transfer the ensnared beast by crane to any other vessel of Granger's choosing, but of course Granger had no such transport. His assault craft was nowhere near large enough. If Granger had told the captain his real plan, he wondered if the man would have gone through with the deal at all, shield or no. For Granger planned simply to release the dragon from its net. To this effect he told Scalton that he merely required the beast deposited in the shallows.

Scalton shook his head in marked disapproval of this lunatic plan, but nevertheless ordered his vessel closer to land. They lifted the ensnared serpent out of the ship's hold by crane, and deposited her in shallow crystal-green water a mile south of Addle, where the topography of the shore allowed Scalton's steamer to get in close to land. Then, with thumping engines and loud and filthy exhalations of smoke and steam, the dragon hunter backed away. Her crew kept the bow harpoon trained on the ensnared beast. Only when Scalton had put a reasonable distance between his ship and the dragon, did he send out a team of welders in the tender to cut the harpoon from her flesh. Granger watched their gas torches from the shore. The dragon's tough scale hide was immune to the effects of fire, and it remained still throughout the procedure, even when the crew yanked the harpoon free of its hind leg.

After the job was done, one of the welders waved to Granger. 'Your boss had better send a ship soon,' he yelled. 'There's no refund if the bloody thing dies.'

Granger ignored him. He waited until they were halfway back to the steamer, and then he hopped across the rocks until he reached the netted serpent.

'Don't eat me if I stand on you,' he said.

She grunted.

Granger climbed up one side of the steel net and found the locking clasp that held the draw cable fast. It was tight and would normally have required a hammer blow to open it, but his power armour made the job effortless. He pulled the clasp open with such force it actually sheared, and the draw cable slackened at once, allowing the neck of the net to be opened like a purse. Chain steel links slid from the dragon's back. She moved her tail and forced her back against the heavy mesh.

'Easy,' Granger said. He leaped down from the beast's back and clambered back to shore. He noted, with satisfaction, that the welding team in the steamer's tender were crying out in alarm. They suddenly gunned the engine of their small boat, and it took off, leaving in its wake a broad tail of froth.

Finally, the last of the net fell away, and the dragon's long neck rose, dripping, from the brine. She stretched out her vast gas-blue wings and let the breeze fill them. And then she gave a violent shudder and the sea seemed to fume and mist around her, rising in smoke-like curls from her aquamarine hide. She gazed after the departing crewmen for a long moment, and then turned her long bony head to face Granger. 'What is your name?'

'Thomas Granger.'

'I am Ygrid,' the serpent replied. 'I was a daughter of Hanmer of Ashellomen. You know the place?'

'It's underwater.'

'Everywhere is underwater,' Ygrid replied. 'I haven't been there in many years.' She flexed her wounded leg and grimaced. 'My father was human once, but said he could no longer remember what it felt like. I myself have never known.' She moved forward through the shallows towards him, and then lowered her neck and rested it on the shore. 'I

have always considered myself to be fortunate in that respect.'
She grinned. 'You may sit between my shoulders. Grip the
riding hoops tightly. You are so tiny that I doubt I would notice
if you fell.'

'Are you fit enough to fly?'

'Let us find out.'

Granger climbed onto the dragon's neck and padded up
to the shallow depression between her shoulder blades. There
he found two alloy hoops emerging from her hide. The presence of such metalwork indicated that this was a very old
dragon indeed. The Unmer had driven these pins into her
bones many, many centuries ago, so that she might carry a
dragon lord to war. She was, then, a war dragon. A veteran
like himself. Granger squatted with his knees wide for balance.
He looped his kitbag strap through the hoops and then wound
it a couple of times around his wrist. He felt Ygrid's huge
muscles moving under him as she turned from the shore.

'You are,' she grumbled, 'considerably more massive than
you appear.'

'If I'm too heavy for you . . .' he began.

'And yet still small enough to eat.' She stretched out her
wings on either side of him.

And then she lifted her head and thumped her wings down
against the shallow waters, once, twice, their powerful motions
creating a tremendous gale. Brine-scented air buffeted Granger
as he clung to the hoops in her shoulders. Ygrid thrashed her
wings again and again and now rose from the emerald sea into
a clear blue sky. She turned, her long neck curving to the left
before him, her wings compressing the air with each ferocious
beat, and it seemed to Granger that it wasn't the dragon who
was turning against the world, but the world turning around
the dragon.

'We make for Peregrello Sentevadro,' Ygrid said. 'The Dragon Isle.'

The harbour at Losoto was full of warships. Briana Marks stood on deck with Acanto as the *Silver Flame* rounded the breakwater. On either side of them the ship's oars dipped and pulled through bromic seawater, leaving little spirals of yellow froth in their wake. The docks were crowded three deep with ships of steam and oil and sail, men-o'-war and frigates and huge iron-hulled cannon ships. A great clutter of mast and funnel. The harbour itself bustled with activity as stevedores saw to the loading or refitting of vessels for war.

Acanto smiled. 'Do you suppose word of an Unmer invasion has reached our good emperor?'

'I sent word of it myself,' Briana said. 'Although, to tell you the truth, I'm actually surprised he's got round to doing something about it.'

'Not a man of action, then?'

'Depends on the action,' Briana replied. 'I mean, if it were bathing . . .'

'The man's a walking cliché.'

'He doesn't do all that much walking.'

The coxswain gave a shout and the oarsmen raised their oars and held them above the water. The *Silver Flame* glided to rest in the lee of a privateer frigate. Acanto ordered the anchor dropped and the tender launched.

'I do believe,' Acanto said, gazing at the various ships' flags, 'that the emperor has mustered every single pirate clan.' He grinned. 'I wonder if they are all lodging in one place?'

'That's one party I intend to miss,' Briana said.

'You are averse to thieves, rapists and looters?'

'I'm averse to ships' captains in general.'

The tender motored them across the harbour, heading for a small quay next to the dragon cannery. None of the large hunter ships was presently in dock, and Briana could see up the cannery's massive blood-stained loading ramp to where the steel hooks clustered at one end of the overhead conveyor. With the presence of so many warships, the normal merchant traders had been forced to unload at one small section of the docks, leaving their associates to queue in the open water beyond. Come nightfall, the shore taverns and lodges would be seething with frustration and bitterness directed at these strange and lawless crews. Blood would certainly flow.

'Are you staying ashore?' she asked Acanto.

'I might dine ashore,' he replied.

'I recommend the Solus Tavern,' she said, pointing to a large white building in the centre of the bay. Scores of foreign revellers packed the street outside, drinking and singing. Crews hollered curses at other crews. A few had already succumbed to the booze and were slumped unconscious against walls.

'The place with the large group of cut-throats outside?'

'It's popular,' she said.

Acanto clicked his tongue. 'Anyone would think you're trying to get me killed.'

She smiled.

They landed at the quay, where Briana bid farewell to Acanto. Actually she had grown quite fond of him. He planned to remain in Losoto for at least three days in order to restock his ship, although he admitted it might take considerably longer than that, given this hellish congestion. If she needed him, he would probably be around.

Briana left him and hailed a horse carriage to take her to the palace. Moments later, she found herself relaxing to the sound of hooves as they meandered up the Yanda Promenade with its countless trinket traders on either side. The quantity of goods on display was so great that it seemed as if the shops themselves had burst, outpouring their wares upon the cobbles. At one crossroads she was able to look out west upon the flooded districts of the capitol, where grids of once noble townhouses had been abandoned to rot under the rising brine. They looked like buildings steeped in tea. Further along the coast would be the Unmer ghetto, where three of her peers yet worked for the emperor. She could sense them in the back of her mind, but chose to ignore their chatter and keep her own thoughts veiled from them. They were expecting her, and yet she saw no reason to announce her arrival. She did not want her presence here broadcast through psychic channels.

Of course such discretion might be superfluous, for the future Unmer queen might be looking through her eyes at this very moment. 'If you are a passenger, dear Ianthe,' she said quietly, 'then you've seen the force arrayed against your lover. For his sake, keep him in Awl. At least until he's all grown up.'

'Beg your pardon, miss?' the driver said.

'Oh shut up,' she replied.

The carriage continued to wind its way up the hill. It left the harbour district and reached the birch-lined avenues wherein the master merchants and Losotan businessmen displayed their wealth in grand palazzos. Orange leaves whispered in the wake of the turning carriage spokes. White stone porticoes flanked black iron doors and black ironwork surmounted white stone balconies. Everywhere one looked one saw precision: in the manicured kerbs and balustrades and in arched blue glazing; in alloy beehive doorknobs and gleaming gold bootscrapers; in the birches themselves, placed like rows of flaming spears.

Utterly soulless, Briana thought. She found herself beginning to hate this place, without knowing precisely why. And then it dawned on her. She despised the *conformity* of it all. Hu's palace had been called the mouth of Losoto in wry reference to its occupant's phenomenal degree of consumption, among other things. If the palace was the mouth, then these buildings must surely be its teeth. Tall and white and uniform. Cleaned regularly.

She was still toying with ways to expand this metaphor when they arrived at the palace gates.

The gates were thirty feet high, thirty feet wide and three feet deep, a jungle of metal vines, flowers, thorns, and small creatures painted in a thousand colours. This was one of four entrances through the massive limestone walls that had once formed the old town boundary. They were also, Briana decided, the only gates in Losoto (and probably the world) that could actually induce despair. Despair that someone had actually designed them to look like this. Despair that someone else had wasted many tons of metal in their construction. And then yet more despair that such an extravagantly ugly creation had then been further debased by what looked like a paint fight. The sight of them now made her feel faintly nauseous. Every noble visitor and warlord who came here would see the same sight. It was like reaching the gates of vulgarity itself.

Thankfully, the palace guards waved her through with minimal delay. Even a buffoon like Hu knew better than to try her patience.

The gates closed behind her carriage and the imperial palace loomed ahead of her like a peach and gold mirage. Acres of gardens surrounded them, the floral sprays and whorls of lawn and box hedge dotted with finely carved dragon-bone gazebos and colonnades and statues of warriors and courtesans in chalcedony and pink quartz. Fountains glittered like broken crystal.

Songbirds shrilled and twittered in gilt wire cages hung from an ancient spreading yew.

Briana despised the sickly sweet beauty of it all. Real grandeur, she felt, could only be achieved through restraint.

But then they reached the Caxus Serpent and, as ever, she fell into silent awe.

The Caxus Serpent was the preserved corpse of an ancient sea snake, some three hundred feet long and twice as tall as a man at its thickest. These monstrous serpents pre-dated dragons and, indeed, were known to have been used as a template when the Unmer set about creating the modern beasts. The specimen before her now had been killed by one of Hu's predecessors over eight hundred years ago. Columns of white alabaster held its great maw open and, as the carriage passed, Briana could look deep inside the creature's gullet, where a hundred gem lanterns marked a sinuous path through its fossilized innards. There was, she knew, a small shrine in the snake's tail – a carved statuette in the shape of an old and forgotten god that Hu's antecedent had believed to be patron of the great snakes. They were hunted by emperors as a rite of passage, but also for ashko, the psychoactive drug extracted from their poison glands. The specimen before her now, Briana mused, would have contained enough ashko to get an entire empire high. And that was just a baby.

The carriage passed the snake and finally came to a halt on a red-brick piazza outside the main palace entranceway. Servants of the emperor helped Briana down, paid the driver, and ushered her on through the doors and into a vast antechamber of white and gold stone. Before her, a broad cascade of stairs rose to a circular gallery hung with hundreds of paintings and statuettes on quartz plinths. A second team of manicured youths arrived, headed by a powder-faced old cretin in an ivory frock coat and ruffs.

This man clutched a handkerchief in one upraised hand, as if cautious that the smell of Briana might offend him. He said, 'His Highness Emperor Hu is presently attending a war council.'

'Take me to him.'

'I'm sorry,' the lackey replied in a tone that implied the very opposite. 'But he cannot be disturbed.'

Briana huffed through her teeth. She spoke with slow, cold precision. 'Do you know who I am?'

The servant smiled thinly. 'It doesn't matter—'

'Answer my question.'

He shrugged. 'I presume you are a Guild representative?'

'I am the head of the Guild.'

His smile suddenly disappeared. 'Miss Marks? Oh, I do beg your pardon. His Highness was not expecting you for weeks yet. Please, please, forgive me. I expect that the emperor would greatly value your input at the war council.'

'I'm sure he would,' she remarked. 'If I ever make it there.'

'Yes, of course.' He bowed and fluttered his hands and then led her up the marble stairs to a circular vestibule that formed the jewel in the gallery's ring. Painted images of Emperor Hu looked down upon them, oozing derision. Onwards they swept, through a sparkling corridor boasting a thousand silver mirrors, eventually arriving at a single golden door.

'The council is within,' he explained. 'Please wait a moment while I inform His Highness of your presence.'

Briana ignored him and barged through.

She found herself in a vast hall with three tall windows overlooking the gardens. Before one such window, a group of

people stood around an enormous map of the Anean peninsula set upon a carved oak table. The war council was rather
more eclectic than Briana had prepared herself for. It comprised
Emperor Hu, an admiral of the Imperial Navy, several officers
and court advisers, half a dozen flouncing young noblemen
who looked like poets or artists, together with what appeared
to be a sizeable retinue of their friends, lovers or courtesans
and at least twenty servants waiting at the far wall. In addition to all of these people were four of the emperor's blind
Samarol bodyguards and three score of foreign warlords. It
didn't look like a council so much as a carnival.

The warlords would not have looked amiss deserting a
burning ship with armloads of loot and women. They wore
necklaces of bones and beads or trinkets of glass and silver
and leather skullcaps or wide-brimmed hats, printed head-
scarves or turbans, beaded sword belts and amulets and they
kept their hair in long braids dyed blood red and green or
spun with coloured thread. Tattoos covered faces, arms, necks,
knuckles and lips. Their jewellery clinked and gleamed. A riot
of jewellery. Their mouths contained marginally less gold than
the chandeliers above their heads and also teeth from men
who were evidently not present.

'You!' the emperor cried, stabbing a finger at Briana.

'A formidable deduction, Hu,' Briana replied.

'What are you doing here?'

The servant had followed her in and was about to make
an announcement, when Briana pushed him aside with a raised
hand and a warning glare. 'I'm here,' she said, turning back
to Hu, 'to make sure you don't mess things up.'

The emperor reddened. Several of the warlords grinned.

Briana marched up to them and regarded the map table
with disdain. 'You have one chance, Hu,' she said. 'Hit

Marquetta's armada with everything you have. Crush it before it reaches land. Drown them all.'

'Don't tell me how to fight,' Hu said. He gripped the table in both hands and fixed his gaze upon the map. 'As a matter of fact, we won't need to engage the Unmer at all.'

'*What?*'

Hu pointed to the tip of the peninsula. 'We merely need to station combat psychics here, and . . .'

'You're not using my psychics,' Briana said.

'They're *my* psychics,' Hu replied in a low dangerous tone. 'I pay you well enough for them.'

'Ianthe will simply kill them.'

Hu snorted. 'Here we have the advantage of surprise.'

'Surprise?' she said, aghast. 'What surprise?'

He said nothing, but the murderous glare he gave her was enough to make Briana suddenly regret having taken such a confrontational approach with him. Here before these foreign warlords he had everything to prove. And they themselves would not prevent him from courting disaster. Men such as these resented the empire. They guarded its boundaries and gathered taxes and for that they were given a certain degree of autonomy. But they knew that Hu would act quickly to crush dissent. If Briana was going to convince him, she had to be subtle.

She swallowed. 'Ianthe's powers are growing,' she said. 'The range at which she is capable of detecting and destroying a psychic's mind is now greater than ever.' She took a deep breath, mustering conviction for the lie she was about to tell. 'And it's no longer just Haurstaf who are vulnerable.'

Hu's eyes narrowed.

'Everyone here is in danger,' Briana added.

'She could destroy *any* of us?' Hu said.

Briana nodded. 'With a single thought.' She paused to allow this misinformation to sink in. 'That's why the armada needs to be attacked at sea. As far from here as possible.'

The emperor studied her warily. 'That strikes me as particularly convenient for you, Miss Marks,' he said.

'You think I'm lying?'

'Actually, I do.'

'Then I won't waste any more time here,' she said. 'I'll take my sisters and go.'

'You are lying,' Hu said. 'And what's more, I think you have threatened me for far too long, Miss Marks.' He turned to his bodyguards. 'Seize her.'

Two Samarol warriors rushed forward, their silver wolf's head helmets grinning. They each grabbed one of Briana's arms and held her firmly. She cried out, 'What the hell are you doing?'

'Your psychics are cowards,' Hu said. 'They are afraid to face the Unmer as long as Ianthe is with them. But they do not understand the value of tactics. They're women, not warriors. I need to offer them some . . . what is the word?'

'Discipline?' one warlord ventured.

'No.'

'Motivation,' another tried.

'Yes,' Hu said. 'Motivation. They need to know what happens to cowards in my army.'

'What are you doing?' Briana cried. 'You need us on your side, Hu. Can't you see that? You need me.' As she said this, she broadcast a message to every Guild telepath who might hear it. *Hu has seized me and turned against the Guild. Send help to the Imperial palace in Losoto.* 'What about all the Unmer you have here in Losoto? Who will guard them?'

'I released them.'

Briana's face fell. 'Released?'

'They sailed for Awl this morning.'

Briana was dumbstruck. 'You think that's going to save you? A token gesture of conciliation? Do you really think Marquetta will forgive you for all the years of enslavement?'

The emperor strolled around the map table and came up to Briana. 'I see no harm in preparing for all eventualities,' he said. 'If the Unmer leave us in peace, then we will not pursue them. Otherwise my combat psychics will be ready and waiting. And they will stand firm, Miss Marks. They will fight or they will suffer the same fate as their leader.'

Her throat felt dry. 'What are you going to do to me?'

The emperor smiled. 'I'm going to have you leucotomized, of course.' Then he laughed suddenly, and turned to address the others. 'The Unmer must appreciate the irony of that.' This statement provoked a smattering of laughter and nods from his guests.

'Please,' Briana said. 'Don't do this. I can help you.'

Emperor Hu turned back to her, his eyes still wrinkled with mirth. Briana searched his expression but she could not find a shred of pity in there, only defiance and triumph. 'You will serve me better as a symbol,' he said. He waved to one of the Samarol. 'Do it now.'

The blood drained from Briana's legs. Her heart froze.

The Samarol to her left slipped a nine-inch blade from the loop in his belt. In some dulled corner of Briana's brain she registered it as one of their famous seeing knives. 'Please,' she begged. 'Don't.'

The other bodyguard seized her neck in the crook of his arm. His free hand clamped her forehead. She watched his companion step forward and press the tip of his blade against the innermost corner of her right eye, angled upwards into the brain.

'Don't,' she said.

She felt her body go completely limp with terror. Had the emperor's men not been supporting her, she would surely have collapsed to the floor. And just as her thoughts began to reel she found she had no more time to think.

She felt pressure in her eye and watched the Samarol push his gauntleted fist forwards, sliding the full length of the knife up into her brain. Liquid coursed down her face. She tasted blood.

There was a moment of confusion, while she tried to remember how she'd hurt herself. She sensed heavy pressure behind her nose. They were holding her firmly. Her face was wet so she must have been crying. And then she remembered that they were severing the two lobes of her brain, so she really ought to remain very still in case they made a mistake. She felt the knife moving up and down next to her eye. More liquid – blood – streamed down her face. The vision in her right eye went dark.

And then the warrior in the wolf's head helmet withdrew the blade. Briana felt a surge of welcome relief. There were people all standing about her, looking at her. She recognized the powdered face of Emperor Hu. There were other men who could only be warlords. And servants.

'Should we put the eye back in?' Hu said.

Was she crying?

Briana touched her face. It was wet. Her fingers came away bloody.

'How do you feel?' the emperor asked her.

. Briana stared at the blood on her fingers. 'I'm hurt,' she said. And then she realized that everyone was still looking at her. She smiled shyly. 'What happened?'

The emperor's eyes glimmered. 'You were ill,' he said. 'But we've fixed you now.'

'Thank you,' she said.

'You know,' the emperor said, 'I think I might follow your advice after all.' He turned to an old man who was wearing an Imperial naval uniform crusted with medals. 'What do you think, Admiral? Should we strike them at sea?'

The old man moistened his lips. 'A splendid idea, Your Highness.'

Port Awl's shipwrights had completed their repairs to the Haurstaf man-o'-war, *Irillian Herald*, and there remained no trace of the damage Ianthe's father had caused. She was moored against the dock, her gilt brass fittings as bright as sunlight and her red dragon-scale hull shining fiercely on the crystal-green brine. The water was so calm and clear that Ianthe could see three former harbours down below the current wharf and the ruins of old stone buildings along what had once been the waterfront. Paulus took her hand and led her up the gangway onto the midships deck.

Sailors were busy with a system of ropes and pulleys, loading crates of provisions and stowing them in the hold. A young man walked past with a goat in his arms and smiled at her. Ianthe thought she recognized him from her journey here with Briana Marks.

They climbed some stairs up to the quarterdeck and entered the wheelhouse – a hemisphere of Unmer duskglass – where Ianthe was surprised to find Captain Erasmus Howlish conversing with Duke Cyr.

Howlish was tanned and wore his black hair in a single

long plait. He had sailed under Briana Marks for years, and his easy manner and broad grin implied he was just as comfortable sailing under his new Unmer masters. The man had been a privateer, Ianthe supposed, and therefore used to selling his allegiance. She could still see the raised white lines across the back of his hands where the Haurstaf had once applied their whips.

'Your Highness,' Howlish said.

Paulus acknowledged him with a nod. 'How soon until we leave?'

'Half an hour, if it suits you.'

The young prince nodded. 'That's fine.' He turned to Duke Cyr. 'And how have your own negotiations gone, Uncle? Do you have everything you need?'

Cyr smiled and bowed. 'As we had hoped, Highness.'

Howlish glanced between them, a trace of unease on his brow. 'We stowed the crated cargo as the duke instructed – on the cannon deck and the powder stores,' he said. 'Away from perishable supplies and the crew bunks.'

'Good.'

'Will it require any . . . special attention?' Howlish added.

The prince wafted his hand. 'Rest assured, Howlish,' he said. 'There's nothing in those crates but a few artefacts rescued from the palace cellars: objects that should make our passage somewhat easier.'

'Weapons?' Howlish asked.

'Not exactly.'

Howlish waited a moment, but when it became apparent that the prince had no intention of elaborating, he turned to Ianthe and added, 'Miss Cooper. Do you have news of the whereabouts of the *Ilena Grey*?'

This was the ship on which Paulus's people were sailing

from Losoto. News that Emperor Hu had released the Unmer from his ghettos had come from one of the palace psychics – a pretty girl named Nera, who had so impressed the prince that he'd brought her along on this journey as his personal seer. Ianthe still felt uneasy about this assignation, but was ill placed to speak out against it. Her objections would only be seen for what they were. Jealousy.

'We shall locate the *Ilena Grey* once my fiancée has rested,' Paulus said. 'We have both endured a rather arduous and jarring carriage ride and need to freshen up.'

Howlish nodded to one of his officers, who stepped forward to escort them to their cabins.

Ianthe found herself in Briana Marks's old cabin, with its opalescent walls and floor dusted with crushed pearls. Bereft of all furniture but the bare minimum, it reminded her of the stark simplicity of the operating rooms and recovery wards in the Haurstaf palace. *Monastic* – that was the word. Briana had undoubtedly intended the décor to be restful, but it left Ianthe feeling uneasy. It felt as cold and lifeless as the grave and she was bothered by a unsettling sense that she was trespassing. Briana had been decent to her on that last voyage. Now there was nothing here except painful memories.

As it would not have been seemly for Ianthe to share a bedchamber with her fiancé, Paulus and Cyr had been allocated their own cabins at the front of the warship, as had Nera.

They had brought servants with them. Ianthe's maid, Rosa, was a young Evensraum girl, no doubt chosen for the connection with Ianthe's homeland. And yet despite their common heritage, they rarely spoke. Rosa unpacked her clothes and put them away and then bowed and left. Ianthe didn't even know where the girl slept. And now that her curiosity had been piqued, she thought about slipping into her mind to find out.

But she didn't.

Using her talents to perform espionage in a time of war was one thing. Spying on the staff was something else altogether. And spying on her prince?

The day she did that would be the day their love died.

She thought of Nera suddenly. And in a moment of jealousy she wondered if the girl had been chosen *entirely* for her telepathic ability. But then almost as soon as the thought had occurred to her, Ianthe felt foolish and guilty. She pushed all such corrupting ideas away. She was going to be a queen, after all.

Soon the anchors were raised and the sails lowered and the *Irillian Herald* slipped out of Port Awl on a stiff north-westerly breeze.

No sooner had they cleared the harbour than Paulus sent a message, telling Ianthe to meet him in Duke Cyr's cabin. A few minutes later she was knocking on the cabin door.

Nera opened the door.

Ianthe blinked with surprise. Paulus and his uncle were hunched over a table under the window. Just why *exactly* did they need a psychic present? She tried to smile at the girl. Nera smiled shyly in return, her cheeks dimpling. She flashed perfect white teeth. Her blonde hair shone like silk. Her blue eyes sparkled. Ianthe hated her. 'I know we haven't really spoken yet,' Nera said. 'But I'm sure we'll become good friends on this trip.'

Ianthe nodded. 'I'm looking forward to that.'

'Ianthe,' Paulus said, beckoning her over. 'I've something to show you.'

She wandered over to the table and found that he had laid out four ichusae – the sorcerous little sea-bottles that were the source of all brine. The glass from which they were formed was old and woozy and each had a copper stopper jammed into its mouth. She looked up at Paulus, only to find him smiling.

'What?' she said.

'Well, what do you think?'

She glanced at the bottles again, but this time they held her gaze as suddenly she realized they weren't ichusae at all. Only one of them was actually filled with brine. The others held different things entirely.

In the first she perceived a tiny flickering light. As she peered closer, she saw that it wasn't a flame or any such glow from a wick, but rather a miniature pulse of forked lightning. She reached towards it, but then hesitated. 'May I?'

'Be my guest,' Paulus said.

Ianthe lifted the bottle and stared into it. She could see a tiny cloudscape in there – dark vaporous forms rolling over each other. Lighting flickered between them, illuminating the underside of the clouds. 'It's a storm,' she said.

'Rather more than that,' Duke Cyr said.

'It's beautiful.'

Paulus exchanged a glance with his uncle. 'Think of them as a wedding gift to us,' he said.

'From Fiorel?'

He nodded. 'Look at the others.'

Ianthe replaced the storm bottle and then picked up the next one. This phial held an inch of inky liquid at the bottom – brine, she supposed. Floating on this brine was a tiny model of a ship, no larger than her thumbnail. She had never seen such wonderful craftsmanship. Every last detail of the ship, from its three masts, to the glass in its portholes, was perfect.

'It's wonderful,' she said.

'Look at the third bottle.'

Ianthe complied. The third bottle also contained liquid, but this was clear and completely filled the space inside. Floating in the liquid was a maggot. She frowned and put the bottle down again. 'I'm not so keen on that one,' she admitted.

Paulus laughed.

The fourth bottle held nothing but some sort of yellow gas.

'What are they for?' Ianthe asked.

Duke Cyr cleared his throat. 'We don't yet know. But Fiorel presented them to me in this specific order and told me to open them whenever I felt that we required assistance. The storm bottle must be opened first, followed by the ship, and so on.'

Ianthe examined the bottles again: the storm, the ship, a maggot, and the gas. She looked up at the prince's uncle. 'You brought these back from a dream?'

He nodded. 'In which I met my patron.'

'What does he look like?' she asked.

The old man huffed. 'Well, that usually depends on whatever mood he's in. At the moment he has a penchant for snakes. It is not the most relaxing form to be in the presence of.'

Paulus took her arm and walked her past Nera, and she realized he was leading her towards the door. 'I can stay,' she said. 'I don't have any other plans.'

'My uncle and I must discuss strategy,' Paulus said. 'You'd only find it boring.' He smiled. 'And we would not wish to disturb your search for Conquillas or your father.'

From then on, Ianthe kept mostly to her cabin. She tried repeatedly to find Conquillas, hurling her consciousness out across the oceans in search of him, skipping from the mind of one dragon to another. She spent whole afternoons flying with the great serpents, thrilling at the rush of the wind on their faces, breathing in the bitter fuel-oil stench of their exhalations. But the dragon lord was nowhere to be found. It was as if he had vanished from the face of the world. Her persistent failure began to dishearten her, but Paulus's optimism never wavered. His support for her was unerring. *You'll find him*, he said. *I trust you.* Lately her beloved had been spending a great deal of time with his uncle Cyr. When they were not pondering the significance of Fiorel's bottles they were going through the artefacts they had brought with them from the Haurstaf palace. On several occasions she heard strange mechanical whistles or saw queer lights coming from the gun deck at night. She restrained her curiosity by priding herself on the fact that she did not know what was going on.

So Ianthe kept herself to herself. She read from some of the books she'd brought from the palace. Her literacy had improved considerably since she'd been able to see through her own eyes, rather than piggy-backing the minds of others. Paulus had given her a fine gold chain for her lenses, to prevent her from losing them. He had also showered her with jewels and rings taken from the palace coffers, although if she was honest she considered them to be rather vulgar and so only wore those in his presence. But the chain was different, more personal somehow.

They sailed south-east, taking advantage of the prevailing westerlies, but soon the weather changed and a storm came hurtling down on them from the north. The Mare Verdant frothed and churned, the waves looming like hillocks of tar behind the portholes in Ianthe's bedroom. But she was long used to the sea and had witnessed more violent weather. The booming and crashing of the ocean, the creak and roll of the hull – it all felt strangely exhilarating to her.

The storm continued for two days and was still raging when they reached the dragon nesting grounds of Carhen Doma. That evening she stood with Paulus and Cyr in the *Irillian*

266

Herald's duskglass wheelhouse and watched the huge serpents soaring over the rocky cliffs and the partially submerged temples. Doma was much smaller than the Dragon Isle and had been abandoned by men even before the seas began to rise. The leaden clouds brought an early gloom to the scene, and the dragons filled the air with fleeting and murderous shadows. Rain lanced down and drummed against the wheelhouse panes while out in the distance spume exploded against stacks of black rock. The sea around them heaved like liquid coal, but in the west the dying sunlight suffused and pierced the storm and turned both cloud and brine to flame.

The duke watched with hooded eyes. 'Our presence here will be reported to Conquillas,' he remarked. 'He will see that we move to Losoto, just as we have claimed.'

'You expected an answer from him?' Paulus said. 'Here?'

'Perhaps,' Cyr said. 'He knows Doma lies on our route.' He was silent for a moment, and then his lips drew back and he smiled and pointed up to the tumultuous heavens. 'Could this be it, I wonder?' He turned to one of Howlish's officers. 'My cloak. Goggles. Come, Your Highness. And Howlish, bring your men.'

To the west Ianthe could see a vast winged silhouette turning against the fiery clouds. It had broken away from the main group of serpents and was now bearing down on them.

Paulus hurried into his storm cloak and face mask and pulled a pair of brass navigator's goggles over his eyes. Howlish and two of his officers did likewise. Ianthe glanced at Cyr, then back out at the approaching dragon, and then she grabbed her own cloak and wrapped it around her and hurried after the departing men.

Outside, the wind shrieked and almost blew her across the quarterdeck. She could smell the sea all around her, the bitter tang of metal salts, but also the clean rain driving against her skin. The ship was pitching heavily, ploughing deep into ocean troughs and then rising to burst through the crest of the waves. Storm clouds thundered overhead. Pale blue lightning flickered in the north.

She slipped on wet timbers but grabbed a support rope lashed to the deck hatches and pulled herself after the others, reaching them just as they clambered up the steep stairs onto the foredeck.

From here she had a clear view of Carhen Doma – its cadaverous temples rising from that black and stinking ocean, roofless, their gables broken and battered by brine and spray, mullioned windows gaping. Whale bones and shark bones and the bones of seals lay mounded and glistening under cliffs of wet and rotten stone. Cold gales shrilled. Sunset lay in a red line across the western horizon, a hot wound in the burgeoning darkness, but the clouds above it were dark and copper veined and monstrous. Against these flew the dragon.

It was a red male. As it grew nearer, its great shadow engulfed the ship. All these dark and cruciform shapes that flitted across the storm-blown heavens were truly monsters.

The dragon descended quickly and then braked hard, thumping the air with wings as vast as warship sails. Its hind claws raked the foredeck and then one of them seized the forecastle rail and crushed it. With a great awkward clatter and stink it thrashed one wing again, inadvertently taking out a line of rigging and a cleat, and then it settled on the bow of the ship. Ianthe felt the vessel tilt forward heavily. The timbers gave an ominous groan. And then the serpent swung its long neck down, under the foreyard, where it huffed and glared at the party with eyes like embers.

Paulus stepped forward. 'You have a message for me?'

THE ART OF HUNTING

The dragon brought its head forward until its huge maw was mere inches from the Unmer prince. Rain and brine streamed from its scales and sluiced down in rivulets across its teeth. Ianthe flinched, but Paulus did not. Her sudden movement drew the serpent's attention for a moment. It huffed oily fumes and then grinned.

'Conquillas agrees to enter your tournament,' it said. It turned back to Paulus with a sardonic expression. 'He looks forward to meeting you and your uncle in combat.' Its breath stirred Paulus's hair. 'Provided you can take the capital.'

Paulus wrinkled his nose. 'You smell like a hag's cauldron,' he said. 'Move your stinking face away from mine, serpent, or die here.'

The dragon's eyes narrowed and it bared its fangs. 'This is Doma,' it growled. 'Only a fool would threaten us here. Only a fool would bring a dragon-skinned boat to this sacred place. To our children's nursery.' Saliva dripped from its maw. 'Is that what you are, boy? A fool?'

Paulus stepped forward suddenly, thrusting his left arm out.

Cyr cried a warning.

But he was too late. The young Unmer prince struck the dragon a blow across its muzzle and then lunged forward. There was a great crackling, snapping sound as Paulus pushed his arm *through* the creature's maw and up into its brain. Blood sluiced across the wet deck, spattered the prince's face. He wheeled savagely, teeth bared, and pulled his fist out of the side of the dragon's skull, leaving in its wake a gaping wound through which its lifeblood pumped. In the blink of an eye he had turned the dragon's head into an unrecognizable mess of glistening bone and flesh.

Ianthe cried out.

The great serpent slumped forward upon the warship deck, dark blood flooding from its ravaged tissue.

Howlish and his men looked aghast.

Paulus stood amidst the blood, his chest heaving. He gazed down at his hands. On his face was a grin of such fierce savagery that it sent a shiver of despair into Ianthe's heart. And then he turned to her, his eyes aflame with battle lust. 'They are treasonous beasts,' he said.

'The others will retaliate,' Cyr warned. 'Captain Howlish, have your men prepare themselves.'

'Prepare themselves?' Howlish said. 'Against a dragon attack?' He looked incredulous. 'In this storm?'

'Your Highness,' Cyr said.

The prince appeared not to hear him. He was listening to something in the skies above. To Ianthe it sounded like a chorus of mournful cries and howls of terrible rage. *The dragons.* They were calling to each other.

'Marquetta!'

Paulus turned.

'The amplifiers,' Cyr said.

Paulus nodded, finally shaking himself free of his madness. 'Of course,' he said. And then he turned to Ianthe. 'Go back to your cabin; it's too dangerous here.' Without a further glance in her direction, he hurried away with his uncle, heading below deck.

Captain Howlish gathered a dozen crewmen beside the slain dragon, and between them they started to heave the huge beast over the side of the ship. Ianthe left them. She would watch the battle through the eyes of others.

Back in her cabin she threw herself upon her bed and with a stammering heart she cast her consciousness out into the world around her. For a moment she hovered in the mysterious sea that lay beyond the reach of all perception but her own – its endless darkness dappled here and there by the vision of others. She could see the man-o'-war as a conglomeration of moving images, the external drawn from the crew hurrying about the deck and the internal drawn from those within its hull. Painted like this, the ship seemed vague and ghostly. Ianthe chose a mind at random and hurled herself into it.

She found herself standing at the port deck rail, one sailor among many watching as the corpse of the great red serpent crashed into the sea with an almighty splash and turmoil of foam. And then its huge carcass slipped under the inky brine. Ianthe's host glanced forward to where Howlish stood gazing up at the sky. She leaped into his mind.

And saw two dragons turning inwards, their wings dark silhouettes against an angry storm, lining up for a pass across the length of the ship, where her cannons would be ineffective. A third beast dropped down to join them from high towers of cloud as black as coal smoke. The wind whipped Howlish's hair across his goggles. He pulled his whaleskin cloak more tightly around his shoulders, then ran for the wheelhouse, waving his arm and crying, 'Bring us round, close reach.'

Howlish ran past Paulus and Cyr, who had at that moment emerged from the midship hatch. The prince and his uncle carried between them a narrow crate with leather handles. They set this in the middle of the deck and tore off its lid. It seemed to be full of ash, but then Cyr rummaged about inside and brought something out. He shook it free of dust.

Ianthe found herself flitting between minds to get a better look. Before she realized it, she was inhabiting Cyr himself.

He clutched in his black-gloved fist a heavy iron ring. Parts of the metal had been wound with rotten old wire. Cyr pulled out another one and handed them both to Paulus. Then he took out two more for himself.

He set these down nearby and then reached back into one end of the crate and pulled out a longer object. It was a silver tube, like a flute covered in fine arabesques. The device was divided into several sections that rotated individually, making different geometric connections between separate patterns. Cyr knocked out the ash from inside the device and blew it clean. Then he twisted several of the sections, and peered down the tube. It seemed to be empty.

'Are we good?' Paulus cried against the howl of the wind.

Cyr nodded. 'We're good, Highness.'

'Did you bring Fiorel's gift?'

'The first of them.'

'We might not need it.'

Duke Cyr tucked the metal tube into his belt and reclaimed the two rings from the deck. 'Don't count on it,' he said. 'I don't know about you, but I haven't used an amplifier in a hundred years.'

'I have a feeling it will come back to us,' Paulus replied.

The two Unmer lords now turned to face the approaching dragons. Each held one ring against their side and raised the other aloft.

The three serpents came low under the storm clouds, flying in a V formation, the tips of their vast wings almost reaching the tops of the monstrous black waves. Lightning ripped across the sky behind them. Gales tore spume from the raging seas and hurled it like confetti. The serpents drew nearer: four hundred yards, three hundred, their powerful muscles gleaming in the pre-dark. The dragon on the left was jade green, the one on the right a shade of lamp-oil brown while the centre beast was the largest of the three – huge and black and battle-scarred. At a hundred yards Ianthe could see its dark eyes shining, white teeth flashing. Its neck reared up. It opened its maw.

Cyr brought both amplifiers up over his head and struck them together. The air crackled. Immediately, a translucent green sphere flickered into existence around him; it was about ten feet across, awash with nebular energies. It warped and blackened the boards where it touched the deck. And now Paulus did likewise, and a second sphere appeared around the young prince. An angry buzzing noise surrounded both men. The sailors nearby looked suddenly queasy and afraid. Several of them dropped to their knees, their stomachs bucking.

As the dragons soared over the ship, they expelled from their throats a great deluge of liquid fire.

Paulus and Cyr thrust the amplifiers out and the sorcerous spheres of light around them grew suddenly huge, merging together, enveloping the entire vessel – yards, masts, sails and all – in a shimmering bubble of green plasma. Ianthe's consciousness flitted between the crewmen on the deck, and yet her body remained in her cabin below. She felt the energy pass through her host and then – an instant later – her own body. Her ears popped. Her skin prickled. A sensation of profound nausea crawled through her guts.

Dragon fire exploded across this luminous shield, drenching the skies in flame. But the wooden ship remained untouched. An instant later, the sky raged with a second blast of fire as both remaining serpents unleashed their breaths against the *Irillian Herald*, and again the ship was protected.

The *Herald*'s shrouds and sails shuddered as the three dragons tore overhead. They split formation, the outermost two peeling away to port and starboard. Howlish had been turning his ship to bring their cannons to bear on the serpents, but Ianthe could see that it was a fruitless endeavour. The *Herald* could not hope to match her attackers' speed.

Now both men lowered their amplifiers and the green sphere surrounding the ship suddenly flickered and diminished. Ianthe felt that Unmer energy pass through her once more and her stomach heaved. The air around her was electric. He own skin seemed to sparkle and itch with the aftermath of that weird energy, but the sensations came from a distant corner of her mind. Through Duke Cyr's perceptions she spied sailors writhing on the deck, their arms clenching their stomachs, their red-veined eyes bulging. Only Paulus and Cyr appeared indifferent to this sorcery.

The duke dropped his amplifiers and then took the silver tube from his belt. He pointed this device up at one of the dragons – the brown-scaled beast now banking high to port, thrashing its wings to gain height. Cyr whispered a word under his breath and the Unmer device in his hand activated with a ferocious burst of red light. Then he put it to his lips and blew through it.

It *was* a flute, Ianthe realized.

A great and terrible note resounded across the heavens – so deep and loud it shook every timber within the Haurstaf warship. Ribbons of black and red energy erupted from the Unmer flute and traced a score of arcs across the face of the storm. The serpent veered suddenly and the coruscating energy missed it entirely, tearing onwards through the thunderclouds, punching holes through the sky itself.

'To stern!'

Howlish had come running out of the wheelhouse, shouting and jabbing his arm wildly towards the stern, where the black dragon was once more swooping down on them. 'Your shield, Highness,' he called out. 'The beast is coming.'

'Hold firm, Howlish,' the young prince yelled. 'That serpent's still dry.'

The captain glanced up in dread and disbelief. 'It's not just the fire I'm worried about.'

But Paulus ignored him. He kept his eyes fixed on Cyr, who raised the silver flute to his lips a second time and blew. Cords of fire and shadow poured from the device, sweeping across the sky like the tails of burning comets. Behind them the storm clouds began to change shape, pulled asunder by these weird vortexes of flame. And still cascades of natural lightning tore across the heavens. Thunder pounded the sky, the sea, again and again. Gales screamed. It seemed to Ianthe that nature itself was being twisted, forced to the point of breaking by some ghastly process. Above their heads the sorcerous inferno dissipated.

'Damn this thing,' Cyr shouted. 'I'll need more luck than skill. These serpents are too quick.'

Howlish stood upon the quarterdeck, his cape flickering in the wind as he shouted orders to the second officer in the wheelhouse. 'Fire chasers!' he cried. 'All stations.'

For the dragon was almost upon them and its dark eyes gleamed like hot coals in the light of Cyr's sorcerous fire. It held murderous claws outstretched as if it meant to rip the wheelhouse from the deck.

Flashes of light lit the stern, accompanied by a series of concussions as the *Irillian Herald*'s rear cannons fired.

The dragon swerved. Its fore-claw snagged one of the aft mast shrouds and tore cleats and rigging free. Its vast wings beat spirals in the rising cannon smoke. A sail unravelled from the mizzenmast, snapped full in the gale, and then tore loose and shot out across the seething waters. The chasers had missed, but had at least succeeded in confusing and disorienting the beast. As it thrashed skywards once more, its tail smashed through the upper yards, sending parts of Howlish's ship raining down around panicked sailors.

'Fiorel's gift!' Paulus cried to Cyr. 'Use the first bottle.'

Cyr grinned at him. 'You think this counts as a crisis?'

'A small one, perhaps.'

Cyr reached into the pocket of his tunic and took out the first of the ichusae Ianthe and Paulus had been given as a wedding present. Ianthe could see a tiny storm raging within, a miniature version of the one around them now. Cyr held the tiny bottle aloft and pulled out the stopper.

For a moment nothing happened.

And then from the bottle there came a massive outpouring of energy, bolts of blue-tinged lightning, flaming cords as white as magnesium flares, all crackling, snapping furiously as they tore through the air. For an instant it seemed as if the duke was wielding a storm far larger than the natural one that enveloped then. Overhead, the energy coalesced in a single point – a sorcerous star that drew the ocean up towards it in a great swell. It flared once . . .

. . . then vanished.

As quickly as it had appeared, the lightning had gone – snuffed out like a candle flame. As Ianthe watched, the bulge of ocean collapsed, the waters rushed outwards in a twenty-foot wall of brine that lifted the *Herald* high and then brought her bow rushing back down again.

Cyr bared his teeth. 'What is this? Has Fiorel failed us?'

The prince's violet eyes flashed. 'No!' he cried. 'Can't you feel it? A rift is opening here!' He raised his hand to where the star had been. And now Ianthe could see a knot of some dark material forming there – it appeared to be composed of shifting smoke-like tendrils. She watched it with growing fascination, unconsciously shifting her perceptions from mind to mind to find the best viewpoint. It reminded her of *something*, although she could not say what. It seemed strangely familiar.

Suddenly from the knot there came a great cataclysm of electrical bolts: blazing forks of light in all directions, illuminating the ocean for miles around. For an instant this alien brilliance bleached the gaping façades of Carhen Doma.

Paulus shouted, 'It is Otiansel Mestra!'

Duke Cyr gazed at the scene with awe. 'Fiorel has opened his first domain?'

As the lightning continued to spread across the skies, Ianthe began to perceive shapes within it. *Winged creatures?* Initially she thought she was looking at dragons, but as the things detached themselves from that crackling mass of light she was able to perceive them more clearly.

They were similar to dragons, but smaller. Each of them possessed two sets of wings – wings that, like their lithe bodies, necks and tails, appeared to be entirely composed of energy. Pale fire rippled across their spines and streamed behind them; white flames jumped and flickered with each beat of their wings. They were ethereal, beautiful, terrible. Their heads were smaller in proportion to their bodies than those of dragons, their muzzles more akin to beaks and yet filled with needle-like teeth. They had no discernible eyes.

This did not appear to hinder them.

The black dragon had climbed high above their ship and now banked to face this strange new aerial threat. A cluster of three electric beasts hovered momentarily, as though assessing this flesh-and-blood foe. And then they swooped on the serpent with terrifying speed.

But the dragon had by now produced in its glands

sufficient venom to create more flames. And, as its foes drew near, it disgorged a torrent of liquid fire against them.

The electric creatures passed through this inferno as though it did not exist. They attacked the dragon from three sides, their wings flaming like wraiths against the dark of the storm. In moments they had ripped the serpent apart.

It fell in pieces into the boiling brine.

Its companions fared no better. The brown dragon burst from the base of a thunderhead, diving hard with its ragged wings outstretched, and fell upon a solitary wraith creature. Teeth and claws met pure energy. The creature emitted a furious burst of lightning, and the dragon's scorched carcass crashed into the Mare Verdant.

A few wraiths had by now reached the roofless spaces and temples of Doma and they swept inside, destroying nesting mothers and their young, while others of their kind converged on the site. Ghostlights flickered far across the dark ocean as lightning coursed the heavens and thunder boomed. And scores of dragons rose from those mouldering halls to meet the threat. They must have known they were going to their deaths and yet they did so without hesitation. They clashed with the electric foes and were slaughtered.

Ianthe spotted the blue, flying high to starboard. Six of the wraith creatures were converging on it, mere wisps of light in the ever-deepening gloom. The dragon hesitated for a moment, thumping its great wings as it hovered. And then it turned away from its enemies and folded back its wings and dived, fixing its murderous eyes upon the Haurstaf warship.

'Cyr!' Paulus yelled.

'I see it.'

The duke snatched up the heavy iron rings from the deck and then struck them together above his head. Around him bloomed a plasma sphere, scorching the deck. His brow furrowed with concentration and the sphere grew suddenly large once more, enveloping the whole ship.

Again Ianthe felt a wave of hideous energy flow through her host body and then through her own body in the cabin down below. She no longer knew or cared whose mind she inhabited. But she looked up in time to see that blue serpent bearing down on them in a reckless, suicidal dive. It meant to use its own massive weight as a missile against the ship.

She realized this a heartbeat before the dragon struck the top of Cyr's sorcerous sphere with sickening force. It felt as if the warship had been struck by a hammer blow from the gods themselves. Masts shattered. Timbers snapped. The whole ship lurched and appeared to *buckle*. Cyr's sphere fizzed and crackled with tremendous fury, but it held. And as the serpent plunged within that bubble of spitting energy, it burned – dissolving into ten million points of light.

Ianthe watched the dragon's remains scatter like so many embers.

But she knew something was wrong. The ship had not righted itself after the attack, but was now listing to port at a shallow angle. She saw crewmen race to the port gunwales and peer over the side. Their expressions of concern and alarm terrified her.

Howlish came striding forward. 'How bad is it?'

One of his men replied, 'Looks like her spine is broken.'

'The amplifier,' Cyr muttered, 'pushed the force through to the keel.'

Howlish singled out members of his crew, barking orders as he strode the deck. 'All teams to the bilge pumps,' he cried. 'Raise the mainsail. Get us to Doma if you can.'

'Can we make it?' Cyr said.

Howlish glanced across to where the temples of Carhen Doma stood above the fuming seas, less than half a mile away. 'We'll make it,' he said. 'But this ship is lost.'

The figure had been encased in molten lead and yet was still alive. Maskelyne's crew stood in silence, struck dumb as it heaved itself out of the coffin and fell upon the deck, its skin and clothes still obscured by a film of grey metal. Liquid metal sloshed across the wooden boards. The figure began to convulse.

'Bring helmic acid,' Maskelyne said. 'We need to dissolve the lead, flush it out of his lungs before it cools.'

'That'll kill him,' Howlish remarked.

'One would have expected immersion in molten metal to have accomplished *that* feat,' Maskelyne replied sardonically. 'This situation, by all appearances, lies beyond our expectations.' He nodded to Mellor. 'Get the acid, and plenty of water too.'

His crewmen returned with a barrel of the caustic solution they used to clean marine deposits from trove, along with another barrel of purified seawater. Helmic acid would have taken the skin off a normal man. Yet clearly this was no normal man. They doused him with it and watched in silent awe as his flesh steamed. He bore the agony of it without a sound. It was not a quick process. But after the acid had been applied several times, enough of the dissolved lead had washed away to reveal something of the man beneath. He was stout and dark skinned with heavily muscled shoulders and arms and a neck like a bull's. He was completely bald, and where his skin showed through the lead it was covered in tattoos.

And then suddenly he thrust his arms out, fists clenched, and gave a terrible cry of rage. White light flickered furiously across his skin, accompanied by a ferocious crackling sound. In an instant, the rest of the lead and acid had boiled away.

Maskelyne's crewmen gasped.

The man sat there naked, breathing heavily, as smoke uncurled from skin that looked as hard as old mahogany. His eyes remained closed. Every inch of his body had been inked with the sort of geometric designs favoured by Unmer Brutalist sorcerers.

And that was an enigma.

Maskelyne had just watched the man decreate a film of lead and acid from the surface of his body – an innate power that only the Unmer possessed. But this man was clearly not Unmer. He had the racial features of a Bahrethro Islander: his broad flat nose and strong jaw were as far removed from the Unmer's waifish looks as one could imagine between any two men. Maskelyne had never heard of another race possessing the Unmer's gift of decreation. Yet here he sat, not only able to vanish matter from the cosmos, but also with his body inked in geometries that indicated allegiance to the Brutalist school of sorcery.

Evidently, the Unmer had trained him. And the Unmer *never* trained outsiders.

His eyes remained closed, but he held out a hand and said a word that sounded like *chirfa*. Maskelyne did not recognize the language, and yet he imagined it to be a dialect of Bahrethro. Still, it was clear enough what the man desired.

'Give him water,' Maskelyne said to his crew.

A crewman placed a ladle of fresh water into the sorcerer's outstretched hand, which he downed at once and held out his hand for more. '*Chirfa, chirfa.*'

'Jashu kaval Unmer?' Maskelyne asked.

The man exhaled deeply, then sniffed and opened his eyes. He regarded Maskelyne with fierce curiosity, then shook his head and replied in perfect Anean. 'I'd rather think of myself as a bastard.'

'You're Bahrethroan, then?' Maskelyne said.

He nodded. 'Half so,' he replied. He stood up suddenly and cast his gaze around at the ship and crew. He was a head shorter than Maskelyne, indeed shorter even than most of the men present. And yet his powerful frame looked to be twice as heavy as any of them. His gaze finally rested on the coffin from which he'd come. He looked at it with marked distaste, then cricked his neck and extended one huge hand towards Maskelyne. 'The name's Cobul.'

The metaphysicist shook his hand. 'Ethan Maskelyne,' he said. 'And this is my ship, the *Lamp*. We are currently seventy degrees south in the Mare Lux confluxes. Welcome aboard, Cobul.'

He nodded. 'May I ask, where did you find me?'

'A samal was using you as a hot-water bottle.'

Cobul nodded, as if this merely confirmed what he already knew. 'I owe you a great deal,' he said. 'I thank you, Ethan Maskelyne, and your crew, for coming to my aid.'

'My pleasure,' Maskelyne said. 'May I ask how you came to find yourself in such a . . . eh . . . predicament?'

'I saw something I wasn't supposed to see.'

'And what was that?'

'A murder.'

'You were imprisoned inside that for—' He broke off. 'How long *have* you been in there?' It had to have been decades at the very least, he thought, since that's how long the Drowned had been bringing him keys.

'What year is it?'

'1447 Imperial,' Maskelyne said.

Cobul made a mental calculation. 'Then I have been in the box for close to three hundred years.'

Maskelyne raised his eyebrows. 'Three hundred years of . . .' He glanced at the box. 'I suppose it would be no exaggeration to say *severe discomfort*, merely for witnessing a crime. One would have thought it would have been kinder just to kill you.'

'Indeed.'

'May I ask who this scoundrel is?'

'A god named Fiorel.'

'The shape-shifter,' Maskelyne exclaimed. 'Cauldrons and what not, isn't that his thing? Who did you see him murder?'

Cobul studied him a moment. 'Knowing that would put you at great risk.'

'Because Fiorel has assumed their form?'

'It was during the dragon wars,' Cobul said. 'After we realized the Haurstaf would defeat us, when all hope had been lost. I was a unit sorcerer with King Jonas's Third Division. We were fleeing Losoto into the Anean foothills when our party came upon Fiorel. He appeared as a faceless man walking the trail. Jonas spoke with him all night and most of the next day. They made some kind of a deal. Fiorel gave the king the means to create ichusae. He saved our race from the Haurstaf.'

'And do you know what Fiorel wanted in return?'

'No, but I can guess,' Cobul said.

'Argusto Conquillas?'

Cobul nodded. 'The man who killed his daughter, Duna.'

'Something went amiss, I take it?'

'I do not know,' Cobul admitted. 'King Jonas consulted with the god and then sent our last bonded dragon west, presumably to deliver a message to Conquillas and Aria in Awl. That is all I know of their scheme. Later that evening I happened, by sheer chance, to witness Fiorel's villainy.'

Maskelyne tapped his fingers against his chin. 'I'm guessing he murdered someone close to the king?' he said. 'Someone in the royal party? After all, it would do Fiorel little good to assume the form of the camp cook. He must have . . .' Suddenly he stopped. 'If a shape-shifter could replace anyone he chooses, then the most logical candidate would be King Jonas himself.' He looked at Cobul.

He nodded.

'But Jonas vanished. He boarded the prison ship in Losoto, but never made it to the dungeons in Awl. The Haurstaf claimed he jumped overboard.'

Cobul pondered this. 'I saw Fiorel murder the king and assume his physical form,' he said. 'And it was in that disguise that he had me confined in that coffin and dropped into the mouth of a samal. If he vanished on the voyage to Awl, then he has clearly assumed another form and escaped. I imagine he went after Conquillas.'

'Well,' Maskelyne said. 'Evidently something went wrong with his plan, because Conquillas is still alive.'

Cobul frowned. 'Alive? Are you sure?'

Maskelyne nodded. 'And as jovial as ever.'

Cobul was thinking. 'Then he has delayed his revenge for some reason. You must fill me in on all that has happened these last few centuries.'

'It would be my pleasure,' Maskelyne said. 'But answer me one last question, please.'

The sorcerer nodded.

'Why on earth,' Maskelyne said, 'did the Drowned want me to come and get you? How did you convince them? What sort of deal did you make with them that their rotting minds could possibly understand?'

Cobul had a grim expression on his face. 'I made no deal,' he said. 'Until this moment I did not even know that the Drowned had acted in my interests. I imagine the truth is that they simply wanted me gone from their domain.'

'Why?'

The sorcerer looked embarrassed. 'Presumably my screaming made them uncomfortable.'

Captain Howlish managed, against all the odds, to run the *Irillian Herald* aground in shallow waters beneath the ruins of a huge stone hall. The landing had smashed her hull beyond repair and now each wave pitched her further against vicious rocks and threatened to tear her apart entirely. Howlish ordered the corbuses lowered and the lifeboat unlashed and dropped, and Cyr organized a hurried evacuation and soon they had decamped most of their provisions onto a broad ledge above the darkly surging waters.

Night was fully upon them now and the surrounding halls and temples of Doma revealed themselves as hulking slabs of darkness briefly silhouetted against the intermittent lightning – or else as grey and crumbling façades burned into the retina. The sea hissed and the winds moaned through empty doors and windows, turning the buildings into so many monstrous throats.

Ianthe took a gem lantern, wiped her lenses clear of brine spray and clambered up some rocks near where they'd made their camp. She soon found a doorway in one wall of the derelict hall and ventured inside. The structure held four nests – crude curved embankments of mortared stone and whale-bones set against the lower walls. The air was rank with the dense musk and blood odour of the dragons. But Duke Cyr's entropic wraiths had left nothing alive. Ianthe wandered among the scorched remains of old and young dragons, blues, greens. She had no idea how many of them had been killed in here, but it seemed to be far more than the number of dwellings would suggest. Evidently other adults had come to the aid of their neighbours' young.

She climbed up the edge of the nearest nest and peered down into it. All three of the eggs had been smashed open revealing the dog-sized pink foetuses within.

It was the same story, she discovered, for the other nests.

She sensed someone watching her and turned to see Paulus standing in the dark a short distance away.

'They destroyed the eggs, too,' she said.

He nodded. 'You feel pity for them?' he asked. 'The young?'

'Don't you?'

'Of course.'

Lightning coursed across the skies, illuminating the vast hall and the broken bloody corpses within. A moment later, the ruined walls resounded with thunder.

'Still no sign of your father?' he said.

The question took her unawares and she hesitated a moment before finally answering. 'There are a lot of people in the world.'

He gave a slight shrug. 'I would understand if you didn't want him found.'

'No, it's not that. It's just . . .'

He waited.

'There are so many people,' she went on. 'More than I could ever hope to visit. And sometimes it's hard to reconcile the visions that I see with the real world. Particularly if there are no landmarks to go by. It's the same with the *Ilena Grey*, harder even . . .'

'It's a big ocean,' he conceded. 'And she might not even sail upon it.'

'You think she could have sunk?'

He shrugged. 'More likely we simply haven't found her yet.'

'But what if we don't find her? Or we can't contact them? How will we escape?'

'We have another ship, Ianthe.'

She gave him a puzzled look. 'What ship?'

'Our wedding present. Cyr is preparing to uncork it now.'

'The bottle?' she said. 'You mean the ship in the bottle?' As outrageous as it seemed, she forced herself to consider it. If a great flock of wraiths had come from the first bottle, could a usable ship come from the second?

Paulus approached her, stepping carefully over the blasted ground. 'The bottles are not unlike ichusae,' he said. 'They act as doors between one place and another. Each of these four bottles accesses a different artificial universe created by Fiorel. They are far smaller and more fragile than our own cosmos. Opening the bottle unleashes whatever is stored there.'

'Fiorel made those wraiths?'

'And the ship, and whatever lies in the other bottles.'

'But how did he know we'd need these things?'

Paulus shrugged. 'The gods are ancient and wise. Fiorel knew that we would pass Doma on the way to the Anean peninsula. Perhaps he anticipated my reaction and the subsequent battle.'

Ianthe thought about this. She couldn't see how anyone could have predicted Paulus's violent outburst that had led to their present dilemma. No one but Paulus himself.

'When the battle raged,' he said, 'were you ever inside me?'

She didn't answer at once. It had all happened so quickly. And in the chaos she had leaped from mind to mind. Had she been inside her lover at any point? 'No,' she said, honestly. 'I made you a promise.'

'What does it feel like?'

'Like this,' she said. 'Like life. Except you're carried. You are there . . . but without control. A passenger.'

He leaned forward and whispered in her ear. 'Do it now. Move inside me.'

'I swore to you I wouldn't.'

He placed a hand upon her cheek. 'I want you to,' he said. 'Just this once. I want to see if I can feel you inside me.'

Ianthe shivered. She could feel his breath upon her neck. And then he pulled back and gazed into her eyes.

She slid her mind inside his own.

And saw herself exactly as he did – a dark-eyed girl, at once sad and fearful and breathless. 'You are there now?' he said. 'Inside me?'

She watched herself nod slowly.

'You see what I see?'

Another nod.

'And feel what I feel?'

He smiled and then leaned forward and kissed her deeply. And then he eased her back against the wall and slid his hands down her body. He lifted her dress. She felt his fingertips between her thighs, each delicious sensation coming to her through a wonderful union of both his senses and her own. He pressed hard against her. She clung to him desperately and shuddered as he pushed inside her.

'How does it feel?' he said.

Her breaths were fast and hard against his neck. She inhaled the scent of him.

He whispered in her ear, 'How does it feel to fuck someone who could kill you in an instant?'

Ianthe smiled. She drew her hands more tightly around him and pulled him deeper inside her.

Ianthe and Paulus returned to the camp to find that Howlish's men had erected a crude sailcloth shelter to protect them from the worst of wind and rain. The prince's uncle, Duke Cyr, had not availed himself of this shelter. He was standing on the edge of the rock promontory, gazing out at the brooding storm-lit sea.

He turned at their approach, and it seemed to Ianthe that he gave the young prince a questioning glance. And yet perhaps she imagined it. A degree of paranoia accompanied her racing heart. A part of her could not help but wonder how anyone gazing upon her flushed and breathless face could *not* instinctively know what had transpired. She had undergone a change so profound that its effect must yet radiate from her.

'Success, Uncle?' Paulus said, in an oddly flat tone that made his words sound – to Ianthe's presently overly sensitive mind – more like a statement than a question.

'I was awaiting your return. If it pleases you, I will open the rift now.'

'Do it. I am growing tired of this rock.'

The duke nodded. From his pocket he brought out the second bottle and held it up before them. It was hardly bigger than his thumb. Inside it, Ianthe could see the tiny ship floating upon a finger's width of brine.

The duke carried the little bottle down to the edge of the sea, where he asked Paulus to raise his gem lantern. By its light he pulled the stopper free from the bottle and peered intently at the contents. He said, 'As I thought.'

'Reflected light?' Paulus said.

'Indeed. Thankfully there's no need to venture closer.' With that he merely set the bottle down on a rock and waved Paulus and Ianthe away.

They clambered back up the rocks to the camp.

'The ship was never in the bottle,' Cyr said. 'Merely the light it reflected.' His gaze scanned the dark waters and then he stopped. 'There,' he said, pointing. 'There! There it is. Yet again, Fiorel has anticipated our plight and come to our aid.'

At first Ianthe saw nothing. But then another flicker of lightning tore across the night, and by that illumination she caught a momentary glimpse of *something*. A mass of faint white lines hanging over the sea? Weblike, but chaotic – without discernible shape. And then full darkness returned to swallow the vision.

But, no . . .

Some trace of it still remained. The lines, she now perceived, were becoming brighter with each passing moment. And yet more of them appeared, gossamer-like, forming in the air a hundred yards from where Ianthe stood. Like a phantasmal drawing, something was taking shape out on that black ocean. And, as she watched, it became recognizable. *A pale and ghostly sailing ship, wreathed in ethereal fire.* Her four masts and square-rigged sails identified her as a barque, albeit of an unusual and seemingly archaic design. She was much larger than the Haurstaf man-o'-war they had so recently been forced to abandon – heavier, bulkier and yet infinitely more insubstantial. Her decks and masts were not constructed from timber and iron, but from the ghosts of those materials. Her hull seemed formed from lightning and liquid fire. Her masts and shrouds were opaque, mist-like. There were moments when Ianthe thought she could see clear through the whole ship.

Upon her decks there stood strange cannon-like devices, each formed of the same pale energy and fronted with a series of sparkling discs.

And how she burned!

Streams of pale fire coursed across the barque's timbers and played in her rigging and shrouds. Every nail and knot and dowel crackled with the same mysterious ethereal energy. And yet down below the waterline, where the keel met the brine of the Mare Lux, the white flames became fierce and angry – a mass of bonfire golds and reds that gave Ianthe the uneasy impression of a funeral barge recently set alight.

'Fiorel has a morbid sense of humour,' Duke Cyr remarked.

Ianthe frowned. 'How so?'

The old man pointed. 'See the name etched on her bow?'

It read: *St Augustine*.

In response to Ianthe's puzzled frown Paulus said, 'Cyr's patron has conjured us a ghost ship. The *St Augustine* has a dark past. She was once a plague ship. King Uten the First requisitioned her to carry plague victims from Galea to an isolated colony on the Herlon coast.'

'Over a thousand years ago now,' Cyr added. 'Before the seas began to rise.'

'But there never was a colony,' Paulus said. 'It was merely a ruse. A frigate of the king's navy escorted her for three days out into the open sea. On the fourth day they opened fire on her. The *St Augustine* sank, taking all eight hundred souls onboard with her to the seabed.'

'That's awful,' Ianthe said.

'But it wasn't the end,' Paulus went on. 'If the stories are to be believed, then the *St Augustine* has been seen many times since then. Her appearance was always said to foretell disaster for any who spotted her.' He leaned closer and lowered his voice. 'Fiorel has given careful thought to this name. Enemies of ours who look upon this ship will see her as a harbinger of doom.'

She nodded. 'Why does the ship glow?'

'It is wrought from light,' Paulus said.

Ianthe looked back at the ship. It burned with ghostly fire, lighting up the seas all around. Indeed, its very fabric seemed to surge between solid and ethereal, fading in and out of existence before her eyes. She could see the waves crashing against its fiery hull, but occasionally she'd catch glimpses of the sea *through* that same hull. It remained, to her eyes, a phantom vessel.

All except in one place.

There was a cubic object within the ghostly timbers – a box or perhaps a room – that appeared consistently solid. While the vessel around it phased back and forth between the corporeal and the ethereal, this one component remained a solid white block. At no point could she see through it.

Captain Howlish and his men had seen the apparition too and now gathered on the promontory around Ianthe, Paulus and Duke Cyr. Howlish said, 'I've seen Valcinder magicians pull whistles from the air, but never a ship.'

Cyr grunted. 'Whistles we don't need.'

'Well, I applaud you, sir,' Howlish added. 'And your good sense. That barque, I see, is well anchored.' He hesitated. 'Assuming it is more substantial than it looks, we'll pull the gear across at first light.'

Cyr wandered over to one of the crates that they'd rescued from the *Irillian Herald*. He grabbed one of the heavy metal rings he called an amplifier and then rummaged around until he found a gem lantern and what appeared to be a small stone sphere on a chain. He slid the ring over his hand and wore it like a huge bracelet. And then he attached the chain to a hook in the lantern's peaked cap. When he released the stone, it floated upwards, pulling at the lantern as though it meant to carry it skywards. Cyr opened one of the gem lantern's metal shutters.

The crewmen gasped and shielded their eyes or else turned away from the fearsome glare emitted by that lantern. Its wide beam shone far across the waters. Then Cyr opened the other two shutters and released the lantern. It floated upwards, blazing like a small sun.

Ianthe marvelled at the sudden change in her surroundings. The sky above remained black and dense with thunderheads, but here the sea now shimmered like the brightest jade, and the halls of Carhen Doma basked in strange daylight.

Cyr turned to Howlish. 'First light,' he said.

The gem lantern remained hovering in the air, several hundred feet above them, for several hours – which was more than enough time, as it turned out, to ferry people and supplies out to the *St Augustine*. Howlish's men regarded the barque with unease, cautious of the spectral inferno that rippled across her bulwarks and yards and even plucked at their own boots as they carried cargo across the decks.

Ianthe stood on the deck with the prince and his uncle, while Howlish's men worked around them. The translucent timbers beneath their feet emitted an eerie glow, and yet they supported their weight as effectively as any plain wooden board. Howlish had sent men to explore below decks. Now he turned to the prince and said, 'We could plunder the *Herald* for more supplies, if you like, but it's a risky business in these seas and we've more than enough food and water now to reach Losoto.'

Paulus's eyes were inscrutable, but Ianthe had the feeling

he was weighing something up. 'No, you are quite correct,' he said. 'Let's not linger here a moment longer.'

'Captain.' The call had come from behind, and Ianthe turned to see one of the crewmen peering out from an open hatchway built at a forty-five-degree angle to the deck, through which steps led down into the ship's interior. 'Your Highnesses, My Lady,' he added quickly, 'we've found something odd down below.'

'*Odd* in what way?' Howlish asked.

'It's a room of mirrors,' he replied, glancing between the captain and the two Unmer lords. 'I'm not sure how best to explain it. You really need to come see it for yourself.'

He led them down the steps, which then turned around and descended a second flight. They arrived in a short wooden passageway from which there led many doors – cabins, Ianthe supposed. The walls around her glowed with soft ethereal light. The sailor, whom Howlish introduced as Gaddich, then brought them to a single door at the end of the passageway, where waited another, younger, man.

Gaddich picked up a gem lantern from the floor and opened the door to admit the party.

They found themselves in one of the strangest rooms Ianthe had ever seen. It was about ten paces across on each side, and yet seemed infinitely larger, for both the floor and the ceiling of the room each consisted of a single huge and flawless mirror. This arrangement of mirrors produced an optical illusion. To look up or down was to see countless copies of the room and its occupants, each marginally smaller than the last one and stacked one upon the other to infinity. The walls of this strange room consisted of regular panels of some dark and polished hardwood. And in each panel there hung yet more mirrors – these of varying shape and size and age and yet all presented in exquisitely carved gilt frames. There were four on each wall and two more flanking the door, fourteen in total.

It was only then that Ianthe realized something was different here. Neither the mirrors nor the panelling upon the walls looked unusual: they did not glow nor pulse nor coruscate with ethereal flame. This was the only room in the ship that looked perfectly normal.

'It gets weirder,' Gaddich said. 'Have a look in one of the mirrors. Any one you like.'

The party separated, each approaching one of the mirrors hung upon the walls, except for Ianthe, who clung to Paulus's arm and walked with him. The first gasp came from Captain Howlish . . .

. . . and before she realized it, she had cast her own consciousness into his mind . . .

He was looking into the mirror and yet the mirror did not return a reflection of his face. Instead it showed a ghostly figure peering out from darkness. The visage before him could almost have been human – perhaps distorted by some warp or sorcery within the glass. Otherwise he was looking at the true image of an alien being. It had a long backward-sloping forehead and an out-thrust chin as sharp as a horn. Its flesh was as hard and white as bone, its eyes oddly elongated and wholly white with mere pinprick dots for pupils. It had its mouth open in a peculiar smile or grin, revealing too many tall and narrow teeth.

She heard Paulus give a sharp intake of breath . . .

. . . and returned her mind to her own body . . .

Her fingers were clutching Paulus's sleeve. The mirror before her now was larger than the one into which the captain had been gazing. And in this glass she perceived something even stranger and more terrible than the apparition Howlish had witnessed.

Again it stood against darkness. But this monster lacked any hook by which one might attach it, however tenuously, to humankind. It was a writhing mass of blood-red tentacles – more like some hideous nest of engorged leeches than a single organism. And yet Ianthe saw that the part before her now was merely a fraction of a much larger creature – the tip of an arm that was itself one of countless more such appendages that flailed in the deep abyss behind the glass.

Other looking-glasses held yet more horrors: one human-like but horned and bestial and clad in mountains of bronze armour, another corpse thin and encased in a queer geometry of metal wire and glass, a spinning box from which peeled arcs of light, pulsing blue things like squid, a vast maze of grey stone paths wreathed in lurid green veins of vegetation. This last structure retreated for untold miles into the void.

In the periphery of Ianthe's mind, she sensed all of them lurking nearby. Even the maze had a discernible presence. Their minds were oddly distant and yet, at the same time, terrifyingly near, as though they inhabited a rift or fracture in the Sea of Ghosts. She understood the mirrors to be membranes through which she could propel her own consciousness if she chose to. But nothing in the world could have persuaded her to send her mind into any of those foul intelligences.

'They are travellers,' Cyr said.

'Travellers?' Howlish said. 'I don't understand. What is this place?'

'It is merely a viewing room,' Cyr replied. 'Entropic sorcerers once used such chambers to gaze into the void that lies beyond the universe. To stare into the infinite dark. The travellers you see before you now have ventured into that void and become trapped, or else they were exiled there. These mirrors are used to lure them to this boundary, so that one might learn from them.'

Howlish stared in horror and disbelief. 'Learn what?'

'Whatever can be learned.'

'Is it safe?' Howlish said.

Cyr frowned. 'In what way?'

'I mean, can they get out?'

'No,' Cyr said. 'They can never escape.'

Howlish gave an immense sigh of relief.

Cyr smiled. 'Come, now, I suggest we lock this room and forbid the crew from entering. There is nothing to be gained here.'

They left the room and, after a quick search, located a padlock for the hasp. Cyr locked it and took the key himself.

It was only later, when Ianthe found a moment alone with Paulus, that she asked him, 'Did the original *St Augustine* have a room like that?'

He seemed momentarily startled. 'No,' he admitted. 'She would have been a merchant vessel.'

'Then why should such a room exist now?'

'Because this is Fiorel's own ship.'

'He made it for himself?' she asked.

Paulus smiled. 'A fine wedding gift, don't you think?'

CHAPTER 7

YGRID

Ygrid soared over the Mare Regis and Granger knelt between her shoulder blades and clung to the alloy hoops in her spine. His cloak was sodden and heavy with rain and pulled at his shoulders in the icy, rushing air. The plates of his armour chilled and grated his brine-burned shoulders and his gauntlets chafed his wrists, but he knew that without their sorcery he would have collapsed with physical exhaustion days ago. And yet there was no escape from mental exhaustion. Another sleepless night had taken its toll on his nerves. He had to rest, and rest soon.

When he pulled off his gauntlet to examine his hand he saw that his flesh looked grey and dead and he could not move his fingers at all. He struggled for a while, concentrating with all his might, trying to force one finger to twitch, but he failed. The effort left him gasping with pain and exhaustion.

He pulled the gauntlet back on.

The dragon's great wings stretched out on either side of him, glimmering aquamarine in the morning sun. The ocean below was an immense crimson slab that changed to the clarity of thin wine in the shallows around the island of Peregrello Sentevadro.

There were other serpents in the sky, but they kept their

distance. Granger could see them towards the south, their wings folding as they dived, their long lithe bodies plunging deep beneath the poison waves in explosions of candy-coloured froth. They would not be hunting for food this close to the Dragon Isle, for they would long ago have stripped the seas here bare. It seemed more likely they were tending to some ichusae hoard, supping at the source of the very drug that had corrupted the oceans of the world.

Ygrid had hardly spoken for the duration of the trip, but now as they neared this mass of black rock and scallops of beach she said, 'Conquillas is absent.'

Granger shouted over the wind. 'How do you know?'

'There are signs,' she said. 'Signs a dragon can read.'

'Well, where is he?'

Ygrid made no reply. As she banked in the air, the sunlight flashed briefly across the scales of her back and over Granger, and for one glorious moment he felt warm. And then she swooped down into the shadow of a vast cavern in the island's cliff face. Her powerful wings thumped at the air, raising a storm of grit and sand and sending smaller stones scuttling across the uneven ground. And then she landed.

Ahead, Granger could see a rare and antique Unmer yacht set amongst pillars of black rock and the scattered bones of the Drowned. A vessel such as this was old enough to have sailed untainted seas. She was exquisitely crafted. Her grey wooden hull still possessed its original metal scrollwork cladding. One of the duskglass portholes lay open and from this he could hear music. Someone inside was playing a lute.

Conquillas?

A sudden loud and bestial *huff* grabbed his attention.

To the right another dragon appeared. He was a young male, half the size of Ygrid, and had been lying curled in a hollow as black as his hide. Now he uncoiled his slender body. His claws shifted a mound of skulls and bones that spilled and clattered across the rocky ground. He raised his head and gave a low growl, followed by a curious clicking sound.

Ygrid reciprocated, making a similar noise.

It seemed to Granger that they were talking in a language he had never encountered before.

Ygrid seemed troubled by whatever was said. Finally she turned to Granger and said, 'Conquillas is unavailable. No one will be able to reach him until Marquetta's tournament in Losoto next month.'

'Next month is no good,' Granger growled. There was no way he would be able to hold out against the sword that long. He might only have days, perhaps a week, before it had complete control of him. He could no longer even use the blade. His own replicates now obeyed the weapon, not him. He shot a glance at the yacht's open porthole. 'I only want to speak to him.' He spoke loud enough, he hoped, to alert the lute player within the yacht, for it must surely be the man he sought.

Now the smaller dragon bared his fangs. 'Your daughter has made this necessary,' he said to Granger. 'Our master does not want to be spied upon. Nor does he want to be targeted by assassins. And, as much as I imagine he's deeply concerned with your predicament and anxious to help you, Colonel Granger, we have our orders. Conquillas is indisposed until the contest. No dragon will help you locate him before then.'

Granger glanced at the yacht again. The music had stopped. 'Your master is in great danger.'

'Conquillas likes it so,' the black serpent said.

'There is no way to send him a message,' Ygrid said. 'We must wait until he resurfaces before we can warn him. Or else we must expose Marquetta's plans at the tournament. Let it be known that Fiorel himself intends to be among the competitors. Perhaps we can force him to reveal himself.'

'But what about me?' Granger said. 'I can't last till then. You must take me to Ethugra.'

Ygrid's great neck curled and she brought her head down to Granger's level. He turned away from her chemical exhalations. She said, 'You pin your hopes on Ethan Maskelyne?'

Granger cast another glance at the yacht. 'Do I have a choice?'

Ygrid spoke with the other dragon in that strange language for a few moments. It seemed to Granger that the small male chuckled. Finally Ygrid turned back to him. 'Ethan Maskelyne is not in Ethugra. His dredger was spotted passing the Clutching Rocks, three days to the south of the prison city.'

'Will you take me there?'

'This news is over a week old. He might be anywhere by now. I will take you to Ethugra if you still desire, but I think you should travel onwards to Losoto to await Conquillas's arrival. If he knows Ianthe's father is looking for him, he might seek you out.'

Granger frowned. *Ifs* and *mights* were not good enough. He didn't like being fobbed off. He glanced over at the yacht again. He could hear music coming from the vessel again.

He untied his kitbag from Ygrid's saddle hoops. 'Let me stretch my legs while I consider your offer,' he said. 'My joints are frozen solid.'

Ygrid bowed and pressed herself flat against the ground, allowing Granger to clamber down her spine and slip off her tail. He hefted his kitbag over his shoulder and then walked around to her front. 'Might I use the yacht's head?' he asked, inclining his head towards Conquillas's boat.

The dragon shook its head. 'I do not possess the authority to grant that request.'

'Two minutes,' Granger said.

'I'm sorry.'

Granger grunted and mumbled under his breath, 'Can I at least take a shit among the goddamn rocks, then?'

'Of course,' Ygrid replied. 'But do not wander far.'

Granger wandered in the direction of the yacht. As he did so, he slid the kitbag from his shoulder and let it drop.

He picked up his pace.

He felt the air stir suddenly, and Ygrid's voice growled behind him. 'Do not approach that yacht, human.'

Granger exploded into a run.

'Stop!' Ygrid cried.

He scrambled up the rocks towards the gangplank, sensing a change in the light as the huge dragon moved behind him. He glanced back . . . to see Ygrid clawing across the rocky ground towards him, closing the gap quickly. He had to hope his shield would repel her fire.

Granger reached the top of the outcrop and pounded across the gangplank.

A hatch led below. Granger rushed across the deck towards it, his muscles tense, the whole time expecting a deluge of fire at his back. His metal boots thundered across solid planking. And still the fire did not envelop him. He reached the hatch and pulled it open just as a shadow loomed overhead.

Granger leaped down six steps and landed hard in the passageway below. He rolled to break his fall, and came to rest on his back, staring up at the open hatchway, and the dragon beyond.

Ygrid glared down at him with murder in her eyes. Her teeth were as large as the opening through which Granger had just passed. Her breath filled the passageway with noxious vapours. She could have burned him to ash where he lay, or ripped the yacht to splinters to get to him.

But she didn't.

For either of those actions would have wrecked her master's home.

She did, however, speak. 'Conquillas is not at home, you fool,' she roared. 'He is not on this island. Your actions have earned you nothing but my distrust.'

Granger got to his feet.

The dragon was probably lying. *Someone* had been playing that lute, and he meant to find out who. He turned away and opened a door at the end of the passageway.

Beyond the door he found a sumptuous parlour with walls inlaid with tropical woods and metal. Dozens of tiny gem lanterns hung from ceiling joists carved to resemble whale bones. In one corner stood a lacquered white harpsichord – one of many delicate objects and furniture situated in this chamber. On a stool next to the harpsichord sat a young girl.

She was younger than Ianthe, perhaps twelve or thirteen years old, and she held a lute in her small pale hands. Her bone-white hair and fair skin were clearly Unmer, as were her violet eyes, and yet she had a rounder, fuller face than most of her kind. Granger suspected her blood might possess a hint of human ancestry.

On seeing him, her eyes widened with alarm, and she rose sharply from the stool, clutching her instrument to her chest. There was a crackling sound and the strings snapped suddenly, loudly – like a series of gunshots. The girl cried out and dropped the instrument.

It fell to the floor in pieces, destroyed by that peculiar

Unmer trick of decreation. Her fingers had evidently passed through wood and wire as easily as air.

And yet no sooner had he registered the surprise and fear upon her face than the expression vanished. She glared at him with a look of utter condescension. 'How dare you intrude here,' she said in Unmer. 'You must leave at once!'

Granger's thoughts stumbled. He had expected to find Conquillas here. The girl was a surprise. At the same time he realized how frightening his brine-scarred face must look to her. He raised his hands in a placatory manner. 'You've nothing to fear from me, child,' he said. 'I'm looking for Conquillas.'

She snorted. 'I do not fear you,' she said. 'And any chance you had of an audience with my father died the moment you came storming into our home.'

Her father? Conquillas has a daughter?

'Is he here?' Granger said.

'He is not.'

'Then where can I find him?'

'You will not *find* him,' the girl said. 'But his arrow will most certainly find you.' She kicked the remains of her lute aside and took a step forward, her brow now furrowed with derision. 'Now get out, before I skin you like a fish.'

Granger raised his hands again. 'Easy,' he said. 'I'm not going to hurt you.'

She laughed. '*Hurt me?*' she said. 'Whatever makes you think you could hurt me?' She advanced across the parlour towards him, her arms now outstretched. From the tips of her fingers came a furious snapping sound as she destroyed the air around her hands, creating vacuum in its place. A single touch from those hands would just as easily destroy him. He felt a breeze stir.

And then a sudden movement to one side snagged his

attention, and he glanced over to see Ygrid peering in through one of the yacht's portholes. The dragon looked furious.

'All right,' he said to the girl. 'I'm going.'

The child halted and lowered her hands. The noise from her fingertips ceased at once, and the breeze died.

From outside came Ygrid's voice: 'The first wise decision you've made since we arrived, Colonel Granger.'

'Granger?' the child said, suddenly tense. 'Your name is Granger?'

He shrugged. 'What if it is?'

Suddenly she shrieked and came rushing towards him in a furious rage, her hands like outstretched claws.

Oh crap. Granger scrambled out of her way, dragging a carved wooden settee between them. She swiped at the settee and her hands simply passed through it. It collapsed into pieces and she kicked those aside.

'Have you forgotten?' she said. 'The trove market in Losoto all those years ago.'

Granger's memories raced. He recalled the incident that had brought him, injured, before Emperor Hu. An incident involving Conquillas, a dragon, an ichusae, and an Unmer child . . .

This Unmer child?

Oh crap.

'You ordered your men to shoot me!' she cried.

He continued to back away. He'd assumed her to be some waif allowed to escape from the Losotan ghettos as a political stunt by the Haurstaf. But now he saw the truth. Conquillas had been in Losoto with the girl – with his daughter – all along. That's why he'd turned up at such an opportune moment. 'We didn't harm you,' he said. 'We only meant to scare you back to where you came from.'

'The ghettos?' she said.

'Well . . .'

She flung herself upon him, her small hands crackling with that strange power. Granger shoved her aside, taking care not to hurt her, but not before she'd reduced his cloak to tatters. Now it hung over his armour like so many ragged scraps.

The child screeched and threw herself at him again.

Again, Granger diverted her attack. A large section of his cloak fell to the floor. Amazingly, his armour had not been compromised in any way. 'Just calm down,' he said. 'I'm leaving.'

'No you're not!' she yelled, and ran at him again.

Granger stepped back, but the back of his leg struck something solid, and he almost toppled. He had staggered into the pieces of broken settee. He turned back, too late. The child leaped on him, her hands outstretched, knocking him back. There was a flash of light.

And then a cry of frustration.

Granger realized that her fingers were scrabbling against the alloy breastplate of his armour, unnervingly over where his liver would be. And yet the surface remained intact, unblemished. White sparks flew from the metal where she clawed at it, but it continued to resist her sorcerous assault.

Granger threw the girl off him again.

'Entropathic armour?' she yelled. 'Where did *you* get that?'

He said nothing.

She began to sob.

Granger let out a deep breath. 'I'm sorry,' he said. 'I'm sorry Creedy shot you in the face.'

She hid her face in her elbow.

'What's your name?' he said.

'Go away.'

'I have a daughter about your age. Her name's Ianthe.'

306

The girl continued to weep into her elbow.

'That's why I'm here,' he said. He sat down on the floor beside her. 'She's gone and fallen for a . . .' He let out a weary sigh. 'An Unmer prince called Paulus Marquetta.'

The girl lowered her elbow and looked at him with red-rimmed eyes. Granger could see that the name was familiar to her. She was curious.

'Marquetta has challenged your father to public contest.'

She sniffed. 'My father will kill him.'

'The prince plans to cheat.'

'It wouldn't be the first time,' she said.

'The contest is rigged. Your father is going to face a god named Fiorel in the arena.'

She stopped and stared at him. 'That's impossible.'

'He's going to be disguised as a human combatant,' Granger said. 'This is what I came to tell Conquillas – that we have a common enemy in Prince Marquetta and that he has found a powerful ally.'

'You came to ask for *help*? After what you've done?'

'I'm sorry,' he said. 'But you have to understand, back in Losoto, you were never in any danger from my men. Our weapons couldn't have harmed you.'

She sniffed again, nodded.

'But I also came to ask another favour of your father. My daughter is still a child. She doesn't know what she's doing. Her fiancé and his uncle are merely using her. I came to beg your father to spare her life.'

'*My* father doesn't kill children.'

'He's vowed to kill anyone who stands in his way,' Granger said. 'And my daughter will certainly try to do that. She can't see beyond this boy's looks.' He noticed the girl's choked noise and looked around for something to use as a handkerchief. He picked up a scrap of his cloak from the floor and handed it to her.

After a moment's hesitation, she accepted it.

'That's why I need to know where he is.'

'I don't know where he is,' she said. 'He always leaves me and never tells me. I only know where he'll be.'

Granger sighed again and rose to his feet. 'Then I have to hope Ygrid keeps her promise to carry me to Losoto,' he said, squinting through the portholes. 'Right now, I think she means to eat me.'

The girl laughed and blew her nose.

'She's very protective,' she said. 'But she'll listen to me. I'll convince her not to harm you.'

Granger nodded. 'Thank you.'

'Wait there while I pack.'

He frowned. 'Pack?'

'Pack! For Losoto.'

'You're not going to Losoto.'

She folded her arms. 'I'm not staying here,' she said. 'Not when my father is in mortal danger.'

'I didn't say *mortal* danger. From what I gather—'

'He's in *mortal danger*,' she said, stamping her foot to emphasize the point. 'And you wouldn't know how to find him. *You* haven't been trained as a hunter.'

'I'm not bringing you with me . . .'

'Siselo,' she said, getting to her feet. 'My name is Siselo. And, no, you're not bringing me with you, Colonel Granger. *I* am going to Losoto with Ygrid.' She smiled thinly. 'However, if you behave, I may decide to bring *you* along with *me*.'

From Carhen Doma they sailed east for five days before Ianthe located the *Ilena Grey*. She had cast her mind adrift in the Sea of Ghosts and finally stumbled upon a shining beacon of perception amidst that vast dark plain lit only by the isolated glimmers of marine life.

She relayed to Paulus the *Ilena*'s position and informed him that all of the passengers were, as far as she could tell, alive. However, she did not speak of their condition lest he fall into despair. Paulus instructed Captain Howlish to sail with all speed towards the other vessel, some three days east and several degrees north of them. Through trial and error they closed the gap and by dawn on the fourth day the crewman in the crow's nest cried out the news that he had spied a sail on the horizon.

By mid-afternoon the two ships – their own strange barque together with a huge Losotan merchantman – lay side by side and their corbuses crashed down with a series of iron-bound *thunks*. Ianthe stood on deck with Paulus and his uncle as they welcomed nine hundred and twenty-three of their kin aboard.

Back in Awl, whenever Ianthe had thought about the Losotan Unmer, her imagination had always painted them as noble lords and ladies, draped in the jewels and precious metals and finery she had come to associate with her fiancé's race. She had expected flamboyance, even ostentation. She had come to understand the Unmer's propensity for extravagance as a symptom of their explosive elevation from relatively humble roots to masters of both creation and destruction. And yet the people who came aboard the *St Augustine* that afternoon were cruelly thin and ragged. They carried with them no possessions other than the filthy vestments on their backs and the simple rations with which the emperor had supplied them. Many of them seemed near death.

Paulus eschewed all formality. He clasped their hands and hugged these pitiful men, women and children close to him.

And while he welcomed his kin with smiles and rousing words of encouragement and victory, Ianthe could see that the encounter moved him close to tears.

It soon became apparent that among the new arrivals the older men and women saw nothing odd in the construction of the *St Augustine*, for their eyes were used to sorcery. And yet the younger Unmer and the children saw the vessel with awe-struck eyes. They marvelled at its shifting translucency, at the pale, ethereal flames that played endlessly across the yards and gunwales.

If Howlish's crew had been nervous with two Unmer aboard, they seemed positively twitchy at the prospect of having more than nine hundred ensconced in the cabins and holds below decks, but the good captain promised Duke Cyr that he'd keep their rum rations low and their workload high: too sober and too occupied for strained nerves to foment trouble, as he put it.

The last to leave the *Ilena Grey* was a very old and frail man named Raceme Athentro, who had been a highly distinguished naval officer in his youth and had thus taken charge of the refugee ship on her voyage from Losoto. Athentro had had the luxury of discovering among his fellows a considerable number of men with sailing experience, and had chosen his crew from the fittest of these. He offered to continue to helm the *Ilena* so that she might accompany the *St Augustine* wherever she might head, but Paulus would not hear of it. Instead, the prince ordered Howlish to find a crew for the *Ilena* from among his own men.

The *Ilena* would be provisioned, Paulus explained, and the refugees would be split between the two vessels. Both ships would return to Losoto, where they would witness Emperor Hu kneel and beg forgiveness for his crimes.

And so, with Howlish's men divided between the two ships, they turned their bows south-east towards Losoto.

Later that evening Ianthe found Paulus at the bow of the *St Augustine*, staring out at the horizon as if searching for the city still over a hundred leagues away. He didn't acknowledge her as she stood by him and she could see that he was in a dark mood.

'There used to be half a million Unmer in Losoto,' he said, his eyes still fixed on the horizon. 'Before the Revolution. When the Haurstaf arrived, they crammed most of those people into sixty city blocks.'

'It must have been awful.'

'My family were luckier than most,' he said. 'Aria's troops captured my mother and father fleeing across the Anean hills, but because of their status they were taken to Awl. They never saw the ghettos.' He shook his head and then stared up into the heavens. He spoke in a furious whisper, forcing the words out between clenched teeth. 'Half a million souls . . . decimated by starvation and disease . . . reduced to this, to less than a thousand.'

'How will you take the city?'

'I shall open our third wedding gift,' he said.

'The worm?'

'No mere worm, I suspect. When we first saw Fiorel's dragon wraiths I recognized them from legend. They are from the Otiansel Mestra – the first of the four Great Rifts Fiorel is known to have created. And if he has given us access to his private domains, then I have my suspicions about that worm's true nature.'

'What is it?'

'The Uriun,' he said. 'It is probably the largest creature in existence – certainly the largest we know of. It is the worm that inhabits a rift as large as this world, Otiansel Vadra – the domain of swamps.'

'And what about the gas?'

'If the third bottle contains the Uriun,' Paulus said, 'then the gas must provide a way to send it back to its own realm. Otherwise it would destroy this world.'

Ianthe shuddered. 'Why did Fiorel create these things?'

'Why does anyone create anything?' he replied. 'Some are weapons, others are useful in different ways. Besides Mestra and Vadra, there is Otiansel Cama, a land which was destroyed by a great war – a thousand leagues of ruin and blasted earth. It is a terrifying place full of the spectres of the dead. The last of the major four is Otiansel Hurulla, the City of Pain, to which Fiorel exiles his enemies. There are just the Great Rifts, but there are countless minor ones. This ship came from one such rift. Your father's sword contains another.'

'His sword?'

'The place where the replicates reside.'

Ianthe wondered where her father was now. She *had* been looking for him, although she would never have betrayed his location to Paulus. But in a world as vast as this, he might be anywhere. She desperately hoped he had freed himself from that terrible weapon.

But, as frightening as Granger's sword had been, it was nothing next to the horror Duke Cyr had unleashed from one of these tiny bottles. Images of the slaughter at Doma still lurked in her mind. And that had been nothing but an isolated clutch of rocks. Losoto was a city.

'A tournament?' Maskelyne said.

'In the Halls of Anea,' Halfway replied. 'Just as soon as the Unmer retake the city.'

'And what does the emperor have to say about that?'

'Don't suppose he's very happy about it, Captain.'

'No, I don't suppose he is.'

They were lunching in the officers' dining room in the rear of Maskelyne's dredger. Mellor and their strange new Bahrethroan sorcerer Cobul had barely touched their soup when Halfway had arrived with this startling news. Maskelyne returned his attention to his engineer, and specifically to the small trumpet fixed to the man's ear. 'To tell you the truth,' he said. 'I thought you'd . . . eh . . . ever so slightly exaggerated the abilities of that earpiece. You still don't know whom it is you're listening to?'

'Only that they're in Losoto.'

Halfway had been picking up excited chatter through his earpiece all morning. If any of it was to be believed, then Losoto was expecting an Unmer invasion. Prince Paulus Marquetta was planning to have his coronation and subsequent marriage to Ianthe in Hu's own capital. What's more, he had already sent word far and wide, inviting combatants to attend the celebratory tournament. And yet before all this could happen, there remained one small detail he had to attend to. He must first depose the emperor and take the city by force. Emperor Hu had mustered his navy and ordered them out to sea with instructions to parley with the Unmer. Or so he claimed. Maskelyne imagined that Hu meant to sink his enemies before they ever got to land and threaten his imperial self.

'That is confidence verging on arrogance,' Maskelyne remarked.

'Argusto Conquillas is coming to the tournament,' Halfway said. 'He has declared vendetta against Marquetta and Duke Cyr.'

'Now *that* would be an interesting match,' Maskelyne said.

313

'If it were ever allowed to happen.' He thought for a moment, wondering how Paulus planned to get out of that one. Would he simply have Ianthe incapacitate the dragon lord? That didn't seem likely.

'Argusto Conquillas never could resist a tournament,' Cobul said. 'I heard he regularly won the contests in Herica, before he left those isles for Awl. They say he got bored.' He grinned. 'But then he never did face me.'

Maskelyne thought for a moment. 'I had intended to speak with Prince Marquetta, although the timing could be better.' He turned to the Bahrethroan sorcerer. 'At full steam we should be able to reach Losoto in a month, less than twenty days with a wind behind us. I imagine your prince will have already taken the city by then, married his woman and declared himself king of Anea.'

Cobul slurped his soup. 'He's not my prince.'

This surprised Maskelyne. 'Surely you don't side with Conquillas?'

'I side with neither of them,' Cobul said. 'Unmer lords have always looked down on men like me.' He looked up. 'Mongrels, I mean.' He dipped a hunk of bread in his soup and stuffed it in his mouth, chewing as he went on: 'But if you're planning to visit the capital, I'd be grateful for a lift there.'

'Of course,' he said. 'You have, eh . . . friends in Losoto?'

Cobul grunted. 'No friends. I'll go because I could use the money.'

'Money?'

'For winning the tournament.'

The dragon flew Granger and Siselo across the Sea of Lights to Losoto. The young Unmer girl stood upon Ygrid's shoulders or skipped lightly between the alloy saddle hoops with the easy grace and confidence of someone who had spent her entire life flying with dragons. Ygrid did not moderate her flight to accommodate her youthful passenger, but swooped and banked as fiercely as she had done before. If anything, it seemed to Granger that the dragon had flown more gently during her first flight with him.

Ygrid had remained in a sullen silence for most of the day. Granger felt sure she would have shucked him from her shoulders and eaten him whole in an instant if Conquillas's daughter had not been present. Perhaps the dragon was still angry that he'd deceived her, or perhaps it was simply that she couldn't get a word in edgeways. Siselo, as it turned out, liked to talk.

'But of course I've been to the ghettos many times,' she said breathlessly. 'There are ways to slip under the Haurstaf radar if you know how, but that takes years of training and I haven't yet mastered it, although Father says I'm nearly there, which is good for someone so young, don't you think?' With barely a pause to wait for his reply, she went on. 'He calls it *mental silence*. You have to sort of empty your mind and think about absolutely nothing because the Haurstaf sense conscious thought even if they can't always read it. That's how they get you! But it's really difficult to do because how can you even walk anywhere without thinking? You can't! You can't stop *all* thoughts, but Father says you have to learn to do as much as possible by instinct, because that's subconscious and is harder to detect. And it won't work if the witches are looking for you, only if they're not really paying attention, which actually happens quite a lot.'

Granger nodded. 'Maybe you could demonstrate?'

He heard the dragon huff.

'I can't do it now!' Siselo cried. 'You have to prepare your-self like when you prepare for a hunt or when you get ready to sneak into the Losotan ghettos. I only tried it once and I nearly managed it, but then one of those witches sensed me and father had to kill her.'

It went on like this for hours. The Mare Lux stretched to every horizon, the waters an endless slab of heavy bromine brown that started finally to glimmer with lighter copper-metal hues as the angle of the sunlight changed. Sunset was still a couple of hours away when they spotted on the northern horizon a great flotilla of ships.

Ygrid then uttered the first words she had spoken all after-noon. 'The Imperial Navy sails west.'

Granger knew better than to question the serpent, whose eyesight was reputed to be far keener than his own. There could only be one reason why Emperor Hu would send his navy so far out from Losoto: to meet the Unmer prince at sea before he reached the capital. They were hunting Prince Marquetta.

And Ianthe?

She had to be at sea with him. He needed her to protect him.

'Head west,' he said to Ygrid.

The dragon growled. 'Is that an order, Colonel? How amusing.'

'Merely a request,' he said. 'They're after Marquetta's ship. My daughter is aboard that ship.'

'And you wish to warn the prince and your daughter? The same two who plan to assassinate my master – and Siselo's father – by their deceit?'

'My daughter has nothing to do with the prince's plan.'

Siselo stood up on the dragon's shoulders and peered out at the ships. 'Is there going to be a battle?'

'Almost certainly,' Granger said.

'Can we watch it, Ygrid?'

The dragon grunted. 'Your father would never forgive me.'

'Please.'

'No.'

Siselo screwed up her face. 'What if *I ordered* you to take us there?'

'I'm not your pet, child.'

Ygrid banked in the air, her vast wings fluttering in the cold air, and turned to the north-east, away from the direction in which the Imperial Navy were heading and away from the setting sun.

The *Ilena Grey* accompanied the *St Augustine* as she sailed east through the night. Ianthe could see the other ship's lights when she looked out of the porthole next to her bed. And sometimes she could spy those lights through the fabric of the *St Augustine*, which continued to shift between the ethereal and the corporeal.

All but that one chamber.

She rolled over and leaned out of bed. Down through the ghostly floorboards and the decks and bulwarks below she could just make out the viewing room; it appeared to her eyes as a solid white cube at the heart of the ship.

In the part of her mind attuned to other people's perceptions, she sensed someone in there. Ianthe closed her eyes and saw the ship as a patchwork of images adrift in the void beyond sight and sound. She was seeing the *St Augustine* through the eyes of all those people around her. Their disparate perceptions formed a composite whole, but that composite appeared to be constructed from normal, mundane, timber. The ship was no longer a phantasm.

A single mind occupied the viewing room. Ianthe slipped inside it.

The room appeared no different to the last time she'd seen it. Its mirrored floor and ceiling induced a giddy sensation of vertigo. Mirrors hung on the wall before her, all of which looked into the rift Paulus had told her about or else framed the weird visages of the creatures he'd called travellers.

Ordinary mirror glass would have immediately revealed Ianthe's host to her, but this was not ordinary glass and so it took her a few moments to deduce whose body it was she now inhabited. Whoever it was, they were pacing, apparently agitated. It was clearly a man, and from his dark grey clothes she supposed him to be Duke Cyr – a supposition that was confirmed a moment later when she heard him speak.

'Volsh nem do-er nem,' he said, angrily waving an arm. 'Hanyewl.'

Ianthe had come to learn a few words in Unmer, but she recognized none of them in his speech. However, she had promised Paulus that she wouldn't spy on him or his uncle.

But just as she was about to leave the old man alone, a strange thing happened. Another voice replied, also in Unmer. It was deep and forceful; it resounded around the room, and yet Ianthe could not locate its source. It seemed to come from everywhere at once. 'Nem katarloes,' it said. 'Par Marquetta yenshlo.'

She heard the duke grunt. He batted his hand at the air in agitation or disagreement.

They continued to converse for a few minutes more, during which time the duke appeared to become more and more resigned to some unpalatable possibility. Ianthe heard Marquetta's name mentioned several more times, along with Conquillas's and two Unmer words she recognized: *olish-gadda*,

318

which meant tournament, and *hesh*, which she gathered meant battle or war. Apparently they were discussing the events to come.

Cyr paced a short while longer, and then turned abruptly and strode up to one mirror in particular.

Ianthe's breath caught in her throat.

While the other mirrors looked out upon the void and the travellers therein, behind this glass there lay an ocean underneath a jet-black and starless sky. And yet it was not dark, for the ocean itself exuded a tremulous light. It shivered and pulsed, the waters changing colour as Ianthe watched. A million scintillations danced across its surface, while scores of sombre hues throbbed in the deeps.

'Olmaneiro hesh ast tobia,' Cyr growled at this image.

'Nem hesh,' a voice replied. And at that moment Ianthe sensed a powerful mind lurking in that pulsing brine. The scope of its perceptions was so vast they seemed to stretch forever. If she had thrown herself into that alien intelligence, she would have been utterly overwhelmed.

Ianthe recoiled, yanking her own consciousness back into her body with a fearsome jolt. Her eyes snapped open and she lay in bed, gazing up at nothing, breathing heavily.

What the hell was that?

She got up and dressed quickly.

And then she slipped out of her cabin and hurried down the passageway. She stopped at the door four down from her own and rapped her fist against it quickly.

She waited a moment, her heart thumping.

The door opened and Paulus stood there, wearing a red silk gown. Looking vaguely annoyed, he stepped out and partially closed the door behind him. 'Ianthe?'

'What is brine?'

'What?'

'Brine!' she said. 'Where does it come from?'

'It's poison. Ianthe, what's going on?'

She hesitated. If she told him the truth, she would have to admit spying on Duke Cyr. 'I had a dream,' she said. 'It scared me. Can I come in?'

He frowned. 'This isn't a good time, Ianthe.'

'I won't—' She stopped, suddenly aware that someone was in the room with him. She could sense their presence hovering behind the door. She felt it at the periphery of her conscious-ness, yet held back from reaching out with her mind to inves-tigate. She stiffened against him, and drew back. 'Who's there with you?' she said.

'What?'

'In your cabin. Who's that in your cabin?'

He glanced away. 'It's just Nera.'

'Nera?' A knot tightened in Ianthe's gut.

'I told you it wasn't a good time,' Paulus said. 'The impe-rial armada is currently two leagues south-east of us. Nera is communicating with it.'

The pressure in Ianthe's stomach didn't lessen. 'Communicating?'

'One of the emperor's psychics has turned,' he said. 'She's agreed to help us in exchange for her own life. She doesn't want to face you, Ianthe.' He closed the door behind him and then took her hands in his. 'But there's another Guild witch with the fleet and that one has already sensed Nera and given our position to her captain. We don't yet know if she's betrayed her colleague, but we expect the Imperial Navy to engage at first light. I must be ready and so must you, Ianthe.' He squeezed her hands lightly. 'Go and get some sleep.'

Ianthe's gaze shifted from Paulus's earnest face to his closed cabin door. She could easily have slipped behind Nera's eyes, or even crushed the girl's mind with a thought, but that path could only lead to despair. She trusted Paulus implicitly, didn't she? Then what was this knot that kept twisting inside her?

'Perhaps I should stay up with you?' she said.

'No,' he said. 'I need you well rested and alert for tomorrow.' He leaned down and kissed her cheek. His perfume lingered on her skin.

His perfume?

'Goodnight, Ianthe,' he said.

Ianthe glanced at his cabin door again. What she wanted to say was, *Do you love me?* But she was afraid she'd see a lie in his eyes. Instead she said, 'Goodnight.'

Sleep was a long time coming for her. Her mind kept replaying the events of the evening: Nera's presence in Paulus's cabin and the sight of that alien sea in Cyr's mirror. He had been *conversing* with it. He had been talking about the tournament, she felt sure.

These thoughts spun around in her mind for hours. She began to feel as if she'd never fall asleep.

And then she awoke suddenly, her eyes blinking at the orange glare filtering through the opaque cabin wall. The sun was already climbing above the horizon. Ianthe felt exhausted. A bell was ringing above decks.

She filled a metal basin and splashed water on her face, trying to dispel the fog of sleep. If only it were as easy to dispel the knot of anguish in her stomach.

There was an urgent knocking at the cabin door.

She opened it to find Paulus standing there, dressed in his finest velvets and leathers. A pale grey sealskin cloak enveloped his shoulders, parting at his waist to reveal the jewel-crusted pommel of an exquisite rapier. On his head he wore a set of brass navigator's goggles, held securely by a leather strap with tiny end-springs. His face was pale and drawn, and yet he exuded a sort of nervous energy. 'They're moving to attack,' he said.

'I've just woken,' she protested.

'Dress quickly and meet me above deck.' He turned to leave.

'Paulus?'

He stopped and looked back at her.

'Do you love me?'

He looked startled, and Ianthe couldn't help but sense a vague air of annoyance in his reply. 'Of course I do,' he said gruffly. 'I'll see you in five minutes.' Then he hurried away.

Ianthe watched him go. His attitude left her with an empty feeling in her heart. He was taking her help for granted. At that moment she wished that she had no preternatural vision and no power over the Haurstaf. She wanted to be normal. But she was also terrified of what that would mean. All this time she had been unwilling to admit to herself the real reason Paulus was marrying her. She had forbidden herself from asking the question because she was afraid to know the answer. She was so used to viewing the world through other people's eyes that she had clung to a comforting *perception* of her relationship with Paulus, rather than look at the naked truth. She had created her own fiction.

But it wasn't enough.

She still felt hollow as she dressed in loose comfortable clothing, choosing the least ostentatious of the garments with which she had been supplied: a light grey spider-silk blouse and dark grey woollen breeches. She draped a patterned scarf around her neck and then grabbed her hooded sealskin cape on her way out.

The eastern sky was starfish pink and the low sunlight turned the *St Augustine*'s deck candle-flame orange. Ianthe spotted her fiancé standing by the starboard gunwale with Duke Cyr, Captain Howlish and Nera. The Haurstaf psychic cast a nervous glance in Ianthe's direction, then folded her arms and looked away. Even now Ianthe felt a stab of jealousy. In this light, the girl's hair shone as brightly as gold, and a touch of pink coloured her pale cheeks. All three of the men were looking out towards the north-east. As Ianthe joined them, her breath caught in her throat. The sight before her cut through her dark mood.

Ships covered the ocean to the north. At least a hundred of them: destroyers, frigates, galleons and men-o'-war, their hulls clad in copper or brass or blue, black, brown, green and red dragon scales in solid swathes or motleys gleaming like boiled candy. Innumerable painted sails rose above the dark waters, their stylized designs depicting ancient gods or weapons or beasts of legend or one of scores of noble crests. Metal-bound bows smashed waves to spume. Purple and gold imperial pennants fluttered from countless masts. From everywhere came the glint of armour and brass cannon.

'So many,' Ianthe said.

Paulus glanced round at her. 'Do you sense the Haurstaf witches? Nera says they're keeping them out to the rear of the armada. Two vessels, both frigates: the *Warhorse* and the *Castle Sky*.'

'Those ships probably won't engage,' Howlish said. 'They won't risk losing psychics.'

Ianthe glanced at Nera, but the other girl wouldn't meet her eye. 'I'll look for them,' she said.

Ianthe cast her consciousness out and saw the armada as a bright patchwork of decks and sails and pools of ocean all hung in nebulous darkness. These were the collected perceptions of thousands of sailors and she raced through their minds, skipping from one to another like a vengeful spirit hunting for a body to possess.

But she could not find either psychic.

'They've kept them away from the crew,' she said. 'If nobody out there can see them, then I can't. I don't know which ships are which, I have to look for someone who's alone, and . . .' And just as she said it, she found someone who was apart from all the others. A solitary figure in a small cabin situated near the stern of one of the frigates. 'I've found one,' she said. 'I think . . . it has to be.'

'Find the other,' Paulus said.

Ianthe sent her mind out again and a few minutes later she located a second person, similarly hidden from the sight of the crew. This passenger was located in a midships cabin of another frigate. Short of glimpsing them looking into a mirror, Ianthe had no way of knowing for sure if these two minds belonged to the Haurstaf witches she sought, but it seemed likely enough, as every other crewmember was in plain sight of another. She hurled her mind above decks, flitting through the ship's crew. Was this the frigate she sought?

She couldn't be sure.

Her assumption had to be good enough. Now that she had the position of the two witches, she could shuttle back and forth between their minds, ready to crush any psychic attack they might unleash against the Unmer.

'Are we set?' Paulus said.

'I still don't know which one of them is on our side, I don't know who to—'

'But you know *where* they are?'

She nodded. 'I think so.'

'Then kill them both if you have to.'

She was about to protest, but then stopped herself. It was best not to question Paulus in public. If it came to it, she would find a way to tell which one of her targets was the enemy. She'd have to.

The prince turned to his uncle and gave him a grim nod.

Duke Cyr held up the third of his patron's sorcerous bottles. The glass glinted in the sun, and the tiny maggot within floated in clear liquid. 'Once this begins,' he said. 'There's no going back.' He glanced at Howlish. 'You know what you have to do?'

The captain nodded.

'In that case, gentlemen,' Cyr said, 'let us proceed.' He removed the stopper and flung the bottle into the sea.

Nothing happened for a few moments, and then a sudden cataclysm of light erupted in the watery depths ahead of them. For a heartbeat the whole ocean was awash with flickering amber luminance. Ianthe's teeth thrummed. She thought she heard a high-pitched tone at the very limits of her perception, although she couldn't be certain. Bolts of energy tore through the brine, fathoms down, turning from yellow to angry red. In those few moments it seemed to her that a great swathe of the ocean before her had turned to fire.

The sea became dark once more, and yet the event elicited a response from the imperial armada as ships immediately began to manoeuvre around the affected area, clearly antici-pating some Unmer trick.

Paulus looked at his uncle.

'It's coming,' Cyr said. Suddenly he pointed ahead of them to where a vast cloud of mist or steam had begun to rise from the surface of the waters. 'There! You see the shift in entropy?'

'Then it is Vadra?'

The older man nodded. 'As we thought.'

Ianthe seized Paulus's arm. 'The worm?'

'The Uriun,' he said. 'The Worm of Vadra.'

The sea ahead of them began to bubble furiously. And then an acre of surface swelled upwards suddenly, rising ten or more feet before collapsing back downwards and forming a great circular wave.

Ianthe clung to Paulus. 'It's vast.'

He grinned. 'This is but a tiny piece of it.'

Howlish let out a growl. 'Two degrees to port,' he cried, signalling frantically to the helmsman to bring the ship's bow more precisely into line with the oncoming water.

But there simply wasn't time. The *St Augustine*'s bow pitched sharply upwards as the wave passed under her hull, and then she plunged down again. To port, the *Ilena Grey*'s mast tilted as she also rode the wave, her hull rocking sharply before settling.

The expanding circle of seawater passed beneath the armada without upturning any of Hu's ships. They were still beyond cannon range, turning now to flank the two Unmer ships.

'I would have expected a psychic attack by now,' Duke Cyr remarked.

Paulus shrugged. 'You think the other witch has turned?'

'I wouldn't count on it.'

From under the sea there came a series of flickering lights, as silent as a distant lightning storm. Ianthe could see a massive shadow down there, a mountainous ill-defined shape rising up towards the surface. It was pulsing with strange jellyfish luminescence, silent explosions of blue, green and red that spread across a great expanse of the sea. The sheer size of the thing afflicted her with awe. It seemed larger than the whole of the imperial armada.

And then suddenly it broke the surface.

A great mass of writhing coils appeared on the face of the waters. The creature was worm-like, but throbbing with colours that streamed across its darkly gelatinous skin. As it uncoiled, Ianthe first thought that she was looking at a great number of serpents, but then she realized that it was merely one creature with many heads and tendrils. They rose now above the sea, bursting up through the waves, dripping brine: hundreds of fat eyeless stalks, each with a vertical slit for a mouth, and each mouth glistening with tiny red teeth; and still hundreds more tentacles, slender and rippling with bright colours.

But then Ianthe noticed something odd about the creature. Its many heads and tendrils were, to different extents, translucent. While some appeared ghostlike, ethereal, others were more solid. As she watched it untangle itself and extend its reach across the steaming seas, it seemed to her that these lashing appendages left gaseous trails behind them, or else faded out entirely, only to reappear again, giving the overall impression of a mirage.

'Why does it seem to blur and vanish in places?' she asked Paulus.

'The worm's body loops through time as well as space,' he replied. 'The necks and tentacles . . . the . . . ah, you see there, the light shining through that cluster of heads? It is merely the same head revisiting the present moment many times over.' He smiled. 'It is one of several . . . unusual defences the worm employs. Such powers make it almost impossible to kill.'

She shivered.

He placed his hand on her shoulder. 'We have nothing to fear from it,' he said. 'But we must be ready for reprisals.'

She nodded.

Several ships of the armada had turned to bring their

327

cannons to bear on the Uriun, and Ianthe now saw a series of bright flashes from their scale- and metal-clad hulls. A moment later the air shook with multiple concussions. *Crack, crack, crack.* The Uriun shuddered and writhed amidst the drifting smoke, and yet the attack did not appear to harm it in any way.

Its tentacles had by now reached the first of the emperor's ships – a galleon armoured in bright copper. The ghostly appendages wrapped around masts and yards, ripping through sailcloth and snapping rope. A larger tentacle coiled around the hull. Crewmen ran, screaming, to the quarterdeck. Rifles flashed. And then the creature pulled hard.

The galleon toppled and crashed into the sea. There was a great cracking of timbers, an implosion of foam and debris, and then suddenly the ship was gone, dragged under the boiling waters.

All around them other ships were being destroyed as the great worm's tentacles reached further into the armada and smashed through vessels and dragged them down into the stinking brine. Its many mouths lashed out and seized crewmen and lifted them high, only to devour them whole and screaming. Larger it grew, and larger yet with each passing moment, until it seemed to Ianthe that its tentacles and necks filled an area of ocean much larger than the entire imperial armada.

Warships opened fire. Their shells and cannon shot caused no visible damage but only drew the Uriun's glutinous arms towards the offending weapons. As the creature continued to destroy the emperor's ships and dash them apart upon the dark waters, a queerly pregnant silence fell over the scene, punctuated now only by the occasional distant cry or cannon report. And then even those sounds finally stopped. Not a man of Howlish's crew spoke.

The Uriun's thrashing slowed and then it paused, as if finally sensing the quiet that had descended upon the ocean. And then, slowly, it began to coil itself inwards again. Thousands of tentacles and necks became hundreds and then scores and when it had shrunk to the size at which it had appeared from the depths, it slipped below the debris-choked waters and waited there several fathoms down, those odd lights still rippling across its flesh.

Where minutes ago the sea around them had been filled with ships, now nothing remained but a few scraps of wood and cork and sailcloth.

'The Haurstaf didn't attack,' Ianthe said. 'Even when that thing—' She stopped suddenly.

Nera was sobbing into her hands.

'You heard them?' Ianthe said. 'What did they say?'

'They begged us to pull the creature back,' she replied. 'They *begged*.'

Paulus grunted. 'By the time the Uriun got hold of their vessel,' he said, 'it was too late. They had moments left. A psychic attack against us would have been futile, vengeful at best.'

'You betrayed them,' Ianthe said. 'You *used* them.'

He wheeled to face her, his expression hard. 'This is war, Ianthe. We must use whomever we must.'

'Including me?' Ianthe said.

Her question stopped him. He stared at her for a few moments, then blinked and said, 'Of course not. Ianthe, why would you think that?'

But she had already seen the glimmer of fear in his eyes.

'We are not landing in the imperial palace,' Ygrid said.

Siselo scrunched up her face and whined, 'But it would be amazing.'

'It would attract considerable attention,' the dragon replied. 'My decision is final.'

They had been flying all night through the freezing air. Conquillas's daughter had wrapped herself in a woollen shawl, lashing it to the dragon's alloy saddle hoops to form a sort of crude papoose. The garment had seemed woefully thin to Granger, and so he'd covered her with the remains of his cloak. Siselo had slept soundly enough, although he had endured a bitterly cold night hunched against the serpent's spine.

Now he welcomed the warmth of the morning sunlight on his face. He could see the Anean coastline ahead of them and noted with satisfaction that Ygrid had not flown directly for the capital, but had brought them to a wild and unpopulated stretch of the country. Ahead, the land rose sharply from the sea, the steep slopes grizzled with forest but thinning to ochre grass and scree and bare rock higher up. Wisps of mist still rested in small bays and inlets along the shore or pooled in the valleys between the hills, but it was lifting fast. Clouds tumbled over scoured rock summits, ragged and cotton-like with pockets of blue sky showing through the greys and whites.

'There is a mine up ahead,' Ygrid said. 'But the earth was spent many years ago and the road is hardly used now. I will set you down there.'

Siselo looked indignant. 'Are we supposed to walk all the way to Losoto? How far is it?'

'Eight miles,' Ygrid said.

'Eight miles!' the girl wailed. 'But that will take forever. Can't you drop us closer, Ygrid, please?'

'That's fine,' Granger said. 'We'll reach the capital by noon.'

'But I don't want to walk all that way,' Siselo protested. 'Why do we have to walk when we can fly?'

The dragon ignored her protests. She swooped over the

tops of the waves and reached the shore. Her vast green wings rippled in a sudden wash of sunlight as she soared over the treetops, rising to follow the sweep of the land so close beneath them. Granger glanced back to see vortexes of mist uncoiling in their wake. The highest forest branches swayed. Now the rushing air carried the scent of blue pine and fresh rain.

Ygrid banked to her right and skirted the top of a forest ridge. The land below them fell away again. She turned left, now moving inland along a narrow valley through which a stream flowed. At the head of this valley, above the tree line, Granger could see a trail running east through a natural cleft in the hills. The rock walls on either side were peppered with rectangular mine entrances.

With a series of great thumps of her wings, the dragon landed on a broad scree-strewn slope before the cleft, rearing back as she did so. Then she crouched and allowed her two passengers to dismount.

Granger was grateful to have solid earth under his feet once more. He let his kitbag slide to the ground and stretched, trying to massage the pain from his neck and shoulders. His power armour hummed lightly and the engraved whorls on his boots began to alter subtly as they drew power from the very land itself.

Siselo walked a few yards up the slope, then turned to Ygrid. 'What if I need to call you?'

Ygrid huffed oily fumes. 'Then call me,' she said. 'But never for trivial reasons, child.'

'How do I know what's a trivial reason?'

The dragon lowered her head until her snout had almost pressed up against the girl. 'Call if you are about to die,' she said. 'Otherwise, don't.'

Granger frowned. 'How can the girl contact you?'

Ygrid's eyes narrowed on him. 'There are . . . secret means. You need not trouble yourself with the details.'

'It's a whistle,' Siselo said. 'My father gave it to me. All the dragons nearby know to come when they hear it.'

Ygrid glowered at the girl and growled, 'You are too quick to trust people, child.'

Siselo rolled her eyes. Then suddenly she grinned and ran forward and threw her arms around the serpent's foreleg. 'Thank you for carrying us here, Ygrid.'

Ygrid grumbled and huffed and raised her head, tilted her chin to peer down at the child. It seemed to Granger that the serpent smiled. But then her expression darkened and she swung her equine face down again until her huge yellow teeth loomed before Granger like an impenetrable gate. 'If any harm comes to her,' she said. 'You will answer to me, Colonel.'

Granger nodded.

Siselo was already making her way up towards the mine road, so he picked up his kitbag, slung it over his shoulder and followed her.

The Uriun accompanied the *St Augustine* and the *Ilena Grey* to Losoto. Ianthe could see the worm down in the brine below the two ships, a great dark mass that did not so much follow them as they approached the Anean peninsula, but rather grew to keep pace with them. By nightfall its shadow stretched behind them for as far as she could see, and also extended to port and starboard so that it seemed as if they were riding the crest of some strange undersea wave.

This is but a tiny fragment of it, Paulus had said. *Any larger and it could easily devour the whole world*. The worm that had grown so large around them now represented seven years of the full creature's life. It was, Cyr explained to her, the part of the creature that had grown in the last seven years. Or would grow in the seven years to come. Ianthe wasn't quite sure. But she understood it to mean that for every heartbeat during a particular seven-year period, the creature's head or tentacles revisited this current moment in time – what Ianthe regarded as the present. The duke called the process recursion.

But you must not fear it, he said. *For it will always obey its creator's will.*

The sight of the monster had so overwhelmed Ianthe that she had taken to watching their progress from the *St Augustine*'s bow, where the winds filled her lungs with clean cold air from the north. And so she was there the next morning when the lookout sighted land, gazing out at the grey horizon and warming her hands around a mug of tea.

Paulus must have heard the cry too, for he joined her shortly afterwards. He was clutching the fourth of Fiorel's ichusae, the bottle filled with amber gas. He rested a hand upon her shoulder, but Ianthe thought the gesture seemed forced. There was a nervous tension between them that she sought to alleviate.

'Do you suppose it gets cleverer each time?' she asked him. 'The worm, I mean.'

'Cleverer?' he said. 'In what sense?'

'When a future head revisits the past,' she said. 'It will have two minds.'

'Being in possession of two minds does not grant a creature more intelligence,' he said, 'particularly when they are both the same mind at different times in that creature's life. It would be wise beyond imagining, however, if Fiorel had given it the capacity to acquire wisdom.'

'It can't acquire wisdom?'

'A pack of dogs can't learn to read any better than an individual dog.'

For the rest of the morning they sailed on with the Uriun beneath them and by noon they could make out a great white city on the shore of the Sea of Lights. Losoto was larger than any city Ianthe had seen before, although most of it appeared to be flooded. Acres of partially submerged buildings sat in shallow water. Most were mere shells, roofless and windowless, with their foundations steeped in brine and their walls crusted with brown ichusae crystals. The streets between them had become canals. East of this there loomed a massive industrial building, the city harbour, and an ugly stone fort situated atop a rocky promontory. The harbour was empty of ships. Not even Losoto's fishermen had elected to stay.

As they drew nearer, Ianthe could see people gathering on the waterfront – ordinary citizens of Losoto. And she could also sense them in the busy streets and houses behind, thousands of them, tens of thousands. Evidently Emperor Hu had not ordered an evacuation.

'Do you see any Haurstaf?' Paulus said.

She didn't answer.

'Ianthe?'

'No, I don't see any.'

'They've gone,' said a voice from behind.

Ianthe turned to find the slender blonde figure of Nera standing there, heartbreakingly pretty, her pale hands clasped at her chest. The psychic wore a patterned woollen shawl around her shoulders.

'They fled north,' she added. Then she looked up at Paulus. 'Emperor Hu has taken them with him. He abandoned the city after you destroyed his navy.'

Paulus frowned. 'Hu isn't there?'

Nera shook her head.

'Well, where the hell is he?'

'I don't know,' she replied. 'They won't say.' She hesitated a moment. 'The Imperial Army has left with him. The whole city is undefended.'

Ianthe rested her hand on Paulus's arm. 'Then there's no need to attack,' she said. 'Can you send the Uriun back to where it came from?'

He made no reply.

'Paulus?'

He shook his head. 'Fiorel gave us the worm for a reason.'

'To destroy Hu's navy.'

'To be a symbol of Unmer power.'

She grabbed his arm. 'Call it off. Please.'

'It is too late.'

He pointed to the shore a hundred yards ahead of them, where the Uriun's tentacles reached the outskirts of Losoto. A swarming mass of them began to crawl through that maze of broken and flooded buildings in search of food, pulsing with luminescence. Ianthe heard a single gunshot from the west, followed by the sound of a man screaming. And then, before her, the roofless husks of buildings began to collapse under the weight of the creature's countless pushing limbs. Two houses and then four and eight and soon scores of walls were falling to dust and rubble.

Those curious citizens who had gathered on the waterfront now started to panic. Hundreds of them turned and ran from the oncoming monster; they filled the streets like a sudden outrushing of water. Many fell under the pressure of those behind and were trampled. Others screamed, frantically kicking and fighting each other to escape. And as the tide of people poured up the market streets that rose behind the shore, the Uriun reached the stragglers.

Ianthe could only look on in horror as hundreds of the

creature's mouths lashed out and struck at men, women and children. It seemed to blur, its limbs continually shifting between the real and the incorporeal. It crushed the fleeing people and pinned them to the cobbles by the hundreds, shivering as it fed. Other tentacles broke through doors and shattered windows and slithered inside the shorefront buildings.

'Can't you stop it?' she cried.

Paulus watched with awe and did not reply.

Now the houses on the land were starting to fall as the Uriun pushed further ashore, a great wave of flesh that flowed over the harbour wall and the promenade and the seafront buildings. The great worm stretched all along the coast, extending further even than the limits of the city. Buildings crumbled under its weight. The streets became slippery with blood. And still it crawled inland, turning block after block to rubble.

Duke Cyr came running up to them. 'That's enough,' he said. 'Open the fourth bottle.'

'Where have you been?'

'End it now, Paulus.'

Paulus hesitated a moment. Then he pulled out the stopper from the last ichusae and held the bottle high. From its mouth poured a stream of amber smoke that soon engulfed the three of them. He threw the bottle into the sea. The brine around them began to bubble and steam, but the mist was building so rapidly they could no longer see ten yards from where they stood upon the *St Augustine*'s deck. A rank smell filled the air, like rotten vegetation.

Like a swamp, Ianthe thought.

The waterfront vanished amidst the clouds of fumes, but for some time afterwards they continued to hear screams and gunshots from the city. Finally a silence fell on the harbour, the stillness broken only by the creak of the ship and the slosh of the sea beneath her hull and by the occasional mournful wail of a survivor left upon the shore.

The *St Augustine* and the *Ilena Grey* remained at anchor beyond the entrance to Losoto's harbour for another half-hour, waiting for the fog to lift. When it finally cleared, they could at last perceive the full extent of the destruction the worm had caused.

Three of every four buildings along the waterfront had been completely levelled. The debris field extended at least a hundred yards inland from the shore, but in many places it was much further still. Whole blocks had collapsed into piles of shattered stone and timbers. Corpses littered the streets and the gutters ran with blood.

On the deck of the *St Augustine*, the crew stood in silence, gazing out at the carnage.

Finally Howlish lit his pipe and breathed in a lungful of smoke. 'Hell of a wedding gift,' he said.

'What is that thing?' Siselo said.

Granger lowered his kitbag to the ground and looked to where she was pointing. They were standing on a ridge over-looking Losoto. From this high viewpoint he could see the Anean coast stretching far into the east. Mist shrouded the distant horizon but he knew the coast turned north at the tip of the peninsula some four leagues away. Hu's capital sprawled across several miles of shoreline and occupied just as much land to the north – taking a great bite out of the Forest of Ai that covered the inland hills. Apart from the white clutter of the city and the breakers, the landscape was entirely ink green or brown – a meeting of forest and brine.

The old mine road had taken them over these very hills.

But now that they had finally reached Losoto, they found it to be under attack by some sorcerous creation. To Granger it looked like a vast mat of weed that had somehow crawled out of the sea and entangled itself in the city.

'I don't know what it is,' he said. 'Something conjured.' There were only two ships in sight, he noted: a Losotan merchantman and an odd, curiously pale barque, both anchored within a few hundred yards of the harbour entrance.

And then suddenly the strange yellow fog rose.

He watched it forming in the sea directly in front of the barque. It was thickening and growing far too quickly to be a natural phenomenon. In mere minutes it had enveloped the whole of the waterfront and still it kept coming, rolling into the streets, filling alleys and quadrangles like a tide. It obscured the monster and the city around it. He heard a few gunshots, but the scene soon became quiet.

He sat on a log beside Siselo and waited.

After about half an hour, the fog began to disperse. The creature had vanished, but it had left acres of destruction in its wake. Granger gazed out at the ruined city with mounting anger. What the hell had been the point of that fiasco? There would be hundreds lying dead down there, hundreds who'd have to be dug out and buried in lime to stop the spread of disease.

'I knew it! I knew it!'

He wheeled round to find Siselo sitting on the ground next to his kitbag. She had untied the draw string and pulled out the replicating sword, the blade of which was still wrapped in cloth.

Granger growled at her. 'Don't touch that, it's dangerous.'

She set the blade down on the ground and looked up at him. 'It *is* a replicating sword. I *knew* it had to be something like that.'

338

'Something like what?'

'The reason why you shine!'

He stared at her dumbly.

'Sorcery!' she said. 'Ygrid was right. You exude sorcery.'

'What do you know about such things?'

She scrunched up her face. 'Isn't it obvious? Dragons are sorcerous creatures, so they recognize other sorcerous creatures. It's like something in the way they see things, like an aura, I suppose. Ygrid said you were shining with so much sorcery it was hard to even look at you.' She grinned. 'It's because of this sword.'

Granger grunted.

'Are you a replicate?' she said. 'Or the original?'

'Original,' he said.

She raised an eyebrow. 'Are you *absolutely* sure about that?'

'Of course I am.'

She looked at him as if she didn't believe it. 'You do know it's killed you, don't you?'

'It's trying to take me over.'

'No,' she said. 'It's already killed you. You must have died three or four days ago.'

'What are you talking about?'

'Ygrid said you were dead,' Siselo said. 'I didn't believe her. But now I think on it, it kind of explains a lot.'

Granger just stared at her.

'Entropathic armour,' she said. 'You know?'

Granger had no idea what she was talking about, and yet she seemed so earnest. 'This armour helps me move.'

She nodded. 'Yes, because your heart stopped. That's what happens when you become a sword replicate. Your body shuts down and then your mind.'

'You really think I'm dead?'

'You are definitely dead,' she said. 'Have you even smelled yourself lately?'

Granger sat down on a nearby rock. He felt suddenly unsteady. The last time he'd taken off his gauntlet, he'd been unable to move his hand at all. Was that because the body inside the suit was dead? And now only sorcery kept it moving? He turned back to the girl. She still looked earnest. 'Let me get this right,' he said. 'You're saying that I died, and this suit is the only thing keeping me going?'

She nodded. 'Don't you know anything about this sword?'

Granger gave a weary sigh. *Evidently not.*

'My father once fought a whole village with one of these,' she said. 'We still have it back home. He's going to show me how to use it properly when I'm older. I've already learned how to phase with it.' She frowned. 'But why did you let the sword do this do you?'

Granger grunted. 'Let it? I didn't have much choice.'

'Why, what does it want?'

'What do you mean?'

'I mean,' she said, 'why is it turning you into one of its slaves anyway? These weapons all have minds behind them. What is this one trying to get you to do for it?'

He shrugged. 'I wish I knew.'

Siselo blinked with surprise. 'Don't tell me you haven't even asked it?'

'How can I ask it?'

'Seriously?' she said. 'You don't know? Nobody told you?'

'Told me what?'

She shook her head with amazement. But then her expression softened. 'Being dead isn't *that* bad,' she said. 'As long as you keep wearing the armour, and maybe use some perfume, most people probably wouldn't even notice.' She looked down at the sword again. 'But you don't want this to take over your mind. You need to find out what it wants and make a deal with it. That's the only way you can use these things safely. If you don't, they'll kill you.'

'How do I make a deal with the sword?'

She smiled. 'I'll show you.' She brought the sword over and placed it on the ground before Granger. 'Now unwrap the blade,' she said.

He did so, revealing the dull metal surface.

'Now place your hand over the runes.'

'What runes?'

'The runes in the metal! There!' She pointed to the place where the blade joined the grip, where Granger spied a series of tiny markings embossed in the steel. He had just assumed them to be ornamentation before and hadn't paid them much heed.

He placed his gauntlet over the runes.

'Now say, *Let me in*.'

'What?'

'Say, Let me in.'

'Let me in.'

And the world around Granger vanished.

It was night and he was standing on an island surrounded by luminous white mist. The ground ahead of him was black basalt and completely devoid of all plant life. It rose in a series of irregular stepped slopes towards a dark fortress formed from the same rock.

There were no windows in that building, merely a single doorway in the centre of a sheer and otherwise featureless façade. The only illumination came from the mist around the island.

Granger set off towards the fortress.

His metal boots clanked against black rock riven with myriad narrow cracks as if a huge hammer had come down and fractured this land. The air was cold and sharp and smelled of metal. No stars shone in the skies above him. He could hear his armour humming as it shifted limbs through which his blood had ceased to flow. He looked out across the mist, stretching away to the horizon like a softly glowing sea, but saw nothing of note.

As he neared the fortress, he spotted a figure he recognized crouched outside the doorway. The man was brine-scarred and wore armour identical to Granger's own.

'You left it late,' the replicate said.

'You might have told me about this,' Granger said.

'They are waiting for you inside.'

'They?'

The replicate grinned and indicated that Granger should enter.

The doorway led to a short passageway terminating in a set of steps leading upwards. Granger spied light coming from the top of the steps. He climbed, his metal footfalls echoing in that confined space, and arrived in a vast hall.

Torches in wall sconces cast a dim flickering light across a vast space. The chamber occupied what must have been the entire floor of the citadel. And it was crowded with people.

Thousands of them. They stood in silence and watched Granger step into that cavernous hall. The majority of them were men, battle-hardened veterans by the look of them, but Granger spied one or two women among the crowd of faces. Most wore armour of some sort. Here and there an epaulette or buckle or shield edge gleamed in the dim torchlight. These people were replicates, he realized, for their eyes were as dull and lifeless as manacle iron.

At the far end of the room Granger could see a dais. Upon this sat a throne of stone. And on the throne sat an Unmer sorcerer. He was a huge man, heavily muscled, with his naked torso and arms covered in the entropic geometries of his profession. Upon his bald head he wore a circlet of lead. His eyes were deeply set and unusually dark for one of the Unmer. On either side of him burned red chemical braziers.

Granger approached.

He passed between the ranks of replicates and stepped up on the dais and stood before the man who controlled the sword.

'My name is Shehernan,' he said. 'And I had expected you to come before now, Thomas Granger.'

'I didn't know this was possible.'

Shehernan shrugged. 'It is too late to come looking for a deal,' he said. 'Your body ceased normal function three days ago. Your mind is almost mine to control.'

'Why me?' Granger said.

The sorcerer was silent for a moment. Then he said, 'You, more than anyone, are likely to supply me with what I want. Your kind possess certain . . . unique abilities.'

'My kind?'

Shehernan's lips thinned. 'How is it that you, of all the people in the world, begot a child powerful enough to free the Unmer from enslavement?'

Granger frowned.

'I imagine you have a little of her talents yourself,' Shehernan said. 'Eh? A fraction of her gifts, but, nevertheless . . . Perhaps a talent for knowing where to look for things, or where to step to avoid a trap? You probably think of it as luck or intuition.'

Granger's men, the Gravediggers, had often said as much.

Whether it was a food panic in Weaverbrook, or spotting the Drowned, or escaping from a warlord in Ancillor – his intuition never failed him.

'These abilities came from one of your parents,' Shehernan said, 'who inherited them from one of their parents, and so on for nearly three hundred years. All leading to the birth of Ianthe, a blind deaf peasant girl from Evensraum powerful enough to smash an entire guild of psychics.'

'You're saying Ianthe was part of someone's plan?'

'She is the result of three centuries of selective breeding,' Shehernan said. 'Desired traits were chosen with every generation until finally a child is born who can do what she can do.'

Granger felt suddenly cold.

'Do you know who your parents were, Thomas Granger?'

Granger spoke through his teeth. 'I remember them.'

'You remember mortal people,' Shehernan said. 'But the creature who actually conceived you merely looked human. It was the same creature who conceived one or more of your grandparents and their parents before them and so on.'

A shape-shifter?

'Almost three hundred years ago, when King Jonas fled from the genocide of his own people, a shape-shifter came to him on a mountain trail. Fiorel made him an offer. In exchange for help in seeding the oceans with ichusae, Fiorel vowed to return the Unmer to power. And now he has succeeded.'

'How do you know this?'

Shehernan steepled his fingers under his chin and observed Granger with dark eyes. 'For many years I have been searching for someone to assist me in a particularly difficult task. When I learned of Ianthe's existence I knew that she was the only one who could help me. But my attempts to bring her to Pertica failed.'

'What do you want from her?'

'I want her to find something for me.'

'And when you couldn't get to her, you sent the deadship to retrieve me in her stead?' Granger rubbed his forehead, thinking. He had been adrift at sea when that strange crewless electric ship had made such a timely appearance. It had brought him far to the north, to an old Unmer transmitting station in the frozen wilds, where he had found the sword among a hoard of trove.

'I saved your life,' Shehernan said.

'Maybe.'

The sorcerer allowed himself a smile. 'And now you are dead,' he said. 'A walking corpse in power armour. We are past the point of any return, Thomas Granger. You cannot now survive without your armour or my sword. And very soon you will be mine to control.'

'I will make you a deal,' Granger said.

Shehernan regarded him in silence.

He wants to deal, Granger realized. 'Back off,' he went on. 'Stop forcing your will onto me. Give me control of my own replicates until my daughter is safe from harm. Agree to that and I'll persuade her to find whatever you want.'

The sorcerer got up from his throne and walked over to Granger. Standing, he was even more intimidating. He stood a full foot taller than Granger. He placed a hand on Granger's shoulder. 'Easier for me to enslave you. I can make you give the sword to Ianthe.'

'I won't do it.'

'You won't have a choice.'

Granger's jaw tightened. 'Even if my daughter accepted the sword,' he said through his teeth, 'you wouldn't enslave her so easily. She'd crush you like a fucking insect. And what about Marquetta? Do you think he'd allow you to corrupt his queen?'

Shehernan lifted his hand again. Granger knew from the other man's expression that he had him. Trying to enslave Ianthe was too much of a risk.

'Now, do as I say,' Granger said. 'And I'll ask her nicely. What is it you want found?'

The sorcerer was silent for a long moment. Then he nodded and said, 'I was old before I created this sword. Much older than my appearance suggests. We Unmer are long lived, but we are not immortal.' He gestured with his hand. 'I created all this to escape death. For four thousand years, I have been passed from warrior to warrior, lost for decades and then found again. My wielders have slain thousands. And yet none of them has been able to find the artefact I require.'

'What artefact?'

'It is another replicating sword. Much like this one.'

'Why do you want it?'

'That does not concern you.'

'Then there's no deal.'

Shehernan growled. 'I want to find the blade because I want to kill the sorcerer who lives inside it.'

Granger opened his eyes, to find himself back on the forest trail overlooking Losoto. The two ships at sea were now adjusting their sails to bring them into the ruined harbour, where the remains of cranes and dockside buildings choked the waters. Conquillas's daughter, Siselo, was sitting on a rock, watching him.

'How did it go?' she said.

Granger rubbed his eyes and nodded. 'It went well.'

'What was the sorcerer like?'

'Old and angry.'

'The usual, then.'

Granger shook his head and got to his feet groggily. Not much time seemed to have passed while he'd been inside the sword. And yet he definitely felt different. His ever-present headache had gone. He felt lighter. He looked down at the weapon and considered picking it up to test if it really had returned to him control of his own replicates. Maybe it was best to wait until the child wasn't around.

'How many sword phantoms can you make?' she said.

Granger looked over at her. 'Eight,' he said. 'Eight phantoms.'

'Oh,' she said.

'What?'

'Nothing.'

'Well how many did your father conjure?'

She shrugged. 'I don't really remember.' Suddenly she rushed over and snatched the sword up from the ground.

'Wait,' Granger said. He moved instinctively to stop her, but then halted. It occurred to him that something surprising had happened.

Siselo waved the blade through the air a few times, looking at it without much apparent interest. 'It's much heavier than our one,' she said. 'Ours was forged in Galea about three thousand years ago and the old Unmer blacksmiths folded the steel over on itself like a million times. This one looks even more ancient. But I don't think it's a very good example.'

'You don't have any replicates,' Granger said.

'What?'

'The sword phantoms,' Granger said. 'You don't have any!'

'Uh, that's not true!'

Granger frowned. 'How do you do it? How do you stop the replicates appearing?'

She looked puzzled, and then a light of comprehension lit her face. 'You mean, how do I do this?' she said. Siselo grinned widely and waved the sword around her head. 'I have four replicates,' she said. 'Can you see them?'

Granger looked around, but saw nobody. They were alone.

Siselo swished the blade in front of her. 'Now I have five replicates. Now six, seven, eight, nine.' She continued to grin. 'Can't you see them yet, Colonel?'

She looked around and then skipped across the trail, over to a large boulder. 'Ten and eleven and twelve,' she said, waving the sword around. 'Thirteen, fourteen, fifteen, sixteen. Sixteen sword phantoms. You still can't see them?'

Still gripping the sword, she stooped and abruptly lifted the boulder between both hands, in what was a seemingly impossible feat of strength. That rock must have weighed twice as much as she did. And then she turned and balanced it on one hand, holding it aloft. 'Seventeen, eighteen, nineteen, twenty,' she said. 'You must see them now, Colonel?'

Granger gaped at her for the second time that afternoon. Here was this waif of a girl, holding up a rock that should have crushed her like a flower. 'Don't you get it, Colonel?' she said. 'Don't you see?'

'How are you doing that?'

She grinned. 'You don't let the replicates wander about on their own. That's hard. It takes concentration.' She shook her head. 'All you have to do is keep them inside yourself. It's called phasing.' She hefted the rock over one shoulder, with little apparent effort, and then hurled it down into the forest below, where it crashed through the canopy and disappeared.

'Right now, you're looking at twenty of me. But you can't see us because we're all in the same place.'

Granger frowned. 'How can two things be in the same place?'

Siselo snorted. 'Easy!' she said. 'Matter is just energy. All you have to do is break a few laws, or something. It's like so simple I can't believe you had the sword all this time and never even thought of it.' She grinned again and thrust out the sword, pointing it at him. 'Phasing makes you stronger,' she said. 'And really, really heavy.' She jumped, and her boots sank three inches into the earth. 'Only Father says it's not good for you. Too many copies puts stress on your body and that can kill you. I'm not allowed to make more than thirty of them.' Suddenly she glanced up. 'But I don't suppose that's going to bother you much,' she said, 'seeing as how you're already dead.'

Ianthe wandered through the blasted city with Paulus and Cyr and the others from the two ships. Captain Howlish had come ashore with a small contingent of his men, as had Raceme Athentro – the old Unmer captain from the *Ilena Grey* – after leaving three of his men to guard the tenders.

Most of the buildings facing the harbour had been destroyed and the streets between them were strewn with rubble and bodies. A heavy silence hung in the air as Ianthe and the others picked their way through this human wreckage. She saw hands and limbs lying amidst piles of stone and rumpled clothing and shoes; mouths open but not breathing, dust-coated eyeballs. In places the streets were still puddled with brine, and the broken mortar had turned to grey mud.

Flies had already begun to gather.

Fifty yards further back, the damage was less severe. Half of the shops and houses still stood, although the Uriun had left many of these on the brink of collapse and so Howlish remarked that it was more dangerous here and they should keep to the centre of the streets. They climbed over a treacherous jumble of wooden joists and roof slates that had evidently been dragged here from further up the hill and then they followed a steep cobbled road flanked by shuttered shopfronts.

Ianthe began to feel as if she was being watched.

She noticed the others becoming aware of it too. They glimpsed people in the surviving buildings, faces that shrank away from windows when spotted, mothers who snatched up small children and ran. It was with an increasingly uncomfortable sense of unease that Ianthe realized that the occupants of this place were terrified. Terrified of the Unmer who now walked among them.

Terrified of her?

She tried to banish such thoughts from her mind, and yet with every step she took through Losoto's silent streets, she felt more like a burglar creeping further into someone's home.

They were not challenged. There were, just as Nera had claimed, no soldiers in the capital. Losoto's citizens continued to watch the intruders from their hiding places.

After a while the party reached a rich and airy quarter where birch trees stood in symmetry between ranks of grand townhouses. Rust-coloured leaves skittered across the street. A terrace of white sandstone and black iron balustrades granted them open views across the distant harbour. Ianthe looked down at the sea and felt a momentary stab of fear that the great worm was still there somewhere. But the waters remained quiet, the waves untroubled by memories of violence.

Howlish must have noticed the anxiety on her face for he smiled and said, 'Remember this moment, lass. I swear you'll never see Losoto this quiet again in your lifetime.'

'It's creepy.'

The captain looked up at a nearby townhouse. 'Bland, I'd call it.' Then he grinned and wandered off to speak to his men.

Paulus and Duke Cyr were speaking quietly with Captain Athentro and the other Unmer survivors, but they fell silent when Ianthe approached them. After a moment's hesitation, Paulus said, 'Can you sense anything unusual, Ianthe?'

'What do you mean? Like what?'

'This feels like a trap.'

She let her mind slip out to the edge of her own perception from where she might look out upon the gathered vision of all those around her. There were people hiding in the nearby buildings, but not many. Thousands more filled the city, clustered mainly in the area through which they'd passed, and – oddly – *below* it. She glimpsed brick vaults, aisles of Unmer objects. Suddenly she thought she understood.

'The market below this city,' she said.

'The trove market,' Paulus confirmed. 'You see people there?'

'Thousands.'

'That's to be expected. But no military? No soldiers?'

'No.'

Paulus sighed. 'Can they *really* have abandoned this place so readily?'

His question was met with silence from the others. None of the Unmer looked particularly convinced. Athentro said, 'The lack of resistance will make the task of assuming authority more difficult. These humans are base creatures. We have no hereditary pedestal here. Real authority requires that opposition is engaged and crushed. A battle should have been fought and won here. Instead we brought slaughter.'

'The tournament,' Paulus said. 'Perhaps they can find a champion in Conquillas?'

Athentro shrugged. 'The dragon lord has never represented these people before. It would be preferable if you defeated one of their own.'

Paulus glanced at Ianthe. 'Any news of your father?'

She shook her head.

He stared at her in silence for a moment, before signalling his intention to move on.

They found the palace gates – a tangle of garishly painted iron – lying open. Indeed it soon became apparent that the palace itself was deserted. They walked through bright halls and along glittering corridors resplendent in gold and silver. They progressed in silence, the sound of their footsteps echoing for miles.

At last they came to the throne room, and here they found the palace's only occupant.

She was dressed in rags and seated on the floor with her wrist chained to the arm of the throne. Around her lay scraps of food and pieces of smashed crockery – plates and cups and the broken remains of a water jug. It looked as if she'd destroyed them in a fit of anger. Her hair was matted and filthy and bruises covered her wrist and upper arm. Her right eye had been blackened and looked swollen and painful. Despite these injuries, Ianthe recognized her at once.

'Sister Marks!' she said, hurrying over.

When Briana Marks looked up at her, Ianthe could immediately see that something was desperately wrong with the woman. Something far worse than a mere beating. Her mouth was slack and trailing a line of spittle. She gaped up at her with bovine eyes.

Ianthe halted. 'What have they done to her?'

Duke Cyr arrived beside them. 'They have leucotomized her.' He examined the Haurstaf witch for a moment, then sniffed. 'A soldier did that to her, not a surgeon.'

Briana Marks rattled her chain.

'Sister Marks,' Ianthe said. 'Do you remember me?'

The Haurstaf witch ignored her and began pulling at her chain.

Ianthe felt tears filling her eyes. Despite everything Briana Marks had done to her, she didn't deserve this cruel fate. *I would have forgiven you*, Ianthe thought. *I'm so sorry.* 'Will someone please help her?' she said.

'It would be kinder to kill her,' Athentro said.

'Nobody's going to harm her,' Ianthe replied. She looked at Paulus, Cyr and Howlish. 'Please.'

Howlish nodded to one of his men. 'Find something.'

'Captain.' The man departed.

He returned with a gas cutting-torch and began cutting through the chains. Paulus, meanwhile, ordered Athentro and the other Unmer sailors to search the palace for anyone else – there would undoubtedly be servants hiding somewhere, he assured them – while he instructed Howlish and the rest of his crew to go back into the city and find out who, if anyone, was prepared to speak for however many of Losoto's two hundred thousand inhabitants remained. Then he took his uncle aside and the pair of them spoke in whispers for a long time. Finally, Duke Cyr nodded and hurried away.

Paulus came over to Ianthe. 'This is a delicate time,' he reminded her. 'The populace despise us. We have gained the palace but we have not yet earned it.'

Ianthe glanced at Briana Marks, but then turned away from the fierce glare of the crewman's gas torch. 'You mean to earn it through violence, don't you?'

He shrugged. 'How else is power earned?'

*

Granger and Siselo walked into Losoto from the north. They found a city in which the more affluent areas had been largely abandoned and everywhere else had been battened down. Every once in a while they caught a glimpse of someone peering out at them from a window or a letterbox, or heard footsteps hurrying away. But most of those who had stayed behind had chosen to stay hidden. The streets themselves would have been empty, but for Granger and the girl and a few scrawny cats.

Siselo was growing bored of shuttered windows and locks. She knocked on yet another door, then listened. 'Anybody there?' she called out in a sarcastic voice. She tried the handle and found it locked and so she kicked the doorstep in frustration. 'Where is everyone?'

'Hiding.'

'From who?'

'The one of us who looks most Unmer.'

'I could open any of these doors with a touch of my finger.'

'That would be illegal and immoral. We talked about this.'

She stamped her foot. 'What if nobody opens their door? Where are we going to stay?'

'We'll find somewhere.'

'But where?'

'An inn.'

'What if there aren't any inns? What if they don't take us in an inn?'

'Shush. Corner.'

She growled.

Knowing that the palace would be Marquetta's destination, Granger gave it a wide berth. Nevertheless, he stayed alert for any sign of the prince's men, listening carefully at each corner before peering around it. He supposed he might have hidden his presence here better, but then it seemed to him that Marquetta had recently become much less of a worry. Now that Granger was dead, he failed to see what more the young prince could threaten him with. His priority now was keeping Ianthe alive. And that meant finding Conquillas.

'I know what you're doing,' Siselo said.

'What?'

'I know why we're marching round the whole city. You want everyone to see us. You want them all to know we're here, so that my father hears of it and comes to find us.'

'Really?'

'I'm not stupid.'

He smiled at her. 'No, I don't think you are. And you're almost right. I'm not hiding our presence from the populace.' He shrugged. 'Then again, I don't suppose I could if I tried.'

'Yes you could,' she said. 'Well, I could. But you're wasting time trying to find my father that way. It's quicker if we just go straight to him.'

Granger stopped. 'You said you didn't know where he was.'

She pulled a face. 'Well I didn't. But I also said I know where he'll be. We've been in Losoto before, you know. There are places we both know, places we frequent.'

'*Frequent?* You know where he is?'

'Yes.' She nodded, then shook her head. 'Probably.'

'Where?'

She pointed at the ground.

Howlish returned to the palace with news that a number of Losotan citizens had organized themselves to the extent that they had appointed a war committee to speak to the invaders on their behalf. The opinion that the Unmer prince was not here to murder and enslave was beginning to filter through the general population. And, as the middle of the afternoon arrived, Ianthe found herself standing at the window of her requisitioned chambers, from where she could see Losoto's newly elected representatives being led through the crowds massed behind the palace gates.

On Duke Cyr's advice, the council was held in the throne room. The representatives were shown in by Howlish's men and presented individually to Paulus, who sat upon the seat of power. Ianthe lingered nearby.

She found the entire process phenomenally tedious and she suspected that Paulus found it so too. The representatives spoke on behalf of various groups: market traders and shop traders and importers; fishermen and farming cooperatives; businessmen and bankers and former council officials; innkeepers, hoteliers and brewers. Mostly they sought assurances from the Unmer that their property would remain in their ownership, that there would be no further appearance of the sorcerous creature that had wreaked havoc on the waterfront and no retaliation against what everyone was now calling *past imperial crimes*. Paulus conferred with Cyr and nodded and smiled and waved them all on. Since the imperial troops had deserted the city, law and order would be maintained by a royally appointed militia. Any men with military experience were to present themselves to Athentro. Salaries were suggested and agreed on, along with a temporary cessation of all alcohol and tobacco and foreign trade taxes in order to boost the city economy and thus better facilitate the transfer of power.

It went on like this for hours. They talked about city defence, the reopening of the port to foreign trade, Losoto's position in regard to provincial warlords, the forthcoming coronation and the reopening of the Halls of Anea. This last subject caused the greatest concern among the Losotan representatives, and Paulus and his uncle were hard pressed to allay their fears.

Throughout it all Ianthe tried to appear regal, patient, interested, but eventually she couldn't take any more of it. She made an excuse about seeing to some palace duties and then left to go for a walk.

She found Howlish smoking a pipe outside the door.

When he saw her, he grinned. 'Well, you lasted longer than I thought you would,' he said. 'Are they still talking about whale oil reserves or have they moved on to dried fish?'

'Actually it's the tournament now. Paulus—' She stopped herself. 'Prince Marquetta seems quite animated.'

The captain observed her for a moment. 'You've seen this great snake in the garden?'

'Not yet.'

He bowed. 'Why don't you let me show you?'

'Now?'

'There's a temple inside,' Howlish said. 'Might be a good time to offer the old gods a prayer.'

'Surely you don't believe in the old gods?'

He shrugged. 'I'll try anything once.'

They left the palace and walked out into the imperial gardens, where ten thousand blooms exuded delicate scents and embellished the verges with a bold but stuttering pronouncement of yellows, pinks and white. There were stone fountains and statues of nymphs in quartz and loops of miniature hedge as green as the waters of Mare Verdant. Songbirds trilled in golden cages hung from an old yew.

Two alabaster columns held open the mouth of the great petrified sea snake. Its maw was large enough to allow Ianthe and Howlish to enter walking abreast. Inside it was cool and lit dimly by hundreds of coloured gem lanterns hanging from the creature's spine. Their footsteps echoed. A sinuous passageway led further inside the creature.

Ianthe pressed her hand against the inside of the snake. It felt smooth and cool to the touch. 'Feels like glass,' she said.

'It's varnished,' Howlish explained. 'They have to keep applying the coats for years. If you ran down the inside of this thing, licking the walls as you went, you'd be as high as Jovram by the time you reached the tail. Or dead, anyhow.' He chuckled and loaded his pipe again. 'There's an old tale about a man who was swallowed by one of these,' he said, firming the tobacco into the clay bowl. 'He lived in there for years, making his fire from the boats the serpent swallowed and eating the sailors aboard them. Sometimes he'd find the sailors alive and he'd have to kill them. And, when he cooked them, you could see the smoke come out of the snake's nostrils. That's how people came to think they breathed fire.'

'They all died out?'

Howlish lit his pipe with a match. 'You'll hear people who claim to have seen them,' he said. 'But it's all grog talk. Nobody's caught one of these things for five hundred years.'

They wandered on, deeper into the snake's body. The path meandered to and fro so that Ianthe could never see more than a few yards ahead. The gem lanterns in here were ancient and cast a particularly gentle light, their soft colours bleeding together – reds into yellows into greens – as they walked. The space around them became larger at the belly of the serpent only to grow narrower again as they neared the tail.

The passageway ended abruptly at a pedestal carved out of a strange glossy red stone. It resembled two serpents coiled around each other vertically, a helical arrangement supporting a shallow bowl. The bowl held a small amount of clear liquid.

'It's ashko,' Howlish said.

'Ashko?' She reached her hand towards it.

Howlish grabbed her. 'A very powerful drug,' he said. 'While it might be fun, I don't think your fiancé would approve.'

She could see thin white lines on the back of his fingers, old scars from the Haurstaf lash. It reminded her that this man had once been a privateer. The Guild of psychics had once hired him, but they hadn't spared his punishment. In that sense they had something in common.

He stared at her hand a moment before releasing it. 'Are you looking forward to the games?' He said this amiably enough, but something in his manner gave the impression that he was troubled.

'Of course.'

'Really?' he said. 'I wouldn't have thought that it was your sort of thing.'

'It isn't; I mean, the prince is eager to show me.'

Howlish nodded slowly. He bit his lip and then raised a hand to his mouth, in a nervous gesture. 'How much do you know about the Halls of Anea?'

'Only what everyone knows.'

'You know that they lie in a rift?'

This surprised her.

Howlish went on, 'I used to work for Hu, you see.' He hesitated, shot a glance at her. 'The halls have been there for a long, long time – nobody really knows how long, but thousands of years. The Unmer's ancestors unearthed them before they abandoned Losoto for Galea. And there's those who say that it was something in the halls that made them leave.' He scratched his chin. 'When you go up to them, you'll see for yourself. The entrance is like a door into the hillside – like going into a mine, except finely carved. More like a temple.

And you think you're going under the hill, it feels that way, but the truth is, you're not even on this world any more.'

'This rift is under a hill?'

He shook his head. 'No, it doesn't work like that. The door to the rift – the halls – that's buried in the hillside. But the halls themselves . . .' He shrugged. 'They might be anywhere. Outside this universe, maybe. I don't know. But I do know that they are far larger than most people think they are. That's why Hu couldn't flood them. There isn't enough brine on this planet to do that.'

'How large is it? Has it been mapped?'

The corners of Howlish's lips twitched. 'Mapped? Oh, we found maps of the parts that have been explored. There are rooms in there . . . rooms Duke Cyr won't show you, rooms full of ancient maps.' He leaned closer. 'Maps of great halls and corridors, stairs, tunnels, lakes and pits and canals – all carved, mind you. Every inch of it expertly chiselled from the stone on a scale that you wouldn't believe. You could sail a galleon through some of the larger doors. And those parts of the Halls of Anea that *have* been explored extend much further than Anea itself – maybe further than it's even possible to travel on this world. Some people think it goes on forever. Endless halls and endless darkness.'

Ianthe frowned.

'Exactly,' Howlish said. 'That's the question that begs an answer.'

'What question?'

'Who made it?' he said. 'And why?'

'That's two questions. Well, who did make it?'

'Giants . . . I don't know. But I know why Hu sealed it up.'

She waited.

'People used to see and hear strange things all the time in

there,' he said. 'Ghosts. Queer lights. Combatants went missing outside the arenas. Divisions sent to look for them went missing. And then armies sent to find those divisions went missing. There are tales of terrible things lurking in the further reaches of the halls.'

'Like what?'

'I don't know. Old gods, maybe.'

'Oh come on, Captain, you know—'

'I saw something,' Howlish cut in. 'Before Hu buried the entrance, I was in there. The emperor used to send criminals in with ichusae. I was . . . helping. It was only a glimpse, but . . .' His eyes looked inward as he remembered, then he shook his head. 'I saw a giant figure in the darkness,' he said wearily. 'It looked at me for an instant and then it slipped away into the shadows. I've never felt such a chill. Never felt like I've been in the presence of such *evil*.'

'What was it?'

He didn't reply at once. He was silent for a moment longer and then he said, 'I'm telling you all this because . . . maybe you'll be in a position to do something about it. The Unmer might seem to be in control of all this sorcery, all this power, but really they're like children who've been given the key to an armoury. Your prince is much older than either of us, but he's not infallible, Ianthe. He's just a man like any other. And there are things in the Halls of Anea that should never be disturbed.'

Granger looked up one last time through the circle of light immediately above his head, then dragged the round iron cover across it. It settled into place with a *bang*, plunging the sewer shaft into darkness.

Siselo's voice came from below. 'You could have waited till I got the lamp out!'

Granger grumbled something non-committal under his breath. He climbed down ten feet of metal rungs in utter darkness until his boots touched solid stone. At that moment, Siselo found her gem lantern and opened the shutter and light flooded into the narrow space.

They were in a brick sewage tunnel running roughly north–south. A runnel of brown, stinking water rushed along a channel a foot below their ankles, but the ledge on either side allowed them to follow its course without getting wet. Granger could hear the sewage gurgling somewhere to the south, where he guessed it must either drop through a shaft, or pass into a basin. However, their light revealed nothing but curved brick walls receding into utter black. The smell made his eyes water.

'This way.' Siselo raised the lantern and scampered away, heading south.

Granger sighed and followed.

They wandered along that ghastly passageway for several hundred yards, and then turned to the right, into an identical conduit. This took them another fifty yards or so, after which they turned left into a narrower, orthogonal tunnel that was barely larger than Granger's shoulders. This section of the sewer system looked older. Dozens of other channels branched off from the main conduit, but they maintained a straight course, all the while following the foul watercourse. After what must have been half a mile, Siselo stopped and examined a section of the brick wall near the floor. Then she lifted the lantern again and proceeded onwards.

As Granger passed, he looked at the place where she'd paused and noticed a number of horizontal and vertical chalk marks on the brickwork. Evidently some sort of code. Before he could examine it in any detail, Siselo had carried the light onwards, leaving him behind in the gloom, and he was forced to jog to catch her up.

It seemed to him that she was counting her steps now.

A short distance beyond the chalk marks Siselo stopped and raised her hand. Granger halted behind her.

'Tripwire,' she said.

She stepped over what could only have been the afore-mentioned wire, and then waited for him.

Granger approached. By the light of her lantern he could see a very fine wire running across the tunnel, a foot higher than the ledge above the watercourse.

'He set traps?'

She smiled. 'Actually, I set that one.'

'You use explosives?'

She looked offended. 'Explosives are for children. I used void arrows.' She turned away and hurried along the tunnel, taking the light with her.

They changed direction three more times, by which time Granger had begun to doubt his own spatial awareness. He'd always had a knack for knowing where he was in relation to anywhere else, and he felt fairly sure they were still moving south. However, now he was less than completely confident: the sort of level of confidence on which one might bet one's own life, if hard pressed, but not the life of another.

Siselo continued to follow the marks on the walls. They negotiated two further tripwires, and – at the girl's firm insistence – avoided a narrow beam of light that slanted down through the brickwork from a hole no wider in diameter than a pencil. Granger became used to the odour, which now reminded him less of human waste and more of stale rain-water.

Finally Siselo stopped. In the tunnel wall beside them was a dark hole about two feet square. She shone the lantern down it, revealing a shaft that sloped steeply downwards. He listened and heard nothing but that peculiarly hollow subterranean silence. He sniffed. The air down there smelled no better or worse than the air up here. Siselo was looking at him expectantly.

'What?' he said. 'You want us to go down there?'

She grinned and squatted down at the edge of the hole. Then she set down the lantern, swung her legs into the shaft, and lowered herself inside it. A heartbeat later she let go and dropped, vanishing from sight.

'Siselo?' Granger called after her.

No answer.

'Siselo?'

After a moment he heard her voice calling back, but it sounded so very distant that he couldn't even be sure what she'd said. He sat down on the edge of the shaft and slipped his kitbag from his shoulder. He dropped the bag into the shaft. It disappeared without a sound. Then he picked up the lantern and eased himself forward. The shaft dropped away below him almost vertically. His armoured boots scrabbled for purchase, but found none. The shaft was lined with rough red bricks, and yet the surface under him was smooth stone or concrete.

Her voice carried up from a long way away. 'Colonel?'

Granger eased his body further into the shaft. Then he let go.

He dropped at a frightening speed. Brickwork whizzed by his face in the light of his lantern. His stomach tightened into a knot.

And then abruptly he realized he was slowing down. The slope under him was no longer so steep. It continued to level out. A second later, he emerged from the shaft and skidded to a halt on his back, his boots thumping into his kitbag. He was looking up at the ceiling of a cavernous space.

Siselo was waiting for him. She giggled. 'You should see your face.'

'What is this place?'

'Just a place.'

They were in an enormous underground cavern filled with what appeared to be treasure. Granger was lying on a stone bench that protruded from the wall under the shaft exit. He swung his legs over and sat upright, raising the lantern.

Everywhere he looked, he saw the gleam of gold. There were gilt settees and footstools and gilded tables, golden vases and pots and pails overflowing with coins and medals and jewellery. Ancient candelabra of different styles held hundreds of tallow candles which Siselo was now busy lighting with a taper. The cavern was undoubtedly natural, Granger decided, and yet the living rock had been decorated with numerous carvings. Some of the stalactites and stalagmites had been fashioned into elaborate spiral pillars, while others had been left in their natural state. Between these towering forms lay exquisite furniture, plumply adorned with cushions of yellow and emerald silk.

Conquillas's daughter continued to light candles. Granger got to his feet and swung his gem lantern around, marvelling at the rippling grey façades that swept up and over his head. The cavern extended for more than a hundred yards and terminated in a huge and outwardly swelling crust of white and pink quartz. There were doorways everywhere, often high up the walls and accessed by ladders.

For all the wealth and luxury, there was no sign that this place had been used recently.

'The trove market is that way,' Siselo said, pointing in a direction Granger thought might be west. 'The way in is hidden, though. That's where most of this stuff comes from.'

'It's stolen?'

She scowled at him. 'Stolen? Who do you think made all this in the first place? Humans?' She scrunched her face into a comical leer. 'No, I didn't think so. We just *reclaim* whatever is useful and some things I like. Lots of trove, obviously, but Father keeps that through there, away from the quartz. You know how crystals affect some artefacts. And rain. Or even people, which is quite funny.' She looked at him. 'Did you ever wonder why some artefacts get attracted to certain types of people? It's like how dragons have a sense for people. Like they read people. Oh, you have to swear not to tell anybody about this place.'

Granger picked up a handful of rings from a wooden box and let then spill from his fingers. There was a fortune in this place, enough to buy a ship. A fleet of ships.

'Colonel?'

'What?'

'You can't tell anyone about this place.'

He nodded. 'Right.'

'No, you have to swear.'

'All right.'

'So?'

'So what?'

'So go on and swear.'

'I swear.'

'At last!' She rolled her eyes. 'Honestly, you're like my father. It's so hard getting you to do anything.'

'Where is your father?'

'He isn't here yet,' she said. 'I'd know if he was. But he'll turn up eventually.'

'How do you know he isn't here?'

She gaped at him, then pulled another face. 'Uh . . . maybe because I'm *not stupid*.'

Right, fine. Granger didn't want to know. He couldn't remember the last time he'd had a decent rest, and right now he was exhausted. Conversing with Siselo was just as wearisome as trying to talk to Ianthe. He dumped his kitbag and then lay down on one of the settees, feeling the plates of his power armour settle under his shoulders.

There was a *crack*, and two of the settee's dainty legs snapped under his weight. The underside of the seat struck the stone floor. Now he was lying with his boots above his head.

'That was my father's favourite settee,' Siselo said.

Granger got up again and then turned round so his head was higher than his feet. He glanced over at the girl and grumbled, 'I'll get him another one.'

'You won't find another one. It's about a thousand years old and it's probably the only one in all Anea or even the world.'

Granger sighed and closed his eyes. 'Get some rest, Ianthe. It's been a long day.'

'My name is Siselo.'

'Right.'

CHAPTER 8

THE TOURNAMENT

The next few weeks saw some major changes in both the city and in Ianthe's life. Paulus announced his commitment to repair the damage caused by the Uriun and met daily with the Citizens' Representative Council, as they came to be known. Work progressed quickly and soon the streets were free of rubble and most of the dead had been laid to rest. A few survivors had been pulled from the wreckage at the beginning, but there hadn't been any for days now. Ianthe feared that those who had still not been found must surely have perished.

And so it transpired that Athentro's refugees, those one thousand souls who represented the last of the Anean Unmer, came to live in the same city in which they'd been imprisoned for much of their lives. Apartments were found for them in the abandoned townhouses near to the palace, but several of the older men and women refused such grandeur, choosing instead to return to the ghettos from which they had been released. Ianthe found this difficult to understand, but Howlish merely laughed and said you get used to calling a place home and some people – even the Unmer – dislike change. He also said that a prison was no longer a prison once the locks were opened and the guards had all departed.

Ianthe was also surprised how quickly and effortlessly the

citizens of Losoto accepted Prince Paulus Marquetta as their new ruler. Howlish said, 'They've had Emperor Hu for the last twenty years. Anything would be an improvement. Anarchy would be an improvement.' Although she didn't count the former privateer as a friend, she enjoyed his company. He would find her in the palace gardens most evenings and always stopped for a smoke and a chat. 'People don't care who sits on the throne,' he said, 'as long as they've got somewhere to sleep, something to eat, and someone to fuck.' Upon leaving her he would invariably wander into the great petrified serpent for a dab of ashko on his tongue before heading back to meet his men at the harbour inns.

Duke Cyr had the council appoint special militias to fill the gap left by the imperial soldiers. These men now kept law and order. Trade began to blossom again. Fishing boats unloaded catches in the harbour, and the morning market reopened. Even the trove sellers in the vaults below the city began to find customers for their treacherous wares. Within a month the city seemed to have recovered, if not to complete normality, then at least to a level of effective functionality.

Word of the city's revived prosperity spread through trade and telepathic channels, as did the announcement of the upcoming coronation and marriage. Soon the palace buzzed with visitors who'd come to pledge allegiance to the future king of Anea and his bride-to-be. Wealthy businessmen and landowners came from Do'esto and Valcinder, and prison-keepers travelled from Ethugra. Warlords filled the harbour with brightly painted and goldspun sails. They came to bend the knee and receive assurances that, while a new kingdom would be born out of the palace of an old empire, nothing of consequence would change. Their properties and powers remained safe under Marquetta's rule.

Emperor Hu had taken fifty cohorts of his men and fled north, a march that was said to have stripped a dozen villages of wheat and pork and cabbages, but the news coming from that part of the world was that this army had begun to unravel near Hesellan and the Friesnan gorges. Deserters had been spotted heading south in droves and it was rumoured that some had already returned to their families in Losoto. Only the emperor's Samarol bodyguards remained loyal to him; their silver wolf's head helmets struck fear in all who saw them.

Weeks passed. And as the day of Paulus's coronation drew ever nearer, Losoto went from a recovering city to something that began to resemble a flourishing one. Ianthe could scarcely believe that such a change could happen in such a short time. She began to notice more people than ever in the streets around the palace as Losoto's upper classes returned from self-imposed exile in the country. Now servants came and went from townhouses that had previously been locked and shuttered. Late summer flowers appeared in window boxes. Horses clopped through the cobbled streets. Ships from every corner of the empire filled the harbour to bursting.

Ianthe stayed in the palace grounds for all this time, for Duke Cyr had warned her against venturing outside. She remained a target for Conquillas or even agents of the emperor. The gardens were so extensive that she never felt claustrophobic. But, as the chain of days grew long, the city beyond the painted iron became less threatening and more enticing. Paulus was always so busy, she hardly saw him. He visited her occasionally to enquire about her ongoing search for Conquillas. She kept looking for the dragon lord but she never found him. She didn't search for her father at all. She couldn't think of him without thinking about his replicates – those dead-eyed fiends who walked with him. She didn't search for him because she was afraid she would find him.

The laying of the crown on her fiancé's head and the placement of his ring upon her finger were to happen on the last day of autumn – the month known as Hu-Suarin in the old imperial calendar, or Reth in the Unmer one. In preparation for the tournament, a detachment of workers was dispatched to uncover the entrance to the Halls of Anea.

But, as the coronation and the marriage drew nearer, Ianthe's doubts continued to grow. Her fiancé's rise to power, the palace in which they now lived, the servants who waited on them, the soldiers who paraded for them, the citizens who paid tax to keep them – none of it could have happened without Ianthe. She was the shield that had kept the Unmer safe from the surviving Haurstaf. And, as long as Paulus was to stay in power, he would need that shield.

But did he love her?

Sometimes Ianthe thought he did. But other times it all seemed like a charade designed to keep her on his side. And still her life rolled inevitably towards the marriage. Could she stop it even if she wanted to?

To keep her mind occupied, she passed her mornings on the terrace outside her quarters, practising her writing and reading dozens of books. Most often she spent her afternoons in one of the many quiet corners of the emperor's gardens, helping the old gardener, Mr Doorum, to root out weeds, or else simply sitting in the cool green shade under a tree and watching sparrows hop and twitter among the branches. Paulus admonished her for helping the servants, but Ianthe enjoyed it. What else was she supposed to do here? She grew to love the gardens. It was the only place since her childhood in Evensraum that she could see wild birds every day.

And before she knew it, the big day was imminent.

On the eve of Ianthe's marriage day the morning was crisp and airy. She found the manicured lawns and the box mazes deep in orange leaves and she saw a convoy of leathershine-black carriages clopping up the driveway to form a queue leading back from the palace entrance portico. She hurried over, expecting guests, only to discover that the carriages were all stuffed to the roofs with wedding dresses.

'Prince Marquetta requested a selection of gowns for your wedding tomorrow,' said a uniformed man at the door. He introduced himself as Mr Greaves from Salamander Street and he had been hired that very morning as the prince's valet.

'Are these all for me?' Ianthe said.

Mr Greaves nodded and said, 'Of course, Milady.'

'But there must be every dress in Losoto here.'

'Far more than that,' said Mr Greaves.

The dresses filled seven of the palace suites. There were garments of spider silk, worm silk and beetle silk, of glazed cotton, flax, lace and velvet in a thousand shades of whites and creams and colours from the daintiest pastels to bloody reds and chemical blues and chocolate; dresses of every possible shape and design, all pinched, puffed, frilled, embroidered, layered, seamed, scalloped and rumpled. Dresses so heavy she couldn't lift them. Dresses as light as newfallen snow. Dresses woven from gold and silver thread or so encrusted with jewels that they stood perfectly upright even without an occupant. Ianthe wandered from room to room, through these glades of silk and sparkles, and then she threw herself on the nearest bed and shrieked with delight.

But she could not choose a dress.

The prince supplied her with an army of maids – maids to carry garments from room to room or pile them high upon the beds, maids who gathered around her or rushed around with pins between their lips and threads wound around their fingers, helping her into one dress after another, forever adjusting cloth, clasping and unclasping, smoothing out or rumpling up, tugging at sleeves and fixing hems.

They were excellent as servants and seamstresses, but made terrible companions, for Ianthe could not extract from them a single word of honest criticism. Each garment, if Ianthe chose to believe these meticulously espaliered opinions, made Ianthe look exquisite, beautiful, radiant, regal and sublime. *Sublime* was a favourite. At one point she swore that if she heard the word again she would send the offending girl to enquire if Paulus had appointed an executioner yet. The servants would not be persuaded to convey anything less than hysterically effusive praise at everything Ianthe tried on, even when Ianthe herself felt ugly and foolish in the blasted thing.

Finally she dismissed them all and sat alone amid mountains of material. At that moment, more than anything, she wished that her father was there.

Siselo shifted the contents of her plate around with a spoon. 'This fish tastes funny. Are you sure it's fresh?'

'There's nothing wrong with it,' Granger said.

The two of them were sitting at breakfast in Conquillas's Losotan hideaway. Half a dozen gem lanterns hung from various hooks and chains around their table, illuminating mounds of gleaming treasure and broken rocks. Siselo wore a tunic and breeches of hunting cloth, as she called it – a vaguely sorcerous material that changed colour depending on her surroundings. It was just one of the many possessions she kept in chests in her room. The cave system down here encompassed more bedrooms and bathrooms than the grandest of the mansion houses in the city above them, although Granger slept on the broken settee in the main hall.

'How many times did you boil it?' she said.

'Three times.'

'And you changed the water each time?'

He snapped at her. 'The fish is fine, Siselo!'

She was silent for a moment and then she said, 'I know why you're so upset.'

'I'm not upset.'

'Yes you are. You're upset because it's her wedding tomorrow.'

Granger said nothing. Siselo was right, of course. He'd been cooped up here for weeks, waiting for Conquillas to arrive. But the dragon lord hadn't shown up yet. And Granger was starting to worry that perhaps he wasn't going to show up at all. Lying low was one thing, but Conquillas seemed to have completely disappeared from the face of the earth. He wondered if Prince Marquetta had actually managed to have the man assassinated. At least then Ianthe would be safe.

Prince Marquetta?

Tomorrow it would be King Marquetta. And Ianthe would be his queen. Inside his gauntlet, Granger's hand tightened into a fist. He stood up and strode over to his kitbag.

'You're not practising now, are you?' Siselo said. 'I was going to read.'

Granger ignored her. He rummaged through the bag and pulled out his replicating sword. The moment his hand closed on the grip, he felt his replicates start to appear. Only this time they did not appear in the space around him, but rather in the space *inside* him. *Phasing*, Siselo had called it. She'd said it was something to do with matter and energy being the same thing, but Granger didn't much care for the science or philosophy behind the sorcery. What he cared about was the effect.

So he gripped the sword hilt and concentrated. He found phasing to be much easier than using the sword to create spatially distinct versions of himself. Those outwith his own body were independent. They possessed their own disparate perceptions and reactions, which made them harder to control. Phased replicates, however, shared the same body as he did and thus shared his view of the world. He didn't have to assign different parts of his mind to different tasks. By creating versions of himself inside himself, Granger found that he was able to increase his strength to superhuman levels. And that was before the power armour amplified it.

Granger willed forth dozens of replicates. In his mind he imagined them as cards falling one on top of the other and yet the card pile never increased in size. He felt his entire body grow massive inside his own armour. The alloy plates began to tremble and hum as hundreds and then thousands of sword phantoms shuddered into existence inside it.

'You're overdoing it!' Siselo said.

Granger grunted and took several steps forward. The stone floor cracked under his armoured boots. His suit began to spark and shed arcs of rainbow light as it struggled to cope with the immense energies contained within. This number of replicates would have stopped the heart of a normal man, but Granger's heart was sustained even in death by his armour and could not be stopped. He strode forward to the cavern wall and made a fist with his left gauntlet and then placed it against the rock.

He pushed.

His fist remained where it was, but his boots slid away from the wall.

Granger let out a roar of frustration. Still gripping the sword, he smashed both fists against the rock, again and again, pummelling it with left and right hooks. His armour whined as it amplified the force of a thousand replicates. The rock broke under his assault. Great chunks of stone fell to the floor. Dust clouded around him.

'Stop!' Siselo cried. 'You'll break the suit.'

Granger halted. He stood there, breathing heavily, shrouded in dust, and surveyed the destruction he had caused. A four-foot-square section of the cavern wall had collapsed around him.

Siselo stared at him as if he was insane. 'What did that wall ever do to you?' she said.

Granger looked at her. 'I can't wait for your father any longer,' he said. 'If I'm dead then I'm dead and I'll just have to live with that. Tomorrow I leave.'

'Leave? For where?'

'I'm going to my daughter's wedding.'

Despite the destruction to the imperial capital, Losoto's harbour was so full that there was no suitably large berth available for the *Lamp*. Maskelyne briefly considered sinking one of the warlord's galleons to make room for his own dredger, but then decided against it. The water wasn't deep enough and he might snag his hull on the sunken vessel's masts.

So he ordered his crew to drop anchor in the centre of the bay and then he clambered down into the tender with Mellor and the Bahrethroan sorcerer named Cobul. The chatter Jones had picked up on his ear trumpet these last few weeks had proved accurate. Marquetta had unleashed some vast and terrible creature upon Losoto, for no apparent reason other than to demonstrate that he could.

As they sped across the choppy waters, Maskelyne gazed out at the damage the thing had caused. From here it looked as if they were rebuilding the entire city.

Other news had been more mundane, if a royal wedding could be called mundane. They had arrived in time to witness Prince Marquetta's coronation and his marriage to the Lady Ianthe Cooper of Evensraum. This would have been fortuitous if Maskelyne had any intention of attending. He didn't, so the timing was more of an annoyance to him. He had hoped for an audience with Prince Marquetta, but that seemed unlikely given the current situation. The prince would undoubtedly be busy until after all this nonsense had passed. And what if the pair then took a honeymoon?

'You look agitated,' Cobul observed.

'That's because I am agitated,' Maskelyne replied.

Cobul looked at him for a minute longer. When Maskelyne did not elaborate, he turned away.

By the time the tender had knocked against the quay, Maskelyne was in a more philosophical mood. After all, he thought, there was nothing like a good honeymoon to cheer a king up. And a cheerful king was more likely than a dour one to offer the metaphysicist a job.

Mellor cut the engines and tied up and the three men climbed the steps up to the quayside.

The docks were busy with sailors, porters and merchants. Groups of men in woollen caps and coats smoked and warmed their hands at braziers. A blind beggar rattled his cup against the ground. Other workers pushed goods to and fro, the trolleys squeaking and bumping over the steel crane rails set into the concrete. The crane itself was currently positioned at the end of the dock, unloading a steamer from Valcinder. It loomed over their heads, a great hissing metal-slatted monster. Crowds parted around the three men as they stood there and surveyed their surroundings. Directly in front of them Maskelyne noticed a board covered in lists.

'Now that is fortuitous, Cobul,' he exclaimed. 'For I do believe these are the tournament lists.'

Sure enough, the names inked onto the papers covering the board were those of tournament entrants. There had to be half a hundred of them down already. Maskelyne peered at the names, but could not find Conquillas's among the combatants. He turned to a dock worker who was slouching against the board with his arms folded and his cap pulled down over his eyes.

'Are you a tournament official?'

The man started, then snatched his cap back from his eyes. 'I am, sir, yes.'

'Are these all the combatants?'

'As of last night, sir. There's another board on Pilemoth and one outside the palace, but I don't have the new additions from there yet. We update the three at dusk.'

'So Conquillas hasn't arrived in Losoto?'

The man tilted his cap and drew a hand across his brow. 'We would have noticed him, sir.' He leaned closer. 'There's a rumour going round that he was killed in Vale.'

'Killed.'

'Assassinated.'

Maskelyne laughed. 'I doubt that.' He glanced at Cobul. 'I suppose my friend here would like to know how much is in the prize fund. What's the cost to enter?'

'The Lord's List is ten thousand sir, so the winner is currently looking at about half a million, but it'll likely be double that by the time the contest starts. There's also a fifty-gilder pit game running for the first three days. That's open to all. The winner of that one gets a ticket to the Lord's List.'

'Warm-up sport, eh?'

'The best, sir.'

Cobul looked concerned. 'I don't have ten thousand gilders,' he said. He grunted and shrugged his shoulders. 'To tell the truth, I don't even have fifty for the grunts' league.'

'I would lend you the ten thousand if I had it,' Maskelyne said. 'Nothing would please me more. Unfortunately I don't carry that much in cash aboard the *Lamp*. If we were only in Ethugra . . .'

'I'd never ask you for a loan,' Cobul replied. 'I'll join the pit contest as soon as I can muster the fifty.'

'Oh, I'll pay the fifty,' Maskelyne said.

'I cannot accept,' Cobul said. 'It is too much.'

'Nonsense,' Maskelyne said. 'I plan to spend more than that on our lunch.' He handed the official the amount in coins and collected a contestant's ticket for the sorcerer. 'Now, let's see if any of my favourite restaurants are still standing.'

As it turned out, none of them was. The Unmer monster had razed them all to the ground. Eventually they found a small place off one of the main shopping thoroughfares, where they ended up crammed into a corner table, drinking rather poor Awl valley wine while they waited on three plates of wild venison and creamed potatoes.

Cobul was attracting glances from all the other patrons.

Maskelyne observed this while he munched on breadsticks. 'I suppose you're the first sorcerer to come here in, what, two hundred and seventy years,' he said to Cobul.

'There were sorcerers in the ghetto,' Cobul replied.

'But they were in the ghetto,' Maskelyne said. 'Out of sight.'

He watched Cobul carefully. 'I expect Marquetta will pay them into the Lord's List.'

'Expect he will.'

'The competition doesn't bother you?'

Cobul sipped his wine and then leaned back in his chair. He looked at the restaurant patrons and they looked back at him. 'King Jonas hired me for a reason,' he said. 'He hired me despite my . . .' He made a gesture, indicating his face.

'Your what?' Maskelyne said.

'My race.'

'Your father was Unmer, though? And a formidable sorcerer too, I imagine.'

Cobul nodded. 'You won't have heard of him, Maskelyne.'

'Try me.'

'Jian Cobul. I'm named after him.'

'I see.'

'He was an old Galean Brutalist,' Cobul went on. 'A veteran of Onlo. You know he washed up on the beach near my village? That's true. At first he claimed that his captain had thrown him off the ship, but eventually he admitted that he'd simply got drunk and fallen overboard.' The Bahrethroan sorcerer smiled. 'He was unorthodox.'

'A man after my own heart. He liked Bahrethroa so much he stayed.'

'Something like that.'

'I admit, I'm surprised I didn't know the name. I thought I knew of all the great Brutalists.'

Cobul finished his wine and helped himself to another. 'I'm sure you know about the ones who wished to make their mark on history,' he said. 'My father wasn't like that. He yearned for a quiet life, a family. He despised politics and war. But he loved the art of sorcery.'

'What about you? What do you want?'

Cobul sighed. 'A quiet life, a family.'

Maskelyne raised his eyebrows. 'That's all?'

'That's all,' Cobul said. 'But Fiorel will never leave me in peace. When he learns I have escaped, he will try to kill me.'

'You'd better hope he isn't in Losoto.'

Cobul shrugged. 'These gods are not so powerful,' he said. 'These entropaths, they try to make us believe that they're omniscient. They seem . . .' He shook his head. 'They are masters of manipulation, people, events. They think, plan, so far ahead. They work out every little eventuality, every possible outcome. And most people never know they've been used, moved into place like chess pieces on a board. They think their actions are governed by their own desires. But they are not invincible. Conquillas proved that when he killed Duna.'

Maskelyne thought about this. 'You know, Cobul, something just occurred to me. The first thing our young Unmer prince did after he was freed was to challenge Conquillas to a fight in a public tournament. Furthermore, it also occurs to me that Conquillas will be expected to fight all sorts of other contestants before he faces Marquetta. Contestants from all over the world. Contestants of all sizes and shapes.'

'You think this is Fiorel's plan?' Cobul said.

'I can see how someone might find it a satisfying way to end the life of a legendary warrior. Argusto Conquillas the dragon lord, gut-stabbed by a nobody in a public arena.' Maskelyne refilled the other two men's glasses and then upended the empty bottle over his own, catching the last few drops. 'Barkeep,' he called out. 'More wine.'

The barkeep brought them another bottle of Awl valley red and set it down on the table. Granger, Mellor and Cobul leaned back in their seats while he poured. 'You gentlemen here for the coronation?' the barkeep asked.

'What coronation?' Maskelyne said.

'Prince Marquetta,' the barkeep said. 'Tomorrow they're going to crown him king of Anea.'

'You don't say?'

The barkeep expressed disbelief. 'It's all everyone's been talking about for weeks,' he said. 'That and the wedding. And the games to come.' He beamed. 'You really haven't heard?'

'Must have slipped my mind,' Maskelyne remarked. 'Exciting times indeed.'

'Certainly are.'

'Now go away.'

'Sir?'

'Fuck off.'

The barkeep stared at Maskelyne for a moment. Then he put down the bottle, shook his head, and walked away.

Mellor let out a sigh. 'How many times do I have to tell you, sir? If you're going to speak to the staff like that, will you please wait until after we've eaten.'

'I can't deal with cretins right now,' Maskelyne said. He turned back to Cobul and lowered his voice. 'Are you sure you still want to enter this tournament?'

Cobul grinned. 'More than ever now.'

Ianthe's wedding day dawned clear and blue, and she woke to the scent of marzipan and to the sound of birds chirruping outside the open windows. She sniffed the sweet-smelling air and wondered if it was her wedding cake. That was a good omen, she thought.

The dresses she had chosen waited on wire-frame mannequins that stood in a line along the wall: a stunning glacier-blue frock for the coronation, and three different cream-coloured affairs for the wedding ceremony. She hadn't yet decided which of these she would wear.

A sudden fanfare of brass trumpets sounded, causing the birds outside to scatter in fright. Ianthe leaped from her bed and hurried across the room, her heart racing.

Her balcony looked out across the uppermost districts of Losoto. The air was cool and fresh and the columns of smoke rising from so many chimneys hung in a single white pall above the rooftops. Slates gleamed as if they had been cleaned and polished. The harbour and city fort were hidden behind a plateau in the landscape, but she could see the Mare Lux in the distance – a flat, empty strip of brown. Oddly, its emptiness unnerved her. Had she expected it to be full of ships? Where was everyone?

Panic gripped Ianthe's heart. Had she missed the coronation ceremony entirely? Had they forgotten to wake her in time? What about the wedding?

The trumpets sounded again – a rousing chorus that seemed to Ianthe to be somewhere between a proclamation and a celebration. She ran across her balcony and leaned out so that she could see the clock tower that stood over the paper market.

It was just before seven. She still had hours before the coronation.

She wandered back inside and lay down on the bed, gazing up at the pale domed ceiling. She would be looking up at a different ceiling tonight, she supposed. She felt restless, frightened. She couldn't back out now if she wanted to. Could she? And why would she want to? Here she was about to marry a king. A man more handsome than anyone she'd ever seen. A man who needed her more than anyone else ever had, whose power and status and freedom depended on her.

She'd be foolish not to marry a man like that.

She bathed and was ready for the trio of servant girls, who arrived shortly before nine to help her into the chosen frock. They told her of the crowds which had been massing outside the gates since dawn, and the great number of dignitaries, both Losotan and foreign, who were already waiting in the palace antechambers. They would bring Ianthe down to the throne room a few minutes before Prince Paulus and Duke Cyr of Vale made their appearance at around ten.

A thought occurred to Ianthe. 'Will the duke's wife be there?' she asked.

The servants informed her that the Duchess Anaisy would not be present. She had remained in Awl.

'But why did she stay?' Ianthe asked, while they fastened the buttons on her back.

'Duke Cyr did not call for her,' one of the servants said.

'He didn't call for her?' Ianthe asked. 'But why?'

'The duke worried that the voyage would tire her overly.'

Ianthe allowed them to finish dressing her in silence.

And so, shortly before ten, the servant girls led Ianthe downstairs to the throne room to await her king.

The throne room was already full of people. Their murmurs died down as Ianthe entered and was shown to a bench at the back of the dais behind a golden throne that had once belonged to Emperor Hu. One of the servants remained with her, and the other two departed. Ianthe let her gaze wander over the assembled audience. Members of the Citizens of Losoto Representative Council stood immediately before and to the left of the dais, all dressed in their official robes of damson and black. Beside them waited a group of at least thirty warlords in savage regalia, each weighted down with gold chains and rings and metal and leather belts and cummerbunds bristling with scimitars and daggers. Paulus's militia commanders stood next to them in plain military garb, along with the sea captains Raceme Athentro and Erasmus Howlish. Behind these honoured guests waited the refugees from the *Ilena Grey*: almost one thousand Unmer. They stood in solemn silence, their gaunt faces haunted, and it seemed to Ianthe that their brooding attire alluded both to their past and to a decision they had made about their future. The back of the hall surrendered its space to an equal number of Aneans. These were the wealthiest and most influential people on the peninsula, those whom the emperor had shielded from the Unmer. Now they stood behind a wall of those same Unmer.

The door opened and Mr Greaves walked in, his shoes polished to a glassy shine, his footsteps echoing. He carried with him a black wooden stick. When he reached the front of the dais, he stopped and rapped the stick against the floor three times.

'Honoured guests,' he said. 'I present Prince Paulus Marquetta and Duke Cyr of Vale.'

Greaves bowed and withdrew. After a moment, a door at the rear of the throne room opened and Paulus entered beside Duke Cyr. There was no fanfare to accompany them. In silence they walked across the dais. Paulus sat on the throne while his uncle waited next to it.

For a long moment Cyr let his gaze roam over the room. He took in the great arched windows and pillared walls and the high domed ceiling. Finally he regarded the assembled guests. 'Many hundreds of years before the rise of Golden Domain,' he said in a sonorous voice, 'this great hall witnessed the coronation of the Unmer kings of old. Prince Paulus Marquetta will be the twenty-fourth sovereign to be crowned, and the first in this modern age to be crowned under this dome.' He paused, letting his words resound around that great space while the crowd watched in silence, then he said, 'The crown of Galea is gone, lost, melted down for its metal. However, the world today is unrecognizable from the one in which that crown was forged. And so it seems to us that its dissolution is fitting.' Again he paused, perhaps to give his words impetus to travel beyond mere air. 'Our king will have a new crown, one that speaks of both our past and our future together.' He nodded to Greaves, who opened the same door through which they had passed.

Ianthe felt a stab of jealousy when she saw whom they had chosen to bring forth her prince's crown. In her gown of flowing silver links, Nera looked astonishingly beautiful. Ianthe could see every curve of the other girl's body through the sheer metal cloth, and it momentarily forced her heart to clench. Nera's golden hair had been lifted and bound with silver wire and diamonds so that it sparkled like stardust. She walked across the dais, holding the crown in both hands.

The crown was made of broken glass. Ianthe could see that Nera's hands were bleeding where she grasped it.

Nera handed the crown to Cyr. She curtseyed to Paulus and then to the duke, and then faced Ianthe and curtseyed a third time, without making eye contact. The myriad chain links of her dress clinked against the stone floor. She seemed pale and unsteady, as if she were drunk or unwell. Ianthe noticed a drop of blood gather at the end of the girl's finger and then fall to the floor.

Duke Cyr lifted the crown in both hands. He turned to the guests and then raised it high above his head. 'We Unmer often recount an old saying,' he said. 'Kordosi peli nagir seen hashent jian awar. In Anean it means: the land is the strength of his bones and the sea is the salt of his blood.' Now he turned to face Paulus, whose violet eyes remained fixed ahead and inscrutable.

'In this blood I hereby anoint Prince Paulus Marquetta, son of King Jonas the Summoner and Queen Hope Constance Lavern, grandson of King August the Seventh of Galea, great-grandson of King Roman the First of Onlo and so forth back along that noble line to the Blood of the Mage Arundel.' The echoes of the duke's words settled. 'And so I, in lawful credence of the first royal law and right, in this holy durbar do right-fully crown this prince of the people.' He set the crown upon Paulus's head and then stepped back and sank to one knee before the throne. 'King Paulus the Tenth of Galea. King Paulus the First of Anea.'

The Unmer cried out, 'King Paulus.'

This call was echoed, with a great deal more uncertainty and mumbling, by a number of the other guests, but finally the coughs and grumbles settled to an appropriate silence.

Paulus rose from the throne. 'The king will take a queen.' He turned and extended a hand towards Ianthe.

Ianthe's heart hammered. She had been instructed in this part. She was to walk over and kneel before her king and pledge allegiance to him. And then she would take his hand and rise and stand beside him. And the duke would utter the words of ceremony and Ianthe would be queen of Anea.

She did nothing.

She merely stood there.

She saw the expectation in his eyes turn to sudden concern, perhaps even a flicker of fear. The duke's expression darkened. His glare was a warning. *Do not do this*. Still Ianthe stood there, her heart thumping wildly.

'The king will take a queen,' Paulus said again, more softly.

Ianthe felt her tears begin to well.

'Ianthe?'

'I'm sorry,' she said. 'I can't.'

Paulus and the duke exchanged a glance and it seemed to Ianthe that some unspoken communication passed between them. The newly crowned king of Anea gave his uncle an almost imperceptible nod.

Unseen by anyone except Ianthe, Duke Cyr reached into the deep pocket of his robe and took something out. It was a small silver sphere that looked vaguely familiar to Ianthe. Where had she seen something like that before? The sphere made a low chattering sound and Ianthe suddenly remembered. The same sphere had kept her father asleep for eleven days. What had they called it?

A somnambulum?

She remembered, just as sleep took her and the world went dark.

As he strode towards the palace, Granger in his anger had lost count of the number of times he'd replicated himself in the same physical space inside his power armour. Hundreds, at least. The sword was sheathed at his hip, but he kept the pommel gripped in his right hand as he walked. He had been thinking about the wedding ceremony to come, letting his imagination replay events over and over again in his head, when he suddenly became aware of his footsteps shaking the streets. He had attained such a phenomenal mass that each step cracked the cobbles under his boots with a sound like thunder.

People were staring out of windows at him. His armour emitted a furious buzz.

Granger eased his grip on the replicating sword. He dispelled scores of copies of himself into oblivion, shedding mass until it returned to a more manageable level. The hum from his armour sounded much less stressed. Now he weighed no more, he presumed, than a small building.

Nevertheless, he could hardly hope to go unnoticed. His footsteps still made more noise than a battalion of marching soldiers. His armour's ever-shifting designs reflected light in strange ways, giving him a vaguely nacreous aura. And his brine-damaged face looked more ghoulish than ever.

Crowds parted ahead of him.

Even at the palace gates, the hundreds of people who had gathered there in the hope of glimpsing the royal bride and groom were quick to step aside to let Granger through. They reacted to his presence the way a shoal of fish reacts to a shark.

The palace guards, however, had enough motive to stand firm. Evidently they were under orders to admit no one. They stood behind that garishly painted hedge and levelled their rifles at Granger. From their demeanour he could see that they were young and inexperienced – two of the militia Marquetta had recently employed. You kept your oldest soldiers near you and your freshest ones out watching the camp.

One of them sneered and said, 'Get back to whatever sea you crawled out of.'

Granger lowered the faceplate of his helmet.

And then his fist tightened on the pommel of the replicating sword. With his free hand he gripped the iron gates and pushed. The massive iron bolts began to bend. The guards opened fire, riddling Granger's breastplate and helmet with bullets. His entropic armour merely absorbed the energy from each impact and turned it into power.

Unable to withstand Granger's sorcerous strength, one of the gate hinges burst from the stone pillars in a puff of dust. Iron bolts sheared, one after the other. *Pang, pang, pang.* A second hinge went. With a great rending and groaning of metal, the gates buckled and then toppled inwards.

Granger tossed the wrecked and twisted metal aside and walked up the palace driveway, doing his best to ignore the bullets constantly rattling off his armour.

Every horse carriage in Losoto must have been present on that driveway. The drivers had a hard time keeping their panicked beasts under control as Granger marched past. He sounded like an earthquake. The heels of his boots struck the bricks underfoot like massive hammer blows. The etchings on his armour continually shifted and re-formed. Behind him, the gate guards had exhausted their ammunition and ran to raise the alarm.

A bell began to toll frantically.

Granger kicked open the palace doors and strode inside. He found himself in a grand entranceway filled with vases of flowers. The floral decorations continued along a central corridor – the route, he presumed, that guests would follow. Granger followed it now, the walls shuddering at the noise of his footfalls. Servants fled at the sight of him. More palace guards came running, drawn by the gunfire, but these were no more experienced than those outside. *Farmers, fishermen, shopkeepers*, Granger thought. They unloaded their rifles into his armour, and when that didn't stop him they had no plan but simply to do the same again.

He marched onwards through a hail of bullets. Vases shattered on either side of him. Petals skirled in the air.

He reached another set of doors and kicked them open.

The throne room was vast and crowded with people – both Anean and Unmer. As Granger walked in, the crowds backed away, revealing a raised dais at the far end of the room.

Marquetta was on his knees beside the throne, holding an unconscious Ianthe in his arms.

Granger lifted his faceplate. 'What's happened to her?' he cried, striding forward. Aneans and Unmer crowded back from him as he approached. 'What have you done?'

Marquetta looked up with surprise. But his expression immediately turned hostile. 'How dare you . . .?'

But Duke Cyr laid a hand upon the young man's shoulder. Then he came hurrying forward, his hands raised in a placatory manner. 'Colonel Granger, your daughter has been poisoned. We must act now to save her.'

'Poisoned?'

Cyr waved a hand at two pageboys standing nearby. 'The satchel in my quarters,' he said. 'Fetch it now. Hurry.'

As the pageboys disappeared, Granger stepped up on the dais and strode over to Ianthe. Her face was very pale, but she appeared to be breathing. 'Back up,' he said to the prince. Marquetta rose slowly and stepped back. Granger knelt down by his daughter's side. He couldn't feel for her pulse with these gauntlets on, so he listened at her lips. There was a faint stir of breath.

'She's alive,' the prince said, 'but not by much.'

Granger looked up at him. 'Pulse?'

'Faint.'

Granger scooped her up in his arms. Compared to his relative mass she weighed nothing. He turned to Duke Cyr. 'Where are her quarters?' he said. 'Show me.'

'The servants—' Cyr began.

'Send someone. Tell them to meet us there.'

Marquetta and Cyr led Granger through the palace. They hurried along several grand marble corridors and then ascended a private stairwell and came to Ianthe's quarters moments before the pageboys arrived with Cyr's satchel. Cyr waved them away. Granger carried Ianthe inside and set her down on a settee.

Cyr opened the satchel and took out a small sharkskin wallet. The interior was cushioned with velvet and held a dozen pins, each with a different coloured jewel in its head. Cyr selected a dark blue pin and wafted it gently before Ianthe's open mouth, as though testing the air coming from her lungs. The jewel changed from blue to clear. Cyr frowned. He replaced the pin in its cushion and selected one with a lighter blue jewel. This time, when he waved it in front of Ianthe's mouth, the colour did not alter.

Cyr lifted Ianthe's hand, turned it so her wrist faced him, and slid the pin up under the skin of her palm. Ianthe shivered slightly, but she didn't open her eyes.

'What's wrong?' Granger said. 'Why isn't she waking?'

Cyr held her wrist between his finger and thumb. 'Nothing is wrong,' he said. 'I've slowed her heartbeat to stop the poison spreading. It'll give us more time to figure out what it is.'

'Then she's not safe?'

The duke shook his head. 'She won't die while she's in stasis. But she won't recover without the antidote. We need to know which poison Conquillas has used on her.'

Granger stared at his daughter. 'Conquillas did this?'

'Who else?' Cyr said. 'He said he would kill anybody who stood in his way. With Ianthe out of the way, he is free to enter the tournament without risk of psychic attack.' He scratched his head. 'We'll start making antidotes to the most common substances . . . gravere, inkgrass, fox birch, the ones used in hunting and so on, but I'm not optimistic. Conquillas has a penchant for more exotic toxins.'

'How did he get to her?' Granger said.

Cyr shrugged. 'An agent of his, perhaps . . .'

Granger couldn't contain his rage. He seized Marquetta by the front of his tunic. 'You let this happen to her . . .'

Marquetta's face twisted with fury. He grabbed Granger's arm. His fingertips sparked and slid across the surface of the strange alloy. When he realized he could not decreate the entropic armour, he reached for Granger's open faceplate.

Granger slugged him.

Marquetta crumpled to the floor, then looked up, aghast. 'I am King of Anea,' he cried.

'Be thankful I didn't break your neck.'

Duke Cyr had raised his hands again. 'My lords, please,' he said. 'This violence serves no purpose. The girl lies on the edge of death. Your fiancée, your daughter . . .' He glanced between Marquetta and Granger. 'We must condemn Conquillas's actions as those of a coward, shame him, force him to reveal what poison he used.'

Granger glared at the young man on the floor, then turned his attention to the duke. 'I know where to find Conquillas,' he said. 'Or at least I know how to flush him out. He'll answer for this.'

Cyr exchanged a glance with his nephew.

'Look after her,' Granger said.

Cyr smiled. 'I will do my utmost to ensure she comes back to us,' he said.

The road to the Halls of Anea was packed with spectators and combatants, far more than could be housed at the only inn nearby, but Maskelyne had sent a rider ahead of them to try to secure them rooms at any price. He had no intention of staying at the tent city that had sprung up around the entrance to that fabled ruin.

They were lounging in the rear of a carriage, clopping along the busy forest track, with their driver shouting obscenities at those on foot and telling them to get out of the way, when an excited rider came past from the city, crying out the news that Argusto Conquillas had poisoned the king's fiancée.

Maskelyne called out to the man, and offered him a gilder to elucidate. 'What sort of poison?' he asked.

'Nobody knows,' the rider said. 'She's at death's door.'

'And how was it administered?'

'I don't know, sir.'

'But Conquillas has admitted the deed?'

'No one has heard from Conquillas,' the rider said. 'He's still in hiding.'

'Then how do we know it was him?'

'The news is from the palace, sir,' the man replied. 'From King Paulus himself.'

'So nobody knows anything,' Maskelyne remarked.

'No, sir.'

'Including you.'

The man frowned.

Maskelyne gave him a dismissive wave. 'Elucidate means expound and clarify,' he said. 'It doesn't mean sit there and waste our time. I'm keeping my gilder. I suggest you leave before my friend here roasts your liver with a look.'

The rider glanced from Maskelyne to the tattooed sorcerer beside him. He seemed about to say something, then closed his mouth again, evidently changing his mind. He flicked his horse's reins and disappeared off along the track.

Cobul said, 'Roast his liver?'

'You see?' Maskelyne said. 'You're well on the way to repaying me the ticket cost already. I'm finding your presence financially beneficial, Cobul. And that's before I've placed a single bet.'

'It doesn't strike me as the sort of thing Conquillas would do,' he said. 'Poison, I mean. It's not his style.'

'A coward's weapon,' Maskelyne agreed. 'And the dragon lord is certainly not that.'

'You think the Haurstaf engineered this?'

Maskelyne rubbed his chin and peered out into the forest, where the afternoon sunlight lit patches of mossy ground between the trees. 'Not Briana Marks,' he said. 'She couldn't engineer a splash from a puddle in her current state.' Who else then? Some other surviving Guild member? One of the prince's own psychics? He noted that the rider had not referred to Ianthe as *the queen*. Had the girl had second thoughts about her marriage?

He chuckled to himself. 'I wonder if Marquetta and Cyr still plan to enter the tournament,' he said. 'Despite their present vulnerability.'

'I don't see that they have a choice,' Cobul muttered.

'No, I don't suppose they do,' Maskelyne agreed.

Granger returned, to find Siselo humming merrily to herself among all the stalactites and golden clutter. She was preparing dinner on a strange device that appeared to consist of a cone of red-hot stone placed in a brass tripod. Steam rose from the iron pot. Whatever she was cooking smelled vaguely fishy, and not particularly pleasant.

'Where is he?' he said.

She turned, smiling, but when she saw the expression on his face, her smile vanished. 'You mean my father?' Her brow furrowed. 'What makes you think he's here yet?'

'I know he's in Losoto. Where is he?'

She was silent a moment, then said, 'I haven't seen him.'

'I don't believe you.'

'What's happened?' she said. 'Something's happened, hasn't it?'

Granger strode over towards her. 'Your father poisoned my daughter.'

'No he didn't!'

He kept walking. 'I want to speak with him, now, Siselo.'

She backed away from the stove. 'My father wouldn't poison anyone. It's a coward's weapon.'

A voice behind him said, 'Colonel Thomas Granger.'

Granger turned to find the dragon lord, Argusto Conquillas, standing in one of the many doorways into the cavern. He was dressed in beggar's rags and wore a wrap of some filthy material around his neck, but there could be no mistaking his sharp, angular features or violet eyes. His long grey hair had been woven into a plait that hung down his back. In one hand he held a slender bow fashioned from bone. His fingers clamped a notched arrow to the grip, keeping it taut against the drawstring. He sniffed and said, 'You have deteriorated somewhat since our last meeting. Please accept my condolences for your recent death.'

'Father!' Siselo ran over and flung her arms around him.

Granger's hand moved to the hilt of his sword. 'I want the name of the poison, Conquillas,' he said. 'The antidote, if you have it available.'

Conquillas regarded him for a moment longer. Then he crouched beside Siselo. 'Are you well?'

'Ygrid brought us,' she said. 'We came to warn you.'

'We?' He glanced at Granger.

She was flustered, excited. 'I knew you'd show up here eventually. I remembered to follow the marks. You're in terrible

396

danger. Marquetta or Cyr – one of them has summoned Fiorel to fight you at this—'

'Did he harm you?'

She shook her head. 'No. An entropath is here in Losoto, father. An entropath! He must be disguised—'

Granger interrupted her. 'Conquillas,' he growled, his hand now closing on the hilt of the replicating sword. 'I want the name of the poison.' As he spoke, he felt the sword phantoms flutter into existence within him, increasing his mass, forcing the entropic armour to tremble and growl as it strained to augment the sorcery of the sword.

'He thinks you poisoned his daughter,' Siselo said. 'You have to tell him you didn't do it.'

Conquillas rose to his feet again, his eyes fixed on Granger. 'I heard news of your daughter's misfortune,' he said. 'However, I can assure you I did not poison the girl.'

'Liar.'

The dragon lord's brow furrowed over his piercing stare. 'I do not lie,' he said. 'Nor do I harm innocents. I give you my word, as Argusto Conquillas former lord of Herica and the Sumran Islands and of Peregrello Sentevadro . . . I give you my word as an Unmer noble and as a *father*. I did not do this.'

'Then who did?' Granger said.

'No one did, Colonel Granger.' He absently placed a hand on Siselo's head and ruffled her hair. 'I do not believe she's poisoned at all.'

Granger took a step towards the dragon lord. He heard the armour whine as it strained under the massive weight of his replicates. Rainbows danced across the surface of the metal. 'Explain yourself,' he said.

'The word is that she refused Marquetta's hand in marriage,'

Conquillas said. 'Had you arrived at the ceremony earlier you would have witnessed this yourself.'

'She rejected him?'

The dragon lord nodded. 'I imagine they have put her to sleep while they try to resolve this problem. There are devices to achieve this, common enough.'

Granger knew them well enough. He had personal experience of such devices. 'They can't force her to marry him,' he said. 'And they can't keep her asleep for ever.'

'No,' Conquillas admitted. 'And if they can't have a queen with her powers, they must settle for someone who appears to be a queen with her powers.'

'The shape-shifter?'

'Fiorel is here to ensure the Unmer's survival,' Conquillas said. 'As a simulacrum of Ianthe, he would not possess her powers, but merely present the illusion that she still lives. And that might be enough to keep their enemies away until an heir is born to take his place.'

'An heir?'

'Your daughter need not be awake to conceive, or to give birth.'

Granger let out a growl of anger. 'I'm going to bring her here,' he said, turning to go.

'Wait,' Conquillas said. 'She's safe where she is for now. Fiorel might assume her identity, but they cannot kill her until she gives Marquetta his heir.'

Granger hesitated.

'Rescuing her now would only reveal how much you know of their plans.'

Granger ground his teeth. 'So what do you suggest?'

'We kill Fiorel,' Conquillas said.

'How? How do we kill a god?'

The archer shrugged. 'With bow and sword,' he said.

The pit battles were set to run for three days before the main tournament. By the time Marquetta's detachment of militia arrived to open the gates to Segard, a sizeable temporary settlement had already grown around the underground city. Tents spread out through several hundred yards of forest behind the Segard View – a rambling wooden mansion built a hundred years before to cash in on curious Losotans come to see the fabled Unmer ruin. By the tumbledown look of the place, Maskelyne decided there hadn't been that many of them. No doubt Hu's sealing the gates hadn't helped business.

The rooms he had secured for Mellor, Cobul and himself on the second floor were probably worth about a hundredth of the price he'd been forced to pay for them, but it was either that or sleep under canvas. So it was with a profound sense of satisfaction that he noted the rainclouds gathering overhead. Maskelyne wiped the grime and condensation off his window and peered out at smoke from a hundred campfires drifting amidst the trees. 'At the rate they're going through wood, out there,' he said, 'there won't be any forest left by dawn.'

'Maybe then we'll get a view of the Segard Gate,' Mellor retorted. 'There ought to be a law against innkeepers making false claims.'

'Just innkeepers?'

'Whores, too.'

'That's one story I do not want to hear, Mr Mellor.'

The Segard Gate was located a few hundred yards further up the hillside behind the inn. Maskelyne had yet to go out and see it for himself, but he'd heard enough to learn that there wasn't much to see – a square stone portal four times as tall as a man, set into a muddy slope. The king's workmen had been clearing earth and rubble from it for weeks and it was only three days ago that they'd finally pushed the massive doors wide and ventured inside.

The ruins were intact, the arenas preserved.

That had been the talk over lunch in the Segard View restaurant. The great dark halls inside the mountain were not only still there, but their greatness and their darkness had been perfectly preserved. Royal officials had been bringing in cartloads of gem lanterns to light the arenas, and merchants had been setting up stalls in the surrounding halls and corridors.

Their new king had yet to officially open the Halls of Anea – as the arena district of Segard had always been known – but Maskelyne felt certain that he would make an appearance soon, if only to show his subjects that Ianthe's poisoning had not rattled him. The show must go on. But, given that the first round of fights was scheduled to start in less than an hour, he had expected the boy to turn up before now.

And then he heard trumpets outside.

Maskelyne wrapped his cloak around his shoulders and he went off with Mellor to find Cobul, wondering at the vagaries of thought and fate and coincidence.

The Bahrethroan was asleep in the bar, his head resting on the table, a battered metal tankard still clutched in his hand. The other punters had gone outside, leaving Cobul alone.

'Cobul,' Maskelyne said. 'You're on.'

The sorcerer jerked awake and rubbed his head groggily. 'What time is it?'

'Have you been here all night?'

Cobul glanced at the tankard in his hand and then downed its contents and said, 'Apparently so.'

'Our king is about to declare the games open,' Maskelyne said. 'Well, the warm-up scrap at any rate.'

Cobul stretched his arms and yawned. 'You often see the best fights at these pit contests,' he said. 'Contestants are less worried about honour and . . . what's the word?'

'Hygiene?'

'Reputation.'

'An ignoble conceit,' Maskelyne said. 'Shall we proceed to the slaughter?'

'When am I on?'

'The first round was supposed to begin at noon.' The metaphysicist checked his pocket watch. 'Forty minutes ago. But the king's here now to make his speeches.'

Cobul yawned. 'Then there's time for lunch.'

It was more than half an hour before the three of them reached the gate that led into Segard and the Halls of Anea. A constant stream of people poured into the Unmer city; from the look of them they were mainly spectators, but a few were armed and thus probably contestants. Scores more lingered outside, their boots and wagon wheels deep in mud, hawking everything from roasted insects to cabbages.

As they walked through that massive stone portal and into an unremarkable square tunnel, Maskelyne became aware of a queer sensation – at first he thought it was in his gut, but then he wasn't sure. He had the distinct notion that some change had occurred. Something that didn't quite chime with his sense of orientation? A vague sensation of dizziness? He couldn't say precisely what it was, but it rankled him. He glanced over to find Cobul grinning.

'Geometry,' the sorcerer said.

Maskelyne frowned at him.

'Did you just walk uphill, or down?'

'Uphill,' Maskelyne said. 'And then we came in and . . .' That's what was so odd. The passageway beyond the gates appeared to lead straight into the mountain on a level plain. But as soon as he'd come through the gate, he'd felt like they were on a gentle downward slope. He looked behind him. They *were* on a gentle downward slope. 'Good grief,' he said. 'This is . . . Not *where* it seems to be.'

'I'm impressed,' Cobul said.

'Where are we?'

The sorcerer shrugged. 'I have no idea,' he said. 'All I know is that we are *not* under a mountain in Anea.'

'How big is Segard?'

'Big enough to hold a city, certainly. Maybe bigger than the world we just left. Who knows? The Unmer's descendants spent thousands of years digging out halls. They might still be in here, for all I know.'

Maskelyne stopped in his tracks, causing the people behind to grumble and steer around him. He seized Cobul's arm. 'What contains it?'

'Explain.'

'What contains the portal through which we've just walked? We're in a rift, aren't we? A *vast* rift.'

Cobul smiled. 'A rift inside a house-sized cube of stone buried in the rock face.'

'But, don't you see?' Maskelyne said. He looked around at the hundreds of people pushing past, oblivious to the idea he'd just had. 'The portal has no relation to the mass of this place – it's just a door. Which means that if we can move it, reposition it underwater, we can use it to drain this world of brine.'

'Moving it is more of a problem than you imagine,' Cobul said. 'Anyway, what if there were still civilizations lost in here? Would you save one world by poisoning another?'

'Of course. Wouldn't you?'

The sorcerer's smile faltered. 'Come,' he said. 'The pits are up ahead.'

The tunnel opened into a hall so vast that Maskelyne thought this one room might just be large enough to contain the entire imperial palace. The ceiling had to be two hundred yards above him, and he could barely make out the far walls. It was illuminated by tens of thousands of gem lanterns, more than he had ever seen gathered in one place, all strung out on lines of cable held aloft by a random assortment of poles, tripods and scaffolds.

Crowds packed the area ahead of them, their raucous shouts filling the air. They had clustered around several huge circular pits in the stone floor. As Maskelyne approached, he saw that the pits were stepped to form descending tiers of seating. Additional braziers and torches burned within these depressions, illuminating the stone floors where the combatants would fight. In the pervading gloom, the arenas glowed like the mouths of furnaces.

To one side of the pits lay a great shambling corral of rope, canvas and rotten timber panels and doors that appeared to have been salvaged from half a hundred old buildings. Signs proclaimed this to be the combatants' area, and King Paulus's militia were busy here, taking tickets and registering names, which they chalked upon slate boards, while bookies surveyed each contestant and spoke with them before hollering out their offered odds on the fights to come. From what Maskelyne could hear, none of the odds was particularly fair.

They registered Cobul, who – unsurprisingly – turned out to be the only sorcerer in the entire pit contest. Since amplifiers were prohibited, neither bookies nor contestants rated his chances very highly, for spells took time and concentration to weave. Even the greatest Unmer sorcerers had used amplification artefacts, or else maintained a safe distance between themselves and their enemies.

'How much should we bet on you?' Maskelyne asked him.

'As much as you can spare,' Cobul said. 'The odds will go down after I win the first fight.'

Maskelyne eventually found a bookie to take a thousand gilders, returning one for two should the sorcerer win – atrocious odds, but the best available. He made the bet and then he and Mellor went over to find seats at the correct arena while a referee led Cobul off into the combatants' area to prepare.

An hour later, the sorcerer had his first fight.

His opponent was a local Losotan – a big man named Renton who worked in the dragon-canning factory. He wore a leather waistcoat and shorts and carried a wickedly sharp skinning lance, a weapon with which he was said to have some skill. As the iron-barred door came up, and the big Losotan walked out to a cheering crowd, Maskelyne felt a twinge of anxiety. Renton looked like a formidable opponent.

On the other side of the arena, the second door shot up with a rattle of chain. Cobul walked out to jeers and howls of abuse. Regardless of his physical appearance, the sorcerer's tattooed skin was enough to mark him as Unmer in the eyes of the crowd.

A tournament officiator beckoned the two men forward, until they stood ten yards apart. Renton took a moment to display his talents, whirling his lance above his head with consummate skill. Cobul just stood there.

Mellor exchanged a nervous glance with Maskelyne. 'That butcher looks fast,' he said.

'Remember where we found Cobul,' Maskelyne replied. He glanced around, hoping to catch a glimpse of their new king, but couldn't see him anywhere. Apparently, His Majesty was not overly concerned with the pit fights.

The officiator had finished speaking to the two combatants. He withdrew to the edge of the arena and raised his arms and called out, 'Let the fight begin!'

It lasted less than two seconds.

The Losotan did exactly the right thing. Knowing that speed was his best hope of success against a sorcerer, he came rushing at Cobul with his lance gripped over one shoulder like a spear.

The crowd roared.

Cobul was whispering something. He clasped his hands together suddenly, and then quickly raised one above the other, palm out, and made a small pushing motion.

His opponent burst into a thousand red embers . . .

. . . which skirled around Cobul like a swarm of fireflies, darkening rapidly, and then fell softly like grey snow. Where moments ago there had been a man, there was nothing but a thin layer of ash upon the ground.

The crowd fell silent.

All except Maskelyne, who stood up and applauded eagerly. 'Bravo!' he called out. 'Bravo.'

Duke Cyr found the king breaking his fast on one of the high palace terraces overlooking the city. The editor of the *Losotan Herald* had given him a sheaf of notes outlining all of the city's news for his approval and selection, but one item in particular had caused him to hurry all the way up here. 'Your Highness,' he said. 'Conquillas registered for the tournament this morning.'

King Paulus paused, a slice of grapefruit halfway to his lips. 'Where did he sign up?'

'At the harbour.'

The king nodded. 'We had expected this, Cyr.'

Cyr nodded. 'There has been an interesting development at the pit contest,' he said. 'A Bahrethroan sorcerer by the name of Jian Cobul.'

'A bastard race?' Marquetta said.

'His father was Unmer,' the duke replied.

The king stopped eating. 'What did you say his name was?'

'Cobul.'

'Why does that sound familiar?'

'Your father, sire, had a sorcerer of that name attached to one of his personal divisions. He had the man boiled alive and exiled for treason.'

King Paulus grunted. 'And now he's back, looking for a reprieve no doubt.'

'That is one possibility,' Cyr said. 'He seems rather talented for a half-breed. After he won his initial battle, no one else will face him in the arena. His opponents are forfeiting. If it carries on like this, he's going to win the pit contest by default.'

The king glanced up. 'He must be using an amplifier.'

'Apparently not.'

'Then how is he able to channel that much power?'

Cyr shrugged. 'Natural ability?'

Marquetta seemed to consider this. 'We'll have to kill him.'

'Of course, sire.'

'It wouldn't do to have a bastard race triumph over one of our sorcerers.'

'I shall make the necessary arrangements.'

The king took a sip of water. 'Has Fiorel revealed himself to you?'

'He has not, sire. But he wishes us to know he is in Losoto.'

'In what form did he last enter your dreams?'

'He came to me in the guise of a white hart, sire.'

The king smiled. 'How fitting, don't you think?'

Granger stayed with Conquillas and his daughter until the morning of the tournament. If today went as well as fate could allow, his daughter would wake up a widow. Such an outcome was far from certain, however, for it depended on Conquillas defeating an opponent who many claimed could not be defeated.

Killing an entropath was hard enough. They were far stronger, faster and more cunning than normal men. But killing a shape-shifter would be more complicated still, Conquillas explained. If the god could change his shape at will, then he could re-form any part of his body that sustained damage.

Their only hope was to deliver a lethal injury to the brain.

But Fiorel would certainly try to trick them. Conquillas had fought an entropic beast before. The brain wasn't necessarily where you expected it to be. And, of course, they wouldn't even know who Fiorel was, until things started to go bad.

Granger listened to all this with growing dread. He neglected to tell Conquillas what Shehernan of the sword had told him – that Fiorel also happened to be Granger's father, and his grandfather, and great-grandfather, and so on, for at least a dozen generations. They were going out to fight half of Granger's entire family tree.

A whole network of ancient Unmer tunnels connected the natural cavern Conquillas used as his bolt-hole to the sewer system and the trove market, and to numerous other parts of Losoto. And it was from one of these tunnels that Granger, Conquillas and Siselo emerged in the forest north of the city.

They found themselves in a hollow, where a natural overhang and unchecked vegetation obscured the tunnel entrance.

Granger had to send three of his sword replicates to cut a path for them. The sky above was white and smelled of autumn. Cold rain coming from the north. The leaves were already starting to wither and brown. The three of them trudged through the forest in silence, following a little-used hunters' trail.

They reached the gates of Segard by late morning.

A temporary settlement had sprung up around the entrance to the Unmer ruins. Thousands of people slept under canvas or warmed themselves around campfires. Hawkers wandered to and fro with baskets of produce or trinkets. Children played. Jugglers juggled. A carnival atmosphere suffused the place. The forest road had been churned black by a constant stream of ox-carts and people – merchants, spectators and combatants heading back and forth between Losoto and the arenas.

There were fewer combatants outside the halls than Granger had expected. He spotted a group of warlords sitting around a fire, drinking from goatskins, two Anean lords waiting on horseback surveying the scene around them with some apprehension, and a few men-in-arms, but the majority of people were here to watch the tournament.

When they saw Conquillas and Granger they stopped and stared.

Siselo had grown weary of walking, so Conquillas carried her on his shoulders. She seemed thrilled by everything and everyone and took no notice of the stares. Granger trudged alongside, scowling at onlookers, his hand never far from the hilt of his sword. He supposed that by now his dead flesh had started to smell foul, but his companions did not mention it. Nevertheless, he noticed the frowns and the wrinkled noses of the people they passed. He thought he might buy a balm or perfumed oil from one of the sellers, but was too embarrassed to approach them.

Finally they passed through the Segard Gate and into the Halls of Anea.

Conquillas had warned him to expect a subtle shift in perspective when he entered the ruined city. They were, he explained, entering a rift – a universe created by sorcerous means to contain Segard. To create such rifts took massive amounts of power, and Segard was one of the largest ever constructed. Nobody had yet explored it all. It might be as vast as the whole of the Anean peninsula and possibly larger still.

Granger merely grunted.

A square tunnel brought them into a huge chamber – a space much larger than any Granger had seen before, where numerous depressions in the stone floor acted as arenas. Thousands of gem lanterns of every colour had been strung on wires across the entire area. To one side, a ramshackle corral of rope and timber enclosed the combatants' area. Beyond this stretched an acre of green canvas military tents, all bearing the royal insignia. Here Unmer lords mingled with the most powerful warlords and Anean nobles. Servants brought food and drink to groups huddled around braziers, while musicians strolled among them with pipes and drums and gourds, and guards patrolled the perimeter. Among them Granger spied the tattooed faces of Brutalist and Entropic sorcerers.

King Marquetta's compound.

They found the majority of the tournament combatants in the corral. There were knights bearing crests of wealthy Losotan families, a scattering of lesser warlords, pirates, privateers, sellswords, mercenaries and soldiers of every description and from every part of the empire, all drinking, laughing, shouting and singing. At least three groups of musicians were playing different, clashing tunes. Merchants sold ale and wine by the cup from great wooden barrels while young lads wove through the throng with planks of hot flatbreads and pies.

As Conquillas entered the corral and stood before the tournament officiator's desk, with little Siselo still perched on his shoulders, and Granger at his side, the raucous chatter fell noticeably. The eyes of everyone nearby turned to the new arrivals.

A nervous official checked Conquillas's presence on the lists, and then tipped his spectacles back on his head and pulled out a sheet of paper from a metal cabinet behind him. 'Is it the Lord's List, sir?' he asked.

Conquillas nodded.

'Ten thousand, please.'

The dragon lord reached inside his tunic and withdrew a fat leather purse. He tossed it onto the table in front of the official. 'There's twenty,' he said. 'For both of us.'

The official glanced at Granger. 'It isn't usual,' he said. 'I mean . . . not common for one competitor to pay for another. I mean, why . . . eh . . . reduce your odds of . . .'

'Winning?' Siselo said from up on her father's shoulders.

'Um, I suppose . . .' he replied.

Conquillas merely stared at the man.

'Very good, sir,' the official said. He took the purse. 'Now, please, come with me,' he said, gesturing to the tent compound. 'The area for the lords is . . . eh . . . this . . .'

'Way?' Siselo said.

He nodded quickly. Then he led them onwards past the gaping crowds and brought them to the entrance to the royal compound, whereupon a guard unhooked a rope and waved them inside.

'Now, I have . . . eh . . .' The official moistened his lips. 'Special instructions, sir. The king himself invites you to join him for drinks before the games . . . eh . . .'

'Commence?' Siselo said.

The official nodded.

'You should eat some coal,' Siselo said.

He looked up at her. 'Coal? Why?'

'So your mind doesn't keep running out of steam.'

Conquillas laughed. 'Take us to Marquetta,' he said.

The official bowed and beckoned them towards a much grander tent situated nearby. This was roped off from the rest of the compound and patrolled by yet more guards, who stepped aside to let them through. Finally, they lifted a flap of canvas and were ushered into the presence of the king.

The King of Anea lounged on a pile of cushions, sipping wine from a crystal goblet. He eyed the new arrivals with apparent boredom, and said, 'I had almost given up hope of seeing you here, Lord Conquillas.'

'Paulus Marquetta,' Conquillas said. 'You haven't aged a day.'

The king offered him a thin smile. Then he rose and came over to meet them. 'And this must be your daughter.'

'Siselo,' she said.

He gave her a nod before his attention turned to Granger.

'Colonel,' he said. 'Must I presume that Conquillas has denied all knowledge of poison and you now blame me for your daughter's condition?' He gave a weary sigh. 'Have *you* come to challenge me too?'

'I have,' Granger said.

A fleeting smile touched Marquetta's lips. 'Well then, I look forward to that,' he said. 'Let us hope you survive the early rounds. But please . . .' He gestured towards the back of the tent, to an area sectioned off by painted paper screens depicting battle scenes from what was presumably Unmer history. 'There is something I would like to show you.'

411

He rose and then led them behind the screens.

Granger's breath caught in his throat. Duke Cyr stood next to a long table, upon which lay Ianthe. Her eyes were closed and her skin was as white as the winter sky. They had dressed her in a light shroud and clasped her hands at her chest, so that she resembled a corpse. If he hadn't seen the gentle rise and fall of her chest, he would have believed her to be dead. He rushed forward and took her hand in his. Her skin was as cold as stone.

'She is safe,' Cyr said. 'For now.'

'Wake her,' Granger said.

'And have her succumb to whatever poison she's been given?'

Conquillas gazed down at her. 'There is no poison.'

Granger turned to Marquetta. 'I know she rejected you.'

'She didn't reject me,' Marquetta said. 'Far from it. This is what I wanted to show you.' He approached the sleeping girl and rested his hand upon her belly. 'She's pregnant.'

Granger could see the truth of it at once – the slight, but nevertheless visible swell of her belly. His mind reeled. *When?* He turned back to the young king, furious, raising his fist to strike him.

Conquillas stopped him. 'The arena,' he said.

Maskelyne eyed the names on the slate board and frowned. 'Colonel Thomas Granger,' he said. 'That man has an uncanny knack of turning up alive against the odds.'

The last time he'd encountered Granger had been on a mountainside in Awl, when the colonel had tried to kill him by crashing an Unmer chariot into the gun emplacement Maskelyne had been using to bombard the Haurstaf palace. Maskelyne had found the wrecked chariot empty, however, and it was only after he'd learned of Granger's replicating sword that he'd figured out what must have transpired. Here was one soldier who really did have nine lives.

Now here he was in Anea again. Maskelyne wondered if, after all this time, Granger still possessed that sorcerous weapon – and what cost it had exacted from him. With Unmer arte-facts there was always a heavy price to pay.

'How would you fare against nine men?' he asked Cobul.

They were in the cleanest section of the combatants' area, where Cobul had become a fixture next to an ale seller's barrel. The Bahrethroan sorcerer drained his ale and said, 'I've faced plenty worse odds.'

'I wonder what the bookies are offering on Granger,' Maskelyne mused. He faced Cobul. 'Are you sure you want to drink that much before the main tournament begins?'

Cobul had won the pit fights by default, since nobody else would fight him. The main event was scheduled to begin any minute now. 'I'm sure,' he said.

Maskelyne turned back to the lists. 'Granger faces some Losotan lord in the first round. I happen to know that Granger carries a replicating sword.'

'Nasty things,' Cobul said. 'I'm surprised he's managed to stay alive.'

'It's one of his most frustrating habits,' Maskelyne replied, checking his pocket watch. 'Come, it's about to begin.'

They located the correct arena and Maskelyne found a bookie who took his bet of five hundred gilders on Granger to win. The odds were, as usual, appalling, but Maskelyne didn't much care. He was starting to enjoy himself. They arrived late, and so were forced to find a place on the uppermost tier, forcing the other spectators to make room. Maskelyne found that people were always willing to make room when you have a Bahrethroan Brutalist sorcerer with you.

Moments later, the bout official wandered out into the stone circle below them and raised his hands to quiet the crowd. 'For this, the third of our matches today, we have two locals armed to the teeth with the most dangerous and wicked sorcery.' He gave a signal, and an unseen operator raised the northernmost gate. 'Firstly, I give you Marek Swale from the Yorburn district of Losoto, representing the Yorburn family itself.' The crowd cheered as through the gate came a handsome young man in highly polished armour. He wore a plain shield strapped to one arm and carried an enormous hammer in the other. Maskelyne eyed that weapon and noted the Unmer markings etched across the metal.

'Facing him,' the referee went on, 'and representing himself, we have a former imperial soldier. I give you Colonel Thomas Granger of the legendary Gravediggers. Exiled from his Losotan home for daring to challenge Emperor Hu.'

Out walked Granger. There was only one of him, Maskelyne noted. But he also noted the deathly pallor of the colonel's skin. He looked like a walking corpse.

'Does he look well to you, Cobul?' he said.

Cobul frowned. Then he sniffed the air. 'That smell . . .?'

'You don't think that's Granger?'

'Men who look like he does,' he said, 'are normally lying down.'

The two opponents faced each other across the arena, while the referee continued to pace the floor between them. 'This is a competition match and the standard rules apply,' he said. 'The fight is over when one opponent yields or is knocked unconscious.' He turned to Swale. 'Are you ready?'

The man nodded.

The referee then turned to Granger. 'Are you ready?'

Granger nodded.

'Then, begin!' The referee backed away to the far wall of the arena.

The young Losotan, Swale, began swinging the hammer over and over his fist. Maskelyne could see that it was powered, for in moments it was moving so fast it had become a blur. It began to emit a humming noise. A blow from that would knock a man clear across Losoto's harbour.

Granger just stood there in his battered old armour, his hand clenching the hilt of the sword sheathed at his hip. And, to Maskelyne's surprise, he remained one man. None of his sorcerous copies appeared.

The noise from Swale's hammer rose to a shriek as it continued to build speed. Maskelyne felt the stone seat under him begin to vibrate. And then his teeth began to hurt. Suddenly the young Losotan came running straight at Granger, now moving the hammer in a figure-of-eight motion so as to anticipate and smash aside any attack.

Still Granger did nothing.

Maskelyne sat up in his seat, intrigued.

Someone in the row before them said, 'Get ready to duck.'

'I can't watch,' Cobul said.

Now Swale was within reach of Granger. He brought his hammer down in a savage blow that connected with Granger's shoulder plate.

Clang!

The arena resounded with an almighty peal of metal on metal, a noise so vast and powerful that Maskelyne felt it in his bones. His skull shuddered. All around spectators groaned and clamped their hands over their ears.

The young Losotan attacker rebounded from Granger, staggering backwards like a man dazed. In his hand he now held, in place of a hammer, a twisted lump of scrap metal.

Throughout all this Granger had not moved. Now he walked up to his opponent and slugged him in the face. The young Losotan dropped to the ground, unconscious.

The crowd fell silent.

And then erupted in riotous laughter and cheers.

'The winner,' the referee announced, 'is Thomas Granger.'

Maskelyne glanced over at Cobul, who was now watching Granger intently. 'An interesting fight, don't you think?'

'Indeed,' Cobul said. 'Although technically the younger fellow won.'

'How so?'

'He was the only one still alive at the end of the fight.'

Granger continued to phase as he left the arena. His hand still gripped the replicating sword, although he was now shedding copies of himself as he walked. He had learned that his armour reacted badly to a sudden change of mass within it and would judder and whine if he were to simply release the weapon. Better to take it easy.

The tournament went on for the rest of the afternoon as matches were held simultaneously in all arenas.

It wasn't difficult to locate Conquillas. After asking around, Granger found himself directed to the arms tent, where combatants could rent or purchase various plain and sorcerous weapons. The dragon lord was testing the weight of a sword in his hand as Granger walked in. Siselo was seated on the table next to him, watching her father with wide eyes.

'What does that one do?' Granger asked.

'This?' Conquillas replied, staring at the sword. 'This cuts.'

'Is that all?'

'It's enough.'

'Enough,' Granger admitted, 'if this Unmer lord you're up

against is all he seems to be. Don't you think Marquetta's fixed the lists? What about your void arrows?'

'I have limited numbers of those,' he said. 'Once loosed, they are difficult to retrieve.'

'Congratulations on your victory,' Siselo said to Granger.

'Indeed,' Conquillas said.

Siselo leaped off the table. 'Do you want your prize?'

'What prize?' Granger asked.

'Your prize for winning!' she exclaimed. 'I bought it for you.'

Granger found himself smiling. 'You bought me something?'

She gave him a small bottle with a coloured bow wrapped around its neck.

'What's this?' he said, lifting it up to have a look. He unplugged the stopper and sniffed. The liquid inside exuded a powerful floral aroma.

Perfume?

'You can put some on now, if you like,' Siselo said.

Argusto Conquillas entered a packed arena to face a tall Unmer lord named Geffen who had made a name for himself in the ghettos as a prodigious swordsman. To Granger's eyes, Geffen appeared to be in his sixties, but he moved with the lithe agility of a much younger man. He carried dual swords, one of which terminated in an L-shaped hook. It was a style of sword-fighting Granger had seen once in the east, in which the hooked sword was used to catch and pull the opponent's own weapons.

Geffen rolled his shoulders and hopped on the spot as the bout official introduced the combatants. And then he crossed his twin swords before him, adopted a half-crouch, and began to circle the dragon lord.

Conquillas held his rented sword out to one side and advanced without hesitation.

Siselo clutched Granger's arm. She was seated next to him, her eyes glued to the arena floor. 'This will be quick,' she said.

And it was.

The two men met in the centre of the arena. Conquillas feigned a sudden thrust, then flipped the blade into his other hand and swung it to strike at his opponent's armpit. Geffen responded with a skilful parry, catching the dragon lord's sword with his own hooked blade and forcing it down.

Conquillas allowed his blade to be diverted, but then he turned his own sword inward and smashed the hilt against the other man's nose. Geffen reeled backwards.

And suddenly the tip of Conquillas's sword was at his throat.

'Yield,' Geffen cried. 'I yield.'

The crowds cheered.

'Told you,' Siselo said.

The first round saw forty-eight combatants reduced to twenty-four. Between them Granger and Conquillas watched as many of these as they could, trying to guess which of them might be the shape-shifter. He kept his eye out for any fighters who seemed more capable than most.

The Bahrethroan Brutalist, Cobul, was certainly capable.

His first opponent was another sorcerer, an Unmer ghetto lord who went by the name of Dominus.

Dominus was a fat man who had his hair in a blue plait and wore loose orange robes. He walked barefooted into the arena with so many bracelets and rings and other objects of power on his person that the air around him bent and shivered. He was of the Entropic school of sorcery and Granger was keen to see how the two disciplines fared against each other.

Conquillas and Siselo joined him just as the bout was due to begin.

'You think this could be our man?' Granger said.

'They say he's good.'

Cobul and Dominus faced each other across the arena floor. Even before the bout official had finished his speech, Granger could see that Dominus was already muttering to himself and drawing sigils in the air with his hands behind his back.

'That's cheating,' Siselo said.

'Hush,' Conquillas muttered. 'Let us see.'

The instant the official declared that the fight had begun, a great bubble of energy appeared around Dominus. It was translucent, but woozy, like old warped glass, but it shifted and roiled as a liquid would.

Now Cobul began muttering to himself and making quick precise movements with his fingers. He held both hands out before him in what appeared to be a placatory gesture.

Dominus strode forward, and as he did so the bubble of energy around him gave a fierce shudder and abruptly doubled in size. Granger felt the air pressure change. He heard a low rumbling sound like a distant landslide. He could still see Dominus inside the sphere, but blurred as the light bent around him. He thought he saw the man make another gesture. And suddenly the bubble doubled in size again. Now it was mere inches from the Bahrethroan.

Cobul stepped forward and placed his hands on the bubble. *Snap!*

The sphere of energy abruptly vanished, leaving Cobul standing alone in the arena. There was no sign of Dominus.

'Overload,' Conquillas muttered. 'This Bahrethroan is as good as they say.'

'What just happened?' Granger said.

'Dominus overextended himself,' Conquillas said. 'He was trying to wield a dangerous amount of power. Cobul merely gave him a little extra to play with. It was too much for the poor man to handle.'

'You think he's Fiorel?'

But Conquillas did not reply.

Both King Marquetta and Duke Cyr won their own matches easily, although it seemed to Granger that neither of their opponents tried too hard. Marquetta fought with a rapier, soundly trouncing a young Anean nobleman named John of Berna in a performance that nevertheless showed an unnerving amount of skill. The duke's weapon of choice was a silver halberd engraved with runes; it moved, so Granger thought, with a mind of its own.

It occurred to him that neither man could be dismissed.

And so forty-eight became twenty-four. Granger's opponent in the second round was a Cabathean warlord named Oshak – a talented swordsman whose prodigious natural skill had been augmented by several Unmer rings that threw wild bursts of disorientating colour around the arena. As good as Oshak was, he was ill equipped to topple Granger, whose sword and armour gave him the effective mass of a city.

Conquillas triumphed over another warlord. Another expert fighter, he fought with a mace and was clad in strange blue glass armour that emitted a tone that caused terrible pain to all those who came too near to it. Several times during the contest, the front rows of spectators cried out in agony and scrambled back over the people behind them to escape.

If the pain affected Conquillas, he didn't show it.

Marquetta and Cyr and the Bahrethroan each won their second-round matches without the shape-shifter revealing himself. And twenty-four became twelve.

*

'The king has fixed the lists for dramatic effect,' Granger said to Conquillas after the third round had concluded. Without any daylight it was hard to be sure, but he guessed it must be close to midnight. The fights would resume in the morning. 'He wants to fight you last. He wants his grand finale.'

'Of course,' Conquillas said.

'Or else he intends to have Fiorel murder you in your tent tonight so he can pretend to defeat your copy in the morning.'

Conquillas seemed lost in thought.

They had found a beer seller in a quiet area at the rear of the competitors' compound, not far from the entrance to their own tented area. Siselo was wrapped in a blanket, sleeping soundly at her father's feet. Marquetta had returned to the palace and taken Ianthe with him, if the rumours were true. And that had left Granger in a foul mood.

'What do you think he's done with her?' he said.

'Your daughter?' Conquillas replied. 'She's in no danger from him tonight.'

'Why would he just take her away from here?'

'Because it hurts you,' Conquillas said. 'Because it shows that he has power over you.'

Siselo murmured in her sleep. The Unmer lord reached down and touched her cheek. 'Paulus Marquetta can be cruel and arrogant and he is certainly misguided,' he said, 'but he is not a monster. He is capable of love.'

Granger shook his head. *But he's Unmer*, he almost said.

Conquillas stroked his daughter's head, but his gaze had turned inwards again. 'I wonder if you would know,' he said.

'Know what?'

'If a shape-shifter killed you and became you,' Conquillas went on. 'If it became a perfect copy of you, every cell and every drop of blood. Every memory. Would you know that you had been replaced?'

Granger had had enough experience with the replicating sword to know that he couldn't answer that question.

'If Fiorel has already killed you,' he said, 'then there's no point in worrying about it.'

The dragon lord nodded. 'It's late,' he said. 'I'm going to get some sleep.' He stooped and picked up his daughter, cradling her in his arms. She didn't stir. 'You should get some rest,' he said to Granger.

'I don't need it,' Granger replied. 'I'm dead.'

Conquillas looked at him strangely. 'Even the dead need rest,' he said.

Granger did sleep. And on the morning of the tournament finale, he was woken up by a chorus of drums. He groaned and fell out of bed, his armour clanking against the stone floor. It whined in protest. He sniffed.

Was that stench really coming from him?

He got up and applied Siselo's perfume to the joints of his armour. It helped a little. And then he wandered outside to see what all the fuss was about.

The drums were coming from the arena in the centre of the hall, and so Granger pushed his way through the crowds surrounding it. King Marquetta, as it turned out, was giving a demonstration of his skill with a blade.

He was stripped to the waist, fighting a cutting box.

Cutting boxes were particularly vicious little Unmer artefacts, and the one facing Marquetta now was typical. A decorated metal cube, about four inches to a side, it hovered before the young king at head height. From one side protruded a simple blade, less than an inch long. The weapon would seem innocuous enough, were it not for the terrifying speed with which the box attacked.

As Granger watched, the artefact shot through the air so quickly he lost sight of it. Marquetta moved his blade suddenly. There was a *clang* and sparks appeared a foot to the left of him. The box dropped to the floor and lay there, buzzing and trembling for a few moments, before it drifted back into the air.

The crowd applauded.

The drums beat again. Someone shouted, 'Seven.'

Granger yawned and left him to it. He went to find Conquillas.

Behind him the crowd applauded again. 'Eight!' came the shout.

He found Conquillas breaking his fast outside his tent. Siselo looked unusually glum.

'She has some concerns,' the dragon lord explained.

'About you fighting?'

Conquillas nodded.

Granger said nothing. She wasn't the only one.

His opponent for the third round was a Valcinder cut-throat named Manfred Barder who fought with dagger and bow and wore archaic tanned leather armour that turned sorcery back upon the sorcerer. He had fried the brain of an old Unmer Brutalist in the previous round and then stabbed him in the liver before the man could even yield.

Granger's armour whined when it came close to the man, but since any sorcery he employed was directed inwards, the cut-throat gained no advantage over him. It turned out to be Granger's easiest fight so far.

Conquillas won his bout against a knight from north Anea. This man had been bodyguard to one of the emperor's rivals and had displayed preternatural skill with a short sword and shield. But he fell before the Unmer dragon lord. The Bahrethroan Brutalist came close to destroying an assassin, also from Valcinder, while Marquetta and his uncle fought solidly against the last two warlords in the games – both of whom were heavily bolstered by sorcerous artefacts.

So twelve became six, and still Fiorel had not made an appearance.

The remaining combatants were Granger, Conquillas, Marquetta and Cyr, the Bahrethroan sorcerer Cobul and a mercenary – a tanned and muscular woman named Golsa who fought on behalf of the lord of the Gunpowder Isles. She was a phenomenally skilled warrior, using mace and blade to devastating effect, and inked in protective sigils that had foiled every sorcerer she'd come up against. She had woven metal wire into her face and arms to give herself a frightening appearance. But the most frightening thing of all was her ability to bend the geometries of the space around her.

Golsa claimed it was a natural talent, and yet Granger suspected her of using some sort of Unmer device – a pin or a chain, or even the wire set into her own skin. He watched her fight one of the Unmer lords – a thin grey-haired man who was one of the most talented swordsmen Granger had ever seen, second only to the Anean knight Conquillas had bested. He outmatched her abilities with a blade – and yet he could not land a strike upon her as Golsa bent the space between them. A blow aimed at her neck would bite into the dust under the Unmer swordsman's feet. His thrusts went wide of the mark, not because he lacked accuracy, but because the space around him constantly changed shape. Her own blows came at him from unexpected angles, pounding him to the ground before he finally yielded.

Golsa was certainly a horror to behold. But was she the shape-shifter? The tattooed Bahrethroan sorcerer had also arrived from nowhere, and he was just as formidable an opponent. Granger had watched him hurl savage energies around the arena without the use of an amplifier.

And yet it also occurred to him that Fiorel might have assumed the form of Duke Cyr, or even King Marquetta. It seemed fitting that the duke's patron should fight in his stead, or else be summoned to stand in for the king whom he had helped bring to power. Neither the duke nor Marquetta seemed overly worried to be facing Conquillas in the arena. Was that because they knew they could not be defeated?

Granger was in his tent, thinking all this over when someone tapped against the canvas door.

'Come in,' he said.

Conquillas entered. 'Marquetta wants to make a deal,' he said.

'What deal?'

'One final bout,' he said. 'Two teams of three, to the death.'

'I'm already dead.'

Conquillas didn't smile. 'He is prepared to overlook that.'

'Who does he want fighting alongside him and Cyr?' Granger asked. 'Golsa or the Bahrethroan? Which one of them is the shape-shifter?'

Conquillas was silent for a long time. Finally he said, 'He wants you to fight alongside him and Cyr. He said he would give you this one last chance to join the winning side. If you refuse, then we draw lots.'

Granger stared at the other man. 'He's playing games with us.'

'That is his offer.'

'I'm not Fiorel.'

425

The Unmer lord did not reply.

'Tell him I refuse. We'll each draw for our third fighter.'

Conquillas nodded. 'So be it.'

They drew the Bahrethroan sorcerer, which left the mercenary Golsa to fight alongside the king and Duke Cyr. Granger wondered if this had been Marquetta's intention all along and his offer had just been to sow doubts in Conquillas's mind.

In all our minds. He thought back to something Conquillas had said: *Would you know? If it became a perfect copy of you, every cell and every drop of blood. Every memory. Would you know that you had been replaced?*

And so, as the tournament drums beat one last time, Granger walked into the arena next to the dragon lord Argusto Conquillas and Jian Cobul, a sorcerer from Bahrethroa who could destroy a man with a whisper and a gesture. Opposite them stood a mercenary from the Gunpowder Isles, Duke Cyr of Vale, and Paulus Marquetta – the newly crowned king of Anea.

Cobul whispered to Granger, 'The name's Cobul.'

'I know,' said Granger.

'Beware the duke's halberd.'

Granger turned to him. 'What?'

'The halberd. I sense sorcery there. Something he hasn't yet unleashed.'

'Like what?'

The Bahrethroan just shrugged. 'Something powerful.'

The bout official stepped forward and raised his hands. 'Ladies and gentlemen,' he cried. 'From more than eight score combatants from across the kingdom of Anea and countless outlying provinces, we are down to the final six. Two teams, here to fight for a purse in excess of six hundred thousand gilders. On my right . . .'

Granger turned to Conquillas and whispered, 'Could you shoot the duke's halberd from his hand?'

'That is a two-handed weapon,' Conquillas said.

'Could you do it?'

'Perhaps.' He opened the top of his quiver, letting the air rush inside.

'. . . and from the distant shore of Bahrethroa,' the bout official went on, 'the legendary Brutalist sorcerer, Jian Cobul, master of the secret fires at the heart of creation . . .'

'I didn't write this,' Cobul said. 'They make it up themselves.'

'I know,' Granger said.

'And on my left,' the bout official said, 'King Paulus of Anea, son of Jonas the Summoner and Queen Grace Constance Lavern . . .'

'How are we going to split the winnings?' Cobul asked.

Granger shrugged. 'I don't know.'

'What do you mean, you don't know?'

'I mean I hadn't thought about it,' Granger said.

'So three ways is fine with you?' Cobul said.

'Yes.'

'Good. I just wanted to clear that up. Sometimes people have different ideas when it comes to sharing—'

Granger drew his sword. 'We're starting now,' he said.

The bout official had backed away and called the start of the fight.

'Oh,' Cobul said. 'Right.' He turned suddenly and unleashed a maelstrom of power at their three opponents – a great surge of light and darkness that tore across the arena . . .

. . . and burst into a million scintillations.

Duke Cyr stood there with his fist clenched at his chest. A hazy green sphere of light surrounded him and his two companions. His barrier had dispersed Cobul's assault like so much smoke.

Granger glanced left to see Conquillas notch two arrows to his bow string simultaneously. Granger himself began to phase. As he summoned forth the sword phantoms, he experienced the familiar sensations of his mass and strength increasing. In a heartbeat he had created a hundred copies of himself within the same space. Then two hundred, then five.

Conquillas loosed his arrows . . .

. . . which struck the green sphere and flared to nothing.

The sphere of energy began to darken.

Conquillas frowned. 'That barrier is too powerful to be Cyr's doing.'

'Fiorel?' Granger asked. He continued to multiply himself, increasing his strength a thousand fold, two thousand fold, four thousand fold. His armour began to whine as it reached the limits of its endurance.

He strode forward and struck the sphere with his sword.

The force should have been enough to split a mountain in two, but the sphere of energy merely darkened again. Now he could no longer see their opponents inside it, just vague shapes. Was Cyr using the barrier to mask some further sorcery? Was he trying to obscure Fiorel's true identity?

Cobul unleashed another blast of force, but it had no effect other than to darken the sphere still further. Cyr's barrier had become almost black.

And now it began to rise into the air before them. Five feet, then ten, then twenty. There it hovered, motionless above the arena floor, a swirling bubble of dark energy.

'He's created a rift,' Conquillas said. 'A new universe. He's been using the power we throw at it to fuel its creation.'

Granger gazed up at it. 'To shield them from us?'

The ground beneath them started to shake violently. Stone cracked underfoot. All around, spectators cried out in alarm and rose from their seats. 'I think not,' Cobul said. 'I think it's to shield them from Fiorel.'

Massive tremors continued to shake the great hall. The whole arena jolted suddenly to one side, throwing Granger from his feet. He landed on his back and looked up at the distant ceiling. And in the arched stonework he saw a monstrous face.

He called over to Conquillas. 'You said Fiorel can assume any form?'

'Any form he knows.'

'Look up,' Granger said. 'We're inside him. Fiorel *is* the Halls of Anea.' As he said this, the whole arena began to crumble around them. Great cracks ran through the tiers of seating. Chasms opened to the left and right of them. Stone snapped, shattered, fell away into darkness. Screams sounded all around them as the spectators fled from the destruction or disappeared into one of the ever-widening holes.

'Siselo,' Conquillas cried.

The three men joined the panicked crowds fleeing the arena as the ground behind them crumbled to nothing. They cleared the top of the stepped seats. Ahead of them the competitors' compound was collapsing. Wires strung with gem lanterns snapped or fell as the poles toppled. People were disoriented, unsure which way to go. Conquillas pushed his way through a group of men. 'Siselo!' he cried.

They heard her calling back somewhere to the left.

'I'll get her,' Granger said.

He began conjuring sword phantoms. Eight disparate replicates that he sent bulling through the crowds in the direction of the girl's cry. Their perceptions all crowded into his mind.

He saw men and women trampled underfoot and others falling over each other in desperate panic and fights and cries of agony or fear. Barrels and tables upended, crockery smashed. Rope and tin and broken stone. A hundred faces. A thousand faces.

He spotted her.

She was crouched in a space between the shattered walls of a compound hut, sobbing with fear. Granger scooped her up in the arms of whichever replicate was nearest. They were all him and he was all of them, and he could hardly differentiate between himself and any of them. Another part of him glanced up.

Cyr's sphere of energy was drifting through the air above his head. And in the ceiling far above that he could see the enormous face of the god Fiorel. It was formed of ever-shifting stone and bore a strangely calm, almost serene expression. Rubble and dust rained down from it. Its eyes opened and then its mouth and it spoke with the voice of a mountain.

'Conquillas.'

Granger's replicate reached them and set Siselo down next to her father. He stooped and picked her up, hugging her fiercely.

'Conquillas.'

Granger, Cobul and Conquillas climbed a mound of rubble to better survey the situation. Stone and dust continued to rain down, smashing to the ground all around them, pulverizing the merchants' stalls and the wreckage of the compounds and the bones and flesh of the fallen. The air was becoming difficult to breathe. Granger could see Cyr's sphere drifting away over it all. It was almost at the exit tunnel. But the ground between them and escape was wreathed in dust clouds and riven with great dark crevasses. There was no way to cross.

Conquillas set down his daughter and aimed an arrow up at that vast face in the ceiling.

Fiorel chuckled. 'Much time has passed, Unmer lord.'

'Let my child go free,' Conquillas said.

Above them, stone eyes narrowed. 'Tell me, why should I show mercy now when you showed none to Duna?'

'I am flawed,' Conquillas said. 'You are not.'

'Not good enough,' the shape-shifter said.

'Then I'll make you a deal,' Conquillas said.

'What deal?'

Conquillas lowered his bow. 'Let her go,' he said. 'And I'll fight you.'

The great stone face frowned. 'This is your deal? I refuse.'

Conquillas sat down on the rubble and set his bow down beside him. Then he spread his empty hands. 'Then do what you will. I won't resist. And you will never know.'

'Know what?'

'Which one of us is the greater being.'

Fiorel roared. 'I am a god. Set against me, you are nothing.'

'Only because you have greater power,' Conquillas said. 'But take that away and what is left? If you assumed *my* form, copied *my* every cell, if you made yourself identical to me and then challenged me to a duel, I would win.'

Fiorel considered this.

'There is no shame,' Conquillas said, 'in admitting that the notion terrifies you.'

The god chuckled again. 'Very well,' he said. 'I agree. But if you lose, then she loses too. I will find her.'

Conquillas nodded.

Fiorel closed his eyes and a great tremor shook the ground. The crevasses between where they stood and the exit all closed, creating a path across the blasted ground by which they might cross.

'Look after her,' Conquillas said to Granger.

'No!' Siselo shrieked. 'No, no, no.' She tried desperately to cling to him, but the dragon lord gently pushed her into Granger's arms.

'Quickly,' he said to Granger.

Granger picked up the wailing child. 'Cobul?'

The Bahrethroan sorcerer seemed indecisive. He glanced up at the massive stone face and then he gazed at the path to the exit. Cyr's sphere was nowhere to be seen. 'Hell, I'm with you, Granger,' he said. 'That thing's big.'

They hurried away, leaving the dragon lord standing alone on a mound of rubble. Granger glanced back once. By then he was too far away to be sure, but it seemed to him that Argusto Conquillas had a smile on his lips.

EPILOGUE

King Paulus gazed down at the sleeping girl. Then he knelt by her bed and rested his cheek against the gentle swell of her belly. He listened, hoping to hear the baby's heartbeat, but there was nothing.

Duke Cyr turned his telescope back to the window. He couldn't see the entrance to Segard from here in the palace, but he could see the pall of dust hanging over a ridge of trees where people were saying the tunnel had collapsed. Of the thousands who had ventured inside the Halls of Anea to watch the tournament, only a handful had escaped with their lives.

'Fiorel should have been here by now,' he said.

'Let him enjoy his moment with Conquillas,' the king said. 'He's waited long enough for it.' He lifted his head from Ianthe's belly. 'I think Jonas, if it's a boy.'

Cyr nodded. But he remained preoccupied. The shape-shifter really ought to have arrived at the palace before now. What could possibly have delayed him? The somnabulum floating in the corner of the room chattered suddenly.

King Paulus glanced up at it, before returning his attention to Ianthe. He looked at her for a long moment. Then he picked up a glass from the bedside cabinet and eased a little water between her lips. 'You know,' he said. 'There's no reason to stop at one child. We might have three or four.'

'That would be sensible, sire,' Cyr said. He turned his head at a sudden noise. A distant thumping, like a blacksmith's hammer repeatedly pounding an anvil.

King Paulus heard it too. 'What is that?'

Cyr came over to join him. The sound was coming nearer. He could hear it much clearer now – a steady *thump, thump, thump*. Like soldiers marching.

Or heavy footsteps.

Very heavy footsteps.

'Do you think it's Fiorel?' the king asked.

Duke Cyr glanced at the glass of water on the bedside cabinet. He could see the surface rippling with each thump. And still it grew louder. Whatever was coming sounded as if it was in the corridor outside. It was definitely footsteps, Cyr realized. Massive footsteps.

They stopped outside the door.

King Paulus sniffed. 'Do you smell perfume?'

extracts reading groups
competitions books new
discounts extracts extracts discounts
competitions
books new events
reading groups
events books
extracts books titles reading groups
new interviews
events extracts extracts events
discounts books
new books events interviews new books extracts
events new events

discounts extracts discounts

www.panmacmillan.com

extracts events reading groups
competitions books extracts new books